ARCANA
NIKI FIXTION

Acknowledgments:
Huge shout out to my editor Megan Mossgrove. I live for your margin comments!
www. mossgrovewrites.com

Thank you, H. Warren, for all the amazing artwork!

Casiddie Williams, thank you for turning my word vomit into cohesive sentences!

For my children who have always been and will always be my biggest supporters. I can say with all honesty, I am the luckiest mother in the world.

For Michelle, the love of my life, your belief in me kept me going every time I felt like giving up.

For Ann, you were the bad-ass main character of your own story from beginning to end. You will forever be missed.

MENTAL ORDER:

High Priestess - Psychic Magic

Hierophant - Absorbs Knowledge Instantly

Strength - Mental Shields and Control of Animals

Judgment - Truth Seekers (can hear lies)

Moon - Dream Walkers/Manipulators

Lovers - Empaths and Emotion Manipulation

World - Null Magic

PHYSICAL ORDER:

Fool - Shapeshifters

Emperor - Strength and Strategy

Chariot - Kinetic Energy

Hermit - Astral Projection

Hanged Man - Portal Creation

Tower - Destruction Magic

Sun - Light Manipulation

Justice - Curses and Blessings

WORLDLY ORDER:

Magician - Elemental Magic

Empress - Nature Magic

Wheel - Time Manipulation

Temperance - Artifact Creation/Alchemy

Devil - Shadow Magic

Death - Necromancy

Star - Healers

Great deeds call for great rewards. Great corruption calls for retribution. Those who seek power will bring about a time of need.

Too long your neighbors and family have suffered for your beliefs. Too long their will has been ignored. What was gifted can be taken away. It started with twenty-two and ends with one.

The time of need is here.

CHAPTER ONE

I've heard bad luck comes in threes. If that's true, I'm due some good luck because this week has been rough. At least that's what I tell myself as I kneel to clean up the mess of splattered hot sauce on the tiled floor.

I'm wound so tight today, the sound of the bell over the diner's door caused me to jump from my skin and drop the glass bottle I'd been putting away. To add insult to injury, I cut my finger during the cleanup. Although, in my case, it might be adding injury to insult. Either way, it's strike four, and I'm over it.

First, my apartment manager notifies me they've sold the building and I have ninety days to vacate. Then, I dropped my cell phone in a puddle of water while rushing to work, and to top it all off, I'm pretty sure I've attracted a stalker.

"What is going on with you today, Kennedy?"

Two dingy white shoes come into view from my position on the floor. Of course Rachel would just stand there and watch me struggle to clean it up instead of offering to help.

"You've been really jumpy. If I didn't know better, I'd think you were on something."

"I swear someone has been following me." I wrinkle my nose, both at the overpowering smell of vinegar from the hot sauce and at how paranoid I sound.

When I'm satisfied no glass or sauce remains, I head to the window to wait for my order to come out. Rachel has already positioned herself there ahead of me. We both drew the short straw of a Monday morning shift, and our respective tables are the first customers we've seen in over an hour.

"Like right now? What makes you think that?" Rachel looks around the diner then stares down the cook even though she's only been waiting all of thirty seconds for her food to come out. I smile internally, knowing he'll take twice as long to make her food just to teach her a lesson in patience.

"I don't know. The last two nights, when I was walking home, I could just feel it." It's like sensing

8

someone's gaze even without looking. Growing up in foster care taught me to be hyper-aware of my surroundings.

I work at Pattie's, a local diner with a shabby interior and subpar food. Our main customers are truckers who use the quarter-operated showers and a few daily coffee drinkers. Since it's so close to my apartment, I walk to and from work every day. When you don't make enough money to survive, saving on transportation helps. But it also means I'm a young woman who walks home alone every night. Not exactly the safest mode of transportation for my demographic.

"I'm sure it's nothing. I doubt even the worst thief would be interested in what we earn working here." She brushes the bangs she's trying to grow out behind her ear. Something I find more annoying than the dismissive tone of her response. She does it a million times a day because they're not quite long enough to stay in place.

I'm two seconds away from telling her how unsanitary it is, but the food I've been waiting on slides into the window. I grab it before she has a chance; we might not be the classiest establishment, but I can at least offer my customers hair-free food.

"Muggers aren't the only danger out there, you know."

We couldn't be more opposite of each other if we tried. Where Rachel has short blonde hair and blue eyes, I have long dark hair and dark eyes. Where she's short and thin, I'm taller and slightly more muscular thanks to the occasional free kickboxing class at the community center. She's also completely self-centered. I just tend to stick to myself, but if someone needed help, I like to think I would be more sympathetic.

Shaking my head at her lack of response, I carry the plate to my customer. I've never had anyone order such a random breakfast, but to each their own, I guess. I set the plate of hash browns topped with pineapple down in front of the man sitting at table two.

"What is this?" he pokes at the two strips of bacon sitting on his plate.

"It's bacon; sorry, I think the cook must have put it on the wrong plate. You're free to eat it, no charge."

He sniffs gingerly at the greasy strips and wrinkles his nose.

"This is flesh, right?" The disgust in his voice pauses my retreat from his table.

"Yes?" My answer comes out as a question only because it's the first time I've ever heard someone refer to meat as flesh. I already don't eat the stuff, but now, after hearing that, I find it even less appealing.

"Can you take it back, please? I don't want it on my plate."

I retrieve a saucer and remove the offending meat from his plate before turning to see Rachel unceremoniously dump a plate in front of her own customer. I have no idea how the girl makes tips.

10

"What was his problem?" She eyes the man I just served and ignores her own.

"I think he's a vegetarian. He had me take the bacon off his plate."

Rachel rolls her eyes, and I know she's about to voice her opinion on vegetarians. The same opinion I have to endure every time she remembers I don't eat meat. I cut her off before she begins because I'm not in the mood to have my life choices questioned today.

"Do you think Gary can give me a ride home?"

Gary is Rachel's boyfriend. He's a total douchebag, but he has a car, and after the last two nights, I really don't want to walk home again.

"Is this about your supposed stalker? Have you actually seen someone following you?" Another eye-roll punctuates her question, and I immediately grow irritated with her. What happened to the "girls supporting girls" movement? I toss the bar towel I just used into a bucket harder than I intended, and water splashes over the lip onto the floor. Perfect.

"Can he?" I don't bother telling her about my walk home the last two nights in a row. A walk that should only take ten minutes turned into twenty because I cut through alleys and doubled back. I'm sure Rachel would be happy to tell me all the reasons I was being ridiculous, but for the sake of my last nerve, I don't give her the chance.

Rachel sighs. "Fine, if you throw him some gas money."

11

I also don't bother to argue the fact that getting from the diner to my apartment will cost him less than a dollar in gas. I've worked with Rachel for four months now, and I learned almost immediately that altruism isn't in her wheelhouse of qualities.

Noticing my customer has finished his breakfast, I hurry over to remove his plate and drop the check. We have thirty minutes left in our shift, and I still need to wrap the silverware before I can leave. Rachel, of course, has no intention of helping with side work. She also won't wait for me to finish when Gary pulls into the lot.

"Have you ever been there?" My customer points to the TV in the corner where a commercial plays, advertising MegaCenter, a grocery store, and a department store in one.

"Sure, you'd be hard-pressed to find someone who hasn't." I take the crisp bill he hands me along with his check.

"Why would one want to get their toes done while they're buying food?"

I force a small laugh at his joke. It doesn't quite hit the mark, but I'm not above faking it for a tip. I use the money in my apron to make his change, and when I look up, he's staring at me with a furrowed brow.

"Oh." I realize he actually wants an answer. "I suppose for the convenience of it? Do both things in one place to save time." My answer doesn't seem to satisfy the question, though, because he has a follow up.

12

"What do they do to your toes?"

I stifle the genuine laugh threatening to bubble up. Maybe he's been living under a rock and truly doesn't know. If he thinks I'm laughing at him, I can say goodbye to a tip.

"You know, cut the nails, paint them, smooth the skin. That kind of stuff." He doesn't look any less confused by my explanation, so I tack on, "Make your feet look nice."

"Interesting," is all he offers in return.

My side-work still needs to be done, so I shake off the odd conversation and get started. Rachel is ever impressive with her ability to watch both me and the clock at the same time. When the phone rings, she doesn't bother to acknowledge it, so I'm forced to stop what I'm doing to answer.

"Pattie's." My tone is clipped. Walking home seems inevitable at this rate. At least it's still daylight.

"I need you or Rachel to work a double today. Steph has the flu, and Shannon can't cover." The unmistakable rasp and failure to offer any sort of greeting tells me it's Ginger on the other end. Owner, operator, and all-around overlord of Pattie's Diner.

Rachel already has her purse slung over her shoulder, even though there's at least ten minutes left in our shift. I find myself caught between needing the money and not wanting to be here anymore. The money wins.

"I'll stay." Hopefully, my voice doesn't sound as depressed over the prospect as I think it does. Ginger

13

probably doesn't care as long as there's someone to serve customers. Before I hang up, I'm sure to make it clear I won't be working a minute over sixteen hours.

Please let my walk home tonight be an uneventful one.

"I guess I won't be needing that ride after all," I tell Rachel, dropping my shoulders with a heavy sigh.

"You know, I'm pretty sure this is the third day in a row he's eaten here." Rachel changes the subject, gesturing to the man who remains at table two, eyes fixed on the TV. "Maybe he's your stalker."

I shiver at the suggestion, but refuse to let her get under my skin, which I think was her intention when she said it.

"Maybe he's stalking you. If he was stalking me, I think I would at least remember serving him three days in a row."

I take a minute to study him. His long, dark hair is pulled back into a leather strap at the base of his head. He looks normal, except for the button-up shirt printed with bright pink flamingos in different poses all over it. I guess the shirt isn't the worst thing I've seen, but it's paired with light yellow jogger sweats and leather sandals. Not the height of fashion. But who am I to judge? I've never worn anything brand new. Everything came from second-hand stores or was handed down to me by a foster sibling.

"He sat in Shannon's section yesterday and mine the day before," Rachel says. "I just thought it was strange how someone who's never been here now eats here daily."

"Isn't that kind of how regulars happen, though?" I point out the flaw in her conspiracy, but the coincidence of it makes my hair stand on end.

Rachel just shrugs. "My ride's here." She's almost to the door when she turns around to say, "Maybe you should consider some pepper spray, just in case."

Great. She went from not believing me to adding fuel to my paranoia fire. Her suggestion isn't a bad one, though. Luckily, that's something I already carry. I might be dumb enough to walk home alone in the dark, but at least I'm not doing it unprotected.

After Rachel leaves, I watch the man at table two a little more intently. I look for any sign that he's a crazy stalker who wants to kidnap me on my way home tonight, but his focus never waivers from the TV in the corner. Eventually, I feel like the stalker. Even so, I don't feel like I can focus on my work until he leaves.

The rest of my sixteen-hour shift passes in a blur, and when it's time to go home, I'm more than ready. With my pepper spray cannister in the unlocked position, I set out as briskly as possible in my overtired state.

I'm not far into my walk home when I hear the shuffle of a shoe sliding on the concrete behind me. My grip tightens on the pepper spray, and I take a deep breath. Rather than doing the smart thing, like finding a public place or crossing the street, I choose to confront the person directly.

Taking another breath to control my pounding heart, I spin around to check. There isn't a soul on either side of the street apart from me. I think I can officially say I've gone crazy. I'm pretty sure I read somewhere that paranoia is genetic, but I know nothing about my parents. It's possible that one or both of them were mentally ill. Maybe that's why they abandoned me at the fire station as a baby.

I'll just add that to my ever-growing list of reasons my parents couldn't keep me. It must put my list in the two hundred range by now. Too bad I'll never get to find out which one's the truth.

I tried looking for them after I aged out of foster care but came up with a big nothing. When those Safe Haven boxes say you can leave your baby anonymously, they're not kidding. I didn't have so much as a baby blanket or a thoughtfully written letter from my mother to go by.

The shuffling sounds again behind me. I resist the urge to turn around this time, knowing I won't find that someone has materialized behind me in the minute since I last looked. *Nobody is following me.* I'm letting my imagination get the best of me. Repeating those words over in my mind does nothing for my increased heart rate. I give in to the small burst of adrenaline and quicken my pace.

It's not until I'm at the entrance to my building that I let myself look again. Sure enough,

16

there still isn't anyone behind me. So why can't I shake this feeling? I won't feel normal until I get inside my apartment and lock the door. Maybe I should reconsider my stance on public transportation.

In the movies, when someone is being followed and they get to their door, they always take an obscene amount of time to get it unlocked. It's like they forget the mechanics of how a key fits into the hole or which way to turn it. I don't have that problem. In fact, even the deadbolt I struggle to unlock on the best of days turns easily with a satisfying snick.

I make quick work of relocking my door and hanging my keys on the hook beside it. My shoulders sag as the tension drains from my body. I smirk a little, thinking again of the way thriller movies portray girls. *They have nothing on me. I'd totally kick some psycho stalker a—*

"It took you long enough. Do you know how hard it was to not only find where you live but to get the coordinates just right to get inside? Yet, I managed to do both, and I still had to wait."

The pepper spray I still hold in my hand drops to the floor and rolls in excruciating slow motion toward the sandal-clad feet of the man I served earlier today. *Holy shit, Rachel was right. And also, I am so getting murdered tonight.*

I look from the man to the can and back to the man again. Can I get to it before he does whatever he's planning? No way I could make it back to the door in time. Neither option looks good for me because even

17

as I'm willing my body to move, I'm frozen in shock, or maybe terror. *Probably both.*

"Grab it if it'll make you feel safer. I'm not here to hurt you. There's something you need to know, and I thought it best if we had this conversation in private rather than where you work."

His words barely register as I scramble for the can. It came to a complete stop right in front of him so I snatch it and back away as fast as I can. True to his word, he makes no move to stop or grab me. I inhale a small breath of relief before I point and push the button on the top of the can.

The liquid flows out in a steady, thin stream, but I must be standing just outside its range because, almost as if hitting a wall, the stream rolls downward to the floor without hitting his face. He sighs and shakes his head in disappointment while I wait for the fumes to hit us. The stinging eyes and running nose never comes and I frown at the now empty can in my hand.

His lips press together in a flat line before he responds, "I was hoping it wouldn't be like this. You seemed half-way intelligent at the diner."

The barely concealed insult penetrates the lingering fog of fear clouding my mind. I'm finally able to string together enough words to complete a sentence.

"How the fuck did you get in here?" It's not the most pressing question I could ask, but it's the only thing I can think of.

18

"I already told you. It was just a matter of getting the coordinates right." He crosses his arms and quirks an eyebrow at me. "Do you mind if I sit? I'm feeling a little drained here."

He doesn't wait for my response before taking a seat on my threadbare sofa and crossing one thin leg over the other. I'm positive I resemble a fish out of water with the way my mouth opens and closes again as I try to wrap my brain around what's happening.

A million different questions tumble around in my head, but I can't hear most of them over the sound of my beating heart. I glance at the closed door behind me. It's not super far. With him sitting, I might reach it before he can catch me.

"I wouldn't. I told you I need to talk to you. Once I've said what I came to say, I won't stop you. But not until then."

I don't know if it's the icy determination in his dark eyes or the fact that he looks relaxed under the circumstances, but something tells me I shouldn't test him.

"Wh—" I have to wet my lips and try again, "What do you need to tell me?"

In a million years, I would have never imagined the words that came out of his mouth next.

"I'm from Arcanum, and I'm here to take you home."

CHAPTER TWO

This can't be happening. I stare, speechless, at the man in front of me. He has to be some kind of crazed stalker. There's no way he's not. Especially after he explains that Arcanum is a city but an entirely different realm. I'm being set up. This is someone's sick idea of a joke, and I'm the punchline.

I search the man's face for any hint that might tell me I'm being played, but all I find is cold solemnity. His piercing, dark eyes seem to bore into my very soul as he waits for my reaction. Not a joke, then.

20

I'm unsure of what to do. He already warned me not to try running, and I believe him. Besides, I doubt my kickboxing classes give me any kind of edge.

Do I play along? I think I read somewhere that it can be helpful when confronting someone having a psychotic episode. I'm willing to try anything to prevent this from escalating. Who knew my obsession with reading everything I can get my hands on would come in handy one day?

"Okay." I don't know if I'm talking to him or to myself, but as far as answers go, I'm fully aware this one is not my best work. It doesn't help that as soon as I opened my mouth to speak, my brain emptied of anything useful. I twist my trembling hands together and let the silence between us grow thicker until it might actually be suffocating me.

After what feels like an eternity of silence, he realizes he won't get anything else out of me and sighs, pinching the bridge of his nose between his thin forefinger and thumb before speaking.

"I can see where this might all be confusing for someone living here, but I need you to understand exactly what I'm saying. Maybe you'd like to sit down? It's rather rude for you to stand over me like this."

Somewhere in the recesses of my stalled-out brain, I note the irony of him calling me the rude one. He lifts himself from my couch and reaches out as if to grab my arm. The action seems to reboot my brain, and I'm suddenly firing on all cylinders again. Him touching me is the last thing I want.

21

"I can sit on my own." The biting tone of my words is in direct opposition to what I'm feeling, but I give myself a mental pat on the back for being able to feign confidence in the face of whatever this is. His hand stops its path to my shoulder and falls back to his side. I wait until he sits again before I do the same.

I want as much space between the two of us as I can get, so I sit in my favorite spot. A beige, overstuffed chair that sits adjacent to my couch. It has the secondary benefit of only being big enough for one person.

Everything I own came from a second-hand store—or I found abandoned on a curb—and this chair is my favorite find. It's perfect for cuddling up with a book because it feels like falling into a cloud every time you sit. I don't relax into it like I normally would, though. Instead, I sit on the edge and hold my back ramrod straight with my hands folded in my lap. In this position, I can spring up quickly should I need to. *I really hope I don't need to.*

The Moroccan trellis rug both my couch and chair sit on suddenly becomes fascinating. I trace the patterns with my eyes to avoid looking at him. My defense mechanism screams 'if I can't see him, he's not really here.'

My apartment is my safe place. It's the first home I've had that could be called my own. Everything in this apartment is something I'd wished I could have growing up. It boasts shelves lined with hundreds of books on every subject imaginable. Table surfaces display tiny figurines of mythical creatures carved from various stones or crystals.

But now, looking around at the space that always made me feel happy, everything looks dull and unsafe. Even the faint scent of lemongrass that welcomes me every time I come home smells bitter. It doesn't feel safe anymore, and it's his fault.

The thought finally gives me a useful emotion. Anger. And with it comes some clarity of mind. My idea of playing along is no longer appealing.

"So, you've been following me around for three days to tell me I belong in another world? Do you know how absolutely demented that sounds? What psych ward did you escape from?"

He sighs again, the sound defeated, one an adult dealing with an overly rambunctious child would use, and I'm a little offended by it.

"Not escaped. Jumped." His head tilts in confusion, and I mirror it with confusion of my own. Jumped?

"I don't know what a psych ward is, but I can guess. I suppose it doesn't really matter. My point is that while we don't know how you got here, we do know that you don't belong in this realm."

I arch a brow before I respond, "I'm not saying I believe anything you're telling me, because I don't. But how can you tell when someone doesn't belong in their so-called realm?"

"I don't claim to understand how the power of a high priestess works, but he felt your presence and sent me to locate you—"

The contradictory terms in his sentence confuse me even more. Leaning forward in my seat, I interrupt with the first thought that pops into my head, "High priestesses can't be men."

"In Arcanum there are many male high priestesses." He waves his hand to dismiss my interruption.

"Well, in the real world, we have high priestesses, and we have high priests. One is male and the other female." If he's going to weave a story before he murders me, it should at least be factual. I cross my arms in front of my chest in challenge.

"Ah, I see." Understanding glints in his eyes. "I'm not referring to your term for a religious leader. In Arcanum, high priestess isn't so much a title as it is a classification of magic."

I blink back at him. Got it. I can add hallucinating to the list of reasons this man is bonkers.

"So, not only are you telling me that other realms exist, but magic does, too?"

He smiles at me, revealing straight, white teeth. It doesn't seem right that his teeth are so perfect. It would be super helpful if someone as crazy as him had outward indicators. I'm not asking for much—a few crooked teeth, maybe even a twitch. *Not important, Kennedy. Get it together.*

24

"That is indeed what I'm telling you. Many people in Arcanum wield magic to some varying degree. A gift from the gods thousands of years ago. I would even venture to say you have magic, or I wouldn't have been sent for you."

This has gone far enough.

"I think I would know if I had any sort of magical ability. Magic doesn't exist, and neither does this Arcanum realm. You need help."

This time, his sigh edges closer to a frustrated growl.

"How do you think I got into your apartment if magic isn't real?"

"That's a good question. One I very much would like the answer to." I tick off the possibilities on my fingers. "You could have picked the lock. Come in through the fire escape. Convinced maintenance to—"

"I portaled in. Every location in my realm has a fixed location here in yours. It was just a matter of getting the location correct, so I emerge in your apartment and not the bathroom of your next-door neighbor. Who, by the way, eats while he bathes." He shudders a little.

Setting aside the very specific yet random tidbit he threw my way, I'm still trying to wrap my brain around any of it.

"So, you came from Arcanum because a high priestess sent you, and you're a . . . what? A jumper?"

His lips curl in a sneer before he says, "I'm a hanged-man."

I hit a nerve with that question. But more importantly, his answer teases at some hidden knowledge in my mind. Focusing on that train of thought, I realize why the term sounds so familiar.

"High priestess and hanged-man. Those are tarot cards." I don't know much about tarot, but one thing I'm absolutely sure of is they're not magical.

"Yes, exactly. You know of the Esotera?" He claps his hands together in excitement, and I startle a little.

"I know of tarot cards," I say, emphasizing the word cards. "People use them to tell the future or get answers to questions. No magic needed."

Now he looks like I just told him Santa isn't real. I almost feel sorry for him. Until I remind myself why we're even having this conversation. My sympathy evaporates. This leads me to another thought. I'm not sure why it didn't cross my mind first. Maybe because of the whole fearing for my life thing I've got going on. There is a way to prove what he's telling me.

"Show me. If you can just portal yourself away and back again, it would be a simple way for you to prove the magic exists."

I lean back in my chair to wait for the show I know will never come.

"I can't. At least not at the moment."

A triumphant smirk twitches at my lips. Exactly what I expected to hear. What I don't expect is the tiny sliver of disappointment that accompanies my triumph. Honestly, though, who in their right mind hasn't wished for magic powers at one time or another in their life?

"So that's it, then? You said if I listen to what you have to say, you would let me go. If you can't prove what you're telling me, then I don't see how this conversation can continue. I can't just take your word for it."

He leans forward again and shakes his head before steepling his fingers together at his chin.

"I didn't say I can't prove it. Just that I can't prove it at the moment. Getting the coordinates of your home just right required many trips back and forth between our realms. I also used my shadows quite a bit to prevent you from seeing me until I was ready. I have just enough energy left for one portal to get me back home until I can recharge. If you come with me now, then proving it will be simple."

There it is. I knew it wouldn't be as simple as he told me it would be. Now he wants to take me somewhere. My conflicting emotions and thoughts offer nothing but chaos. I'm at a loss once again for what to do. If I accept, does that mean I'm accepting something else? Will saying no anger him? Do I keep him talking and hope he gives me the key to getting out of this situation unscathed? I feel like none of the puzzle pieces I have been given are from the same puzzle.

I grip the arms of my chair and adjust my feet so they're planted flat on the floor. "You really are crazy if you think I'm going to agree to go anywhere with you. Not without a fight, anyway."

"This isn't going as I imagined it would. It was naïve of me to think a person from a magic-less world would believe my words easily. I didn't sign up to argue with a child. I already told you no harm would come to you, so this act is wearing thin on my patience."

"Well, I didn't sign up to have a stranger break into my home and force me to listen to their psychotic hallucinations about other realms and magical powers."

Both of us sit glaring at each other for far too long, neither one of us willing to be the first to lower their gaze. I watch as several emotions play out on his face under my scrutiny. Irritation melts into disapproval, followed by weariness, then eventually he settles on resignation.

"I've said everything I intended to say for tonight. I won't hold you any longer."

That's it? I don't want to look a gift horse in the mouth, but if he truly believed what he was telling me, why give up so easily? Trepidation over what he might do next keeps me in the chair. This feels way too easy.

28

I was right. Instead of leaving like he promised, he slips down the short hallway and disappears into my bedroom. I don't wait to see what he has planned before jumping to my feet and racing for the door. My only priority is getting to a phone.

Mrs. McKinney, who lives across the hall from me, opens her door within seconds of my knocking on it. Her smile of greeting falters as I push past her and shut the door before using the peephole to watch my apartment.

"What in the world are you doing?"

I cringe at the indignation in her voice. "I'm so sorry; there's a crazy man in my apartment who won't leave. Can you call the police for me?"

As old as she is, Mrs. McKinney can move swiftly when the occasion calls for it. She doesn't question me, just goes straight to her phone and dials those three numbers.

I don't take my eyes off my door across the hall as I listen to her relay my words to the person on the other end. I keep expecting him to walk out, but he never does. Is he so far gone in his own head that he doesn't even consider the police?

Even as I think it, it doesn't feel right. He's crazy, I have no doubt in my mind about that, but he was also totally coherent. Nothing about him, other than the words coming out of his mouth, seemed crazy in the slightest. Yet he's still in my apartment, seemingly without a care in the world.

29

Logically, I know it doesn't take long for the police to show up, but it feels like I've been waiting for days. I'm almost surprised the vision in my left eye hasn't warped into the fishbowl view of the peephole.

When the uniformed officers show up, I pull the door open to reveal two men who couldn't look more opposite of each other if they tried.

The taller of the two men is young. I would put him somewhere close to my age of twenty-one. He's tall and bean-pole thin, with a clean-shaven face and a shiny name plate that reads J. Lawson. He stands with his hands resting on his belt, his chin high, and his shoulders pulled back.

The second man is shorter, closer to my height of five feet ten inches. Most of the hair on top of his head has fallen out, leaving a strip of graying hair that wraps around the bottom of his head. Unlike his partner, he has a couple days' worth of hair growth on his jaw and a thick mustache that holds pieces of whatever he ate just before answering this call. When he speaks, the bits of food seem to wave at me from their nest.

"Good evening, ma'am. We're here about a break-in. Was that you who called?"

I force my gaze away from his mustache before I respond. "Yes, he's in my apartment across the hall."

Simultaneously, they turn, so they have both me and my door in their view.

"Your name?" the younger one asks, pulling a small notebook and pen from his pocket.

"Kennedy Marston."

"Okay, Miss Marston, tell us what happened," the older man says, pulling his pants a little higher over his gut that's threatening to pop the button on his shirt.

I walk them through what happened as quickly as possible, emphasizing the possible mental health issues they may be dealing with. They ask so many follow-up questions, I can't help but wonder if they're even trained to deal with this. Especially when they take so long to ask me to describe him. We've been standing in the hallway for about fifteen minutes; all the while, that man is still in my apartment and it doesn't look like they're any closer to going in than when they first got here.

"Look, I understand you're trying to get all the details, but it's late, and I would like this to be over. Is there any way you guys can get him out of my apartment now? Tomorrow I can go down to the station and give you all the information you need."

The older of the two stiffens.

"That's what we're trying to do here, sweetie. We need to ascertain any potential danger before we go in."

His endearment sounds very much like an insult, but I ignore it. I don't want this to drag out any more than it has to. After a few more questions, they tell me they have everything they need and ask me to go back inside my neighbor's apartment to wait for them.

31

Watching them gingerly push the door open and poke their heads in rapidly is almost comical. I probably should have mentioned he didn't seem to be armed, but in all their "danger ascertaining," they didn't ask. I'm not going to tell them how to do their jobs.

It doesn't take them long to come back out, shaking their heads.

"Miss, there's no one in there."

They seriously can't be this incompetent, can they?

"That's impossible. He never left. Did you check under my bed? It's a tight fit, but I know from experience that it can be done."

The two officers share a glance before the younger one speaks. "When you say he has magical powers, what exactly did you mean by that?"

Seeing where this line of questioning is going makes me want to pull my hair out, but I manage to restrain myself. "I never said he has magical powers; I said *he said* he has magical powers." I cross my arms over my chest and give them my best scathing glare before I add, "I know English can sometimes be a little difficult to understand."

The last bit I tacked on wasn't my best idea, but at least Mrs. McKinney enjoyed the sentiment, if her snort is any indication.

"I don't appreciate the snoot. We're just trying to help you. I promise there isn't anyone in your apartment, and it's safe for you to enter. Maybe just make sure to keep your door locked, so this doesn't happen again."

It's obvious I'm not getting any further help from the two of them, so I say thank you to Mrs. McKinney. Before I make it across the hallway, I toss over my shoulder, "FYI, I don't appreciate the left-over burrito you're saving in your mustache. Maybe just make sure you use a mirror so this doesn't happen again."

I shut the door with a firm click and lean against it for a moment to center myself. I can hear Mrs. McKinney's laughter from the hallway, and a satisfied smile twitches at my lips. What is it with men in power positions always having that condescending attitude? I'll never understand it.

My humor fades when I look at the spot on my couch he occupied less than an hour ago. I won't be satisfied he's gone until I've looked around for myself, but I also really don't want to look on the off chance he's still here. I double check that my door is bolted and all my windows are locked so there's no chance of a repeat performance.

Once I'm satisfied no one can get in, it only leaves my bedroom. I squeeze my eyes shut and steel myself. I'm a big girl; *I can do this.*

CHAPTER THREE

I'm not sure this is your best idea, Aarond. The girl is sleeping with a kitchen pot."

Two voices penetrate the heavy fog of sleep holding me in its grasp. I doubt I'd slept more than an hour or two. Last night, I'd spent several hours searching every inch of my apartment before being satisfied enough to contemplate sleeping. I'd emptied my pepper spray canister and it didn't do me any good considering it was defective, but it left me with little else to defend myself. Which is why, when I couldn't resist the lull of my bed any longer, I took a cast iron frying pan with me. It's only ever been a decoration in my kitchen until now.

I grip the handle tighter and squeeze my eyes shut, willing this to be a dream I need to wake up from. This can't be happening again.

"Perhaps it's an Earth custom?"

I would know that voice anywhere. It's the man from my apartment last night. He brought a plus one, apparently. Her voice doesn't sound at all familiar when she answers.

"I think it means she's been ashga touched. Are you sure this is her?"

"They don't have ashga here. Or any beast that can drive a man mad by touching them, as far as I know. I think she means it as protection." His voice is laced with amusement. "I'm sure. Bren confirmed it when I returned last night."

"Well, what are we waiting for? You'd think sleeping the day away when expecting guests would be rude in any culture." A hand shoving at my shoulder follows her haughty reply, sending my body into high alert.

I scramble from under my blanket to crouch at the head of my bed, still clutching the cast iron pan in my fist. The woman jumps back, emitting a startled gasp before pulling the man she called Aarond to stand in front of her as a living shield.

35

The fact that she's scared, despite me being the obvious victim here, leaves me dumbfounded. As far as I know, the fluffy kittens printed on my pajamas aren't meant to strike fear in the hearts of my enemies. I might be brandishing my cast iron pan like I'm a knight preparing to wield her sword in battle, but I'm sure I look more like the court jester putting on a show.

Aarond clears his throat, "I wouldn't exactly say she was expecting guests . . ."

He trails off with a shrug and shifts his gaze from me to the woman still standing behind him. She glowers at him and adjusts the long sage-colored cloak she wears around her shoulders. It appears to be made from hundreds of overlapping pieces of fabric. The pieces are all shaped like leaves and ripple with her movements. The effect is almost mesmerizing.

"Aarond! You mean to tell me we portaled into this girl's home uninvited?"

Aarond has the decency to look embarrassed in the face of the woman's indignation.

"She didn't leave me much choice. Bren said we need to bring her over quickly. In order to do that, she needs to see magic is real."

The woman's face pulls down in a frown of skepticism, giving me a tiny sliver of hope. She must not know about his magic fantasy. Maybe she'll realize he needs help and get him out of my apartment once and for all.

"Tell me again why this required my help. Why couldn't you just conjure your shadows and be done with it?"

Not her, too. That sliver of hope withers and dies in my chest before it can form anything substantial. Dealing with one crazy is already over my capabilities, but now I have two?

"I've been using so much magic the last few days. I'm barely managing to open the portals just to get here. Once we get her there, it's going to take days to recharge."

I really hope he isn't referring to me because there is no way in hell I'm going anywhere with them. I grip the pan a little tighter.

"Look at the poor girl. What have you done to her? She's so scared I doubt anything we have to say is going to get through to her." The woman clucks her tongue in what I imagine is supposed to sound like sympathy.

"I didn't do anything to her. How am I at fault for her inability to see what's right in front of her?"

My inability? How does neither one of them realize how completely off their rockers they sound? Is it possible to lose touch with reality so completely? Both of them, no less.

My legs begin to tremble from the strain of holding my crouch on such an unstable surface, and I don't know how much longer I can hold my position. The woman, who seems to be the more observant of the two, must realize it because she grabs the man's elbow and tugs him backward.

As soon as they're no longer within arm's reach, I crab-walk to the edge of the bed and set my feet on solid ground. They watch my awkward movements with amusement flashing in their eyes, but make no move to come closer. I don't lower my weapon, but I relax my grip a little so blood can return to my white knuckles.

"Allow me to apologize for my friend's poor handling of this. We mean you no harm—" The woman speaks in a soft voice the same way you would speak to a frightened animal, but the man interrupts her.

"I've already been through this with her. I didn't bring you here to coddle the girl," He huffs out in exasperation.

"Obviously not or she wouldn't be waving that pan around like it's her only chance of survival." The woman crooks a single eyebrow in challenge, and gestures toward me without looking my way.

"I can't be held responsible for her not being able to see what's right in front of her face," he snips back.

They continue to argue between themselves and seem to have forgotten the fact that I'm still standing here clutching my cast iron. Ironically enough, even though their voices rise and the argument grows more heated, I start to feel less threatened.

I'd be dead already if they planned to kill me. The man has managed to break into my apartment twice now and even bring a friend. Who knows how long they were watching me sleep, and I don't have so much as a scratch to show for it.

I feel almost certain I can cross serial killer off my list, and focus on the fact that they're both just run-of-the-mill crazies. It doesn't really make them any less dangerous, but honestly, how dangerous could these two be when they're so busy having a petty argument over me they've forgotten I'm here? I could slide right by them and out the door without them noticing.

My eyes trace the path. If I give them a wide berth and inch my way slowly, it might just work. But before the plan can solidify, the room grows quiet and they're both looking at me again. Since I tuned them out, I have no idea what the outcome of their discussion was.

Neither says anything, and the silence stretches long and awkward. I clear my throat a little and stare longingly at the door just on the other side of my unwanted guests.

A sudden calm washes over me. My shoulders relax and my arm, still brandishing the pan, drops to my side. Somewhere in the back of my mind, a tiny voice is telling me this isn't right, but I can't seem to find the motivation to care. I struggle to remember why I was so tense in the first place.

The woman shoots me a look of sympathy and begins talking again. I'm thankful it's not Aaron, or whatever his name is, because there's a soothing quality about the woman and strangely enough, she doesn't seem crazy.

"I know this is hard for you. I promise we're not going to hurt you, and we will leave you alone if that's what you truly want after we've explained everything."

I don't know why, but I believe her. The heavy weight that sat on my chest all but disappears at her words. I nod as my body relaxes more. I'm safe here, of that I have no doubt.

"Pull back a little. You're going to put the girl to sleep if you relax her any more."

I understand the words, but they make no sense, and a small giggle slips from between my lips. But just as suddenly as it came on, the fuzzy feeling in my brain starts to lift, and with it a healthy dose of weariness returns.

"Did you drug me?" I don't know what their definition of harm is, but in my book, this qualifies as harm.

"Of course not!" The woman's indignant reply comes quickly. Almost too quickly for comfort. Like she was expecting the question. But then, from one second to another, I don't care again. She wouldn't lie to me.

"What are you doing to her?"

I giggle at the silly question. No one is even touching me.

"I don't know! My magic is harder to control here. I can't find the appropriate level."

My heart rate speeds up again and I lift my pan. "What is wrong with you people?" I all but shout.

The woman grunts a little and the rest of the fog releases me from its grasp. *What the fuck was that?* "I can't maintain it. She's stronger than I am, or magic is too unpredictable here."

"Let's just do what we came to do. This has consumed more of my day than I wanted." He's annoyed again, but that's not my fault. I didn't ask them to come here.

"Will you grab that empty pot of soil for me?" She points at the small planter on my windowsill. The plant that once inhabited the pot was long gone. It was a record for me. It only took twelve hours to kill the plant after bringing it home.

His long legs take him to the window in just two strides, and he comes back with the empty pot. She takes it from him, looks at me to ensure she has my attention, and blows her breath across the dirt.

Nothing happens, and once again I feel that small twinge of disappointment. Then a tiny stem unfurls from the soil and stretches toward my ceiling. After another second, leaves bud on either side of the stem and grow until they're about the length of my hands. Immediately after, beautiful pink anthurium flowers burst from the foliage. I almost can't comprehend what I'm looking at. This is what my plant was supposed to look like before I killed it.

41

What. The. Fuck?

Forgetting all the reasons I needed it, I drop the pan and reach for the now bloomed plant she holds. The pan hits my floor with a loud clang, barely missing my toes, but I'm too focused on the sight in front of me to care.

In my haste to grab the pot, I cup my hands over hers and the scent of fresh spring rain washes over me. I take a deep breath, enjoying it more than I care to admit.

Now that I'm so close to her, the cloak she wears is even more amazing. Each individual leaf is so detailed, I can see veins branching out from the stems into the leaves. I know if I were to reach out and touch one, it would feel smooth and slightly furry, just like a real leaf. But they can't be actual leaves, right? That's not possible.

She slides her hands out from under my own, leaving me the only one touching the pot now, and bringing my attention back to the fact that I just watched an entire plant grow from nothing in real time.

I lift the plant so I can look at the bottom of the pot, then spin it around when I find nothing out of the ordinary.

I don't know what I'm looking for, but there must be something here that can tell me how she did it. Nothing pops out at me, but I'm not one to give up easily, so I run my hands all over the bottom, side, and rim surface of the pot. Nothing.

I rub one of the soft pink petals between my thumb and forefinger. It's real. The flowers smell sweet and feel velvety soft, and the leaves are dark green and healthy. The plant may be real, but I can't let myself believe it just magically sprang from a pot of dry soil.

"How?"

Aarond rolls his eyes in exasperation. "Must we go over it again? Misara is an empress."

The title means nothing to me other than I know it's yet another tarot card. I wait for him to expand on his cryptic explanation, but he only watches me with a cocked eyebrow as if daring me to reject what I just witnessed. Once again, I find myself locked in a silent battle of wills against him.

Misara swings her arm out and smacks Aarond in the stomach. A universal sign for that's enough already. "My primary gift is nature magic. Among many other things, I can encourage the growth and health of plant life. As you saw, I can quite literally breathe life into the earth."

My brain revolts against the idea that any of this can be real, and a dull ache forms between my eyes. But I can't deny the plant I hold between my palms. I take a deep, calming breath and blow it out in a steady stream, watching the leaves sway while I try to organize my thoughts.

It's hard to focus, knowing they're watching me and waiting for a response. I need space. My room feels overcrowded and too warm.

43

A small vibration tickles my palms, startling me out of the spiral of panic that threatened to take control. A thin crack forms in the terra cotta and travels from the base of the pot to the rim before it splits in half and a second anthurium springs from the soil fully formed and already blooming.

"Another empress!" Misara's excitement is drowned out by the sound of the pot shattering as it hits the floor.

Soil and fragments of the broken pot spread across the floor in front of me, but I only have eyes for the two plants laying side by side. Their roots tangle together as if they cling to each other for comfort in the aftermath of losing their home.

Misara claps her hands together and smiles, "I've never seen an empress grow a plant so fast! You must be quite powerful."

"You can't possibly think I did that? Even if everything you've been telling me is real, there's no way I've gone twenty-one years of my life without ever showing a hint of magic until today."

"But you did do it. Aarond is right. You don't belong here. Especially now that you've manifested. What would happen if you accidentally manifested in front of someone with no understanding of the arcane?"

Images of being captured by some obscure branch of the government flash through my mind. I've read enough books to realize how bad that could be and cringe at the thought of being dissected on a cold stainless-steel table. The logical part of my brain doesn't let it go any further.

"This is a mistake. I can't have magic." It doesn't escape my notice that I've gone from protesting the existence of magic to protesting that I have magic. This is all too much.

"Now that you see the truth, will you come back to Arcanum with us?" Just the sound of Aarond's voice is enough to grate on my nerves. He really should leave the talking to Misara.

"No." My blunt answer invites no argument, but he does anyway.

"You can't be serious. What more could you need to be convinced to come?" He swipes a hand across his face.

"You say that like all of this should be easy for me. I'd like to see you have your world view shattered like that planter and handle it any better than me." The idea of leaving my entire life behind is too daunting a prospect to think about right now. I can't accept everything and move on like it's just another day.

"You wouldn't see me clinging to a life wasted away, serving food to ungrateful people for next to nothing in return. Not when I could live in a place where my life would mean something."

His retort hits too close to home.

"You know nothing about my life. You can't expect to throw all this at me, then have me begging to leave everything I've ever known behind."

45

The more I think about the way he handled this situation, the angrier I become. I need space or I'm likely to blow up.

"Time!" Misara interjects and brings my focus from Aarond's scowl to her understanding smile. "You need time to work through your feelings. Aarond and I understand you can't be expected to make such a big decision in such a short amount of time."

Aarond looks like he's about to interrupt her and say the exact opposite, but she holds her hand up to stop him. He glares at her but stays silent.

"The least we can do is give you a little space. Aarond will be happy to return at a later time for your answer. Right, Aarond?" She stares at him with pursed lips until he sighs in defeat.

"Right . . . yes, that's fine. I'll be back this evening."

To keep myself from strangling him and to allow myself time to formulate an answer, I kneel to pick up the plants still laying on my floor. A few hours won't make much of a difference. I just don't see myself going with them. It sounds amazing in theory, but the idea of starting over terrifies me. I may not have family or anything tying me down, but I have myself and the life I carved out of nothing. There, I would have even less.

"I don't think I need time. I'm not going with you . . ." In the short time it took me to pick up the plants, both Aarond and Misara have vanished from my bedroom as if they were never here to begin with.

After six hours of apartment hunting and coming up empty, my day has not improved in the slightest. I slip through my apartment door, half expecting Aarond to be waiting for me again. When he isn't, I breathe a sigh of relief.

My skin is still crawling from the last apartment I looked at and, for the first time since this morning, I'm focused on something other than magic and other realms. A shower.

Every apartment I could find within my price range was infested with bugs, bad vibes, or the stench of human waste. The last one boasted all three. Needless to say, I'm no closer to finding somewhere to live when my ninety days are up than I was when I received their notice of eviction.

Maybe when I find a place, it'll have a decent shower that sprays more than a lukewarm dribble. Rinsing shampoo from your hair with what amounts to a faucet drip is challenging, to say the least. My next day off is a week away on Tuesday. Maybe in that time, the perfect apartment will magically become available.

Magic. I went all of five minutes without thinking about it. What am I going to tell Aarond when he comes back? The obvious answer should be no, but a little voice inside me keeps questioning if that's the right answer.

I've always wondered about my parents. What could have happened in their lives that forced them to leave their baby behind? Knowing they may not even be from this world somehow makes it worse. They needed or wanted me so far away they resorted to sending me to a whole other realm.

Does that mean Arcana is unsafe? What if they never meant for me to be here? What if they've been looking for me this whole time?

Standing under the tepid water and speculating over the choices of someone I've never met isn't doing me any good, so I rinse the remaining suds from my body and turn off the shower.

I haven't been able to stop thinking about those plants all day, either. During my hunt for a place to live, I hadn't been able to stop myself from entering a small nursery and purchasing a couple pots to replant them. While I was there, a display of wildflower seed packets caught my eye and before I knew it, I was throwing a packet down on the counter along with a small bag of soil.

Now, still in my towel, I rush to fill a pot with some soil and a few of the seeds. I need to know if I can do it again. I suck in a deep, shaky breath, and heart pounding, I blow into the soil, willing those seeds to grow.

Nothing happens. I blow again, this time hard enough to send some of the soil scattering over my countertop. Nothing.

Maybe I'm crazy too. Is it contagious? I push the barren pot away from me with a frustrated growl after my tenth attempt. This wasn't doing anything except making me light-headed and I need to get dressed before Aarond's inevitable visit.

As I do, I realize something. I told myself I was dreading his return because he's not going to like the answer I give him. But that isn't the truth. The fact that I so desperately wanted to make another flower grow proves it. Why would I be trying so hard to prove him right, only to turn around and refuse to go? Am I really going to pass up the only opportunity I've ever been given to find out about my family?

Just because I dislike everything about the man doesn't mean he isn't right. Nothing is holding me here. I've never had time to make friends or set down roots outside of work. I won't miss anyone when I'm gone. I own nothing of value. The only thing keeping me here is myself.

My stomach flips and my heart flutters with anticipation. I might be crazy. If I say yes and it all turns out to be a giant hoax, I'll worry about having myself committed. The only thing I need to figure out right now is how to pack for traveling to a different realm. I scoff out loud at the absurdity of the thought, then groan. This better be real.

I do my best to pack all my necessities into the two suitcases I own. It's easier than I expected, even though I know I'm leaving behind almost everything I own. When I finish, I sit down to wait for Aarond. Time ticks away slowly, but before I know it, it's after midnight.

And I'm left wondering why exactly I'm upset when he doesn't show.

CHAPTER FOUR

The sound of something being dragged across the floor startles me awake. Pain flares through my neck when I jump from my chair with all the grace of a newborn giraffe. A solid reminder of why I had to ban myself from falling asleep while reading.

I sway on unsteady feet and blink in confusion until I realize why I jolted awake. The sound of my fridge closing, followed by a drawer opening, pulls my attention to the kitchen. It's not until I hear the clinking of silverware that I realize someone is helping themselves to whatever meager supply of food I have.

I find Aarond standing over my counter, wrestling with a container of yogurt, and my stomach flutters a little at the sight. Last night, I waited hours for him to show. The whole time, I was a ball of nerves and excitement. When I realized he wasn't coming, my excitement turned to disappointment, then regret. Regret that I believed it could be possible. I was envisioning being able to start over and even find my family.

That regret turned to anger. Mainly at myself for believing the impossible. Despite having doubts, I believed what I saw and heard because I crave a better life. I want to feel like I belong. More than anything, I want a family. I've never had that.

I lean against the door frame, crossing my arms over my chest to exude an air of irritation rather than the relief I'm feeling.

"Help yourself."

In response, Aarond sticks a heaping spoonful of lemon yogurt into his mouth and savors the flavor before swallowing. Today, he's dressed in all black and his shoulder-length hair hangs loose and wavy. His pants look to be made of leather, which I find both confusing and revolting. The former because just two days ago he refused to eat an animal but now he's wearing one. The clothes hug his lanky body as if they

52

were custom made for him. I realize now that while he is slender, the loose-fitting clothes he was wearing before were hiding a good deal of muscle. Something tells me it didn't come from frequent visits to a gym.

My perception of him shifts. He might be more dangerous than I initially thought. But then he breaks through my internal perusal with that pretentious voice.

"Were you planning on bringing this with you, then?"

He's right, even if he's aggravating. I can't take everything with me. A fact made glaringly obvious last night as I sorted through my belongings. My fake irritation gives way to real irritation at the knowing smirk he shoots my way.

"I never said I was going."

He stares pointedly at the suitcases behind me. That explains what woke me up this morning. I'm pretty sure I left them in my room last night after packing. He has no understanding of personal boundaries, and I can't tell if it's a cultural thing or just indifference.

"I'm curious to know the number of people you've convinced using this same method." It's hard to picture him achieving any level of success in this. If I wasn't so desperate to leave this endless cycle of struggle, it's doubtful I would have ever considered his offer.

53

For a moment, the only sound is the spoon scraping the plastic container. He takes his time scooping every drop into his mouth before he speaks.

"As much as I dislike coming here, this yogurt may have been worth it. It's a shame you don't have anymore." He tosses both the spoon and empty container into the trash and finally deigns to look at me, and completely ignoring my question "Are you going dressed like that?" His upper lip curls a little in disdain as he takes in my boxers and tank top.

"Just because I packed a few of my things doesn't mean I can't change my mind." I think back to yesterday and the conversation I overheard. Someone had sent him to come find me, which meant this was a job. He might pretend not to care whether I stay or go, but I imagine whoever sent him will. "I still have questions and conditions before I accept. I'm assuming it wasn't your choice to come find me, which means someone else expects you to get me there and if you want me to come, then maybe stop with the whole arrogant asshole routine. Surely it hasn't worked for you very well in the past." When he drags his hand through his hair and sighs, I know I'm right. *Kennedy one, Aarond ziltch.*

"Fine. Zero," he finally answers.

I press my lips together to stop a laugh from escaping. I'm not surprised nobody has been willing to go with him. Maybe he should consider a different profession. His mouth pinches at my reaction.

"But only because there has been no one else."

The mirth I'm feeling grows. "I'm your first? Don't worry, I'm sure your technique will improve with experience."

"As my husband can assure you, there's nothing lacking in my technique." The corner of his mouth lifts in amusement. "When I say there has been no one else, I don't mean for me. I mean ever. For anyone."

The implications of what he's saying hits me like a ton of bricks. It makes even less sense to me.

"How can you be so sure I belong in your realm, then? How did you even find me?" I struggle to pick just a few questions from the onslaught of tumultuous thoughts tumbling through my mind.

"I told you, a high priestess found you. He sent me here to bring you back." He cocks his head to the side and glances upward in annoyance.

"Okay, but that tells me nothing. I know nothing about your realm, so you need to explain it to me like I'm a child. Why do you, or I guess him, want me to go?" I'm still leaning against the doorway but I can't sit still any longer. To expend some of my nervous energy, I pace the cheap vinyl flooring of my kitchen.

"I believe you call them psychics. He saw you and sent me to find you. I don't know how much more I can simplify this for you. As for why, you would need to ask him."

He isn't telling me everything, so my distrust rachets up another notch. I let it slide because I'm not done asking questions.

"I need to know what I can expect when we get there. I don't want to step into a world where women are second-class citizens and you've sold me into a life of servitude."

At that, he rolls his eyes. "Everyone is equal. In fact, if you want to see a world where women are treated as second-class citizens, you only need to step out of your current home."

I can't argue with that. "You have a husband, so obviously gay marriage isn't an issue . . ." I trail off because it's not really what I want to talk about.

"Actually, we don't have gay marriage."

I give him a blank look, not sure how to respond.

"We just have marriage. In my lifetime, I've been to many realms, but only Earth emphasizes gender in relationships."

Well, shit. That alone is enough to make me want to hop ship and join the citizens of Arcanum. I clear my throat instead of asking another question. Mostly because I don't know where to go from here.

"Anything else?" He places both hands on his hips and raises an eyebrow. I can tell he's anxious to get this over with.

Just moments ago, I had a billion questions coursing through my mind, but now that I'm able to ask, I can only think of one.

"What about my parents? If I agree to go, I want to look for them." I lean in and hold my breath. This is the question I wanted an answer to all along. The hopeful tone of my voice betrays me, and his eyes soften the tiniest bit. He hesitates before placing a hand on my shoulder.

"I can't promise you'll find anything, or that if you do, it'll be what you expected, but I can promise you that you won't find them if you choose to stay here."

My eyebrows pull together at his words. There are no expectations, but it sounds like, once again, he knows more than he's telling me. It doesn't change anything for me. All my talk about changing my mind was just that. Talk. My answer was always going to be yes.

Imagine my surprise when, just an hour later, I find myself following him into a bowling alley.

"You're kidding, right?" It's mostly empty other than the man spraying shoes behind the front counter and two men in the furthest lane from the entrance. Even though it's only noon on a Wednesday, the music overhead is deafening. An old Beastie Boys song greets my ears and almost drowns out my question. "I'm walking away right now if you tell me I

57

have to slide down a lane in order to get through the portal."

Aarond, who has already passed the front desk and food concessions counter, turns to find me still standing at the entrance. He nods his head toward the arcade area of the bowling alley to indicate where he's heading. When I'm satisfied he's not going to tell me to throw myself down an empty lane, I grab the handle of my suitcase and follow him into the arcade. He drags my other suitcase across the floor on the opposite side where the wheels are attached until he arrives at a door marked "Staff Only" and stops.

"Why is the portal to your realm in a bowling alley?"

"It isn't yet. Take this." He hands me my suitcase and turns the knob, but the door doesn't open.

"Perfect, so you brought me to a bowling alley maintenance closet for what, exactly?" I can't imagine explaining if someone sees us here. My life was already declining, but getting arrested for attempting theft of bleach and toilet cleaner would be the final blow. "What's the point of us being here if the portal isn't?"

"I have to create it. Why must you question everything I do? Where are we going? What are we doing? How far away is the portal?" He mimics in a high-pitched voice, making me sound way more whiney than inquisitive.

"That's not how I sound. Why did we need to come here if you have to create it? Also, the door is locked. It doesn't matter how many times you twist the knob; it's not going to magically open for you."

A thin stream of black shoots from his fingers into the keyhole and a muffled click sounds from the lock.

"You were saying?" He smirks over his shoulder and wiggles his eyebrows up and down.

I take it back; the door *is* going to magically unlock.

"When do I get to learn that?" I peer inside and find shelves lined with cleaning products and supplies.

"You don't. I can create portals because I'm a hanged man and I can create the shadows because I'm also a devil."

"Yeah, I still don't get it."

"You will if we can ever get to Arcanum."

"At least explain the whole portal thing to me. Why does it need to be here, and is it going to hurt?"

The inside of my cheek hurts because I've been chewing on it since we got here. I swear I'm trying not to come off as whiney and irritating, but the apprehension is killing me. Besides, who in their right mind would agree to do something before they understood all the details? Never mind the fact that I already agreed.

"Okay, fine. Imagine different realms as being layered over each other." He holds one of his hands out and flattens it, then hovers the other over it in the same flattened position. "Every point here corresponds to a fixed point in Arcanum and other realms. If I opened the portal in your home, we would step into Arcanum in the middle of the wild. By opening it here, I'm taking us to the location we need to be on the other side."

"So, you can't open portals to travel from one point to another in Arcanum?" If that's the case, I'm not sure his magic is as cool as I thought it was. I was imagining unlimited vacations since the cost of travel would be nonexistent.

"I can if I want to burn out again. Using magic here is much harder and requires way more energy. I've been using so much in my search for you, I'm nearly empty. That's why I didn't come back until this morning. I needed a little longer to recharge."

"How do you recharge?"

"Food and rest. The same way you do, I imagine."

"You're funny." Hopefully, they understand sarcasm in Arcanum. "One thing bothers me about all this."

"Only one?" Aarond crosses his arms and looks upward while I try to organize my thoughts.

"How is it that the exact place we need to be when we cross over just happens to be where I've lived my whole life?"

If every location has a fixed location in his realm, that would mean whoever brought me over did so in this general area. Does this mean my family lived close by to wherever we're going? I have been living here ever since someone abandoned me at a fire station not even ten miles from this bowling alley. It's too coincidental to just move on.

"I can't give you any answers as to how you got here, but I'm positive you weren't brought over from where we're going."

He's standing in the middle of the doorway and reaches his hands out on either side to run them downward along the wood frame. I can only see his profile from where I'm standing, but the ticking muscle in his jaw tells me he's clenching his teeth. I just don't know if it's because he's not being truthful or if whatever he's doing to the door is taking effort. How can he be sure this isn't the exact spot I was brought over unless he knows where?

I don't have much time to think about his evasive answer because the scent of ozone fills the air. It reminds me of the way the air smells during a lightning storm. He takes a step backward and turns to wink at me.

"Ready?"

I look around in confusion. "For what?"

Nothing has changed around us except for the scent of lightning that still hangs heavy in the air.

"You just need to walk through the door."

Inside the small closet, I can see the metal shelves lining the walls. They look slightly warped, though, like I'm looking at them through a puddle of water. Aarond clears his throat and swings his hand out, signaling me to step through ahead of him. When

61

I make no move to walk forward, he presses his lips together in a flat line.

"Fine, I guess I'm going first. Just step through when you're done letting fear rule your thoughts."

With that, he steps into the closet and disappears. Not just steps to the side to make room, but blinks out of my vision in such a way that I'm questioning whether he was here in the first place.

Holy shit.

Am I really doing this? He's wrong about it being fear holding me back. More like healthy suspicion. Just two days ago, my entire world flipped upside down, and I experienced a complete change in my perception of the world. I dare anyone to handle it better than I am.

I reach a single finger out toward the doorway and an iridescent ripple moves outward from the tip. When no pain reaches my nerve endings, I take a deep breath to steel myself for what I'm about to do. Without taking my eyes off the door, I reach down to grab my suitcase handles, only to be met with air. That asshole took my suitcases with him. No doubt thinking it would prevent me from changing my mind. Little did he know changing my mind was never an option. As much as I might appear to be struggling with this whole situation, almost anything would be better than the life I'm currently living.

I step through with my eyes squeezed shut.

The throbbing beat of music cuts off, but the silence that takes its place is almost as deafening. I keep

62

my eyes screwed shut, not quite ready to face whatever I'll see when I open them.

The distinct sound of a pile of paper being tapped against a desk greets my ears. A feminine sigh and a masculine snort of amusement follows. The knowledge that it's not just Aarond waiting for me snaps my eyes open.

I find myself in an office of some sort. There is a large wooden desk directly in front of me, and it seems to have been carved from a single piece of an enormous tree trunk instead of being constructed from multiple pieces cut and nailed together.

Large stones of different sizes, shapes, and shades of gray make up the walls. To my right are two massive windows that run floor to ceiling and take up almost the entire wall itself. Outside, a path wraps from what I assume is the front of the building and continues between rows of trees and plants, forming a canopy over it. It looks like a tunnel with only one entrance and exit.

Beyond the plant tunnel, in the near distance, spires jut to the sky from the tops of several buildings. A few fluffy white clouds dot the cerulean sky, and I feel like I've stepped into the pages of a fairy tale.

"Welcome to Arcanum, Kennedy. I'm Elara."

The woman's greeting jolts me back into the room. I was so intent on taking in the surrounding scenery, I had completely forgotten the reason for my being here. I find her watching me with what I can only describe as amazement. She's sitting behind the desk with her head tilted slightly to the side. Her long auburn hair hangs loose in waves around her shoulders. There's a single braid, no bigger than half an inch in width on one side, and it's tipped with a feather matching the color of her hair to perfection. That, coupled with her aquiline nose, flowing silk robes the color of soft fawn, and quick flickering movements reminds me of the bird one of my foster parents had. I envied that bird. It had its own room and a never-ending supply of treats and toys while I slept on the floor in a linen closet.

I have to force myself back to the present and the woman waiting for my reply. Under normal circumstances, I wouldn't allow myself to dwell on my past, but today has my mind a total jumble.

"Thanks." I look at Aarond who, for once, is patiently waiting for me to take it all in. I try my best to convey a 'what now?' look his way without coming off as rude or ignorant of everything to the lady across from me. For a second I swear the the irises of his eyes swirls in a whirlpool of colors before they revert back to the brown I know them to be. Weird.

Aarond, ever oblivious to tactful handling of weird situations, remains unmoved by my look. Meanwhile, the lady continues to watch me with an air of expectancy.

"I'm sorry. I have no idea what I'm doing here." I look around the room again, as if the answer will spring up.

"You're to be enrolled, of course," Elara responds, as if I would understand what that means.

"Enrolled in what? Is this for citizenship or something?"

Aarond starts shuffling his feet and I know immediately I'm not going to like whatever she has to say because he purposefully kept it from me.

"Enrolled in Arcana Academy, of course!"

You've got to be kidding me.

"You brought me to be enrolled in school?" I turn to face Aarond and cross my arms over my chest. There's no way that piece of information slipped his mind. The look on his face tells me it wasn't accidental, either. He holds his hands up and takes a small step backward. Good. He should be worried. I'm twenty-one years old, for crying out loud. I did the whole school thing, and it wasn't for me.

High-school flashbacks tumble through my mind. I hated everything about it. From the teachers that either ignored me or paid far too much attention, to the other students who branded me as "trash" and went out of their way to make me miserable. A shudder rolls through my body, and I glare even harder at the man in front of me.

"I'm not going back to school." The firmness of my words leaves no room for bargaining.

"I'm afraid you don't have a choice." He scrubs a hand over his face and I can tell he's frustrated with me but honestly, he should just be used to it by now.

"I just made a choice, and it was that I'm not attending school. I completed school and I'm not doing it again."

"As soon as we arrived, the presence of a new magic wielder was recorded. School is mandatory for everyone as soon as their magic manifests." He shrugs nonchalantly.

Frustration simmers beneath my skin and my face grows hot.

"There has to be a work around for someone who has already completed their schooling. The fundamentals of reading and math can't be that different from realm to realm. Especially for someone who didn't manifest until adulthood."

Now I'm plagued with visions of being the only adult in a classroom filled with children. I'll go back to Earth before I subject myself to that kind of torture.

"Magic doesn't manifest for anyone until adulthood. Think of this as college, like you have on Earth. You'll live at the school and attend for four years."

That calms me down a little, but not enough to agree.

"There's a reason I didn't go to college. I hate school and regardless of the realm I live in, I won't change my mind."

I walk to the large windows and stare out toward the buildings I saw earlier. It must be the school.

"If you don't attend the academy, you'll never be able to yield your magic." He's trying to reason with me like I'm a child throwing a tantrum.

Maybe I am, but school is my hellscape. I can't think of anything worse.

"Then I'll just have to learn by myself. That's pretty much how I got through life up to now. I'll be just fine on my own."

"You misunderstand. I meant that in the literal sense. You'll be forfeiting your magic and will be sent to one of the mundana villages to live out your life. Meaning you won't be permitted to enter a mage city."

"What the hell is a mundana village?"

"Mundana is a place where non magical people live in Arcanum."

I'm thinking I should have asked more questions. I've never been a leap of faith type of person before and I'm reminded now why that is. Just my luck that the one time I do something out of character, I wind up in a no-win situation.

If I don't attend school, I can say goodbye to my chances of finding out why I was abandoned. If I do attend school, I may subject myself to four more years of trauma. I don't have the mental capacity to dwell on the obvious division of society he just let slip.

"How am I supposed to pay for it?" When we left my apartment, I brought about two hundred dollars with me. All the money I had. Not that it'll do me any good, considering it's Earth money and probably worthless here. I don't even know what jobs there might be available here or if I'm qualified for anything, really.

"You don't pay to learn here. Nor will you need to pay for food, living quarters, or supplies." He quirks a brow at me as if daring me to find another excuse and waits while I work out the fact that I'm running out of reasons.

My shoulders drop in defeat. Elara, who's still watching us in rapt fascination, taps her long nails against the desk. For a split second, they look curved and come to sharp points just like bird talons. But when I focus my eyes on them, all I see are regular fingernails. Great, now I'm imagining things.

"Fine. What do you need from me?" Arguing up to this point has done me no good, so I might as well agree now. I can figure out how to get out of it later.

"I just need your thumb and your order." She holds up a smooth square stone with a thumb shaped indent in the center.

"For what?" I can't help the wariness creeping into my voice.

"To record your information. After you're registered, I'll be able to print out your class schedule, house assignment, and a map. Your order decides which house you'll be in."

I have no idea what order means, let alone where I fit into it, but thankfully I didn't have to come up with an answer before Aarond speaks for me.

"Worldly." Just a single word that holds no meaning for me, but she accepts it and extends the hand holding the stone further out for me.

When I press my thumb to the smooth divot, the stone warms under my thumb. It only lasts a few seconds before fading back to its original room temperature. It must have done what it was supposed to though, because she pulls it back.

Next, she removes the stopper from a glass inkwell before tipping it over above a stack of papers and letting a couple of drops fall. She places the stone right on top of the droplets of ink. The ink under the stone runs across the paper in thin rivulets that contain a lot more ink than what she dropped onto it.

In a matter of seconds, they form the shape of buildings and pathways across the paper in what can only be a map. I watch in amazement as they draw one large building after another onto the paper, complete with directional symbols. But just as fast as it appears, it disappears, leaving the paper blank once again.

Elara picks up the small stack of paper and slides it across the top of the desk to me before she stands and comes around to my side with what looks like a purple ribbon. She holds it taut between both of her hands. I reach out to take the ribbon, but her snort of amusement stops me.

"I need to wrap it around your wrist."

Even though there was no way I could have known that, heat rises to my face, anyway.

"Why?" I bite out through clenched teeth. It sets me on edge to feel like I'm the only one in the room who has no idea what's going on. My entire childhood was spent at the whim of the adults in my life and, for some reason, I feel like I've somehow landed myself right back in that role. I made myself a promise to allow no one to have power over me again, and it's a promise I intend to keep. Even if it means asking questions other people might deem stupid.

"It's a sizer. A temperance charmed it to collect fitting information for your uniform," she wraps it around her own wrist and holds it out for me to see. "You won't feel a thing."

The smile she flashes me is genuine and her voice lacks the annoyed undertone Aarond is so fond of using. I turn around to tell him to take notes, but he's no longer in the room. He really just left me here without a word. *Asshole.*

"He seemed to be in a hurry or I'm sure he would have said something," Elara offers, the pity in her voice clear.

"It's fine, let's just get this over with." I arrange my features into a look of indifference and hold my wrist out for her. When she wraps the ribbon around my wrist, a warm tingle spreads up my arm and travels down my body. It doesn't hurt, but I squirm a little at the unfamiliar sensation, anyway. When she pulls the ribbon away from my wrist, I rub at the spot to disperse the tingling.

"There, see? The magic is so subtle you probably couldn't even tell it was doing anything."

There wasn't anything subtle about that ribbon. Either I'm a freak or I imagined the whole thing, but I decide to keep my mouth shut about it.

"Yeah," I reply as she walks back around to the other side of the desk to sit down.

Her brows furrow when she looks up at me, still rubbing the spot on my wrist. "Everything okay?"

I drop my hands back to my side and shoot her an unaffected smile. I'm sure my imagination is just getting the best of me.

"Yep, all good. What else do I need to do?" Earlier, she mentioned room assignments and the thought of being able to lock myself in my own space to process everything sounds amazing right now.

"We're all finished. You'll start classes tomorrow. Everyone else started a few days ago but you shouldn't be behind yet . . ." she tapers off and rubs the feather laying on her shoulder. Her unspoken realization hangs between us.

I'm about twenty-one years behind, actually. Not only am I starting from scratch with magic, but I know nothing about the world itself. The fact that Aarond left me here to sink or swim without arming me with any knowledge of what I'm getting myself into makes me even more angry with him.

Elara puts on an encouraging smile. "I'm sure you'll be fine. The map will take you to your room.

71

After you're settled, you can head to dinner in the commissary."

It's obvious I'm being dismissed, so I grab the papers she set on the desk earlier and turn to grab my luggage, only to find it missing from the platform Aarond had set them on when we first got here.

"Where are my bags?" There's a distinct edge of panic in my voice and I wince at the show of vulnerability. Those bags contain everything I own now. My entire life is in them.

"They're already in your room. That platform is another temperance artifact. It transports things from one place to another. You'll see platforms like it all over the school." She dismissively waves her hand at it.

I release the breath I was holding and look down at the empty paper in my hand.

"How is this going to lead me to my room?"

The moment the words leave my mouth, ink begins to form lines and shapes on the paper. The path I noticed earlier when I was staring out the window takes shape and a single drop of ink slides from the image of the building to that path. I'm guessing the drop of ink is me.

Here goes nothing, I guess.

CHAPTER FIVE

The ink droplet continues to trace a path on the page for me to follow, leading me through the tree tunnel I noticed earlier while looking out the window.

It's warm outside, but not uncomfortable. The trees offer cool shade and the sweet scent of wet earth and greenery. I take a deep breath of the clean air, so different from the stale scent of pollution and exhaust I'm used to. When I finally make it out the other side of the tunnel, I come to a dead stop.

In front of me are three identical buildings standing side by side. They're made of the same gray stone as the building I was just in and are connected by two arched bridges that run from the middle building to the other two on either side of it. The bridges sit about halfway up the buildings, causing me to gulp a little at the thought of having to cross them so high off the ground.

The foundations of all three buildings are square and have pillars topped with pointed spires at each corner. At each level of the buildings, the corners have spire tipped pillars, and sit slightly smaller than the level under it, reminding me of the way a tiered cake looks. The buildings come to a single pointed spire at the very top. It's breathtaking. They look more like fairy tale castles than the school I know them to be.

The path I'm on forks off into two parallel walkways that lead between the buildings under the bridges before curving in the opposite direction. Little ink drop me takes the path on the right so that's what I do too.

The two paths form a circle around a large courtyard with several other paths that branch out from it. Inside the circle, dark green clover covers the ground, with little white flowers peeking out from the leaves. A tall white statue sits nestled in the middle, depicting a man, a woman, and another person with androgynous features. They stand back-to-back, clasping hands to form a circle while a floating white orb spins above their heads. I want to get closer to it to see how the orb is suspended, but stone benches line the outside of the circle, so I don't think I'm allowed to enter. A bell chimes from behind me while I'm contemplating crossing the circle anyway. It seems regardless of the realm you're in, schools rely on a bell schedule.

I make a hasty retreat from the courtyard to find my room. If the school has just let out for the day, I'd rather not have to navigate the unfamiliar area and people at the same time. My map takes me down the third pathway branching off from the courtyard circle and leads me to a cul-de-sac. A small wood cottage sits in front of me at the end of the path while two buildings reminiscent of large five-star hotels sit on either side facing each other. The ink dot moves inside the right building, so I follow it.

Once inside, the map goes blank again. Perfect. I have no idea which room I'm in, and from the size of this building, there could be hundreds. I look around the lobby, hoping to find someone to help direct me, but it's empty. My steps echo against the marble flooring as I walk around the spacious room. There are two hallways on either side of me and a large imperial staircase leading up to the next floor. Beyond the two staircases, on the far wall, I see a board that looks like it contains some information. When I get closer, I realize it's a directory with a list of names and room numbers. I hope they've already added my name.

I skim the directory looking for Marston in the m's and find my name listed already. Room 208. According to the accompanying map on the board, each level has eight rooms, with four on each side of the building. The rooms must be huge. It looks like my room is on the second floor and will be the last one on the right side.

My room is bigger than my old apartment. I had to press my thumb to another stone box that is mounted next to the door in order to get inside. The first thing I see is a comfortable seating area right as I open the door. There's a small kitchenette beyond it and a dining area right next to that. On the other side of the table is a set of windowed doors that open onto a balcony.

There are two doors on opposite sides of the room. I'm assuming one is my bedroom, and the other is a bathroom. I'm halfway across the room to find out what's behind door number one when someone opens the main door and lets themselves in.

A small gasp escapes me before I can prevent it. I clap a hand over my chest and whirl around to face the intruder.

"Sorry! I didn't know you'd be here. I was starting to think I was getting this room all to myself!"

A woman who looks to be about the same age as me stands in the doorway and offers a hesitant smile. She's petite, standing no higher than my chest, and has soft pink hair that falls over her shoulders and back in loose curls. In fact, she has more hair than height and looks like she's being swallowed whole by it.

"How did you get in?" You'd think I'd be used to having people barge into my home after dealing with Aarond. If this is the social norm here, I'll never get used to it. I like my privacy way too much.

"I'm Falyn." She steps further into the room and closes the door behind her. "Your roomie." She points to the door I had been heading to just moments ago. Each door must be a separate room.

Taking another look around the room, I realize it does look lived in. There's an open book face down on the table beside the sofa and a couple of plants sit on the island that separates the kitchen from the living space.

When I turn my attention back to her, I realize she's waiting for me to respond. If I have to live with her, I should probably put some effort into being cordial if not friendly.

"I'm Kennedy. I didn't know I had a roommate." It comes out sounding stiff even to my ears and I flinch a little internally. She doesn't seem to notice my awkwardness and breezes by to stand in front of the plants.

A vine emerges from a plant and wraps around her wrist, but when I blink, the vine is no longer there. I rub my eyes and blow out a breath. That's the second time today I've seen something that wasn't there. The stress is getting to me.

"What province are you from? I don't think I've ever heard your accent before," she asks while running her flattened palm over the leaves of the middle plant.

I clear my throat awkwardly, "I'm not actually from around here . . ." I trail off because I'm not sure if I should announce how foreign I am to everyone. Although I have no idea how I would go about hiding it from the person I'm expected to live with.

"I'm from Emritch but my mom is a hanged-man, so I've been to all twelve mage provinces at one point or another. I've even been to Mundana a couple times." She faces me and leans her back against the counter, relaxed. "That's the only reason I asked."

I don't know how to respond, so I just go with, "I've never been . . ."

"To Mundana or Emritch?"

"Neither. I've never travelled anywhere until today."

"Oh, well Mundana kinda sucks but Emritch is beautiful—"

My mouth pulls down a little at her dismissal of Mundana. The idea that they created a province just for people without magical abilities doesn't sit well with me.

"What's wrong? You're not from Mundana, are you?" She worries her bottom lip between her teeth. "I just meant they don't have magic there . . ."

"I'm not from Mundana, but why is there a separate province for non-magical people? They told me they're not even allowed in mage cities."

"What do you mean? It's always been like that. Well, ever since the disunion, anyway. Where did you say you're from?"

"I'm not sure you've ever heard of it." Somehow, I doubt my vague answer is going to satisfy her question.

"Try me. Like I said, we travel a lot. Perks of being related to a hanged-man."

"Have you ever been to Earth?" It's probably better to just rip the band-aid off now and get it over with.

"No way!" Falyn's gray eyes widen and her mouth hangs open in astonishment.

So much for thinking I could use the rest of my afternoon to decompress and figure out my next move. The fact that she's staring at me in utter amazement tells me this is going to be a long conversation.

I use the moment of shocked silence to study her a little more closely. She's wearing what I assume is the school uniform and I have to bite back my snort. It's like the designer asked themselves what the most cliché style they could think of was and called it a day. It features a white-collared button up blouse tucked into a green and gold plaid skirt, complete with attached suspenders of the same pattern. The skirt is barely long enough to hit her at mid-thigh. I bet the men wear blazers, khakis, and ties. Being forced to wear this for the next four years is a whole new kind of torture I never could have imagined. Even so, Falyn manages to make it look amazing. The combat boots she paired with the outfit somehow work to complete it instead of detracting from it. And makes her look like a badass. Something I doubt I'll ever be able to pull off.

"Why are you staring at me like that?"

The ridiculous images of me walking around in that same outfit fly from my mind as I snap back to reality at Falyn's question.

"Is that the only uniform option we're given?" The dread in my voice betrays how I feel about it.

"This isn't the uniform." She laughs at my obvious relief and smooths her hands over her skirt. "The uniform is black pants and shirt, but they don't enforce it unless we're having a dignitary visit. No way I'd be caught dead wearing black on black otherwise."

"Oh." Did I just insult her outfit? "I mean, you look great in it, but nobody wants to see these knees."

"I'd kill for legs as long as yours," she responds with a wink. "But back to the whole Earth thing. I have so many questions. I don't know where to start!"

She's not the only one. I've had nothing but questions since the moment Misara showed me her magic and nearly all of them have gone unanswered.

"Can we trade question for question? I'll answer yours if you answer mine." The tension releases from my shoulders when she gives me an eager nod and heads to the sofa to sit down. It's definitely going to be

80

a long afternoon, but I'm suddenly not as exhausted by the idea as I was earlier.

"You can go first," I offer, after taking a seat on the other side of the sofa. It's going to take me a minute to organize my thoughts enough to form coherent questions.

"I think the most obvious question is what you were doing on Earth in the first place. What was it like living there and how did you figure out what your power is? We've always been told Earth doesn't have magic."

"That's like three questions." I chuckle at her enthusiasm. "I have no idea how I got to Earth. From what I was told, I was born here, then abandoned there to be adopted. Living there is all I've ever known, so for me it was normal. It's way more polluted than here, but I don't really have much to compare it with. They're right about the magic. Earth doesn't have magic, let alone believe in it. Unless you practice wicca, but it's not the same because they don't have actual powers as far as I know."

I suck in a deep breath. This is already shaping up to be the longest conversation I've had in a long time, and we just got started.

"How did you know you had magic, then?"

"I didn't. Aarond found me and at first, I thought he was crazy but then he proved it and after I made a flower grow, I had no choice but to believe him. So, he brought me here and for the second time in my life I was essentially abandoned on a doorstep."

81

That last part slipped out of my mouth before I realized I was saying it. Apparently, his disappearing on me affected me more than I thought it did.

Before she can ask me another question, I hurry to ask one of my own.

"So far, I think I've figured out that everyone's powers are different, but what's the difference between an order and classification? What does worldly mean?"

That first night Aarond was at my house, he said high priestess was a classification and Misara called me an empress, but then when I was registering, Aarond called my magic worldly.

"That one's easy. There are three orders of magic: mental, physical, and worldly. We're worldly because we can affect the earth or the elements. Mental affects things of the mind, and physical, I'm sure you can guess, affects things in a physical nature. Classification is the specific magic. For instance, my classification is empress because I have nature magic, a lover's order is mental because their empathic, and a fool's order is physical because they can shape-shift."

That was only my first question and my head is already spinning. Another question springs to my mind. She's an empress, and I had imagined a vine wrapping around her wrist when she touched those plants. Earlier I swore Elara's fingernails looked like bird talons.

"My turn. What magic did you manifest?"

To give myself time before answering, I adjusted my position on the sofa, drawing my legs up to hug my knees. It felt like a complicated question.

"I'm an empress too . . ." It doesn't quite feel right when I say it. "But I've only ever manifested once, and I'm not convinced it was me who actually did it."

Falyn cocks her head to the side and furrows her brow, but says nothing.

"I've tried to do it again multiple times after, but nothing happened."

"Oh, that's normal sometimes. When a mage is born in Mundana, they usually take longer to get a grasp on their magic, so I imagine someone who lived on Earth would have just as much trouble, if not more, in the beginning. I think it's because you weren't raised around magic."

It makes sense, I guess, and even helps alleviate some of the anxiety I'm feeling over not being able to do it again. But something still doesn't feel right. I hurry to ask my next question before she notices.

"Is the lady that works in the office a shifter?"

"Elara? I think she's a bird of some sort. Why do you ask?" Her nose scrunches a little in confusion, but I ignore her question in favor of asking what I really want to know now that she confirmed my suspicion.

"How do you tell the difference between what's real and the visions you get when you figure out what someone's magic is?" If I'm going to be walking around seeing things all the time, I want to know about it ahead of time.

She sucks in a quick breath. "Are you saying you can tell what someone's magic is just by looking at them?"

"Well, yeah. Is that not something everyone can do?"

"It's not something anyone can do . . ."

We both fall silent after that little revelation. Me, because I'm trying to figure out how big of a freak this makes me and who knows what Falyn is thinking. Confusion, curiosity, and wariness play out over her features in quick succession.

Just when I think she's about to ask for a different roommate, she shrugs her shoulders and says, "We should probably keep that to ourselves for now. Magic doesn't vary a whole lot here and I don't know how people would react to find out you might have a power no one else does."

I release the breath I was holding and shoot her a grateful smile. Maybe having a roommate isn't going to be such a bad thing. For however long I'm here, anyway.

Our conversation continues, but we both carefully avoid the topic of me being able to see magic. I learn a lot over the next couple of hours. Like the fact that there are twenty-two classifications of magic that fall under the three orders. Just as fast as she lists them, I forget most of them. They're all the names of tarot cards, I think, but I'm not an expert. It wouldn't surprise me if the origin of tarot cards on Earth has something to do with a hanged-man traveling between realms. Not wanting to bombard her with the burden of having to be responsible for my entire magical education, I file it away to look into another day.

We move on to other topics and Falyn goes over my class schedule with me. It turns out all first years share the same classes, so I'm a little relieved to find out I won't be completely by myself. Third year is when students are separated into classes tailored to their specific magic.

It's not until I'm trying to explain Earth's cinematic portrayals of magic using shows like Sabrina and Charmed as examples that we realize what time it is. In fact, I still haven't seen my room or checked on my bags, but it's already time for dinner.

Our walk to the commissary is short. We retrace my earlier steps back to the courtyard circle, then take another path that branches off from it until we come to another gray stone building. I'm starting to see a theme here. This building has a lot more glass, though. Inside, people are sitting at tables or standing in line for their food. More people than I was prepared to face, so I hesitate at the door. As soon as I think about turning back, my stomach emits a very loud protest and I know missing dinner isn't an option. Especially since in all the excitement of traveling here, I failed to eat anything today.

Even with hunger gnawing at my insides, I still hesitate with my hand on the door. Why does it feel like I'm preparing to walk into a viper's den?

"Everything okay?" Falyn shuffles her feet behind me.

"Yes." No. This is too much like walking into my high school cafeteria for lunch. "Just nervous, I guess." How do you tell someone you just met that one of the worst moments of your entire life happened in a similar setting?

"If you're not going in, then move." The feminine voice is accompanied by two arms shooting out to shove both me and Falyn aside. I lose my balance and reach out to the only thing I can find to steady myself. The same arm that caused the situation in the first place.

Words hover on the tip of my tongue to chew the girl out for her blatant disrespect, but as my hand wraps around her forearm, they're swallowed back by the hair-raising force of what I can only describe as a vision.

Everything is blurry, but slowly the scene takes shape around me. I'm surrounded by tall trees and foliage. In the near distance, a stream trickles and flows. The sound would be soothing if not for the steady pounding of my heart inside my chest. The kind of pounding that can only be elicited by fear.

Two hazy figures stand in front of me and a long shadow on the ground tells me there's another at my back. Whoever is standing at my back has my arms in

86

a grip so strong, I'm surprised I can't make out the individual grooves of their fingerprints.

I squint my eyes and shake my head, hoping to bring everything into focus, but it remains shadowed and blurry. Even without my sight, the animosity rolling off the people holding me captive is obvious.

Pain ratchets through my arms as the person behind me pulls them even tighter. At any second, my bones are going to snap and I can't do anything about it. That burst of pain is momentarily eclipsed by the sting of a hand meeting my cheek. The force of the blow whips my head to the side and the tang of iron coats my tongue.

A tinkling laugh greets my ears as I struggle ineffectively against the immense strength of the person behind me. My breath rushes in and out of my body in quick succession.

"Did you think you were going to pass? You don't belong here, Zero." The girl in front of me speaks as if we know each other. Nothing about her is familiar. Nothing about anyone or anything is familiar.

"Yet you're the one who had to use an emperor to best me. Not to mention there's three of you and only one of me." Her satisfied smile fades into a glare before her hand snakes out and catches me across my other cheek. It's such a strange sensation . . . being here but knowing I'm not really here. The words I spoke came from my lips and were in my voice, but I didn't choose to say them. I'm not even sure I know what an emperor is. It's like even though I'm inside my own body, I'm watching the scene unfold from the outside.

87

On the heel of that thought, my knees jerk upward. My shoulders take the brunt of my weight and one of them makes an audible popping noise. Somehow, I manage to ignore the searing pain and break free. My body spins around with an unfamiliar grace and my foot slams into the body standing behind me. I don't know how I'm able to deliver a kick so hard his feet lift from the ground and he slams into a tree. I don't have time to wonder because the third person in their trio has decided now is the time to jump into the action by way of grabbing a fist full of my hair and yanking me backward. I hit the ground hard and roll away from the foot swinging in my direction before launching back to my feet.

The three of them surround me, all of them glaring at me with such hatred in their eyes, I'm not sure I'll survive whatever it is they're planning. The girl, who seems to be the ringleader, steps forward with an evil glint in her eyes while I search over their shoulders for who knows what. I get the feeling this is the end. There's no way I can take on three of them at the same time.

She raises her hands with her palms facing me and the air fills with the smell of sunbaked stones . . .

"Are you deranged? Let go of me!"

My captors and the forest disappear, leaving me standing once again in front of the commissary. I have to blink my eyes a couple times to kill the vertigo washing over me. When the world stops spinning, I realize I'm gripping the girl's arm tight enough to leave crescent-shaped marks on her wrist. She yanks her arm

88

away from me and mutters, "Go be a freak somewhere else."

After she disappears into the commissary, I turn to Falyn and notice she's watching me with a concerned frown on her face.

"What was that?" She reaches out to pull the door open for me.

"I think I just had a vision?" Can that be right?

CHAPTER SIX

As soon as we walk through the door and the smell of food hits my nose, the post vision daze evaporates. The only thing on my mind is getting through the line and filling my plate with as much food as it can hold. Thankfully, the line moves quickly.

In my experience, school lunches aren't very vegetarian friendly, but when we get to the front of the line, I'm pleasantly surprised to find there isn't a single offering of meat in the entire buffet style setup.

Thinking back to when Aarond got offended over the bacon on his plate, I have to ask, "You don't eat meat here?"

"Gods, no." The immediate look of disgust on Falyn's face was answer enough. "There are some who do in Mundana, but it's very rare."

Most of the food looks and smells unfamiliar, so I follow Falyn's suit and load my plate with everything she does.

"Do you?" she asks, wrinkling her nose.

"Definitely not." It was a sore subject with a few of the homes I was placed in. "I'm just curious because it's popular on Earth."

"We don't. Eating animals is barbaric when so many people here can communicate with them as easily as they can with other people."

She's referring to the strength classification she told me about when we discussed the different kinds of powers earlier and I can't imagine being able to control or communicate with animals. What is there to even talk about? Just as I'm about to ask as much, someone yells Falyn's name from across the crowded room.

She motions for me to follow as she weaves her way through the commissary to an area in the back. Four people sit at a table against one of the giant windows overlooking more woods. Even though I haven't explored yet, I can already tell I'm a fan of being surrounded by trees. I didn't realize how much I disliked the bustle and smells of the city until today.

91

How could I? It was all I knew. But already, the clean air and forest feels like it's washing away a lifetime of dirt and oppression.

All four of them, two girls and two guys, watch our approach. Rather, they're watching *my* approach. Just what I wanted out of dinner tonight. I was preparing myself to feel like an outsider tomorrow; I didn't expect it to start so soon. I'm not sure I'll have room to fit my food around the pit that just formed in my stomach.

Falyn plops herself down and grins at the four of them before she pats the seat next to her.

"Everyone, this is my roomie, Kennedy. She's awesome, so no starting your bullshit today."

She points first to the girl she sat directly across from, then moves down the line as she lists names.

"This is Sona, Ciena, Rostan, and Noric."

Ciena has her bright red hair styled in a spiky pixie cut. Her pale skin, freckle-spattered nose, and bright-green eyes scream innocence, but when she smiles at me and shows off a pair of sharp elongated canines, I know instantly she's not only a shifter, but a dangerous one. The teeth disappear before my eyes move to the next person Falyn introduces.

Sona is the opposite of Ciena in every way. She has dark skin, dark eyes, and long hair tumbling down her back in hundreds of tiny braids woven with strands of silver. She nods at me but doesn't smile. A crack forms on the table in front of her and bits of it tumble to the floor. Nobody else seems to notice, so I'm

92

assuming this is another power vision. I just don't know what it means.

Next up is Rostan. He smiles and nods, causing a lock of brown hair to fall forward into his eyes. He pushes his hand through his hair in a practiced motion, telling me it's something he does often. When he waves at me, it reveals a tattoo covered arm. Some kind of foreign lettering scrolling upward to disappear into his sleeve. I want to get a better look, but when I lean in, the tattoo disappears. Blinking, I look up to find him watching me with curiosity in his eyes—brown eyes that glow for a brief second as lightning arcs through them then disappears. I really need to get a grasp on this whole vision thing before someone realizes what a freak I am.

Finally, there's Noric. He smiles at me briefly, but barely takes his attention away from Falyn. Interesting. I'm not the only one who notices, either. Falyn's face pinkens under his stare and she shifts in her seat before lifting a bite of something to her mouth. A smile plays at my lips but somehow, I hold it back, filing it away to ask about later. Noric smirks before he follows suit and shovels some food into his own mouth. The black band on his wrist changes shape and color until I'm no longer looking at a bracelet, but instead a thin gold chain that glints in the light before reverting to its original form. Another power vision. I also need to memorize the different categories so I can figure out what these visions are telling me. So far, the only one I understand is Ciena's.

93

"Where are you from, Kennedy?" Ciena asks around a leafy green mouth full.

Falyn and I share a look. Her eyes glint with excitement, and I know she's dying for her friends to know.

"Earth," I say simply.

Ciena chokes on her food while everyone else's eyes shoot upward in shock. Here we go again.

"No way," Rostan challenges in wonder.

"How?" Noric looks like he's struggling to formulate a coherent question.

Sona remains as stoic as she was when Falyn first introduced me, but she's now taking a second look, as if seeing me for the first time.

"How did you get here?"

"I thought Earth didn't have magic."

"Does everyone really burst into song and dance throughout the day?"

It's my turn to choke on the bite I shoved into my mouth to give myself a moment's reprieve. The questions came so rapidly, I couldn't tell who was asking what, all of them except the last one are just repeats of Falyn's earlier questions.

"What does that even mean?" I have no idea what could have spurred that question from Sona. "I came through a portal, Earth doesn't have magic, and I've never met anyone who bursts into song throughout the day."

The table grows quiet for a few seconds as everyone absorbs my answers. I take the opportunity

94

to stuff my face, not caring I don't recognize a single thing on my plate.

"What power did you manifest?" Apparently, I've become interesting enough that Noric can tear his eyes from Falyn for a few seconds.

"She's an empress like me," Falyn answers and shoots me a look that says we're still not talking about the other thing I can do. "With a high priestess secondary."

"Which one is high priestess again?" I feel stupid for asking when everyone gapes at me.

"Relax guys, she's from Earth, remember? She didn't grow up knowing all this." Falyn turns to me. "It's the psychic manifestation. I'm just assuming because of the vision you had right before we walked in."

I can't even get my primary power to manifest and now I'm being labeled as having two? Just another thing for me to fail at, I'm sure.

"What was your vision about?" Ciena props her hand on her chin. "Noric is the only one here who has had a secondary manifest so far." Her voice is a little wistful.

I'm not sure I'm ready to talk about what I saw. Mostly because I'm hoping it was a fluke and not something that's going to actually happen.

"It was kinda blurry, so I'm not entirely sure." I shrug my shoulders and attempt to change the subject. "So not everyone has multiple powers, then?"

It's Sona who answers, "No, most people manifest two at some point in their lives, but usually one is significantly less powerful than that other."

"It's very rare that someone will manifest three anymore, and never more than one from the same order," Falyn adds.

"Anymore?" My ears picked up on the single word.

"Yes, when the triple gods first blessed mages with their gifts, everyone manifested three powers of equal strength. But not everyone was blessed and when mages started forming families with mundanas, it weakened the blood line and powers started fading. That's why the disunion was necessary." Sona sounds like she's quoting a PSA or something.

"That's the second time I've heard about the disunion, but I have no idea what it means." I'm sure I can guess, though, and I doubt I'm going to like the answer.

"When it became obvious that our powers were fading, the king proposed the disunion as the solution. Mundanas were given their own cities to live in to keep us from intermarrying and diluting our powers even more," Ciena answers me this time.

I'm not surprised to learn their government is a monarchy. Especially considering they still practice segregation.

"That really limits the dating pool, doesn't it? So do you guys pick your potential mates based on the amount of power they have?" Why that's the question that springs to mind is beyond me. It's not like I'm looking to be in a relationship right now.

"We don't pick them." Falyn's simple answer causes my brain to stutter. When she casts a longing glance at Noric, I realize the implications of her answer.

"Are you saying marriage is arranged here?" I battle down the rising acid in my throat. I'm glad I've already finished eating or I would have lost my appetite.

"Kind of. That's one of the reasons they started the academy. It determines our future positions in the realm, but also before we graduate, it pairs us with potential mates based on our power levels and ability to use them. It's all part of the king's plan to restore our power to the way it was. We're matched with other mages of a similar power level and have the freedom to choose from that specific pool, but not outside it." Noric exchanges an indecipherable look with Falyn when he answers.

"The pool is much smaller the more powerful you are. If you're an eight or above, you almost have no choice. It's easier for those of us in the middle." Sona shrugs like it's no big deal.

It seems like for every question they answer, two more pop up.

"How do you find out what your level is? Is the scale just to ten?" Even if I don't really agree with the politics of everything they just told me, I'm still interested to know where I would fall on that scale.

97

"It's gauged by our teachers and the school throughout the year, but the trials at the end of every year narrow it down more." Sona's eyes light up at the mention of trials. "My parents are both eights."

"Do you guys have an idea of what your power level is already?" Inside, I'm cringing because the fact that I can't seem to manifest on purpose probably puts me really low on that scale.

"Me and Ciena will land somewhere around a five, and Sona and Noric are definitely going to be eights or higher, Rostan hovers around a seven, so we won't know which side of the line he falls on until the end of the year. But the scoring doesn't actually matter until fourth year." The look Falyn and Noric shared makes sense now. If he's that much stronger than her, there's no way they'll be in the same pool of potential partners.

"The pool is almost non-existent for tens because they're only allowed to match with other tens," Rostan interjects, looking over my shoulder.

I follow his gaze to a small table where three people sit by themselves.

A girl with long blonde hair sits leaning forward over the table to put her chest on display for the two guys sitting across from her. One of the guys has coloring similar to my own: dark hair and eyes with pale skin. Even without seeing him standing, I can tell he's tall. He's taking full advantage of the view offered by the blonde and even hooks his foot around her chair to pull her closer. She doesn't seem to notice, though. Her eyes remain fixed on the other person at the table.

He's leaning back against the seat with his legs stretched under the table. My eyes travel upward over muscled arms crossed over an equally muscled chest, then to his face where I find he's not paying any attention to the girl trying so hard to get his attention. He's looking directly at me. I scramble to turn around, which is probably completely pointless considering he already caught me.

"Who are they?" Hopefully, my face isn't as hot as it feels.

Falyn looks behind us and sighs. "They're three of the five assumed tens in the whole academy. All three of them are first years, which is pretty unusual considering it's so rare. The one with the darker hair is the king's son."

"The prince?" England still has a queen and princes, but it feels more fantastical here.

"We don't really have princes, but I guess you can call him that. I'm sure his ego will appreciate it." She rolls her eyes and turns back to the table.

It sounds like there's a story there, but I save my question for later because when I sneak another glance at the table behind us, I make eye contact with the blonde, and she is not happy. It no doubt has something to do with the fact that the muscled guy is still watching me and not her.

"How do you not have princes if there's a king?" I rush to continue our conversation and keep my mind on the people in front of me.

"Our rulers don't inherit the throne. A king or queen takes the throne by being the most powerful mage." Noric answers my question this time.

"Take?" The way he phrases it makes it sound ominous.

"A new king can't be crowned unless the previous king dies. King Gefred got the throne after winning a mage duel against his own father and killing him," Ciena answers as she's getting up from her seat. There's a hint of glee in her eyes while I'm struggling to not shudder at the thought. "I'm gonna head home, combat was all endurance today."

Combat class? Suddenly, going to school doesn't seem all bad. That's a class I could enjoy. I hope.

"Heads up." Sona nods her chin to a spot over my shoulder.

I don't have to look over my shoulder to know who's standing behind me. The animosity rolling off her thickens the air around us.

"Who are you?" The icy, disdainful voice belongs to the blonde, who was staring daggers at me.

Being in a situation like this isn't new to me. I've had to deal with people making me feel inferior my whole life. So, instead of taking the obvious bate, I choose to ignore her.

"Does everyone get to take combat?" I ask no one in general.

The only answer I get is a snort from the girl standing behind me.

"I asked you a question." My shoulders tense when she pokes me with a bony finger.

If there is one thing I dislike, it's being touched without my permission. Turning so my whole body is facing hers, I'm met with yet another glare. "Oh, were you talking to me? I wasn't sure, since people usually have to get to know me before they hate me."

I relax into my chair as if completely unaffected by her. It gets exactly the response I expected.

"You must be the zero from Earth. They apparently don't teach manners there." She flips her hair behind her shoulder and crosses her arms over her chest.

"I see news travels just as fast here." I arch a brow at the four still seated at the table. Sona ducks her head. Bingo. Although, I have no idea how she told anyone since she's been sitting here the whole time. "Manners must not be my strong suit because I was under the impression it was you who interrupted us. Not the other way around."

Warmth rises to her face, and her blue eyes momentarily turn white before flashing with a bright light. I glance at Falyn, but she's too busy covering her snort with a cough. It faded just as quickly as it

101

happened, so I think it's another magic tell? I really need a name for this power.

"That's funny coming from someone who—"

"Who are your new friends, Ser?" The prince or whatever he is slings an arm across her shoulder, bringing my attention to the black lines swirling just under his skin. I know this one! Aarond manifests shadows too and said he was a devil classification.

"No one you guys want to know. Just a few freaks and their zero friend from Earth." She shrugs and moves to stand between the two guys as if to stake her claim.

Not that she has anything to worry about. To call me uninterested would be an understatement.

"I'm Michan; this is Serresa and Drayzen," the non-prince says, then seems to realize exactly what Serresa said. "You're from Earth?"

I'm taken aback by the frown Michan casts in my direction. I'm aware of how the mages I've met so far feel about magicless humans, but his distaste seems a little more extreme, and I can't help but take offense at his reaction.

"Yep, just a dirty little earthling here to pollute your air with my stench." I roll my eyes and look over at Falyn, who's watching our interaction with wide eyes. Since everyone is done eating, there's really no point in hanging out here when we have an entire apartment to ourselves. I'm about to suggest we head out when Michan speaks again.

"I wasn't trying to be rude. I've just never heard of anyone from Earth having magic, let alone traveling outside of their realm to attend here . . ." his voice trails off and he studies my face intently for a moment. I don't know what he's looking for, but I'm starting to wonder if there's food on my face. I swipe a hand across it just in case.

Michan shakes his head, and the line between his brows smooths out before he wrenches his gaze away from me and locks onto Serresa again. She, of course, is still glaring at me like I stole the last slice of pizza and she hasn't eaten in days. Drayzen has yet to say a single word to anyone. If I hadn't seen him walk over here, I could have mistaken him for a statue. As hard as I've been trying, I can't seem to keep my eyes from darting in his direction every few seconds. Partly because I can't tell if he's purposefully flexing so his muscles are more pronounced or if this is another vision. And also because although he's completely silent, he seems to take up the majority of the space in here. This time, when I look, I make eye contact and even though I know I've been caught, it doesn't stop me from acting as if it never happened. *Real mature, Kennedy.*

"Well, don't worry, your friend is probably right. I'm not anyone you'd be interested in knowing. Besides, I'm not so sure your girlfriend approves." I shake my head and shoot a pointed look at Serresa.

She immediately shrugs Michan's arm off her shoulder and scoffs in disgust. "We're definitely not worried. There will never be a reason, in any realm, for us to know a zero."

"Perfect, because there will never be a reason, in any realm, for me to care." I'm pretty sure Drayzen snorts, but since I've already turned my attention to Falyn, I can't be sure. "You ready to head back yet? It's getting a little crowded in here for my taste."

I give a little finger wave and shoot Serresa a sugary sweet smile before leaving them behind without another glance.

"So, that was fun. I'm so excited we get to deal with more of that for the next few years," Falyn says after a few minutes of silence.

"You more so than me. I really don't see myself staying here the whole four years. I only came to find out more about my family and whatever happened that landed me on Earth." Falyn stops walking when I respond.

"I'm assuming they didn't tell you what happens to mages who don't graduate then?"

"I mean, they told me I might have to live in a mundana village. I don't really understand why that's considered a punishment."

"Living there isn't the punishment. Unless you're okay with having your magic stripped . . ."

CHAPTER SEVEN

It's obvious to me now that everything Aarond told me was half the story. I only have myself to blame for not asking the right questions, I suppose. When he told me I would have to live in a mundana village, it didn't sound so bad. I spent my entire life surrounded by non-magical people. Hell, I was a non-magical person until three days ago. But to be stripped of my power? I may not understand what that means, but there are a lot of things in my life I don't understand. The thought of having my magic stripped causes my stomach to dip and my heart to race.

Even if I can't manifest with purpose yet, I have to admit it was something I was looking forward to. I haven't had a lot of that in my life. Now I waver in my resolve to leave the school at the first whiff of finding my relatives. Maybe I can do this whole school thing and come out unscathed. I'll fade to the back and do my best to stay under the radar, learn what I need to, and use my free time to figure out where I come from. I don't see any other option right now. At least not one that won't leave me with regret.

"Are you almost ready? If we don't leave now, we'll be late!" Falyn taps at my door, pulling me from my early morning thoughts.

Perfect. Day one of staying under the radar is already super successful. "Coming!" I work to yank on my sneakers while simultaneously hopping to my door and yanking it open. I have no idea how my hair looks, but I don't have time to care. "Please tell me my hair doesn't look like a wet mop."

She gives me a cursory once over but hesitates to answer, so I grimace and say, "You know what, never mind. Let's go."

Yesterday, as soon as we got back from dinner, I headed straight to my room. The day's events had caught up with me and the only thing I wanted to do was put away my meager belongings and stew in my over stimulated mind. But my brain and body took that as their cue to shut down. It's a miracle I woke up with enough time to shower, considering I don't have an alarm. Yet another thing I need to ask about if I can't find one in my room after class today.

I only vaguely remember setting out my clothes for the day and had opted to wear the uniform, hoping to blend in. Now that Falyn and I are racing to one of the three buildings to make our first class, I realize what a mistake that was.

Not a single person I can see is wearing the black pants and button-up shirt combo that was sent to my room. Normally I would have no problem with black on black, but the stiff collar and straight leg slacks make me feel like I'm getting ready to perform an a cappella version of some funeral song. I should have taken Falyn's words to heart when she said no one wears their uniform.

Our first class is History of the Realm. Something I very much lack in, among almost everything else, if I'm being honest. Much to my disbelief, I'm eager to dive into it. Very different from my school days on Earth when I could barely be bothered to show up, let alone learn anything.

The classroom is set up much like a smaller version of a college lecture hall. Each row of wood carved desks sits higher than the one before it. Book-filled shelves and jars of unfamiliar flowers and herbs line the walls.

When the teacher walks in, she's dressed in the same uniform as me, causing me to sink into my chair and cover my face. *Perfect.* Falyn elbows me and shoots me an 'I told you so' look from the seat next to me. I just shake my head and sink a little further to hide my growing embarrassment.

I peek up to find her facing sideways, browsing through a stack of papers that were sitting on her podium. I have a clear view of her long, thin neck and watch as a living tattoo of words and symbols scrolls from below her ear to disappear under her collar. Another power vision, I'm sure of it.

"What classification is she?" I lean toward Falyn, whispering under my breath and nodding to the front of the classroom.

"Professor Elwin? Hierophant. All teachers are here," she replies. "Why?"

"Just trying to figure out this vision thing. Remind me what hierophants do again . . ."

"Instant knowledge. They can absorb knowledge from anything and anyone with just the touch of a hand."

Interesting. Although I'd be lying if that power even makes my top ten list.

"Welcome to day three of History of the Realm. Today we'll be learning about the forming of the various unions and how it played a key role in shaping the government as we know it today," Elwin begins in a monotone voice, and I wonder how I'll be able to stay awake during her lectures with a voice like that.

"Who can tell me how many unions were in the first council?"

"What's a union?" I look at Falyn, feeling out of depth. Everyone here already has a basic knowledge of the realm. How am I going to catch up?

"I'm assuming you know the answer, since your attention is on another student and not up here with me. How many unions, Miss . . . ?"

I jerk my attention back to Elwin, who has that stern teacher look down cold and she's aiming it right at me. Her almond-shaped eyes narrow when I hesitate to answer.

I gulp and look around. All eyes are on me. "I don't know?" I hate the shake in my voice when I answer.

"Do try to pay attention then and maybe you'll have half a chance of passing this class."

A few smothered snorts punctuated her admonishment and my face grows warm. This was not the blending in I had planned for the day. *Fantastic job, Kennedy.*

"Anyone else?" She looks around the classroom, her gaze landing on Serresa with a small smile. "Serresa? Care to enlighten our new student?"

Serresa smirks at me before responding, "Four, Professor Elwin. Each representing a different order.

Worldly, physical, mental, and mundana." Her nose wrinkles in disgust on mundana.

"Very well said." Elwin nods her head before continuing. "The council was formed as a sort of ruling body for the realm. Each council member was chosen to represent their order. This, of course, was before the monarchy was established. Now, who can tell me how the original union council was formed?"

The hour and a half long lecture continued much the same way. Elwin would ask a question, look down her pointed nose disapprovingly at a student when they answered incorrectly, then call on either Serresa, Michan, or Drayzen for the answer without bothering to hide her obvious favoritism for the three who sit together in the back of the class.

As much as I dislike the classroom dynamic, I have to admit I learned quite a bit. I don't know how much I retained, but I feel slightly less ignorant walking out than I did walking in. My head is still reeling over how backward the political system feels. But I don't know if I'm letting my American views color my perception. I've always thought of monarchies as something needing to be overthrown and not something that comes in later.

According to Elwin, who I assume must be an expert on the subject considering her magic category, the council was formed shortly after the three gods blessed some of the population with their gifts of magic. The council became necessary as the population of the realm grew to prevent it from falling into chaos. The Esotera chose the first four council members themselves. People who were known to be fair and well respected among their communities.

It's harder to follow along when she brings up certain key events everyone else seems to already know about. Like how the council's failings lead the realm to decide having a single ruler would be a better idea. Then, of course, there's the whole disunion thing. I still don't understand how that came about or why they claim it was necessary.

Even with her monotone voice, I manage to pay attention the entirety of the class without falling asleep. I'm almost surprised when Falyn announces its time to head to our second class of the day: History of Magic.

I would be lying if I said I wasn't looking forward to a class all about magic. The desire to learn how to manifest with purpose has been at the forefront of my mind since trying to grow that plant in my kitchen.

The teacher of this class was much livelier than Elwin. After introducing himself, which I'm sure was for my benefit, since everyone else has already been here for two days, he points at a small statue on his desk. It's a replica of the one I saw in the courtyard with the same floating globe.

"What makes us deserving of the gifts bestowed upon us by The Esotera?"

The question was met with silence, but he doesn't continue, instead choosing to look from

111

student to student, patiently waiting for someone to gather enough courage to answer. The silence stretches only to be broken by the sound of giggling as the door opens and the three elites walk in without a care in the world.

"So good of you to bless us with your presences today . . ."

Serresa, unbothered by Professor Monyae's admonishment, rolls her eyes and takes a seat once again at the back of the classroom. Michan and Drayzen at least have the decency to look apologetic over their disruption.

"Let's start with you, Serresa. What makes you deserving of your gifts?"

I'm not afraid to admit the fact that she's being called out in front of everyone amuses me. Especially when she flounders at answering.

"My bloodline," she finally answers.

"Tell me, how did you earn your spot in your family, then?"

"By being born . . ." she replies sarcastically, then looks at Michan and rolls her eyes again.

"And that's what makes you worthy of your magic?" Professor Monyae lifts a droll brow before continuing. "It's a wonder we have any magic left at all, if that's the attitude the rest of you share."

Serresa's face turns red, but she refrains from saying anything more. I think I'm going to like this class.

"When the first mages were granted abilities, it wasn't because of their lineage. It was their actions. Each of the twenty-two original mages did something so profound with their lives that the gods stood up and took notice. I'm willing to wager not a single one of you here today can, nor will you ever be able to boast such an accomplishment."

Class passed quickly after that. I was so enthralled by Professor Monyae's lecture that it felt like no time had passed at all before the subtle sound of rustling caught my attention and I realized people were getting up to leave.

Listening to him outline the feats of the original twenty-two felt more like listening to a storyteller weave a tale. The original fool earned his magic and ability to shift, when he got caught by a krensel hunting pack looking to make him their dinner. I don't know what a krensel is, but it sounds like a cross between an alligator and a wolf. Something I have no interest in seeing or being near.

The fool managed to get away from the majority of the pack, but one krensel was especially determined to get his dinner. Unfortunately, while trying to sniff out the fool's location after he climbed a tree, he fell into a hunter's pit.

The pit was only four to five feet in depth, but sharp stakes lined the bottom, and when the krensel fell into it, he was impaled by no less than four of them.

The fool, unable to bear the suffering of another living creature, worked tirelessly to pull the

113

animal from the pit and even went as far as to treat its wounds for days until it could care for itself.

I can't imagine a person being so selfless they would risk their own life to save that of another. But apparently the gods found it as impressive as I do because they granted him the gift of shifting. Unlike the shifters today who can only master one, maybe two forms, the fool's shifts were limitless.

We heard four more stories of the originals, each one just as fascinating as the last and making history of magic officially my favorite class. Not that the only other class I have to compare it to was really even a contender in that category.

Arcanum government and its intricacies comes next. It doesn't take me long to decide this is one class I would much rather skip than attend. I learned absolutely nothing of value and I'm almost positive the only reason it's even a class is to satisfy the king's ego. If I have to sit through one more minute of the professor waxing poetic about all the great things the king has done for Arcanum, I might actually vomit.

I don't think I'm the only one not interested in the class either. Falyn and I wound up having to sit just one row in front of the elites, so my peripheral vision was nothing but Serresa grooming herself for the majority of it.

Of the three, it seemed Drayzen was the only one with any intention to actually learn. Not that I was paying close attention to him or anything. Serresa makes such a show of everything she does. It's hard to not glance back every once in a while.

At one point, she leans forward to whisper to the guy sitting in front of her and when they both look up at me, warning bells sound in my head. If this school is anything like the ones on Earth, I can almost guarantee by the end of the day there will be some kind of nasty rumor floating around about me.

Just in case, I angle my body so I have a better view of them without being obvious about it. I have no idea what is and isn't acceptable behavior here and for all I know, one of them is about to turn me into a toad.

I set my notebook and pencil down on my desk, since there hasn't been anything worth taking notes about, and let my eyes wander. Falyn is having a hard time staying awake next to me, as are quite a few of the other students. I can't say I blame them in the slightest.

This classroom is identical to the first two we were in. Apparently, they don't like variety here. The only difference is the royal crest adorning the wall behind the professor's podium. It's a gold sun that looks as if lightning bolts are shooting from it instead of sunbeams. In the center of the sun, a man's profile is carved into the gold. It's painted black, and framing the whole thing are swords crossed over each other to form a pattern of X's. Ugly and garish are the only words I can find to describe it.

Movement to my right distracts me from my appraisal of the royal crest and I turn just in time to catch the guy Serresa was talking to a few minutes ago, reach down to grab my notebook. I clamp my hand over his wrist and cluck my tongue.

"If you're that hard up for some paper, I'm sure there's someone here willing to loan you the money to get some. Sorry, I'm not really the sharing type." I didn't say it very loud, but some of the closer students snicker around us.

His face turns a light shade of pink before he yanks his wrist out of my hand and twists his lips into a disgusted sneer. "Like I would want anything you've touched. It's bad enough I have to spend lunch scrubbing the mundana off my skin. I would never stoop so low as to need anything from a zero like you."

What is it with these people and their classism? Why is being human seen as less than here? It's disgusting. Not to mention the fact that we don't even know what my power level is. Not that it matters. The more I think about it, the angrier I get. Who is he to make such a snap judgment about me? Since reaching adulthood, I've never allowed another person to make me feel inferior and I'm not about to start with him.

Before I can get up to tell him what I think about his little display, a gust of wind comes out of nowhere. Papers fly off the podium at the front of the class and the royal crest rocks back and forth, threatening to fall off the wall. Students grumble as the wind whips their hair around their faces and into their eyes.

The wind current doesn't seem to have any effect on me. Everyone else is struggling to keep their papers, bookbags, hats, and everything else from being caught in the hurricane level wind, but it seems to part around me before joining in front of me to form what looks like a sideways tornado. The only reason I can see it is because of the classroom debris that's caught up in the spinning cyclone. It's heading straight for the guy I just talked to as he trudges back over to his seat directly in front of Serresa.

He's unprepared for the force that hits him in the back, and he launches face first into some desks before falling between them and rolling onto his back with a groan.

Just as suddenly as it started, the wind stops, and the room is completely silent except for the sound of a few papers still fluttering their way to the floor. The entire classroom is in disarray and every person in here is glaring at him with open hostility. Including the professor.

What the fuck was that?

"Are you quite done yet, Mr. Calisk? If you can't control your magic, we'll have to resort to other measures to ensure this doesn't happen again."

"That wasn't me. Why would I knock myself down?" The guy looks around the class before his eyes fall on me in a hateful glare.

It obviously wasn't me. That would be impossible according to what everyone has explained

117

to me, so I don't know why he's looking at me like it's my fault.

"Of the three students with the magician category in my class, you are the only one with wind as your element. I expect you to stay after and clean up the mess you made if you want to make it to first year trials."

The guy sputters but doesn't argue. The other students take that as their cue and gather their things strewn across the classroom. Lucky for me, my notebook and pencil still sit exactly where I left them on my desk. I can't say the same for Falyn. Her hair is a frizzy, tangled mess and her face looks wind burned.

"Let's get out of here. I need to fix myself before we walk into combat. You're so lucky to have been standing where you were. What was his problem, anyway? I wouldn't be surprised if that wind funnel was actually aimed at you."

I'm only half listening to what she's saying because, looking at the chaos, I don't understand how the exact spot I was sitting is the only part of the classroom untouched. Is it possible I created the wind?

Reaching into my stomach where I felt the stirring of magic when I grew that plant, I try to find any spark of energy I can grasp and pull out. If I created the wind, maybe I can do it again. Putting all my focus into manipulating the air around me, I almost don't hear Falyn's next question.

"Why are you making that face? Is your stomach okay? You look like you're about to be sick

118

and trust me when I say you don't want that to happen in here."

I relax my face immediately. So much for that theory. I don't know why I tried, really. I can't even manifest the magic I know I have and now I want to manifest one I couldn't possibly have? Still, his face was genuinely surprised. I don't think he created the wind and if that's the case, then who did?

CHAPTER EIGHT

I don't know what I was expecting out of combat training, but this isn't it. It's my fourth lap of the small dirt trail behind the combat arena and I'm moments away from passing out. The trail runs through the forest behind the arena and consists of steep hills, sudden drops, and surprise rocks jutting from the ground to trip you up at every opportunity. I swear it shifts on me every time I complete a lap, because the obstacles are never where

120

I encounter them in my previous pass. I don't know how it's possible, but I jerk to the left to avoid tripping over a root I know for a fact wasn't there when I came around this bend during my second and third laps.

This is absolute torture. I thought I would learn to fight for real or maybe use a weapon other than my cast-iron skillet. Never did I imagine running until sweat soaks through the white t-shirt and black shorts I found waiting for me in the locker room before class.

Falyn and I are evenly matched for the first two laps, but she's been steadily lagging further behind with every step. Even though there's only one other student lagging behind the two of us, I'm determined to not make a fool of myself. I won't be the last to finish, so I push through the muscle cramps and the stitch forming in my lower stomach. I ignore my need to stop and take a moment to fill my lungs with a breath that doesn't hurt. Then I lower my head and tell myself this is the last stretch; I only need to make it about a hundred more yards, then I can collapse into the soft grass waiting for me at the end.

The rest of the students are already headed back into the massive arena when I round the final bend of the trail and my heart plummets when I realize this means I won't have that moment with the grass I'm craving. Struggling to rein in my heavy panting, I hobble toward the door while trying to apply pressure to the now burning stitch in my side. I have no idea how I'm going to get through the rest of whatever that sadistic asshole of a professor has planned for class.

121

When we got here, Falyn told me he's the only teacher on staff not of the hierophant category. Which makes sense, because no matter how much you read about the art of war or combat, I don't think it's as easy as applying the knowledge. Professor Brextin is an emperor.

Emperors are the warrior class of magic. Their ability is supernatural strength, and the ability to master any and all fighting techniques quickly and efficiently. I'm a little jealous of that ability. I would kill . . . not literally—or maybe a little literally—to have that ability.

Thankfully, the rest of combat isn't as brutal. We're allowed to stretch our muscles out on the mats littering the floor and even drink some much-needed water. While we do that, Professor Brextin paces between the mats and surveys every student individually. When he stops at my mat last, I feel like a bug under a microscope, but I lift my chin and meet his gaze head on. I'm not a delicate house plant ready to wilt at the slightest stirring of unease. I wish I had some mind reading magic right about now.

He's a giant of a man. Almost as broad as he is tall and there isn't a single part of his body not rippling with muscle. I would not want to be in battle against this man. Everything about him screams danger. Even his eyes are so dark they look black. His nose is oddly shaped, like it was smashed into his face so many times it couldn't bounce back anymore.

After a moment, he nods at me, then turns away. I have no idea what that means, but I don't have time to analyze it before he starts talking.

"This will not be an easy class for most of you, if what I saw out on the trail is any indication. In fact, more than half of you probably won't pass." A few faces darken with anxiety, but everyone is paying attention. Even Serresa and Drayzen, who I'm sure were the first two to finish the trail run, look a little sick at the prospect of not passing.

"This first month will focus solely on your endurance. I expect every one of you to be able to run that trail with ease by the end of the thirty days. Some of you will need to fit in additional running time to your days if you have any hope of making it past the first month of my class. I won't bother to call you by name, but you know who you are." His eyes flit from student to student, pausing on a few, including Falyn, before coming to a stop on me. "Before you decide to ignore my warning, know this: if you don't make it past the first thirty days, you're out. Dismissed."

He walks out without another word.

We eat lunch with the same group of Falyn's friends from yesterday. Sona actually smiles at me from her place next to Ciena today.

"We heard Lefrin had a magic misfire in HOM today. Did you guys see it?" Ciena snickers in between bites of the rusty orange-hued leaves on her plate. They're shaped like classic spring mix, so I'm assuming it's their version of lettuce, but who knows? I haven't seen a single plant I recognize since arriving.

"He was being a total Frelch to Kennedy, then when she called him out on it, I think he lost control. Fell face first into a desk." Falyn can barely hold back her laughter while recounting the image of Lefrin knocking himself down with his own magic. "I wish I had thought to bring out my crystal to record it."

"He deserved it. Seriously, what does everyone have against mundanas?" Apparently, that was the wrong question to ask because the table goes quiet. Thinking quickly, I add, "Also, what the hell is a Frelch and crystal?"

Sona snorts. "A Frelch is a huge hairy beast that looks really scary, but is too dumb and slow to be a danger to anything other than the plants it eats. But I think what Falyn was referring to is the fact that even though the males are as big as four of us put together, their . . . uh . . . organ? Is about the size of my little finger." She holds her finger up and shakes it up and down.

Everyone dissolves into another round of laughter, and I have to join in. I couldn't have come up with a better description for that asshole if I tried. After the laughter dies down, Falyn pulls a small rectangular object from her back pocket and hands it

124

to me. It just looks like a thick piece of glass with rounded edges. I can see the table through it. Flipping it around in my hands, I can't figure out what she wants me to do with it.

"What's this?"

"It's my crystal . . . we use it to communicate with people who aren't right next to us."

"Oh! It's a cellphone!" She looks at me quizzically. "That's what we call them on Earth. I lost mine right before getting here. They connect through signal towers, but you have to have one within a certain range for them to work. Can you surf the internet?"

"I have no idea what you just said. We just use them to communicate and story memories sometimes . . ."

"How do they connect to each other?" I ask, still flipping it between my hands, looking for buttons or something to turn it on.

"Magic . . ." Noric answers, this time amusement lacing his voice. "They're made by a temperance from the glass that forms when lightning strikes sand."

I hand the glass back to Falyn. "How do you turn it on?"

She taps her finger against the glass twice and it glows with a soft yellow light. She taps the screen a few more times, then holds it up in front of her face. A small chirping noise comes from Noric's pocket so he pulls his own crystal out and taps the screen before holding his up.

125

Falyn leans over so our shoulders are touching to show me the image of Noric being projected onto her crystal. Understanding dawns on me. They're essentially video chatting. Noric crosses his eyes and sticks out his tongue, eliciting a small giggle from Falyn. It would be cute if it wasn't so nauseating.

Behind Noric, I have a clear view of Drayzen sitting at his table. It looks like he's watching us, but the angle is a little confusing since I'm looking at it through a video chat on someone's phone. When I look away from Falyn's phone and toward the elite's table, I find myself looking right into his eyes. Was he watching me? During combat, I swore he was doing the same thing, but every time I looked up, his focus was on something or someone else. Usually Serresa, not that I care.

"Can you access like records or public files with these?" I yank my gaze away from him because I have more important things to figure out than why he's watching me.

"I don't know how that would be possible, why?" Noric asks while Falyn ends the video and slides her crystal back into her pocket.

"I want to know if there's any record of me being born. The guy who brought me over said I was born here and left on Earth. I have no idea who my family is, so let's just call it curiosity. Do you guys have anything like that here?"
"Do you know what territory you were born in?" Ciena questions. "I'm pretty sure The Star Guild keeps

126

record of births since, as healers, they attend almost every one. But every territory will have different records. What do they do on Earth for children without families?"

If only she knew how loaded that question was. I give her the simplest answer I can think of, "Sometimes they pay families to take children in temporarily, sometimes they just live in group homes with a bunch of other kids who lost their families, and sometimes the kids get lucky, and a family permanently adopts them into their families." I shrug, not wanting to talk about my own experiences. "I don't know anything about my birth. Is there one close to us we can try? Anything is better than nothing."

"All of them can be close by . . . all we need is a hanged-man willing to portal us. But we could start with the one here, since there's an always open portal into town for students and teachers who need supplies and stuff. I'll take you on our off days from classes." Falyn, thankfully, chooses not to question my upbringing any further.

The rest of my first week flies by. History of Magic remains my favorite class, but surprisingly, combat is a close second. By day four, I was able to get through the trail without feeling like I would keel over and die by the end of it. I suppose the extra running

127

Falyn and I do in the evenings is helping with that. We aren't the only ones either; half our combat class runs the trail a second time in the evening. I guess everyone took the professor's announcement to heart.

The rest of my classes seem to be utter failures. Or at least I seem to be an utter failure. Not once have I been able to manifest my magic. My practical applications professor is probably the nicest one I have and when every suggestion she makes inevitably fails, she gives me a sympathetic smile and suggests something else. That empty pot has sat on my desk for five days now and hasn't so much as sprouted a weed. .

My classmates, on the other hand, aren't as sympathetic to my plight. Serresa has very quickly become the bane of my existence. The never-ending snide remarks about my lack of magic are really wearing me down. I'm even starting to wonder if I belong here. If it weren't for the constant visions of other people's magic, I would think they got me completely mixed up with someone else.

Falyn keeps telling me that people born in the mundana villages who wind up being gifted always take a long time to get the hang of their magic, but I can see the shadow of doubt in her eyes and hear the slow hesitation in her voice.

It seems the school runs the same way schools do on Earth. Five days on, followed by two days off, so when I woke up on my own and not to the sound of Falyn pounding on my door, my mood improved drastically this morning. We opt out of taking a

128

morning run so we can head straight to the village after breakfast. I wanted to make sure we have plenty of time to browse records, considering I don't have a whole lot to go off.

This time, I don't hesitate to step through the portal. The smell of ozone is as still off putting, as it was the first time I used one, but at least I know it's not going to send my body parts to different places.

"Why are you making that face?" Falyn asks when I step out of the portal after her.

"I don't like the smell. It reminds me of burnt rubber." I relax my nose but purse my lips.

"I have no idea what rubber is, but I don't smell anything." She makes a show of sniffing the air then herself.

"I mean the portal. The last one I went through smelled the same."

"Portals don't have a scent that I'm aware of. I'm gonna guess this is another weird high priestess thing." She gestures toward a large open gate about twenty feet from where we came out of the portal. "After we check with The Star Guild, we should hit the market. They have the best stuff on sixth-day."

I follow Falyn down three separate cobblestone streets until we come to a small wood building. An eight-pointed star hangs above the door Falyn knocks on. Slow, steady footsteps shuffle inside just before the door creaks open.

129

"Can I help you?" an older woman with white gray hair answers. She holds a cane in one age spotted hand and the door in her other.

I step forward. "Hello, ma'am. I was hoping to look through some birth records today, if that's possible."

She squints against the sunlight shining in her eyes, causing her laugh lines to become more prominent. "Whatever for? I don't think we've ever had anyone make such a request in all my years serving in the guild."

"I'm trying to find out more about my family and where I come from," I answer honestly, praying she doesn't send me away. This is my best and only chance right now.

"I don't see any harm in it, but wouldn't it be easier to just ask your parents?" She widens the door so Falyn and I can step through.

"That's actually why I'm here . . . I don't know who my parents are. I'm hoping to find out."

"You poor thing. Tell me what you do know, and maybe I can point you in the right direction."

I hesitate because there isn't much I do know and I'm beginning to see this may be a futile effort.

"I know I was born in the beginning of September twenty-one years ago . . ." I trail off at the look of confusion on her face.

"September? I don't think I quite understand what you mean by that."

130

Falyn interjects, "I think we're going to have to give her the complete details of your beginning if we have any hope of finding a record on you."

I clear my throat and rub my sweaty hands against my thighs. "Right . . . I don't have any details because someone took me to Earth as an infant and left me there. September eighth is the day I was dropped off in the care of an Earth healer. They said I wasn't more than a day or two old."

The woman's gnarled fingers stiffen on the handle of her cane as the rest of her body goes still. Her face pales and the skin around her mouth tightens for a split second before she adopts a mask of indifference. I don't have time to wonder about her reaction before she turns away to head for a chair.

The interior of The Star Guild is not an office like I expected it to be. Two-seater tables topped with doilies and floral-patterned teacups dot the room we're in. "What exactly is The Star Guild—are you sure they have records here? This seems more like a tea shop or a club for old women." I lean in to whisper to Falyn as we both watch the woman lower herself with a sigh of relief.

"I may be old, but I'm not deaf, child. Your friend is right. The Star Guild keeps a record of every birth we attend. We also enjoy coming together to discuss new healing techniques or decompressing after a hard day. Both men and women, young, and as you said, old. In this room, knowledge that could very well save your life or someone you love was passed from one

131

healer to another," she admonishes me with a stern voice. "Now, what is your name and what in the seven realms is a September?"

Falyn covers her mouth to hide her forming smile while I clear my throat to answer, "I'm Kennedy. September is the name of a month on Earth. A period lasting around thirty days or so—"

"Ahh, you're referring to a moon cycle!" She claps her hands together in understanding.

"Right . . ." This is going to be harder than I thought. "It's the mon . . . moon cycle, I mean, when leaves are turning, and the weather starts to cool . . ." How the hell do you describe a month to someone with no reference for it?

"How far away from now is it?" Falyn asks, giving me the obvious solution and making me feel slightly dumb in the process.

"If time runs the same here, then it would be the next moon cycle after this one."

"The harvest moon, then. How many harvest moons have passed since your birth?" The woman asks.

"This will be my twenty-second harvest moon. How far back do the guild's records go?"

"Far enough. Follow me and we'll see what we can find." She struggles to lift herself from her chair, and both Falyn and I rush to her side to help. She swats our hands away as soon as we offer them and, using her cane for balance, gets to her feet on her own. "I'm fine.

It just takes a minute to get these old bones to do what I want them to."

We follow as she leads us on uneven steps to another door at the back of the room. The room it opens to is smaller than the one we were just in. In the center of it sits a single round table with three chairs. Floor to ceiling bookshelves line the walls, overflowing with hundreds if not thousands of journals.

She browses the shelves, running her fingers over the spines of the books until she finds what she's looking for and begins pulling a few down. "Well, don't just stand there, I'm too old to carry all this by myself." She shakes her head in disappointment.

I shoot a glance at Falyn, remembering only minutes ago when she admonished us for trying to help. She just shrugs her shoulders and takes the books from her to set them on the table. Four journals in total contain all the births of this territory from around the time I think I was born. I stare at them, hopeful and terrified at what I might find inside. One of these books may have answers to almost twenty-two years of questions. Or they might have nothing at all.

"That's it. If you need anything, just yell for me, I'll be around . . ." she hesitates for a moment at the door. "Some questions are better left unanswered . . ."

"You say that like you know what I'm going to find. Do you know who I am?" I knew when I told her where I'm from, something wasn't right about her reaction.

133

"No, I just mean to say if a parent abandons their child, I would expect it to be for a good reason. You may not like what you find out." She smiles to soften the blow of her words. "Anyway, my name is Anzlee, if you need to get my attention. Good luck, girls." She leaves us with the journals and me with twice as many questions as when I came in.

"That was kind of weird," Falyn says pulling a book from the stack and opening it to the first page. "Also, I don't know what we should even be looking for. How do we know if any of these births listed are your birth specifically?"

She has a point. Each page is dedicated to a single birth. It lists the parents' names and the baby's name, gender, time of birth, and order of the baby being born. There's also a few notes on the delivery itself. I don't know how any of this will help me.

"How do they know what order babies are in when they're born if magic doesn't manifest until adulthood?" That piece of information will help narrow it down a little. We just need to pay attention to females born into the worldly order.

"Healers say the three orders give off different vibrations or something. So, when a baby is born, they can tell what order, but not specifically what category of magic they'll have, I guess."

We spend several hours pouring through the books but find nothing helpful. Halfway through my first journal, Falyn realizes the pages had been enchanted by a temperance. Swiping a finger down the page adds extra information to the journal. The new information includes a date of death, if there is one, and the symbol for their category of magic appears next to their name. This helps narrow it down even further because now all we need is to find people with the stylized leaf next to their name indicating they manifested empress magic. We find ten names in total, but I can tell by the look on Falyn's face she's about as hopeful as I am. All we have to do is check the names against the student directories for the four academies in Arcanum and hope one doesn't match.

After saying our goodbyes to Anzlee, who peppered me with a hundred questions about growing up on Earth, we step back out into the fading daylight of early evening. I'm still trying to figure out why Anzlee was so interested in my personal experiences rather than the generalities of living on Earth when we round a corner and come to a bustling street market.

It reminds me of the swap meets one of my foster parents would drag me to on the weekends to sell their stolen electronics and bags of who knows what. Although this one is way more clean and friendly. Every booth owner has a smile on their face and welcomes us when we step up to browse their wares.

135

I'm admiring a beautiful bracelet made of polished blue stones when a familiar shirt catches my eye a couple booths down. Those fucking flamingos.

CHAPTER NINE

Aarond is having an animated conversation with the man behind the booth and neither one of them notice as I drag Falyn over with me to confront him.

"Has anyone ever told you how big of an asshole you are?" I demand forgoing any other greeting and am a little satisfied at the slight tightening of his shoulders when he recognizes my voice.

"I think you may have a time or two, actually." He smirks at me but shifts his eyes to the man he was talking to before I interrupted.

I watch as they carry an entire conversation with their eyes as if I'm not even here and huff out my irritation. "I just wanted to come over here and thank you."

Aarond breaks eye contact with the man and looks at me in shock. "Really? For what?"

"No, not really!" I all but yell. "You left me in that office with no idea of what I was supposed to do. You didn't even tell me you were leaving!"

"Is this who brought you over?" Falyn interrupts what was about to be a magnificent tirade on my part.

"Yes, unfortunately. Although I still have no idea how he found me or how he knew I existed." Aarond opens his mouth to interject but I cut him off, "And don't give me that bullshit line about the high priestess. I want to know why you were looking for me in the first place."

There's a tiny part of me that really wants his answer to be that he was hired by someone related to me, or who at least knew my family. I don't know why I'm so hell bent on finding people who obviously didn't want me. The only thing I can come up with is closure. I just want to know why.

"Look, all I know is you're—"

The man behind the booth clears his throat and Aarond snaps his mouth shut mid-sentence. I narrow my eyes at them both and cross my arms over my chest.

"Okay, seriously, this all feels very cloak and dagger and it was amusing for about two whole seconds but I'm over it, so can you just—"

A loud crash from across the street cuts me off. A man and a woman wearing chest armor consisting of overlapping gold and silver scales are destroying a vendor's booth as he cowers against the building behind him.

The woman lifts the entire booth and tosses it aside as if it weighs nothing and stalks forward to stand over the huddled man. "Lochwen, you have been accused of conspiring with rebels and acts of treason against the king." She grabs the man by his neck and hauls him up until his feet dangle above the ground.

I take a step forward but Falyn's hand on my arm stops me. "Don't. They're the king's warriors and both of them are emperors."

"I have no idea what you're talking about. I've conspired with no one!" he gasps through the grip she has on his throat.

"That will be for the king's high judgment to decide," she responds before dropping him. He stumbles to catch his balance but before he's able to right himself all the way, she pulls thick black cuffs from the band of her pants and shackles his wrists together. "We've been commanded to bring you in for questioning regarding your activities four days ago."

139

The blood drains from his face, leaving him a ghost of his former self.

The woman uses the cuffs to drag the helpless man behind her while her partner stays to continue wreaking havoc on his booth and wares. He leaves nothing unbroken or usable. The satisfied smile on his face when he surveys the damage makes my gut churn.

"Why didn't anyone stop them? Even if he's being accused of something, how is it okay for them to destroy his things and drag him off like that?" I ask no one in particular, but need to know all the same.

"You can't interfere with the king's warriors unless you want to be locked up, too," Falyn answers.

"They can just grab anyone they want off the street and throw them in jail on a whim?"

"Not exactly a whim, but the king's warriors are an extension of his power. Their word is as good as law in the territories." This time it's the man Aarond was talking to who answers my question.

I turn away from the wreckage to look at all three of them. "How is that okay?"

"It's not," Aarond states simply. "On that note, I'll need to go let Lochwen's wife know what happened." He looks at his friend. "We'll have to continue this later, Bren."

Falyn tugs on my arm. "We need to go too. I'm not starting first year trials with a deficit because we get caught up in rebel activity."

140

I let her tug me back toward the portal. So much has happened in the last ten minutes. I'm not sure I've fully absorbed it all.

"Who are the rebels and what are they rebelling against?" I ask, following behind her at a much slower pace.

"Nobody really knows who they are, other than the majority of them are mundanas. They're trying to overthrow the king and go back to the old ways."

I pick up my pace to match hers. I don't know enough about the history of the realm to understand. "What was wrong with the old ways?"

"Before the disunion, magic was fading at a much faster rate because of bloodline dilution. Magic weakened with every generation born. If the king hadn't stepped in and took the throne when he did, magic might have disappeared." She shrugs as if that explains everything.

But something doesn't sit right with me. If mingling with humans was causing such a substantial loss of power for mages, why would any of them side with a faction of rebels to return to the old ways? That can't be all there is to the story. Also why is it, every time I ask anything about the disunion, I'm fed the same line repeatedly? It's like everyone has been coached on what to say.

Instead of voicing my concerns, I change the subject. "What did you mean by starting with a deficit?"

141

"The first-year trial is usually about testing your ability to use your magic in high-stress situations without a whole lot of training. The actual trial changes every year, but we compete against each other for the highest score. If you start with a negative score, it'll be that much harder to pass, let alone score higher than other people. If you rank really low, you won't move on to the next year."

"So even if you can manifest magic, it doesn't guarantee you'll pass? And everyone is just okay with that?"

"What do you mean?" She looks at me quizzically.

"I mean, if you don't pass, they strip your powers and you have to go live in the mundana territories, right? The parents just agree to this?"

"They don't really have a choice. It's the law. And the only way to prevent magic from disappearing completely." She stops in front of the arches that house the portal to get back to campus.

I don't say much the rest of the way back. There's just too much for me to process. The fact that people aren't given a choice about going to school in the first place is bad enough. But also knowing you could have your magic ripped away from you as a product of not doing well is just plain horrible.

Before we head up to our room, we stop at the directory board to compare it with the names I wrote down during our visit to The Star Guild. No luck. Each name is assigned to a room in our building, which means there's no way any of them could be me. *So much for that tiny sliver of hope.*

Sleep eludes me for a long time after laying down. I can't stop thinking about the market. I feel like there's something I forgot to do, or something I lost, but for the life of me I can't figure out what it is. It's just a constant buzz in the back of my mind and every time I try to grasp it, it slips through my fingers like water.

Falyn wakes me up for breakfast, as is our usual morning routine. I really need to see about getting an alarm, so I don't have to rely on her. Plus, she's one of those annoying people who get up early every day regardless of whether we have school, and I would have much rather slept in than ate breakfast.

"Did you guys see the warriors?" Sona asks before Falyn and I even get a chance to sit down.

"We just woke up. I haven't seen anything except the inside of my eyelids and the path to the commissary." I hunch over the table, ignoring the plate of fresh fruit in front of me. I miss coffee. And sleeping in.

"How could you miss them? A whole squad showed up late last night and have been patrolling the campus ever since." She leans in and lowers her voice to almost a whisper, "My father said a few people in

143

Emberbell have gone missing and they think it's happening all over again."

"What's happening all over again?" No longer struggling to wake up, I give her my undivided attention.

"A bunch of people went missing over the span of a few years back when my parents attended the academy. No one knows what happened, but they think it was the rebels."

Ciena rolls her eyes. "It's always the rebels."

"You don't think it is? The king himself said they were behind it." Sona crosses her arms over her chest in challenge.

"The only reason he even thinks that is because everyone who went missing was a high-level mage. I don't think the mundanas are smart or powerful enough to manage something like that. For all we know, they could still be alive and living happily in other realms."

I take a closer look at Ciena, surprised to hear her defend humans, even if it was in a back-handed way. She picks at the green fruit on her plate and doesn't look up while she talks. Sona glares at her, but doesn't respond. I'm pretty sure this is the first time I've heard them disagree on something. Even though they couldn't look more opposite of each other, I've been thinking of them as 'the twins' until this point. I haven't seen one without the other and they practically share the same brain, so it's surprising to see them disagree on such a big topic.

Noric clears his throat to break up the awkward silence that falls over our table. Of course he chooses the last thing I want to talk about as the diversion.

"How's manifesting coming along, Kennedy?"

"Well, it can't get any worse, right? At least none of you will have to worry about scoring the lowest in the trials, because I'm sure that'll be my honor," I groan.

"Maybe we can help. I don't have anything planned today, so if you and Falyn are free, we can try to help." He's not looking at me when he says it though, and I take it for what it really is. He's looking for a reason to hang out with Falyn today without outright asking her to hang out. It would be cute if it wasn't for him using me as a way to get to her. Even so, I'm not dumb enough to turn down help when I so obviously need it.

"I'll come too," Both Sona and Ciena say at the same time.

Perfect. Four people to witness my failure as an empress. Exactly how I wanted to spend my day.

Rostan chooses this exact moment to join us at the table. He smiles at Ciena, who blushes under his gaze, before asking, "Where are we going?"

Make that five witnesses to my embarrassment. I release another groan and flop my forehead against the table before responding. "To watch me begin my descent into the mundana villages, probably."

Falyn snickers next to me and I kick her leg under the table in retaliation. I have nine months to either figure this magic stuff out or find my family. Since I don't have high hopes for my standing at the end of first year trials, I really need to visit The Star Guilds in the other territories and check their records.

The spot we wind up in is beautiful. Blue crystalline waters lap at a sandy beach just beyond a grove of dense trees not too far from campus. I don't think I'll ever get over how vivid the colors of plant life are here compared to Earth. The greens are deeper, and the reds, pinks, oranges, and yellows are brighter. Everything smells better here, too. It makes me realize how much the pollution on Earth has affected plant life as much as it does animal.

We find an open spot of soft grass dotted with tiny purple and white flowers to sit on, and I spend a few minutes just taking everything in. I've been to lakes before, but none as serene and beautiful as this one.

Falyn, Noric, and I sit in a circle together while Ciena, Sona, and Rostan take turns showing off their magic. I watch as Sona picks up a large rock and stares at it with total focus. After a few moments, her expression changes to a beaming smile when the rock

146

disintegrates into sand that slips between her fingers to land at her feet.

Rostan kneels next to Ciena and puts both palms against the beach sand before closing his eyes. It doesn't take long for a burning smell to permeate the air. The sand in front of her glows red for a few seconds before fading and leaving behind what looks like a shiny lump. When Rostan removes his hands from the sand and reaches over to pick it up, I realize he made glass from the sand, and it wasn't a lump. He holds a small figure in his hand, but I can't quite make out what it is other than an animal of some sort. The fact that he can direct his lightning so precisely leaves me speechless. It looks like the gift he made for Ciena does the same to her.

But then she tosses her head back in a loud tinkling laugh before taking it from him to admire. She hands it back to him before dropping to her own knees, as he did just moments before. By the time I realize what she's doing, it's already over and I blink several times to be sure I'm actually seeing what I think I'm seeing.

A huge red cat now stands in her place. She's about the size of a large lion with two sharp horns jutting backward from her head right behind feather tufted ears. Her tail starts as one, then forks into two about halfway down. Each one tipped with a sharp barb. She circles Rostan, who only looks slightly concerned to have such a dangerous animal so close, but he doesn't let her get behind him.

My heart rate kicks up a notch when the front half of Ciena's cat body lowers to the ground. A clear sign she's getting ready to pounce. Looking at the two-inch claws on her feet, I don't think Rostan wants that to happen. Even in play. When her hind legs coil to launch her in the air, I yell out, "Move!"

Rostan pays me no attention. He's about to have his head taken off by one of the biggest cats I've ever seen, and he's just standing there. I jump to my feet as if I could do anything about it, but I can't bring myself to watch when she leaps. Squeezing my eyes shut, I wait for the sound of impact but only hear laughter. Everyone's laughter.

My eyes snap open and I see Ciena once again in human form, straddling Rostan on the ground between her legs. However, she, like everyone else, is focused on me. She must have changed back mid leap to avoid hurting him.

I glare at them both before turning around to rejoin Noric and Falyn, who are both obviously fighting a losing battle with their own laughter.

"It's not like I knew she could do that," I grumble, but my own lips are twitching. "Whatever. Just wait until I can grow some vines and hang you all upside down from the trees. We'll see who's laughing then."

I watch wistfully as the three of them continue to play around with their magic. I want to be able to do that. I look at Falyn, who holds her hand over one of the tiny flowers with that same look of focus on her face. Three more spring up around it. She grins at me as Noric takes the small twig in his hand and presses it into the skin at my wrist. After he pulls it away, a tiny set of black wings resembling those of a bat appear on my skin tattoo style. At the top of each wing sits a sharp talon. They're both beautiful and dangerous looking.

"How did you do that?" I question, admiring my wrist. I've always wanted a tattoo but never had the funds to get it done.

"I can remove it if you don't like it. It's temperance magic. I can imbue objects with my magic to make them do anything I want. We call them artifacts," he responds proudly. "Your name almost sounds like the name of an animal here that has those wings. They live in the trees and you only see them at night, but they're called kendees."

I pull my wrist inward to press it against my chest. "Don't you dare remove it. I love it! Is it permanent?"

"As permanent as you want it to be."

"My turn." Falyn shoves her wrist in front of him. "I want wings too, but pretty ones."

I elbow her. "Mine are pretty. You must be blind."

Noric shakes his head and presses the same twig to Falyn's wrist. Hers looks like butterfly wings and fits her personality perfectly. Falyn squeals and holds her wrist out for me to see.

149

"Okay," Noric says, blushing, obviously liking Falyn's reaction to his creation. "We came here to figure out Kennedy's magic, not mine."

"I kinda want the tattoo power though," I say, still admiring my wrist.

"Once you get a grasp of empress magic, you'll think differently." Falyn smiles softy. "We literally create life."

"You create life. I just stare at dirt for hours at a time," I mutter, glaring at the grass I'm touching. I've been trying since we got here to make something grow, but I won't admit that out loud.

"Where do you feel your power?" Falyn asks. "It can be different for everyone. For instance, when I'm pulling mine forward, I feel it in my hands."

I have to think about it for a minute, because that day in my apartment, I felt something at the top of my stomach just below my chest, a warm tingling sensation had started, then spread throughout the rest of my body. I haven't felt it since though, nor have I felt anything anywhere else.

"I guess my stomach? It kind of radiates through my body, but it starts just below my chest."

"Good, now I want you to close your eyes and focus on feeling that spot," Falyn urges me with her head cocked. I roll my eyes at the cliché, but do as I'm told.

Nothing.

No matter how much I focus inward, the tingle isn't there. After a few minutes, I groan and open one eye to find both Noric and Falyn watching me. "I'm starting to think everything until now has just been a fluke, and maybe I don't belong here."

"Don't say that. It'll come. I seriously doubt a high priestess would have a vision about a powerless girl in a completely different realm and send someone to look for her. Maybe there's something we're missing." She smiles at me reassuringly. "Maybe you need a trigger. The first time you manifested, what were you doing?"

I open my mouth to answer, but she triggered something different than my magic. The thing I was trying so hard to figure out when I laid in bed last night.

A high priestess sent Aarond to find me on Earth. A high priestess he referred to as Bren. I'm almost positive Aarond also called the man he was talking to in the market Bren. How did I miss that? I was standing less than two feet from someone who could answer most of my questions, if not all of them.

Fucking Aarond. Once again, he fails to give me the important details. Every time I see that man, I wind up regretting it later. Okay, maybe that's not entirely true. I would never admit it to him, but I'm not having the worst time here. Sure, things can suck just like anywhere else, but this is the first time in my life I feel like I might actually be discovering myself. Or at least my history.

"Kennedy?" Falyn breaks through my revelation. "What's wrong?"

"Do you remember that guy Aarond was talking to at the market?" She nods and waits for me to continue. "I'm pretty sure he was the high priestess."

Her mouth forms a small O.

"We have to go back," I urge, getting to my feet. "I need to talk to him."

CHAPTER TEN

We don't end up going back to the market. According to Falyn and Noric, it would be pointless since it's not open today. Instead, we spend another couple of hours trying unsuccessfully to make my magic manifest. When my head starts throbbing, I call it quits.

I mostly just pick at the food on my plate when we make it back to the commissary for dinner. While everyone is still riding the high of our afternoon at the beach and chatting animatedly, I'm a lot more subdued. Partly because of my still present headache and mostly because I feel like a total failure.

Falyn tries to draw me into the conversation several times but eventually she gives up and I can tell my mood is bringing down the rest of the table, so I give in to the temptation for a nap.

"Guys, I think I'm gonna go lay down for a while. My head is killing me," I say, pushing back from the table. Falyn moves to stand also, but I wave her back down. "Stay, I'm fine. I just need to rest."

She searches my face with a frown but sits back down. "If you're sure. I don't mind going back with you or taking you to the healer."

"It's fine, I promise. You don't have to constantly babysit me. I'm a big girl."

"I'm not babysitting you, Ken. I was just trying to help you acclimate to Arcanum. That's what friends do, but if it's annoying you, just say something."

I flinch. "I didn't mean it like that. I just meant you don't have to disrupt your life to cater to mine. I'll be fine."

"Fine, I'll see you later, then," she responds, but I can tell it's not fine. I just don't have it in me to hash out whatever her issue with me is. I send her what I hope is a reassuring smile before I turn to leave.

Outside, the sun is still shining brightly and when I get to the courtyard where all paths on campus branch from, I decide to sit on one of the benches for a few minutes and enjoy the quiet. It's frustrating me to no end that I figured out who Bren is too late to do anything about it. I'll have to wait another week before I can go back and talk to him.

Footsteps crunching on the gravel path behind me bring me out of my thoughts. I should have known I wouldn't get to enjoy the quiet very long, considering the courtyard is the main junction point between all campus locations.

I turn to find three warriors walking side by side. None of them spare even a cursory glance my way as they come from the physical path and head to the worldly path across from it. I almost didn't believe Sona this morning about them being on campus, since I hadn't seen a single one all day, but I guess she was right.

Does that mean she's also right about rebels kidnapping people? Even as I think it, something doesn't feel right. What could the rebels gain by kidnapping mages? If returning to the old ways is what they're ultimately after, wouldn't causing harm to mages just because of who they are accomplish the exact opposite? Just like my short-lived time with Aarond, I feel like I'm getting a bunch of puzzle pieces, but none of them fit together.

The warriors fade from my sight, so I turn back to the statue only to hear another set of footsteps

155

on the gravel. I guess this place isn't as quiet as I initially thought. Of course it has to be Serresa and her tribe of lackeys who would find me sitting here by myself. I don't have the brain power to deal with them right now.

I get up from my bench hoping I can just head to my room without having to interact with her, but after taking only two steps toward the worldly path I find myself unable to move thanks to a vine wrapped around both my ankles. Perfect. It's going to be one of those interactions.

"What do you want, Serresa?" I sigh, already over her mean girls mentality.

The two girls she's with smirk as she takes a step forward with a nasty glint in her blue eyes.

"I want you to go back to where you came from," she replies, putting her hands on her hips. "You're not wanted here."

"Someone obviously does, or I wouldn't be here. Are you forgetting I didn't even know Arcanum existed until someone came to get me? Must mean I'm important to someone around here." I cock an eyebrow at her, refusing to back down.

"An obvious mistake that needs to be rectified before you dilute our blood lines even further. You might as well go ahead and move to the mundana territory now since you have no magic and there's zero reason for you to be here."

I shake my head. This again. She really needs to come up with another schtick, this one is getting old real fast. "Don't you ever get tired of hearing yourself say the same thing over and over? We've already been through this. I'm not going anywhere. Why are you so focused on my existence, anyway? I would have thought you'd be out practicing your light work, so what happened in class the other day doesn't happen again." I know my jab hit its mark when her face turns red at the mention of the hole she burned through the wall separating our classroom from another during practical applications.

"I'm glad you find it so amusing, considering your magic seems to be nonexistent." I sober at the cold reminder.

"Well, I'm sure now that I get to take two classes in one thanks to your hole, I'll catch up soon." I struggle against the vines, still holding my feet together. "Are we done yet?" I stare pointedly at my feet.

"Actually, I don't think we are. Since you can obviously use some tutoring, why don't we give you a lesson in empress magic?" She looks at one of the girls standing behind her. "Maybe something that suits her thorny personality?"

The girl smirks and the vine slowly crawls from my ankles, up my legs, and wraps itself around my arms and torso until I'm completely bound. I struggle against it for a moment but realize very quickly it's no use. My heart rate kicks up a notch. I don't know how far they're going to take this, and I'm not stupid enough to bait them further.

157

When the girl controlling the vine meets my eyes, icy dread works its way up my spine. I'm no stranger to the glint of malice I find there and whatever she has in store for me, I know it's not good.

No sooner does the thought pass through my mind that the first sting pierces my skin. I bite my lip to keep myself from gasping in surprise. I won't let them have the satisfaction of a reaction. But then it's not just one sting, but several, starting at my ankles and climbing everywhere the vine touches my skin. Thorns. She's making it grow thorns. It doesn't take long to become overwhelming, and I cry out when they break skin and begin imbedding themselves.

Serresa leans her face in so close I can feel her breath on my skin. "First lesson: you should quit now."

They leave me standing there, still wrapped in the thorny vine with no way of escaping. The slightest movement causes the thorns to tear at my skin, shooting burning pain through all four of my limbs.

"Kennedy?" I twist my head to see who's calling my name, sending another round of pain through my body and causing me to moan out loud.

Michan rushes to me at the sound and slices a finger downward. A black shadow follows the same path and cuts through the vine with ease.

"Thank you." I gasp when I can take a full breath without the vise around me. My arms and legs are covered in hundreds of cuts and punctures wounds dripping blood. How could anyone be that cruel?

"What happened?" he asks through clenched teeth.

"You should ask your girlfriend." I turn from him with disgust. If he hangs out with her, then I have no doubt he's as cruel as she is and I want nothing to do with any of them. He stops me with a hand on my shoulder.

"You need to see the healer so those don't fester." I search his face and find nothing but genuine concern etched on it.

"I don't know where it is." Frustrated by the tears in my throat, I don't say anything else. Thankfully, he points me down a path and falls into step next to me when I limp in that direction.

"Are you gonna tell me what happened?" he asks after we walk in silence for the first few minutes.

"I fell," I reply, not wanting to hear him make excuses for her. "You don't have to walk me. I'm assuming the path will take me straight there?"

"I'm just making sure you get there, okay?"

If only I could believe that. "Look, I'm not going to tell anyone if that's what you're worried about."

He frowns at me. "What do you mean? Tell what?"

I sigh and try to push my hair out of my face, but the motion pulls my skin taut and stings too much, so I drop my arm back to my side. "I just want to make it through the school year. I don't know what the deal is with you guys, but I'm not interested." I pause

159

outside a door with an eight-pointed star above it. The symbol for healers. "I'm sure I'll only be here for this year, then you won't have to worry about it, so can you please just leave me alone?"

I leave him standing there before he can say anything back. My headache is very quickly becoming a migraine, and I feel like one giant paper cut. I just want to see the healer, then go home and sleep it off.

Inside, there are six beds, three lined on either side of the room with curtains between them that would allow for privacy if needed. There's a woman sitting behind a desk at the back of the room. She gets up as soon as I enter and rushes forward as she gets a better look. My arms and legs are still dripping blood from the larger gashes and there's very little skin visible through the now drying smears covering me.

"What in the triple gods have you done to yourself?" she says, taking my hand and leading me to the nearest bed. Before I can answer, she's halfway across the room, headed for a closed door behind her desk. When she re-emerges, she has a large bowl of water and several small cloths in her hands.

"I had a little issue with some magic," I reply, purposefully avoiding mentioning that someone else had done it to me. The last thing I need is to make a big deal about it and having Serresa seek retaliation for it.

"I'd say," she responds and dips one of the cloths into the water before using it to clean away the blood on one of my legs. "Hmm, it doesn't look as bad as I initially thought." Her hands are soft but deft as she continues to wash away the blood and dirt.

The room doesn't have much in the way of things to hold my attention, so I spend my time tracing the rows of even parts in her dark hair between her braids and trying to figure out where the scent of lemon grass is coming from. One thing I miss from home is my lemon grass candles, soaps, and pretty much anything else I could get my hands on.

Her cloth climbs higher to the gashes on my thigh, and I tense, knowing those are the ones that are going to hurt. But when she gets there, the scent of lemon grass grows stronger and when she pulls away, not only is my leg clean of blood but there also isn't a single cut on it.

"That's amazing," I breathe out before I can stop the words from coming. "I mean, I didn't expect it to be so easy and painless."

"You've never been to a healer?" She looks up at me quizzically and gives me a genuine smile. I find myself returning her smile and relaxing against the bed.

"I've been to a doctor, but they heal with medicine and not magic on Earth."

"Aah, you must be Kennedy, then." Her face is still serene and holds none of the shock or distaste I'm used to receiving. I instantly like her. "How would your doctors treat this?" she asks, stumbling over the word doctor a little bit.

161

"They would probably just clean it, apply bandages, and give me medicine so it doesn't get infected." I shrug.

"You would have to walk around with the cuts until they heal on their own?" A small wrinkle forms between her eyes at the thought. "That sounds awful."

I laugh out loud, but before I can tell her about the side effects of taking antibiotics, the door opens and two men carrying a third between them walk in. They half drag, half carry the limp form and lift him onto the bed next to mine.

The healer sighs, but she finishes the last bit of cuts on my arm before she turns her attention to them. "Training again, I see." She cocks one dark brow and rests a hand on her hip.

The two conscious men who sport a few scrapes and bruises answer by way of sheepish grins, as if this is something they've done before. "You two are fine. It'll do you some good to live with those bruises for a while and I'm going to need every bit of my magic for him, so you can go." She shoos them out with a stern look that invites no argument.

I'm impressed such a small woman has the ability to command the largest men I've ever seen. Something I've noticed about all emperors, including the women. They're extremely large and intimidating. I wonder if they're born large or if they all have magical growth spurts when their magic manifests.

"I don't think I'm going to be able to heal this completely. I'll do what I can, but a temperance salve will have to do the rest. It'll be slower and probably hurt worse, but I'm sure you can handle it. As often as you're in here, I'm gonna put a plaque above one of these beds that says Drayzen."

I was so busy being impressed by the healer and imagining people growing a foot in a matter of seconds, I never looked at the person laying on the bed next to mine. My head whips around at the sound of his name and we immediately make eye contact. I don't know how long he's been awake and staring at me. He only looks away to respond to the healer.

"Aw, come on, Maylah, I'm your favorite patient and you know it. Who else allows themselves to get injured as often as I do just for the benefit of being in your presence?" He winks at her and even I blush a little. But she's not buying into it in the slightest.

"Boy, I think you've taken one too many blows to the head if you think for one second any of this impresses me." She shakes her head with a smile. "Besides, I'm pretty sure my wife can take you."

Drayzen is still smiling when she disappears into the same room she got the supplies for my cuts from earlier. I don't think I've ever seen him smile. Or look this relaxed. He doesn't seem like such an angry anti-social jerk.

I take a minute to give him a once-over. He's only wearing a pair of black sweats and sneakers. His upper body is completely bare, giving me the full view of his shoulders and muscular arms. When I get to his chest, I feel a little faint at the sight.

He has a burn that covers the majority of his stomach and chest. The center of it is so bad, most of his skin is missing and the surrounding areas are red and blistered. How is he so relaxed and smiling? There's no way he's not in agonizing pain right now.

"She's probably right." I whip my eyes away from the massive burn to find him watching me with amusement.

"Huh?" What I lack in eloquence, I obviously makeup for in intelligence.

"About her wife. She could take me."

"Oh. I mean, with how badly you're injured right now, I could probably take you," I say without thinking.

He tips his head back and snorts out a laugh. "It takes a lot more than a little burn to take down an emperor. I've had much worse." I might think he's cute if it weren't for the massive ego.

I roll my eyes. "Doesn't sound like it the way Maylah was talking. It seems like you're in here pretty often. Are you sure it's hard to take you down?" He scoffs at my quip.

"This is not me being taken down." He seems almost offended by my summation of his abilities. "This is me allowing a fire mage to blast me so I could get close enough to incapacitate. Sometimes you have to let them get the upper hand for a second so you can take it back long term."

164

I have no idea what he's talking about. "You let someone do this to you? That's sounds really stupid if you ask me."

"How stupid could it be if it worked?" he asks, cocking a brow.

"Did it though? You're the only one in here besides me." I make a point of looking around the room to prove my point. "Besides, if Maylah's wife can take you, I'm not sure you should be bragging."

He laughs even louder this time. "Maylah's wife is captain of the elite guard. There aren't very many people alive who could take her on and live."

"Oh." I laugh a little with him. "I guess it's not that shameful, then."

"So, what brought you in to see Maylah?" His abrupt change of subject throws me. Then I realize I was enjoying the easy banter session with a guy who would just as soon wrap me in vines and torture me as he would joke around with me. The thought sobers me immediately and I get up from my bed.

"I lost a fight, too. Anyway, I should probably head out. Good luck with all that."

I gesture to his chest, trying not to flinch when I look at him. When I sway a little, he reaches out to steady me, but I jerk away from him and wind up landing right back on the bed I was trying to get up from.

"Easy. Healing can do that to you. It makes your body really relaxed for a bit afterward," he tells

165

me, choosing not to comment on my reluctance to be touched by him. "By the way, I'm Drayzen."

"I know who you are. We have three classes together." Of course he wouldn't recognize me.

"I know. You sit next to Falyn, right? And you're Kennedy."

I'm surprised he knows my name. I didn't see him interact with anyone other than Michan and Serresa the whole first week of classes. My stomach does a little flip when we grasp forearms. To be honest, I'm not sure if it's because I'm weary of what he might do or because his hand is warm and firm and he holds my arm for two beats longer than necessary.

"Well, Drayzen. As fun as it's been, I really do need to get going." And it has nothing to do with how small the room suddenly feels.

"Sure, I'll see you in class tomorrow," he says, nodding his head slowly.

"I'll be there. You may want to reconsider, though."

He tilts his head to the side. "Why's that?"

"Well, I mean, it just sounds like you're gonna be draining Maylah tonight and if you have to face any of the other elements, I'm not sure she can save you. Wouldn't want some wind to be your ultimate downfall, would we?"

"It was a blast from a fire mage, not a natural element." He puffs his chest out in indignation. "Like I said, I won that fight."

166

I only laugh and lay a hand on his bare shoulder. By the time I realize what I'm doing, it's already too late. My hand makes contact with the soft skin encompassing hard muscle and twitches a little.

"Maybe with a little more practice, you won't be such a regular here." I don't know what comes over me other than the sound of Maylah laughing behind me, but I throw a wink at him before walking away.

I have to force myself to not look back at him. Am I just imagining his eyes burning a hole in my back?

"That's odd. This is nowhere near as bad as I thought it was," Maylah remarks. "That's the second time tonight I've misjudged an injury. I must be off my game." I can't keep myself from looking back in curiosity when I hear her words. His chest looked horrific to me. I don't know how she could think it's anything less than. But looking at it now, it does seem to be way better than I initially thought too. Weird. Even weirder is the confused expression on Drayzen's face when our gazes meet across the room. I'm sure he's just not used to the woman being the one to leave first.

167

CHAPTER ELEVEN

After what happened with Serresa three weeks ago, I decide I need to get a handle on my magic. I can't imagine that will be the last I see of her and having dealt with bullies my whole life, I know it's only going to get worse. The only problem is figuring out how to manifest my magic when I can't seem to feel it.

Now that I'm taking everything more seriously, I discover I really enjoy the majority of my

classes. Surprisingly, my favorite is potion making—
outside of combat. Only they don't call it that. It's
simply called "Brewing", but potion making sounds so
much more magical.

Things are starting to click thanks to practical
applications. I understand magic a little better and
how when two categories work together; the
possibilities are limitless. When a temperance, empress,
and star get together, they can create the healing salves
like the one Maylah was going to use on Drayzen.

But not all of it was necessarily good. I learned
that a hanged man could travel to the beyond, the place
souls go to wait for their next life and bring them back
from death to use when re-animating. They're still
technically dead but have the ability to problem solve.
They outlawed this practice a long time ago, but
according to Falyn, there are still death mages who do
it.

I just wish some of the knowledge I'm soaking
up could help me figure out how to use my magic. I
feel like I'm running out of time. Every day I don't
figure it out. I'm a day closer to being sent to the
mundana villages, where I'll lose any hope of finding
out about my family.

"Are we still on for a study session in the
library today?" I ask Falyn and Noric as we walk into
combat together.

"I don't think the books are going to help,
Ken," Falyn groans. "We should be actually trying to
practice, not reading about it."

169

We've had this discussion before, and I don't know how many times I have to prove that I can't manifest no matter how hard I try. There has to be some record of another person with the same problem, and I'm determined to find it.

I don't have a chance to give her my usual answer because Professor Brextin walks in and starts class. When he speaks, you listen. "Today we find out if you're moving on in my class," he states, cutting to the chase.

Me and Falyn are ready, though. Besides all the studying and manifesting sessions, we've also been running the course every evening before dinner. Neither one of us is willing to be dismissed from Brextin's class. It wouldn't mean having to leave the school, but it wouldn't look good come the end of the year when trials start.

We share small grins because we know we're ready. Every time we run the course, we do it faster and with much more ease than the time before. Our last four runs didn't end in us collapsing in sweaty panting puddles of arms and legs. There's no way we're coming in last again.

"What are you waiting for? Go!" Brextin shouts when no one moves after his announcement.

As one, we scramble for the track to begin our run. As soon as my feet hit the dirt of the trail, I know something is wrong. The ground feels spongy, and my feet sink into it with every step, slowing my pace and making it impossible to get any real speed. I look at

Falyn, who is having the same issue. The rest of the class is already pretty far ahead and we're not gaining any ground.

"Fucking magicians," Falyn pants, trying to pull a foot from the quicksand we're navigating.

Ahead of us, Serresa turns around to jog backward and waves. Of course, she has something to do with it. "What do we do?" I ask, trying to come up with a solution. "The edge of the path—it doesn't look soft like this. If we catch up and keep pace with everyone else, whoever's yielding the earth magic won't be able to keep it up without also hurting their own chances."

Falyn smiles and a spark of something flares in her eyes. "I have a better idea, but let's start with yours."

We move to the edge and begin running full speed to eat up the ground between us and our classmates. It's not until the second loop around that we finally see them not too far ahead. By this time, we're both already struggling, and we still have this lap plus two more.

"I hope your idea involves some kind of energy boost because I'm already dying." So much for not being last again. Having to expend so much energy catching up is going to kill us the last half of the run.

"There's no better pick me up than revenge, don't you think?" She flashes an evil smile before sweeping her hand from one side to another. "See that girl running beside Serresa? She's a magician with power over the earth element."

I squint against the sun in my eyes and she comes into focus just as a root pulls up from the ground and sweeps her feet out from under her. She topples over, taking Serresa with her, along with about four other unsuspecting students.

I would snort if I wasn't already having enough trouble breathing. I don't like the fact that Falyn is fighting my battle for me, but until I can figure everything out, I'm doomed to be the non-magical amongst a sea of mages.

When we catch up to the group, they're still rolling around on the ground trying to untangle themselves from Falyn's roots, I throw a wave at Serresa and keep moving. Falyn smiles but ignores them. Determination glints in her eyes as she pumps her arms and legs beside me. I guess we're still going all out. *I can do this.*

The smell of burning wood pulls my attention back to Serresa in time to see her direct a beam of light to the roots around her feet to burn them away. All out it is. I'm not about to be on the receiving end of that sun magic.

It doesn't take us long to reach the rest of the group ahead of us and we only slow our pace once we are safely sandwiched in the middle. Hopefully it's enough to prevent Serresa from trying anything else. I feel a little guilty about the bystanders who got caught up in it, but there's nothing we can do about it now except hope it doesn't get them removed from combat.

The third lap feels almost impossible. Even with all the extra training we did, I'm worried we'll drop with exhaustion before we make the fourth. I steel myself with as much determination as I can muster, but Falyn is still pulling ahead of me to join the group in the lead. When the group behind me starts pulling ahead, it's time to worry. I don't think Falyn has realized I'm not at her side and without having a buffer between me and Serresa, I can guarantee it's about to get ugly.

Footsteps pound behind me at an alarming speed, but regardless of how hard I dig, I can't seem to find a burst of energy to get me moving faster. It wouldn't be enough, anyway. Because I know the moment I hear them, it's already too late.

This time, when my feet sink into the soft earth, it's midway to my knee and there's no hope of navigating to the side of the trail. I can't do anything but watch as they pass me by. Even once I manage to pull free of the ground, I know it's futile to try. By this point, everyone else is already hitting their fourth and final lap of the trail while I still have half of the third. There's no way I was going to keep my spot in combat.

Disappointment surges through me at the thought, but it's not a new feeling. In fact, if anything, it puts me back in my comfort zone and reminds me why it's pointless to want things. If I could leave the trail before the end of my run, I would do it, but once we start, it becomes a closed loop with no way to leave.

I just want this to be over with, so I put my head down and pick up my speed. I just need to finish the course, then get through the rest of the day, and after dinner I can hide in my room and wallow in self-pity.

Thankfully, I manage to keep a speed that prevents everyone else from bypassing me in their fourth lap. I don't think I could withstand that humiliation. When I make back to the arena, Falyn is waiting by the door with concern all over her face.

"What happened? You were right next to me. Then when I looked up, you were gone. Serresa and her groupies caught up to us just as we finished the course," she says wringing her hands.

"I fell behind." I rolled my eyes upward because I refuse to let something as inconsequential as getting kicked out of combat class make me cry. "I got stuck in the mud again and couldn't get out."

Whatever Falyn is going to say is interrupted by Brextin clearing his throat. "I have to say I'm surprised so many of you passed." He looks around the room before landing on me. "All but one. Kennedy, I want to speak to you after everyone leaves." In true Brextin fashion, he doesn't wait for my response before turning on his heel to leave.

Falyn promises to wait for me outside before leaving me behind to face my fate. I gulp back my nerves and set out to follow. I find him in a small room

174

with hundreds of weapons lining the wall. I take a minute to admire a few before I work up the courage to face him.

"Not only did you come in last, but you had the worst time of any student I have ever taught during my career here." He definitely isn't one for beating around the bush.

"I would have had the same time as Falyn, but I was trapped by magic," I respond through my wince.

"I teach combat. Do you honestly think telling me another student used magic against you and won would earn you my sympathy?" He pulls a sword down from the wall and walks over to a whet stone. "I made myself clear on the first day of class. Endurance is everything to be an effective fighter."

"I haven't learned to manifest yet. I had no way of fighting back." My voice sounds too small and I hate it.

"You didn't have magic on Earth either. Did you run around making excuses for yourself when things got too hard?" My face grows hot under his penetrating stare. I stand a little straighter, refusing to let it get to me.

"Did you ask me to stay after so you could shame me before kicking me from your class?" I cross my arms this time.

"I suppose not. You'll need to see Elara this afternoon to be assigned to another class." He waves his hand toward the door in a shoo motion and dismisses me.

"We're taking class outside today," Professor Maceen announces as soon as practical applications starts. It's a welcome relief.

I walked out of combat and could only muster a shake of my head to let Falyn know it was over for me, leaving me feeling uncomfortable in my own skin. I did't say anything else because it was pointless. If I don't find my answers before trials start, I'll find a way to pass without combat. I don't need it . . . even if it feels like I'm failing before I was even given a chance. Either way, having to sit in a stuffy classroom would have just made it worse.

She instructs us to leave all our things behind and to follow her. A man I didn't notice when we first came in touches his hands to the door frame and, having seen Aarond do it once before, I realize he's creating a portal for us.

Maceen goes first and, one by one, we follow. I recognize where we are as soon as my eyes adjust to the sudden brightness of the sun. It's the same shore Falyn and Noric brought me to the day we were trying to get my magic to appear. Not exactly the same spot,

176

but close enough that it serves as a reminder of yet another of my failures. Can this day just end already?

Falyn must see my internal struggle because she reaches out to grab my hand and pulls me along with her. "We're gonna figure this out. I refuse to believe you were brought here by mistake," she leans in to whisper before choosing a spot for us to sit while we wait for Maceen to situate herself.

I pull my hand out of hers but shoot her a grateful smile for the pep talk just as Professor Maceen separates us into categories and tells us all to start working with our magic so she can see what our power levels are. *Perfect.*

Watching everyone manifest so easily leaves the bitter taste of jealousy in my mouth. Their faces are practically glowing with happiness and exhilaration while I sit here and contemplate all the ways I could escape after the trials to prevent them from stripping my magic and shipping me off to the mundana villages. You'd think in all that magic there would be a way to just strip me of my memory and send me back to Earth. Even if I do wind up being able to produce some semblance of magic, at this point I seriously doubt I'd score higher than a one or a two on the scale. If I was stronger, wouldn't I be able to feel it?

"Are you gonna tell me what happened with Brextin?" Falyn asks, breaking through my thoughts and pulling me back to the present.

"There isn't anything to talk about. He cut me. After he let me know I broke the record for worst time running the course." I can't bring myself to look at her. No doubt her face will be full of pity for the human girl pretending to be a mage.

A flash of lightning shoots across the sky, coming from the magician group who set up a few hundred feet from us. At the same time, loud cheers sound from Noric's group, and both Falyn and I strain to see what's going on.

In the center of it all stands Noric, a huge grin on his face. At first, I'm not sure what all the cheering is about until I realize the person standing next to him is also Noric. I'm seeing double. Rubbing my eyes to be sure I really am seeing two of him, I stand to get a better look. Falyn stands with me and I can see the moment she realizes exactly what's going on. Her face goes slack, then she breaks out in a beaming smile.

"He's a hermit!" She claps her hands together in pure glee. For a second I forget that's another classification and wonder what the hell she's talking about. When I remember, I give myself a mental slap to the forehead. He just manifested a second magic. Astral projection.

"Holy shit. That's amazing," I say, trying my best to sound excited for him. I mean, I am, but it's completely overshadowed by the fact that he now has two while I'm struggling to have one. I don't know if that makes me selfish, but I can't stop the thought from happening.

Falyn jumps up and down as one of the Norics saunters toward us while the other stays in the middle of the circle. He almost reaches us before an invisible string snaps and yanks him back hard enough for his feet to leave the ground. When the two bodies collide, Noric flies backward and is once again just a single body. He rubs his forehead and grimaces before rising to his feet again and calling out to us.

"Maybe I'll practice that a little more before I try it again."

"I hope you don't think I have to share my snacks with two of you now, because that's never gonna happen!" Falyn warns him.

"I second that! I don't think the commissary is equipped for this new development!" I join in.

He makes a face at the both of us before turning back to his group. We do the same, but I'm more reluctant than Falyn is because reality is setting back in. It would be totally fine with me if we just spent the whole class admiring Noric's new power instead of my nonexistent one.

But when I notice Professor Maceen watching me, I know I'm going to have to at least attempt to manifest something. Falyn reaches over and squeezes my hand, giving me a knowing look before turning her focus to her own manifesting. I take a deep breath but can't bring myself to put any real effort into it. Mostly because I don't want anyone to see me genuinely try and fail. If I'm only half trying and nothing happens, it doesn't count, right?

Falyn is weaving together a live flower crown from one of the seeds we were given when we first got

179

here. I watch as the leaves and stem grow and wrap around each other before a host of flowers spring up from nodules along the stem to complete the crown. She sets it on my head, and I strike a pose with pursed lips and a majestic wave. She smiles and sets about to create another for herself.

I know she's trying to take my mind off everything, and it probably would have worked if I wasn't currently surrounded by people reminding me of my inability to manifest even the most basic of magic. I know I've stalled long enough when I see Professor Maceen start walking toward us. Doing what Falyn and Noric are constantly telling me to do, I close my eyes and search for that hidden spark I'm supposed to be able to feel at all times.

When I actually feel something, I'm so surprised I gasp audibly and my eyes snap open. Falyn gives me a questioning look, but I don't want to speak and risk losing whatever it is I'm feeling right now. Instead, I dig a little deeper and picture my power as a cord that I can grasp and tug to flow through the rest of my body. It responds easily, so I direct it outward to my hands and press them flat to the ground while imagining flowers blooming. All I need is for a single flower to sprout. It doesn't even need to be big. Anything that would let me know this whole thing isn't some big joke being played on me by the universe.

This time, the audible gasp doesn't come from me. Falyn, Maceen, and several other people all suck in a breath simultaneously. I keep my focus for a few seconds longer because I'm too nervous to see if it worked or not.

"Blessed three, Kennedy," Falyn whispers from beside me. I look up at her, but she's not looking at me. With her mouth hanging slightly open as she stares toward the grassy field in front of us. I follow her gaze and almost fall when I see it.

When we first got here, the field was mostly grass dotted sparsely with tiny wildflowers, but that's no longer the case. Thousands of flowers have sprung up from the earth in varying colors, shapes, and sizes as far as I can see. I stare in shock, trying to figure out who did it because there is no way it was me. Right? Falyn wrenches her gaze from the field to look at me in stunned silence. Actually, everyone is.

For the longest time, the only sound around us is the water lapping at the shore and the occasional sea bird calling out. Nobody seems to know what to make of the flowers, myself included. Until Maceen clears her throat and claps her hands to get everyone's attention. "We're just about out of time here, so let's head back to class." She gestures to a newly opened portal and everyone moves toward it, all the while still gawking at the field. Falyn and I bring up the rear, but before I can step through, Maceen holds me back with a hand to my shoulder. "I'd like you to stay a few minutes late, if you don't mind."

Even though her words say I have a choice, her tone says I don't, so I just nod my head and walk through, still in a daze. Noric and Falyn are waiting for

181

me just on the other side, both with huge grins covering their faces.

"That was amazing, Kendee!" He says using the name he's been calling me ever since giving me the tattoo. "I've never even seen a ten do that much so quickly!" He slaps me a little too hard on the back and I stop to glare at him.

"A high five or fist bump would have been fine," I mutter, trying to rub out the sore spot.

"Sorry. Next time I can five bump or whatever . . . as soon as you tell me what that is . . ." He shrugs but continues grinning.

"High five or fist bump. I show him each one as I say the name by grabbing his hand to teach him the motion. After our third fist bump, Falyn interrupts.

"Looks like we're not the only ones impressed," she says, nodding her head toward the rest of the room. Everyone is watching me like they're waiting for me to manifest right here in this room.

"Why are they all staring?" I ask out of the corner of my mouth. "Feeling super uncomfortable right now."

"Probably because you just manifested the strongest magic out of everyone in this class. Probably in the entire school. And up until today they haven't seen you do anything," Falyn replies. "Even I'm having a hard time not staring."

I guess it makes sense, but it doesn't make me feel any better about it. Especially when I make eye contact with Serresa and she looks like she's contemplating lighting me up right here in front of everyone. I think things just got worse for me.

CHAPTER TWELVE

My conversation with Professor Maceen was strange and disappointing, to say the least. After everyone else left to eat lunch, she handed me an empty pot and asked me to grow something. My confidence deflated in the span of two seconds when I reached for my power and discovered it missing again. I clung to her explanation of completely draining myself with such a huge burst of magic and tried to keep my steps light when I joined my friends.

Every time the conversation swings toward my burst of magic, I do my best to steer it away. I'm not ready to admit it may have been a fluke, but only time will tell. Falyn, who I swear is a lover with empathic powers, seems to sense my reluctance to talk about it, so she helps as much as she can. It's almost impossible when several people stop by our table to tell me how impressive my power is. Each time it happens, an uneasy feeling settles in my stomach. These are the same people who turned their nose up at me when they thought I was a zero and now they want to be best friends?

Now that classes are over and Falyn and I are sitting in the library for yet another of my study sessions, I feel like I can breathe again.

Until I come across something in the old text I'm reading about the high priestess magic.

"Holy shit. Did you know about this?" I point at the passage I'm reading and Falyn leans across the table to read it.

"No, we don't learn about joining powers until fourth year. You would need an empress, temperance, and a high priestess to do it," she responds.

"Well, I'm two out of the three and I'm sure Noric would help if you asked him to." I wag my eyebrows at her and get an eye roll in response.

"We'd have to go to the market to get a lumi pod. They're pretty expensive, though. I don't know what we could trade for it."

The passage describes how a brew can be created to grant the high priestess the ability to choose any vision, whether from the past or present. It says a temperance can imbue the power of an empress into a lumi pod, whatever that is, and brew it into a tea for a high priestess to drink. Now that my power is finally coming in, it should work for me. All I would need to do is focus on the events surrounding my birth and maybe I'll be able to see something that would set me on the right path to figuring out where I come from.

We copy the instructions down, then call it a day. I think both of us are getting tired of spending every free moment either running or studying. I don't know how long Falyn is going to keep joining me for these sessions. Especially now that she's continuing with combat class and I'm . . . I don't even know what I'll be doing. Another twinge of disappointment hits me, but I shove it down with everything else. I don't have time to stew over it. If this potion works, I could potentially find the answers I'm looking for. I don't want to think about what happens if it doesn't. At least I know I may be powerful enough to not have to worry about the mundana villages at the end of the year. As long as being booted from combat doesn't hurt me too much. Knowing my luck, it'll be the very thing that makes or breaks my ability to pass the trials.

"Do you have any idea what to expect from trials? I mean, you don't think not being in combat is going to destroy any chance I have of passing, right?" I finally ask. The question has been weighing heavily on me all day.

"All I know about the trials is that they test everything you learned up to that point . . ." She trails off because since combat is something most of the students will be learning, it means I may not have what I need to pass after all.

Story of my life. "Why would they just allow students to be kicked from classes then? You'd think the goal would be for as many as possible to pass."

"The goal is for the strongest to pass." She cringes when she says it, and I think she might actually be seeing the system through my eyes. "I think the goal right now is to stop the decline of magic. The king said we have to focus to on our best hope. The strongest mages give us the best hope."

The king said. Every time I question a custom or rule, the answer always comes in the form of "the king said." Do they not see the issue with that? It's like no one has the ability to form their own beliefs or thoughts. Everything is riding on this one man who, the more I hear of him, the less I like. What if the loss of magic has nothing to do with diluting bloodlines and everything to do with us not being worthy of the gifts we were given? That reason seems just as likely, if not more so than anything else I've heard.

I don't voice any of those thoughts. I can't imagine they'd be accepted coming from someone who's only been here for slightly over a month. All I can hope for right now is whatever new class they stick me in does something to help make up for the loss of combat.

I'm up before Falyn pounds on my door after a restless night of almost no sleep. Between getting kicked from combat, finally manifesting, and possibly finding something to help me in my search for family, it's a wonder I got any sleep at all.

I'm already dressed and ready to go see Elara for my new assignment by the time Falyn emerges from her room with a frizzy tangle of pink curls and groggy eyes. "Do you want me to come with you?" she asks over a yawn she's trying to suppress.

"Nope, I'm sure it'll be quick. I'll just meet up with you in class." I wave to her as I walk out the door.

Elara smiles as soon as I walk into the admin building. "Kennedy! So good to see you. How have you been liking Arcanum?" She doesn't wait for my answer before moving on. "So sorry to hear about combat. I'm sure you'll do fine though. We're keeping your combat time open instead of assigning you to a new class."

188

"Why? Is there not anything available?" Panic rises in my chest. Have they already decided I'm a lost cause? "There has to be something."

"Don't worry, dear. It's not a bad thing. It was the dean's idea. He wants to meet with you directly after this and explain." Her voice is bright and positive, but I don't miss the slight tightening around her mouth and eyes that tells me maybe it is a bad thing.

If she's not assigning me a new class, I suppose I should get this meeting over with. "Where do I find him?" Or maybe I'll just run for the hills now.

"His office takes up the entire top floor of the middle building. Just knock on the door, he's already waiting for you." That doesn't sound ominous or anything.

The doors are dark, solid wood with the name Dean Galen carved into them with elegant script. A metal knocker in the shape of the school crest sits right under the name. It has a seam that lines up with the seam between the doors that allows them to swing inward to open. I use the knocker to announce my arrival and wait.

The man who answers the door is at least an inch shorter than I am and very thin. The suit he's wearing is a size too big and drapes over his body oddly, like he's playing dress up with someone else's clothes. His lips flatten into a smile when he sees me, but it doesn't quite reach his emotionless blue eyes. He gestures for me to sit in one of two chairs in front of his desk and he takes the other, crossing one leg over a knee.

"Hello, Kennedy. It's nice to finally meet you." His voice is unexpectedly deep, and I think he's trying to project some warmth into it, but it makes the whole sentence sound forced and unnatural.

"Thank you. Elara said you wanted to see me?" I'm really hoping we can get right to the point and not draw this out.

"Yes, yes. I spoke with Professor Maceen yesterday as well as a couple of other professors about your progress since arriving." He weaves his fingers together over his stomach and leans back. "There seems to be some concern about your power."

"Oh?" I don't know how else to respond to his statement.

"I hear you made quite a show of manifesting yesterday. I'm just a little curious how you did it since everyone else seems to think you've shown no aptitude for magic since your arrival."

Why does it sound like he's accusing me of something? "I really don't know how I did it, if that's what you're asking. I was starting to think I didn't have magic."

"What about your other gift? I hear you're also blessed with the power of the high priestess. Has that manifested as powerfully for you?"

"It's only ever happened once and mostly the vison was a blur." I answer honestly, trying to figure out where all this is going. "Is this about combat?"

190

Each time I answer a question, tiny orbs of light flicker in his eyes. I know it's another power vision, but I can't figure out what power he has. I haven't seen this one before.

"No, not at all. I'm merely trying to figure out what to do with you. If what Professor Maceen says is true, then you're quite powerful. You really had no idea you had magic before coming here?" It hits me. He's a judgement. The power to know whether what someone is saying is truthful. They can quite literally hear lies.

"None at all. What do you mean do with me?" There is something seriously not right with this guy and it's making me nervous.

He leans forward and pats my hand as if to soothe my worry, but the only thing it does is make my skin crawl. "I think the best course of action is to use the time you would have been in combat to set you up with a tutor."

That honestly doesn't sound so bad, but why do I feel like that's not the whole truth?

"I already have a tutor. My friends have been helping me figure this all out, but thank you for the offer."

He chuckles deeply and replies, "It hasn't got you very far. No, it would be better if we pair you with someone a little more advanced, don't you think?" He taps his chin as if trying to figure out who would be best for the job.

191

I somehow doubt anyone he deems a worthy tutor would have my best interests in heart. Why is he so concerned with my schooling all of a sudden? I've been here a month and didn't even know he existed until today. None of this feels right, but I also know I probably don't have a choice.

"Don't look so concerned, Kennedy. This is for your own good. I'm only here to make sure you get the schooling you need in order to become successful." He smiles at me, but I know his statement for what it is. A lie.

I wipe my hand on my shirt as soon as I walk out of his office. My skin hasn't stopped crawling since he patted the back of my hand, and the friction of my shirt helps to erase the lingering sensation of his touch. I don't know how someone I don't know can skeeve me out so much.

I'm going to have to rush to class to have any hope of making it on time. He offered to walk me down, but I didn't want to spend a single second longer in his company than I had to. Luckily, class hasn't started, and Falyn is waiting for me right outside the door.

"What took so long?" she asks, concern etched across her features.

192

"I had to meet with Dean Galen," I reply, shaking my head. "Apparently, I'm not being assigned a new class. I get a tutor instead. I'll tell you everything after class." She's going to want every detail, and we don't have enough time before class to unpack it all.

Paying attention to Professor Elwin's is difficult enough on a normal day, but today even more so. My head is still reeling from my meeting with the dean, and he never did tell me who was going to be my tutor. Only to meet them in the courtyard during my free period.

On the way to our next class, I tell Falyn everything. His strange questions, the fact that I could tell he was using his judgement on me, and how uncomfortable the whole thing made me.

"Why would anyone lie about their magic? I don't understand why he would be so interested in you either. Maybe we're looking too deep into the whole thing, and he really is just trying to help you." Even as she says it, I can tell neither one of us believes it.

"Maybe, either way, I'll be stuck with a tutor hand picked by him, so I'm not feeling super confident about it."

"He didn't tell you who it would be?" She frowns.

"Nope, I'm supposed to meet them by the statue in the courtyard during my free period. We should leave our next class early so you can come with me and check it out," I tell her as we walk into History of Magic.

193

"I definitely want to find out who it is. Let's do it." With that settled, we take our seats and wait for class to start.

Even with this being a class I enjoy, I find it hard to focus or sit still. Falyn has to glare at me several times to stop my fidgeting and I wind up missing the entire lesson on how the first empress was blessed with her magic. I really hope Falyn was paying attention because I wanted to hear that one. I told her as much on our way to the statue.

"You could always just get The Lore of Arcanum Magic. All the stories are in there. My parents read it to me when I was a child," she responds with a smile. I make a mental note to see if I can find a copy of it. Sometimes I envy everyone for the fact that they were raised here and have a whole host of knowledge I'll never have access to.

We leave Arcanum government about ten minutes early and when we get to the statue to wait for my tutor, Falyn lets out a gasp. It's surrounded by a host of warriors, making it hard to see from where I'm standing. Since I doubt this was what the dean meant when he said he was assigning me a tutor, something is up.

"What's going on?" I ask when she stands on her tiptoes and cranes her neck to get a look.

"I don't know, they're all in the way. I think something happened to the statue." I mirror her pose and rise to my tiptoes. I'm a full head taller, so maybe I'll be able to see something. I manage to make out a flash of red before one of the warriors realizes we're here.

"You two, head to class!" he barks.

"This is my class," I respond and shrug my shoulders. "At least according to Dean Galen anyway."

The warrior shares a look with the woman beside him. "Find somewhere else to have class then. The courtyard is off limits right now."

Falyn grabs my hand to pull me away, but the curiosity has me in a choke hold. I want to know what that flash of red was and why it requires so many warriors' attention. I tug her in the opposite direction. "Come on, I think we can see it from the other side."

"I don't think you want to disobey a warrior, Ken," she says, but doesn't resist.

"We're not. They told us to find somewhere else to be, and that's what we're doing." I wink and keep pulling her along. We're the only two students out here. Whoever my tutor is, still isn't here, which means class hasn't let out and we have some time before she has to be in combat.

We round the courtyard looking for a better view just as a woman shows up and pushes through the warriors. "Definitely temperance magic. I'll try to pull it out," she muses loud enough for us to hear. "Did anyone see it happen?"

"No, luckily we got here before any of the students were able to see it." One of the warriors responds to her as the smell of lavender permeates the air.

195

"She's a temperance," I tell Falyn.

"How can you tell?"

"Her magic smells the same as Noric's did when he made that tattoo stick."

"Have I told you lately how weird you are?" Falyn laughs. She mostly gets a kick out of the fact that I can see and smell magic, but I know she's also not lying about it being weird.

"Only twice today, so far. You're really lacking."

Finally, we make it to the opposite side of the courtyard just as Drayzen emerges from one of the connecting paths. I ignore him in favor of trying to get a look at the statue again.

"What's going on?" he asks, but he's also focused on the scene in front of us.

The warriors haven't noticed our changed positions yet, which makes me wonder about their ability as realm protectors. I have a clear view of the statues and now know why I saw red from the other side.

They're bleeding.

"Blessed three," Falyn murmurs when she sees it.

I want to say I know it's not real blood, but honestly, I don't know. I've lost track of how many things I've seen this last month I previously thought to be impossible.

"Is that real?" I ask, hoping it's not a stupid question.

196

"Probably not. It looks like a temperance spelled it to do that. That's why they have Prin here. As another temperance, she can pull the magic out," Drayzen responds. "Do you see that paper?"

I follow his pointed finger and find what he's talking about. Someone attached a note to the female of the three. "What do you think it says?" I ask.

He smirks. "Only one way to find out."

Drayzen walks over to the closest warrior and leans in to talk to him. They clasp hands and smile at each other. I roll my eyes and look at Falyn.

"Really? We're told to leave, but he's allowed to just walk up and question them?"

"Benefits of your mother being one of the king's elite," Falyn replies.

"You mean like those two we saw in the market?"

"Exactly like those two. The woman we saw is his mother and one of the highest ranking members of the king's guard." She gives me a look I can't quite decipher. "Drayzen is training to take her place when she retires."

"Oh." I see what that look was for now. Those two we saw in the market were needlessly cruel and every single person who was there that day was terrified of them. That's who Drayzen is going to be. I suddenly find him way less attractive. Not that I found him all that attractive in the first place, I mean.

"I'm gonna wind up being late for combat, so we should probably head out. I don't think your tutor is gonna show since this area is supposed to be off limits," Falyn says when it doesn't look like Drayzen is going to come back over to us any time soon.

"You're probably right. I'll just go hang out in our room until lunch and meet you at the commissary."

Falyn takes off in a brisk jog, but I hesitate. I don't know why I'm so curious except that I'm just naturally nosey.

Drayzen and two guards stand joking and laughing with each other while I'm awkwardly shuffling my feet back and forth, staring like a stalker, so maybe I should just leave. It's probably a stupid prank played by one of the students, anyway.

I take the path that leads to my room, and it doesn't take long for the crunch of footsteps to announce someone behind me.

"Why'd you leave?" Drayzen calls out as I turn around.

"I got tired of the view." I smirk at him.

"Did you not want to know what I found out?" he asks, even though he knows I do.

"Let me guess, a student thought it would be funny to get the warriors all riled up and imbued the statue with magic to make it bleed?"

"You're half right." He hesitates to continue, searching my face for I don't know what.

"Who did it then?" I ask.

When he finds whatever he was looking for, he finally answers. "They think the rebels somehow got

198

on campus. They left a note too. It's just a quote from an old book of prophesies made by The High Priestess Guild a long time ago."

"What does it say?" He's obviously messing with me by making me ask to get it all out of him.

"What was gifted can be taken away. It started with twenty-two and ends with one. The time of need is here." He shrugs. "Most of what was in that book was proven false, so I wouldn't worry about it."

"I wasn't worried. Just curious," I reply, but then think of something. "What were you doing there, anyway?" I wouldn't be surprised if he had something to do with it.

"Oh yeah, I'm your tutor."

Y ou're not my tutor." It's the only thing I can think of in response to him.

"Dean Galen told me you already knew about it. Did he not tell you?"

"No . . . I mean, yes, he told me, but I don't need a tutor."

Drayzen cocks an eyebrow. "Are you forgetting I've seen you in class? I know you still can't manifest.".

"You must have missed the show yesterday then because not only can I manifest, but I'm pretty strong too." I don't know why I feel the need to defend myself, but I do it anyway.

"Let's see it then." He crosses his arms over his chest. "If you can grow something right now, I'll leave you alone and tell Galen you don't need a tutor."

"Fine." This should be easy, and as long as he keeps his word, I won't have to worry about having a tutor outside of Noric and Falyn. But when I reach for that spark in my lower abdomen, it's still not there.

Squeezing my eyes shut, I search deeper, but it's nowhere to be found. Why is this happening to me? It makes absolutely no sense that I did what I did yesterday and now today I'm back to square one. It feels like the universe is playing a joke on me. After a few seconds that feel like years, he sighs loudly.

"You need a tutor."

"I have a tutor. Two, in fact, so your services aren't needed, but thank you." That last thing I need is one of Serresa's groupies to be able to report anything back to her. With him, it would be two-fold. I wouldn't be surprised after meeting Galen yesterday if he also wants to be reported to about me. Not to mention the fact that Drayzen is who he is. I don't think I would learn anything valuable from someone

201

whose goal in life is to become an elite guard to a man who promotes classism, among other things.

I would never say that last thought out loud because I don't know what the criteria is to be charged with treason, but when he asks, I give him the condensed version of my truth.

"Your tutors aren't helping if you're still having issues with manifesting. And don't try to use yesterday to prove they are because that was obviously a one off. By this point, you should be able to call on your magic with purpose and not accidentally grow an entire field of flowers."

"So you do know about yesterday. I'm probably just still burned out. If I did it once, I can do it again. I'll figure it out myself without your help."

"What do you have against me?"

"Forgive me if I'm not falling all over myself to be subjected to spending time with a glorified bully."

"Me? How am I a bully? The only one who has said or done anything remotely bullyish is you."

I think back to our only interaction besides today and realize he's not wrong, but it's only a matter of time before he shows his true colors. "Okay, that might be a little true, but in my defense, look who you hang out with. I'm just trying to get ahead of it. I can guarantee Serresa won't like it if you're spending time with me."

"What does she have to do with you needing a tutor?" he asks, annoyance dripping from every word.

202

I ignore his question and continue, "Not to mention the fact that I'm not dumb. You might be my tutor, but that isn't your primary role. Galen asked you to keep an eye on me, right? Make sure I'm not team rebel or whatever he thinks I am?"

"No, he just asked that I help you figure out your magic. That's it," he says between gritted teeth.

"I'm sure. And like the good little soldier boy you are, you accepted. There's no other reason behind it, right?"

"Does it matter? There's not really a choice here when you consider the fact that the man who can determine whether we fail or pass at the end of the year is the one telling us to do this."

I know he's right, but I really don't care. "I don't want to be followed around the rest of the school year by the dean's watch dog so I'm gonna pass."

"For one, it's only a couple hours a day and two, you can't pass or you really will have me following you around the rest of the school year."

"Whatever. I'm not doing it. I'm gonna go home until lunch, then meet up with my friends and you can do whatever it is elites in training do."

I leave him standing on the path and rush to the worldly building to get away from him.

"It's Drayzen," I say as soon as I sit down at our usual lunch table. Everyone else is already halfway done with their food, but I spent way too much time trying to figure out how to get out of the whole tutoring thing and wasn't watching time. It doesn't matter, I'm not feeling very hungry at the moment anyway.

"What's Drayzen?" Falyn asks, yanking her plate further away from Noric's wandering fork.

"He's the tutor Galen assigned to me."

"Oh, I guess that explains why he was in the courtyard earlier. It's kind of strange Galen chose another first year, though."

"I'm more concerned about the company he keeps than anything else." I nod my head toward their table, where Serresa just sat.

"What did we miss?" Ciena asks around a mouth full of her lunch. "When did you get a tutor?" I sigh because so much has happened over the last twenty-four hours, I don't even know where to begin.

After telling everyone about being kicked from combat, then manifesting the field of flowers, and having to meet with Galen, shocked silence stretches on for what feels like ages. Finally, Sona breaks the silence. "So instead of being stuck in the arena with thirty other students, you get one-on-one tutoring with that." She gestures over to Drayzen, who is watching me from his table with narrow eyes. "And you're unhappy about it because . . . ?"

"You're about to be trained by the best emperor in all four years. You don't even need combat," Ciena adds.

"That's not the point. It isn't about me needing a tutor. It's obviously about having someone keeping an eye on me. I just don't understand why." Since Falyn's plate is closer to me now in her bid to keep it away from Noric, I reach over and grab the soft breadstick hanging over the edge and bite into it. Noric snorts at her indignation, but I'm too focused on my immediate problem to find it funny. "I really don't need Serresa to be witness to my every failure, all while probably making it worse for me. Think about it. When was the last time you saw any of them by themselves?"

"You're missing the point, Ken." Falyn elbows me. "You can still get your combat training. You just have to convince Drayzen to tutor you in everything. Not just magic."

I toy with the idea for a minute before visions of having to spar against Serresa play out in my brain, then immediately dismiss it. No, I'm better off just avoiding that group all together.

"I don't know, can we talk about something else?" I'll figure my shit out later.

Falyn rolls her eyes but complies. Kind of. "Not to bring him up again, but did Drayzen find out what was going on at the statue?"

"Oh yeah, the note was a line from a prophecy or something," I reply trying to remember what it said.

205

"Wait, what happened at the statue?" Noric leans in. "Why does everything seem to happen when none of us are around?"

Falyn launches into an explanation of what we saw at the statue, but I don't hear anything she's saying. Much to my annoyance, my eyes have found their way back to Drayzen, who is still watching me. When I meet his eyes, he leans back in his chair and cocks an eyebrow. By the way he's been watching me since I came in, I can tell it's going to be harder than I thought to avoid him. I suppose I shouldn't be surprised, since he did say he wasn't above following me around the rest of the school year.

"Ken . . . ?" Falyn pulls my attention away from Drayzen and back to the table. I didn't hear a word she said. *Oops.*

"Sorry, I zoned out. What were we talking about?"

Sona looks over at the elite table and chuckles. "I think you mean zoned in."

"What did the note say?" Falyn nudges me, smiling at Sona's remark.

"Oh yeah . . . What was gifted can be taken away. It started with twenty-two and ends with one. The time of need is here." All three of them stare like I've grown another head. "What? Drayzen said it's from a high priestess's book of prophecies that were all false or something."

"That's not exactly accurate, actually," Rostan says hesitantly. "At least, not according to my father."

206

"I don't understand. What does your father have to do with this, and why are you all acting so weird?" They're all looking at each other as if deciding whether to let me in on a secret.

"Rostan's father is the head high priestess for his guild," Ciena explains. "The same guild that book of prophecies came from actually."

"That's pretty convenient," I quip. "What's the big deal about it?"

"It's not that they were wrong, just that they haven't happened yet," Rostan says.

"I don't even know what it means. Well, besides the obvious part about starting with twenty-two. Twenty-two original mages, right?"

"Yeah, that line isn't the whole prophecy, but it seems to be the line everyone focuses on. They think it's warning about the fall of magic." Rostan shrugs.

"Well, whatever it means, it seems the rebels are super interested in it, if that's really who spelled the statue," I reply.

We spend the rest of lunch discussing the possibility of rebels and eventually the school, with the increased presence of the warriors. Or why they would even feel the need to do it, for that matter. I'm happy to just listen to everyone else's opinions because it means not having to talk about the downward spiral my life is currently taking. Especially since I can feel Drayzen's eyes boring a hole in my back and it takes everything in me to not turn around and meet his stare.

"Anyone up for a trip to the market today? I need to pick up a lumi pod for something I want to do this weekend," I ask before everyone heads off to their respective classes.

"Did you figure out how you're going to pay for it?" Falyn asks.

"Not yet. But I brought a few things I don't think you guys have here, and I'm hoping a vendor will find them valuable enough to trade."

"I wish I could go, but I have to meet up with a group of hermits to practice my new manifestation." Noric shoots me an apologetic smile.

"We can't go either," Sona replies. "We're holding extra sparring sessions in the evening for combat."

Falyn looks at me with guilt in her eyes. "I can't go either. I'm sparring tonight too."

"It's fine. It'll be a quick trip anyway," I say, doing my best to hide my jealousy.

"I can go," Rostan offers, and I breathe a sigh of relief. I really didn't want to navigate the village by myself. I'm honestly a little surprised he offers since I don't spend nearly as much with him, Ciena, and Sona as I do with Noric and Falyn.

"After dinner then?" I ask. That should give me enough time to find something to trade.

"Sure, we can head to the portal right after. What do you need a lumi pod for?" He asks as an afterthought. He looks over at Ciena like he wants to ask her to join but stops himself. Interesting.

208

"I want to try a guided vision now that my power is manifesting." *Maybe manifesting . . .*

Right after dinner, we went to the portal that would take us to the village. After searching through my things, I decided my best bet would be the computer tablet I brought. On a whim, I'd packed it along with a portable solar charger. It has movies, books, and music downloaded to it and is the only thing I think might garner interest from someone not from Earth. I have no concept of money here, so I'm really hoping it's enough.

The market is full of people rushing to and from booths and I have no idea where to start, so I'm glad Rostan agreed to come when he leads me straight to a booth filled with different plants and seeds to choose from. It didn't take much convincing for the woman at the booth to agree to the trade. One look at the movie I queued up on the screen for her to watch was all it took.

The lumi pod is a soft, opalescent pink rectangle with rounded edges that glows every time it's jostled in the jar she hands to me. It's so beautiful, I almost feel guilty I'm going to boil it.

"That's all I needed unless you want to look around," I tell Rostan, not looking away from the jar I

209

hold in my hand. It's hard to believe this seed pod may be the answer to everything.

"Actually, I do need to get something, but it's on the other side of the market. You can just stay here and look around while I go grab it if you want," he says, but doesn't wait for my response before sprinting away.

I'm not sure why I couldn't just go with him, but whatever. I got what I need, so I'll just hang until he's ready to go. I wander from one booth to another, marveling at the clothing, jewelry, and artifacts created by the temperance users.

"Hello again, Kennedy." I snap my head to the next booth over and make eye contact with none other than Bren. The man who started all of this.

"You." Even after having held multiple pretend conversations in my mind with him, I can't think of anything else to say.

"The lumi pod is a good idea, but don't be surprised if it doesn't work in the way you want it to." He gestures to the jar in my hand.

"What does that mean?" I ask. "Wait, don't answer that. I'd rather you tell me how you knew about me and why you brought me here."

"I didn't bring you here. Aarond had that honor."

"Semantics. You know what I'm asking." I can see this is going to be just as easy as getting an answer out of Aarond.

"I can't give you the answers you want. Not because I don't want to, but because I don't have them. Things are changing every day."

"What's changing? What do you know about my family?" Desperation edges my voice. I feel like everything is spinning out of control. If I can't figure this out by the time school ends, I don't know what I'll do. There's a good chance I won't pass.

"I don't know anything. All I can offer you is this: family isn't created by birth. Nor by the blood you carry in your veins. The family you make will be your light when blood seeks to take it all."

"That tells me nothing. I don't care about making a new family or whatever you're going on about. I just want to know what was so horrible about me that it required shipping me off to an entirely different realm."

"I wish I had the answers you're so desperate to find, but I don't. Being a high priestess doesn't mean I can access everything I want to know. I only know what the Esotera see fit to let me know. But for now, all I have is this gift." He hands me a small wood box with tiny symbols carved into it. I immediately recognize the leaf and eye symbols for empress and high priestess classifications. The only two I know, if I'm being honest.

Inside the box is the same bracelet I was admiring from a vendor the last time I was here, only now it has a much larger and flatter circular stone

211

centered among the smaller green spheres. Before I can reach in to grab the bracelet, Bren snaps the lid closed.

"Don't wear it yet." I cock an eyebrow at his cryptic demand. "Wait until the moment you're truly tested. You'll have need of it then."

Seriously, who is this guy? "This is ridiculous. How hard is it to just give a single straight answer? You have to know something, or you wouldn't have sent Aarond for me in the first place." I want to shove the box back at him, but a tiny voice tells me to hang on to it. He's still a high priestess, even if he's a crappy one, in my opinion.

"Just be careful in your search, Kennedy. Sometimes the answers we think we need only serve to make things worse."

I'm just about to tell him what I think of all the confusing and completely unhelpful information he threw my way when Rostan comes up behind me. "You ready to head back?"

"No, but it's getting close to curfew, so we probably should . . ." I trail off because when I turn to answer him, he's looking at Bren in a way that seems much too familiar. Like they know each other. But that would be super coincidental, right? When I turn back to Bren to question it, all I see is the back of his shirt as he slips through the crowd to who knows where.

"Great," I mutter. Then refocus on Rostan. "Do you know him?"

He hesitates just a fraction of a second, but it's long enough for me to know he's about to lie.

"Yes," he says, and proves me wrong. "He knows my father." He doesn't elaborate, though. I don't know if I'm just being overly paranoid, but it feels like there's way more to it than a mere acquaintance. "We should go." He gestures for me to lead the way, but before I can sweep past him, he stops me with a hand on my arm. "I don't know what you guys talked about, but it looked pretty serious. My father and he have known each other for as long as I can remember, and my father has nothing but respect for him. I just thought I'd throw that out there . . ."

I nod but don't say anything.

When we get back through the portal, we're greeted by four people waiting for us on the other side. Three of them are warriors and I don't know about the fourth. As soon as we're through, one of the warriors turns to the unknown fourth and says, "These are the last two who went through today, you can close it down now."

"Why is the portal being closed?" Rostan asks but everyone ignores him as the woman who I'm now assuming is a hanged man runs her hand along the edges of the portal and it disappears.

"You both need to get to your rooms. It's not safe out here." One of the warriors responds while the other two step up to stand beside us. "Lafrel and Clin will escort you."

213

The walk back is long and quiet as my escort refuses to give me a single answer as to what's going on. It's not until I'm inside and Falyn comes rushing out of her room in a panic that I realize something might have happened.

"Thank the three, you're back. I was so worried." She envelopes me in a bone crushing hug.

"What happened?" I ask when she finally releases me. "Why are they closing the portals?"

"They started closing them right after you guys left and sent everyone back to their rooms. Four students have gone missing."

CHAPTER FOURTEEN

The school doubled the warrior presence and established an earlier curfew before Falyn and I even sit down to talk about the missing students. To add icing to the cake, we're no longer allowed to leave campus without first getting it approved by Dean Galen. I have to breathe a sigh of relief at the fact that I got my lumi pod before the school essentially locked down. Even so, the idea that I'm no longer able to come and go really puts a damper on my search. Between this and what Bren told me, I have to wonder if it's a sign that maybe I should stop looking and focus on getting through the school year.

The sky matches my mood today. Dark and gloomy. This is the first time I've ever seen anything other than clear blue with perfect fluffy clouds, but it seems fitting. If this high priestess tea fails, I'll officially be hitting a brick wall I won't be able to scale.

After returning to our room last night, Falyn called Noric and got him to agree to infusing the lumi pod for us to use tonight. I bring it with us to lunch in the commissary to hand over to him. Now the only problem lies in how inconsistent my magic works. I can't so much as draw up a single spark of empress magic for him to infuse the lumi pod with.

Frustrated, I let out a growl and swipe a hand through my hair. "Unbelievable. There's no way my magic is still drained. I think I just need to face the fact that I'm broken."

Noric shoots me a sympathetic smile while Falyn reaches across the table to grab the seed from him. She focuses a moment and just as a tiny seedling emerges from the pod, Noric puts his hands over hers. The smell of damp earth after a rain shower washes over me, then dissipates just as fast. They share a smile, Falyn's cheeks turning a soft pink before she slips her hands out from under his and allows him to place the lumi pod back into its jar.

"There, it's infused. And Kennedy, we're going to figure out your magic situation. You're not broken," Falyn says.

Before I can respond, the rest of our group flops into the remaining chairs around the table. Sona's eyes are bright with excitement and her body practically vibrates with unspent energy. She leans forward and smiles. Something she doesn't do often, so I know whatever she's about to say is going to be good.

"I got my second! Looks like you're not the only high priestess at the table anymore, Ken."

"That's amazing, Sona!" Noric says, then immediately looks at me like he's checking to make sure I'm not going to have a meltdown. "What was your first vision?"

"Actually, it was about that." She points at the jar sitting on the table. "Whatever you're doing with it, I'm supposed to do with you, I think."

I hesitate for a second. Why does it seem every high priestess I meet is getting visions about me? But it's not a horrible idea. This tea is basically an experiment and what's an experiment without a control?

"It's a brew that lets a high priestess choose their vision. I don't even know if it'll work, but I guess the more the merrier, right?" I shrug.

Sona eyes the jar with skepticism. "Any vision I want?"

217

"That's what the book I found it in says. But it only works for a couple minutes at most. We're gonna do it tonight in our room if you want to join," I respond, sliding the jar from the table into my bag. I should probably get this back to our room before something happens to it. That would be my luck.

"I want to come too," Ciena says, nudging Sona with her elbow.

"Vision party in the worldly building!" Rostan pumps his fist in the air, not giving us a choice. I groan but smile because if I'm being honest, it really doesn't bother me having them around. In fact, I kinda like it. Something I'm definitely not used to.

"It's settled then. Tonight we're gonna find Ken's family, and hopefully that'll solve her magic issues." Falyn claps excitedly. "In the meantime, we have another sparring session to get to." Her smile falls as soon as she says it, and she looks over at me. "I can skip though, if you want to do something today?"

"It's fine. I already accepted it and I'm moving on. I'm not going to dissolve into a puddle of tears every time you mention combat. Go. I'm sure I can find something to keep me occupied."

"I'm sure you can too," Ciena says and nods her head at something over my shoulder.

When I turn to see what she's talking about, Drayzen is making his way toward our table, his eyes fixed on me.

"On that note, I'm gonna head back to the room," I say, getting up quickly. Falyn giggles when I push away from my chair so hard it falls backward and hits the floor. My cheeks flame.

"Coward," she says, amidst everyone else's snorts of amusement.

"I am not. I just have things I need to do today, and he's not one of them." The laughing grows louder around the table. "That's not what I . . . you know what, never mind. You all are children and I'm not sinking to your level." I glare at them, my face even hotter than it was before.

Back in my room, I put the lumi pod on my desk and look around for something to occupy my time. Grabbing the copy of Lore of Arcanum Magic I picked up from the library, I try to focus on the story of the first hanged man, but after reading the opening line six times in a row, I know I'm not going to be able to focus. I'm too amped up about drinking the potion tonight. My body practically buzzes with nervous energy, and I need to find a way to expend it or I'm going to go crazy.

It's been over a week since I've run and I have to admit once my body got use to the exertion I was starting to like it. Not giving myself a chance to change my mind, I quickly change into some loose clothing and head outside. I remember seeing a trail behind our

219

dorm I can use. It won't be as hard to run as Brextin's, but I'm not looking to kill myself. I just need to do something other than pacing back and forth.

I start slow since I don't know how quickly someone can lose their conditioning, but pick up my pace when I realize my slow speed is doing nothing for me. Soon I fall into a steady rhythm that increases my heart rate and exhilarates me. I really do enjoy running. Imagine that.

The trees lining the trail are changing from green to the gold and red of fall. They call it harvest season here. I should probably get used to using their terminology if I ever want to fit in.

The thought gives me pause. How long have I been here? I calculate the days since my arrival and do some math. Holy shit. I stumble a little bit. I've been so hyper focused on finding my family and trying to figure out my magic, I completely forgot. I can't be a hundred percent sure since I don't have calendars to compare, but I think tomorrow might be my birthday. Then again, I've never been one to count down the days. I've had very few good birthdays in my life and I doubt my change of scenery is going to effect that.

"If running makes you so sad, why do you do it?"

I trip over my own feet when the voice comes suddenly from beside me. This time, I'm not able to right myself and pitch forward with all the grace of a toddler learning to walk. Before my face hits the ground, a strong arm captures me around the waist and yanks me backward against a hard chest.

My shirt slipped up, so I feel the hand holding me steady splayed out against the skin of my stomach. A tanned, callused hand against pale smooth skin. The sight and feel of it sends a small shiver up the back of my neck. Then reality crashes in, thankfully. I don't even know who's behind me.

I slap the hand away and whirl around, not surprised at who I see. "Why are you following me?"

Drayzen smirks. "I did warn you. Consider me your shadow from here on out."

"I don't need a tutor and I especially don't need a shadow. I have enough to deal with without you constantly being here to remind me there's something wrong with me."

"What do you mean?"

I scoff at his attempt at ignorance. "You're going to act like Galen didn't ask you to spy on me and figure out what's wrong with my magic?"

"Nobody said anything is wrong with you or your magic." He scrubs his hand across his face before continuing. "Look, he did ask me to report anything unusual, but he wasn't specific. I don't plan on doing that. I just couldn't refuse the assignment, okay?"

"That's why I don't need you as my tutor. It's hard enough to figure this out by myself. Having to watch my back while doing it will just make it worse. Why can't you tell him no?"

"Let's just say you're not the only one with eyes on you here."

"Right. Your mom. You know, I saw her in the market the first time I went."

"Oh yeah?" He gives me a weary look.

"She was arresting someone . . . and destroying their booth." I pause. "You're slated to become one of the king's guards too, right?" I ask with more disdain than necessary.

"I see now. You think because of who my mother is, I'll be just like her."

I don't immediately answer, even though that's exactly what I think.

"I mean, isn't that a prerequisite to being in the king's guard? Blind loyalty and obedience, right?"

"You think it's wrong to be loyal to our king?" He lifts a single eyebrow in question.

"I think it's wrong to support someone fully if they don't deserve the support just because of who they are."

"And what makes you think our king isn't worthy of support? You just got here. How much could you possibly know about our society?" He crosses his arms over his broad chest. "And just because I want to hold the same position as my mother doesn't mean I also hold her values."

I sigh. This isn't where I intended the conversation to go. "I think we got off track here. My only point is that I don't think a student tutor relationship will benefit either one of us. You should ask Galen to choose someone else."

"I can't do that. Besides, how do you know it won't work if you don't at least give it a chance?"

"It's not just because of your mother. What about Serresa? She already has it out for me and you spending time with me isn't going to make that any easier."

"So then we don't let her find out . . . what makes you think she has it out for you?"

He sounds like he's genuinely curious, making me wonder if he knows any of the things she's done to me. If not, I'm not about to bring light to it.

"Never mind. I'm obviously not getting anywhere with you. Also, I'm not going to play dirty little secret between you and your girlfriend. Can I finish my run now?"

He frowns at me in what I think might be confusion, but chooses to keep his mouth shut. Instead, he gestures for me to move past him on the trail. I set out in a light jog again and it takes me a couple of seconds to realize he's keeping pace with me.

"What are you doing?"

"I thought we were running?"

"No. I'm running. You were supposed to leave me alone."

"I already told you that wasn't going to happen." He shoots me an annoyingly cocky smile and I groan. "Besides, you never answered my question."

223

"What question?" I ask because I can't help myself.

"Why running makes you sad."

"Running doesn't make me sad. Why do you think that?"

"When I caught up to you, you just looked really sad."

I glance over at him. He's focused on the trail in front of us, giving me a view of his profile. A thin scar runs from under his ear and traces the line of his jaw. It's a nice jaw. I've heard the term strong jaw, but I don't think I've ever understood it until now. I wonder where he got the scar.

His head swivels toward me and I quickly avert my eyes, but I'm sure he saw me. I struggle to remember what we were talking about for a second.

"I wasn't sad. Just thinking about stuff."

"What stuff?"

I clear my throat. "I think tomorrow is my birthday." I don't know why I'm telling him. The only reason I come up with is it must be easier sharing stuff with someone you have no emotional attachment to. Right?

"You think?"

"I don't really have a calendar, and I don't know how the calendar translates to over here, but I'm pretty sure based on how many days I've been here." I try to sound indifferent, but I obviously fail.

"You're disappointed they closed the portals. You can't do anything with your friends, right?"

224

If only it were something as trivial as that.

"Not really. I don't celebrate my birthday. I never have. It was just a random thought that popped into my mind is all." We round a bend and the worldly building comes into view. The trail must loop. "Guess the run is over. I'd say see you later, but I'm hoping you change your mind about this whole stalker thing you've got going on." I wave before increasing my speed until I'm at the door of my building. Not a moment too soon. I already said way more than I intended to and I'm pretty sure I would have kept going.

After taking a quick shower and a much-needed nap, everyone arrives and it's finally time to brew my lumi pod tea. There's nothing special about the brewing itself. I just have to steep the pod in hot water the same way I would a normal cup of tea. I'll know it's ready when the color of the liquid changes from the same pink as the pod to brown.

All of us watch the tea pot with single-minded focus waiting for the color to change. It seems to take forever, but when it does finally happen, I can't help but think it looked so much more appetizing when the liquid was pink. Now it just looks like lake water after kicking sediment up in it.

225

Falyn pours a cup for both me and Sona. She swirls the liquid around for a moment, her nose wrinkled in disgust. "I don't know if I want to drink this anymore."

I laugh because if I wasn't so desperate for answers, I would probably agree. "Let's do it on three." I gingerly sniff the warm brew. At least it smells good. That gives me hope for the taste.

"One . . . two . . . three." We tip our heads back and swallow the contents of our cups in one gulp.

The taste isn't anything like I thought it would be. I imagined everything from sulfur to floral, but the tart fruitiness that bursts across my tongue is wholly unexpected. I find myself tipping the cup into my mouth, hoping for one more drop to find its way onto my tongue.

Sona drops her cup before she can place it back on the table and it falls to the floor with a dull thunk just as her eyes roll back, leaving only the whites. Right before her lids close, all expression falls from her face and she becomes nothing but a living statue. Until her eyelids flicker.

Everyone watches her with rapt attention while Falyn pats my shoulder and offers a small smile. Oh. It hits me. She's having a vision and I'm not. Of course I'm not. Because why would anything go the way I need it to for once?

"It's fine." I shrug Falyn's hand off my shoulder and stand to gather the teapot and cups Falyn set out for us earlier. I need something to keep my hands and my mind busy.

True to what I read, Sona's eyes snap open after just a couple of minutes. She looks around the room in confusion before her eyes settle on me with a frown. "Your brew didn't work. I can't believe I swallowed that vile crap." She gags a little to punctuate her sentence.

"What do you mean? It tasted fine to me."

"Yeah, fine if you enjoy drinking stagnant pond water." She shudders and gives me a disgusted look. "I did have a vision, but I definitely didn't pick it. I don't even know what I was watching."

"Oh, I guess that makes me feel a tiny bit better about it not working at all for me. What did you see?"

"I wanted to see my future. What power level and assignment I'm going to receive after school. Instead, I wound up in a dark cellar or dungeon or something. It was made of stone and there were no windows or anything." She stops talking and her eyes take on a slightly glazed look before she finds her voice again. "It was so cold. I could hear voices, so I followed them into another area of the dungeon. I couldn't see who was talking, but it was definitely a man and a woman. He was telling her to get rid of it."

"Get rid of what?" Rostan asks, smoothing a hand down her back in comfort.

"There were so many beds . . ." she whispers, eyes darting around before she closes them. "Then another man shows up and takes something from her. I'm pretty sure he portaled in."

"What do you mean about the beds, Sona?" Ciena asks, puzzled.

"She told him to hurry before he finds out."

"Finds what out?" The hair on my arms stands up. Even without being able to manifest my high priestess magic, something tells me whatever she's about to say is important.

Sona's brows scrunch before her eyes pop back open and she looks directly at me. "Not beds. Cribs. I think she gave that man a baby."

CHAPTER FIFTEEN

After everyone left last night, Falyn and I stayed up late talking about Sona's vision. We figure it's way too big of a coincidence that Sona has a vision about a baby being hidden away for it not to be about me, but it's not much to go off of. Why would I have been in a dungeon with a bunch of other cribs? Sona didn't know if there were other babies in them, but I imagine

229

if someone put together that many cribs, there's a reason for it. She also couldn't see anyone's faces, which does nothing to help me. I'm left with more questions than ever, and I can feel my hope of finding the truth slip through my fingers.

Just before we parted ways to get some sleep, an announcement came across Falyn's crystal. They're giving us a three-day weekend in light of recent events. Whatever that means. Ciena told us they may have found one of the missing students, but that was all she heard.

I really need to get a crystal of my own. Having to rely on someone else to relay information makes me feel way too dependent. Especially when she tells me someone is hosting a party near the lake, and we were invited, so she already agreed to go for the both of us.

I am not a party person. I don't drink or enjoy large crowds in the slightest, so it would have been a firm no from me had she not answered without asking.

"Come on, Ken. You need to let loose for once. Going to one party isn't going to kill you." Falyn pops her head out of her closet long enough to roll her eyes at me.

"You don't know that. What if we get attacked by a pack of krensel? You're going to feel really foolish crying at my funeral."

"I just won't go then," she calls out.

"Good, I'm glad you finally see it my way. We can stay in and do something else! I wanted to see about getting a crystal for myself anyway and we can't do that if we're getting ready for some lame party."

"No, I mean I won't go to your funeral. We're definitely going to the party." She emerges with her arms full of clothes she tosses on the bed next to me. "Now let's find you something to wear."

"Absolutely not. You're like half my size. I might as well go naked if I'm borrowing something from you."

"I already checked your closet and you don't have anything remotely appropriate to wear to a party, so it's this or nothing."

"We could just not go . . ." I reply, pressing my hands together in fake prayer.

"We're going. Everyone will be there and you're going to have a great time and forget all about your problems for one night." Her voice rings with a finality that says, I don't really have a choice.

"Fine. But I'm not wearing your clothes."

Imagine my surprise when I'm standing in front of a mirror several hours later in a nude-colored gauzy top that definitely came out of her closet and not my own. She at least let me wear my own jeans with the top after I tried on one of her skirts and couldn't get it over my hips.

I have to admit it's cute. And even though it leaves my entire midriff exposed, I like the way it shimmers when I move. I can't wear anything under it since it's a halter top, so thankfully it's supportive and only gives the impression of being see through.

231

We pair it with my favorite light jeans and she doesn't have any choice but to let me wear my converse since there's no way I can squish my feet into a pair of her shoes. Falyn also does my makeup, giving me smoky eyes and dark red lips. She leaves my hair down to fall in waves over my back and claps her hands in excitement after putting the finishing touches on my makeup.

"You look gorgeous!" she gushes. "Every guy there is going to be falling over himself to talk to you."

"You need to go get ready yourself since you're the one so dead set on going. Even if Noric is the only one you want falling over himself."

"Maybe. Maybe not. What if I'm tired of waiting for him? What if there's another boy there who grabs my attention? The possibilities are endless tonight, Ken!" She sweeps out of my room in a flurry of pink hair and makeup brushes. I smile. She's not fooling anyone but herself. I've never seen her look at anyone but Noric, and I doubt she'll start tonight.

The party is already in full swing by the time we get there. It took Falyn two hours to get ready, making me wonder why I had to get ready first. Probably because she didn't want to give me time to back out of it.

232

There's probably a hundred people scattered across the banks of the river. Most of them with drinks in hand. Loud rock music I don't recognize drowns out the sound of conversations with a loud almost hypnotic drum beat. When I look around, I don't see any music equipment. I'm sure we can thank a temperance for that.

Noric and Ciena wave at us from the edge of the tree line where they're standing by a makeshift table covered in cups filled with different colored liquids. Falyn grabs my hand and pulls me behind her through the crowd to get to them.

"Hey, you made it! That means Sona owes me a week's worth of her dessert after dinner, so thank you for that!" Noric gloats proudly.

"You guys bet on whether I would come?" I scoff, then turned to Falyn. "You drug me here to help Noric win a bet?" I shake my head in amusement.

"I didn't know anything about the bet! I promise." She laughs.

"Here, try this." She hands me a yellow drink from the table. "It's made from the petals of yellow briar flowers and super yummy!"

I sniff the drink before taking a sip. It smells similar to lemons and has a tart bite to it that I love. I finish the rest in two gulps. Ciena and Falyn watch in amusement. "You may want to drink your next one a little more slowly. It has a way of sneaking up on you." Ciena warns me as I grab another yellow drink from the table.

233

Warmth is already spreading through my limbs, so I choose to listen to her warning and only sip my next one. The music changes to something with an obvious dance beat and since I'm feeling pretty good, I let Falyn pull me away from the table toward the crowd of people dancing.

It doesn't take long to adjust to the music and soon I'm throwing my hands up and swaying my hips with the rest of them. I don't know how long we dance. I lost count of the number of songs, but I'm actually having a good time. Just like she promised. This might actually go down as my favorite birthday when the rest of our group joins us and they start teaching me the steps to a dance when a specific song starts playing. It's pretty similar to line dancing, only with way more twirling. Enough that I'm starting to get dizzy. Although that could be from the alcohol too, considering I'm on my third yellow drink of the night.

I mistake a forward step for a backward one and wind up stepping on the person behind me. I whirl around with an apology on my lips until I see who it is. Serresa. Standing on either side of her are Michan and Drayzen, both of them watching me with amusement in their eyes. Serresa, on the other hand, is trying to melt the skin off my bones with her stare.

"Watch what you're doing, zero," she bites out.

"I would if I had eyes behind my head, but since you're the one who could see me, maybe you should watch what you're doing . . ."

234

Drayzen's laugh is cut short when she shoots the same glare his way.

"Whatever. Let's go somewhere else. Where the air doesn't smell so much like mundana."

I stare pointedly at Drayzen as she drags him away. She just proved my point for me. He shrugs and rolls his eyes but follows her anyway, like the good little elite soldier he is. The whole interaction is enough to kill my buzz, so I pull away from the group to catch my breath. They all follow me.

"Don't let her ruin the night. There's still drinks and dancing to be had!" Rostan is the first to speak. "Come on, I'll show you how a pro dances." He doesn't give me the opportunity to say no before he's pulling me back to the crowd and dipping me until my head almost touches the sand.

I dance with Rostan for a couple of songs, in which he twirls and tosses me around like a rag doll until I'm laughing so hard I can't dance anymore. I hold my stomach, panting, and shake my head to let him know I'm officially out. The rest of our group stand on the outskirts cheering and clapping. Clapping coming from behind Rostan captures my attention and I find myself staring into the smiling eyes of Drayzen. Michan and Serresa aren't anywhere near him as far as I can tell, but I know where there's one, the others are probably close. My smile falters but not completely, because Rostan grabs my hand and motions for me to bow with him. When we straighten up, Drayzen is out of sight.

235

"Thank you," I shout over the music. I know the dancing was his way of distracting me and it worked. He winks at me, but he's already grabbing Ciena around the waist to pull her to the dance floor.

"Admit it. You're glad you came." Falyn smirks and hands me my drink once I'm standing next to her again.

"I guess it's not all bad." That's as much of an acknowledgement as I'm willing to give her.

"Looks like it might be getting better." She tips her chin toward the crowd and I follow her gaze.

A guy I've never seen before heads straight for us and he's looking directly at me. Falyn elbows me and slowly backs away to merge with the crowd by the drink table. The guy stops right in front of me.

"Hey." He smiles, revealing slightly crooked teeth, but it somehow adds to his cuteness.

"Hey."

"Do you want to dance?"

I hesitate. I'm not sure I want to, but I know I'll never hear the end of it from Falyn if I don't. I tip back the rest of my drink before I respond.

"Sure." I glance over my shoulder to find both Noric and Falyn grinning at me. Falyn has both her thumbs in the air. *I really hope he didn't see that.*

He leads me out to the crowd, but instead of staying on the outside, he keeps going until we're right in the middle of everyone else. I'm not entirely comfortable with it but I can manage one song then make my excuses. The dancing comes easily as the alcohol floods my body. I'm just sober enough to realize I've had too much to drink but not sober enough to care.

He wraps an arm around my waist and splays his hand across my bare back to pull me in until we're dancing chest to chest. I sway my hips against his and tilt my head back as the world around me spins. *Definitely too much to drink.*

"I'm kind of glad Serresa asked me to dance with you," he whispers in my ear when I lift my head up. His words are enough to sober me almost instantly.

"What are you talking about?" Icy dread is already working its way up my spine. There's no way he's not up to something.

"If she hadn't, then I wouldn't have got to see this . . ."

I register two things at the same time. The first being that I can feel the cool night air against skin that shouldn't be able to feel it. The second being that everyone has stopped dancing to look at us. No, not us. Me. I look down to find the last scrap of my shirt disintegrating between his fingers. *Fucking towers and their destruction magic. If I wasn't so tipsy maybe I would have realized it sooner.*

Laughter echoes in my ears, but the sound of my own blood rushing through my veins drowns it out. My vision narrows to the disgustingly satisfied smirk on Serresa's face when she comes to stand right behind him.

"You seem to be missing something, zero," she says while I scramble to cover myself from the eyes of probably half the students in our school. I search the crowd for a familiar face but realize this was exactly why he pulled me into the center. So my friends would have no idea what's happening.

My eyes burn and I have to draw in a deep breath and look upward to prevent the tears from spilling over and showing them exactly how much this is affecting me. Serresa starts chanting something, but it's not until everyone joins her that I realize what they're saying.

"Take it off . . . take it off . . . take it off . . ." As if it was my choice to be standing here shirtless in the first place. The triumphant glint in her eyes gives me the fuel I need to move beyond shame into anger. She thinks she's won, but I'm not done yet.

I have lived through being abandoned as a baby, countless foster homes in which I suffered everything from mental and emotional abuse, to physical abuse. There were times in my life I had no idea where my next meal was coming from and I did it all alone. I didn't have anyone to hold my hand or tell me it was going to be okay. I only had myself.

That's why this is nothing. I drop my arms and let my hands come to rest on my hips. I'm fully exposed now, but it doesn't stop me from lifting my chin in defiance. Meeting Serresa's in the eye, I smile before lifting my hands in a flourish and twirling in a circle to really give them a show. The clapping and cheering increase tenfold and I tip my head back and laugh.

"Who wants to go swimming?" I yell out, doing my best to raise my voice above the crowd while unsnapping my jeans to push them down my hips.

One by one, the students around me follow suit, tossing their clothes to the side. I wink at Serresa, waggle my fingers in a small wave, then run into the lake until I can dive in headfirst. The water is icy cold, but a welcome distraction. As much as I pretend it doesn't bother me, being able to hide under the water is a welcome relief. I'm just not sure what I'll do when it's time to get out.

Naked bodies splash through the water around me, but I only have eyes for Serresa, who is still standing on the shore completely dumbfounded by the turn of events. She narrows her eyes at me and clenches her hands into fists. I know this is far from over, but I'm counting this as a win even if it will also go down as one of the worst birthdays in history. Funny how quickly my perspective changed on that.

I still have to figure out what I'm going to do about a shirt because I don't know how much longer I'm going to be able to stay in the water. My teeth are already chattering like crazy, but Serresa maintains her spot on the shore and I'm hesitant to try my luck with her so soon.

Drayzen and Michan choose this moment to return from wherever they were when everything went down. Their presence makes me want to leave the safety of the water even less. I can't hear their conversation over the sounds of laughing and splashing, but it's evident who Serresa is talking about when she points directly at me with hate in her eyes. The guys frown and look my way, neither one of them seeming impressed.

I can't stay in here forever and my group of friends haven't seemed to notice my predicament yet. I take a deep breath and steel myself when an idea formulates. Crossing my arms over my chest, I stand in the waist height lake before wading through the water and sand until I'm standing right in front of the three of them. Serresa wrinkles her nose at me.

"There's more alcohol that way if you don't think you've already had enough for one night."

Well, at least now I know what she was telling them when I was in the water. It's probably no use defending myself, so I choose to play the part instead.

"I seem to have lost my shirt . . ." I bat my eyes up at Michan first, because he seems like the type to fall for it. Except he's doing everything he possibly can to avoid looking at me. Not what I expected from him, if I'm being honest. I would have pegged him for the type to jump at talking to a shirtless woman.

Serresa gloats at me and presses her lips together like she's holding back a laugh. I momentarily close my eyes, refusing to be embarrassed by his blatant lack of interest. That leaves Drayzen, who's still watching me with that damned look of disappointment on his face. I stiffen my shoulders. He can believe what he wants to believe. It's probably easier this way. If he wants to think I'm a vapid drunk, maybe he'll leave me alone about the whole tutoring thing.

I reach over, keeping one arm securely crossed over my chest, and tug at the hem of his shirt with an empty smile plastered to my face. "I don't think anyone would mind if you were to loan me yours." I look up at him from under my lashes.

He sighs heavily, but tugs the shirt over his head and hands it to me. I may have been playing the part up to this point, but the appreciative look I give him at the sight of his bare chest is anything but an act. Defined muscle under tan skin and covered in tattoos. I definitely don't mind that he loaned me his shirt.

"Are you going to put it on or just hold it all night?" he asks, clearly annoyed with me. I ignore the twinge of disappointment and slip his shirt over my head.

"Thank you," I murmur once I'm fully covered. "I need to go find my friends."

I turn toward the drink table where I saw them last, but before I make it too far Drayzen calls out behind me. "You should probably think about avoiding that table for a little while. You wouldn't want to lose another shirt."

I cringe and stiffen my shoulders at his words, but I don't turn around. I don't care what any of them think. Even so, when I'm halfway to the table, I decide I'm not ready to talk to anyone, so I detour into the

241

copse of trees just to my right. I don't venture too far because the last thing I need is to get lost, especially considering I'm in nothing but a t-shirt and my panties. I didn't even grab my shoes.

I just need a moment to gather my thoughts and deal with the events of the last hour. Am I just a magnet for bullshit? I let Falyn convince me it would be an amazing night, and I dropped my guard too much. Now I'm buzzed, soaked, and half the school has seen my boobs.

Leaning against the closest tree, I scrub a hand across my face and take a deep breath. I'm ready to go home. I just want to sleep and forget this night ever happened. I'm sure I made it worse by asking Drayzen for his shirt. I would bet everything I own that he's the reason Serresa instantly disliked me. Well, that and the fact that I don't come from a long line of tens like she does. As far as she's concerned, I'm no better than a mundana, and she enjoys reminding me.

The more I think about it, the angrier I become. She is bound and determined to make sure I'm miserable every time we cross paths. And for what? Amusement? To prove she's stronger? I'm well aware of how much stronger she is. That's why I haven't done anything about it. There's nothing I can do, and she knows it.

Without warning, the tree behind me disappears and I fall backward onto my ass. I stay on the ground for a moment, just staring at the sky and wondering what else could go wrong tonight. I don't have to wait long for an answer.

"How did you do that?" Serresa demands.

"I don't know what you're talking about. Aren't you bored with me yet?"

"You dissolved the tree. Only a tower can dissolve objects like that and last I checked you weren't registered as a tower. How did you do it?"

"Really? Why would I destroy the tree I was leaning against? Why are you following me anyway?"

"I watched you, zero. Tell me how you did it, or I'm going to report you to Galen tomorrow."

"Report me for what exactly? Did I dissolve this tree the same way I got too drunk and dissolved my shirt? Where's your little tower friend? The one you sent to do your dirty work, since you're too much of a princess to get your hands dirty."

Serresa's eyes flash white momentarily and I know she's about to do something I'm going to regret. I roll out of the way just as a thin beam of light shoots from her fingers and singes the ground where I was just lying.

Fuck. I scramble to my feet, scraping my knees in the process. Just as she's gearing up to send another one my way, the sound of leaves crunching underfoot stops her. The fear of being caught has her slinking off further into the forest before whoever it is finds us.

"Kennedy? What are you doing out here?" Michan approaches, looking at my blood covered knees.

243

"Oh, you know. Just hanging out . . ."

CHAPTER SIXTEEN

I grabbed your shoes and pants when I saw you head this way. I thought you might need them, but it seems I might be too late." He squats down to inspect my knees.

"I'm fine. Just a little scraped up," I reply, grabbing my pants and yanking them over my legs in a hurry. First the shirt and now this. It's definitely going to cement me as the class drunk.

"Did you find your friends?" he asks, shoving his hands into his pockets.

"I haven't looked for them. I think I'm just gonna head home so I don't ruin their night."

He runs his hand through his hair and shuffles his feet awkwardly. "I could walk you if you want?"

"To the portal?" I raise one eyebrow because I'm pretty sure the portal is less than a five-minute walk from where we're currently standing.

"I mean, back to your room. We don't know how safe campus is yet and with you having so much to drink, you may need help getting past any patrols." He shrugs.

"I'm not drunk. I mean, I was definitely feeling a buzz earlier, but I'm fine now."

"Oh. I can still walk you if that's okay?"

Okay, this has officially gotten weird. Less than an hour ago I stood in front of him completely shirtless, and he acted like it was the last thing he wanted to see. Now he's determined to walk alone with me? Actually, this smells like Serresa all over again.

"Let me guess, Serresa asked you to be nice to me?" I cross my arms over my chest. I have no interest in letting her make a fool of me three times in one night.

He snorts. "I'm not sure if you've noticed, but Serresa is the last person to do anyone favors. Nice isn't a word I'm sure she even understands. I just thought I'd offer . . ."

I hesitate, searching his face for any sign of bad intentions, but find nothing that sets off my warning

246

bells. Maybe being walked home by a good-looking guy is exactly what I need to salvage something from tonight.

"Okay," I respond. I mean, he walked me to the healer after a different run in with Serresa and I made it there fine. It is kind of interesting that he's shown up right after her twice now. Something I'll have to analyze later because he's already walking in the direction of the portal and I'm still standing here like an idiot.

"So how'd you hurt your knees?" he asks once I'm walking by his side.

"I fell," I echo the same words I used the day he caught me in those thorny vines.

"Have you always been so clumsy?" He smirks, and I know he's remembering the same thing I am.

"Just since coming here, apparently. It must be the air."

He shakes his head in amusement.

"How did they find you anyway?"

"A high priestess had a vision, I guess. That's all I know."

"I never would have expected a family of mages to choose a realm where magic doesn't exist to make their home."

I cringe a little on the inside. "Actually, it was just me. I don't know anything about my family. I don't even know how I wound up on Earth."

247

He doesn't seem surprised when I tell him. In fact, it's almost as if he already knows. Before I can comment on it, he changes the subject.

"How did you like your first Arcanum party?"

"I think like is kind of a strong word to use if you're talking about my experience tonight . . ." I trail off.

We arrive at the portal, and he pauses in front of it.

"For being so last minute, it didn't turn out bad." He steps through the portal, and I follow him, confused.

"Last minute?"

"Yeah, Drayzen of all people planned it. I've never seen him approve of partying of any kind, but yesterday he was adamant the school needs a morale boost . . ." He grins. "Not that I'm complaining. It's my birthday in a couple days, so I'm pretty sure it was his way of doing something for me since we're pretty much on lock down."

"You guys are good friends, then?" I don't mention my own birthday. At this point, it's not worth the effort. If it ever was.

"We've known each other since we were small. Our mothers went through school together."

"Must be nice," I respond without thinking, twisting my fingers in the hem of the oversize shirt.

"What's that?"

"Nothing, I was just thinking how nice it must be to go to school with your best friend."

248

"Oh," he shrugs. "I guess I've never really thought about it. Even though we've known each other for a long time, we didn't exactly get to grow up together."

"How come?"

"I didn't get to leave the palace often and Drayzen's mother takes her job far too serious to ever bring her son with her."

"It must have been so hard growing up the king's son in your giant palace." I can't help the bitterness creeping into my voice. Luckily, he doesn't take offense.

"It definitely had its perks."

"Did you sleep in a crib made of gold?"

"Until I grew out of it and demanded a bed made of precious gemstones instead." He winks and I snort.

"Ha ha. Seriously though, what was it like growing up like that? I can't fathom having a father, let alone a king for a father." His smile drops a little at my question.

"Honestly? It's probably not anything like you're imagining. I was raised by my nursemaid and had very little interaction with my parents until I got older. They're still just the strangers I eat dinner with every now and then." His voice sounds almost wistful. "Liandris was great though. She did her best to shield me from my fa—" he stops suddenly. "—from becoming too spoiled."

249

I choose to ignore his almost slip up. "Tell me about the king. On Earth, it's very rare to have an outright monarchy."

"What do you want to know?" I don't miss the tightening around his eyes when he asks.

"How does it work? Does he just make all the laws and everyone has to follow them? No questions asked?"

"Something like that. I mean, he has a council of advisors, but he doesn't have to listen to them."

"Have you ever been to a mundana territory? If they're separate, do they have their own ruler?" As much as I've learned over the last month, the one thing I can never seem to find answers about is the mundana villages.

"No, they still fall under the king's rule. Why?" He frowns.

"Then why aren't they allowed to enter mage cities?" I ask a little more abruptly than I intended.

"You'd have to ask the king himself if you want the answer to that question. I don't know the reason behind half the things he does, and it's not my place to question him." He kicks at a rock and it skips ahead on the path.

"How is it not your place? You're his son. You just support everything he does, no questions asked?" It's wild to me that no matter who I ask, I get the same response.

"Being his son doesn't earn me special privileges, and it's not anyone's place to ask. I don't

250

support him because he's my father. I do as I'm told because he's the king and his word is law."

"What do you mean, you do as you're told? Do you share his beliefs that people without magic are less than?" I kind of want to strangle him at this point.

"It doesn't matter if I share his beliefs or not. He's the king. I never said I like him or his views, but I don't need to in order to acknowledge that fact," he replies. "I have nothing to do with any of it."

"So you just stand by and accept everything he lays down? That makes you no better than him. What good is growing up privileged if you do nothing with it? You stand complacent while other people are treated unfairly? I have no idea what it's like living in a mundana village, but considering it's used as a punishment, I can't imagine it's a good place to live. Honestly, I'm not surprised there's a whole faction of people who want to dethrone the king."

Michan stops walking all together. "You're right. You don't know what it's like. You have no idea what anything is like here. Who are you to condemn anyone for something you have no understanding of? And you may want to remember who you're talking to the next time you declare your approval of the rebels. I'm still the king's son." With that, he turns on his heel and walks away, leaving me standing by the courtyard statue.

The faces of the Esotera mock me with their serene features. I feel anything but serene. My insides are churning, both from his not-so-subtle warning but also from frustration. That definitely could have gone better.

When I get home, I waste no time jumping into the shower to wash the lake smell off me. I wash, rinse, and repeat several times before I'm satisfied I don't smell like fish. I still have Drayzen's shirt, but I hesitate to toss it into the washing basket. As soon as it's halfway full, the temperance charm will activate and clean everything in it, destroying any lingering scents in the process. I lift his shirt and inhale deeply before I realize what I'm doing. I must still have a buzz from earlier because there's no way I would do this otherwise.

Warm sandalwood with hints of citrus invades my senses and I breathe more deeply before shaking my head in disgust and dropping it into the basket. As soon as it's clean, I'll return it to him and forget about the whole night. As far as I'm concerned, it never even happened.

The front door slams open, followed by Falyn's panicked voice. "Ken? Are you home?" She doesn't wait for me to answer before she barges into my room in a flurry of unsteady feet and shushing noises from Noric, who's doing his best to keep her from falling over. "I was worried about you. Why didn't you tell us you were leaving?" she slurs. I pull

252

my towel tighter around me and glare at Noric over her head.

He shrugs. "She's an adult. Besides, she's fine. She didn't wander off and disappear like someone else we know."

"I'm standing right here. And I'm perfectly capable of making my own choices." She punctuates her sentence with a hiccup and slaps her hand over her mouth. "Fine, maybe I had a little too much, but we have no idea when we'll get to do it again, so I have no regrets." The whole time she's speaking, her body sways one way then another as she over corrects herself each time. She may not regret it right now, but tomorrow is going to be a different story. "Well?" she asks.

"Well what? I came back early and didn't want to ruin your fun. Michan walked me home, so I was perfectly safe."

"Safe? He's the worst of any guy I know. I'm surprised you have clothes on right now. Wait . . . did you just shower? Please tell me you didn't do anything?" She exaggerates a gagging noise, but in her state, I'm worried she'll manifest it into existence.

"Nothing happened. He offered to walk me home. I may have told him I agreed with the rebels, then he went home, that's all."

"You what?" Falyn shrieks at me. "You can't say that to the king's son! Are you trying to get sent away?"

253

Her high-pitched tone is enough to make me wince. "Calm down. He's not going to have me arrested for treason. At least I don't think so . . ."

Falyn pulls away from Noric and staggers to my bed before flopping down on it. "See, this is why you can't just disappear and not tell anyone where you're going. Also, why is your bed so much more comfortable than mine?"

"I think I'm gonna go now . . ." Noric says, still hovering in my doorway. "It looks like you've got this handled, okay?" Falyn waves at him between yanking her shoes off and crawling toward my headboard.

"You realize you're still in my bed, right?" I ask when she starts working her way under my blankets.

"Mine is too far away, and yours is big enough for both of us." She pats the space next to her.

"Whatever. Let me get some clothes on." I head to my closet but pause at the basket sitting just outside of it. Drayzen's shirt is still sitting on top unwashed. I peek up at Falyn, but her eyes are already closed, so I hurry to pull it back out and rush into my closet to change. I tell myself I'm only doing this because his shirt is big enough to be a nightgown, and I didn't bring a whole lot of pajamas. It has nothing to do with the owner or his smell.

When I slip in next to Falyn, her eyes pop open and she rolls over to look at me. "Are you gonna tell me why you really left?"

I sigh. I'm not sure I want to unpack everything so soon, but I know her well enough to know she's not going to leave this alone. I tell her everything. From the magically dissolving shirt to the impromptu skinny dipping, then my petty attempt at pissing Serresa off even more by trying and failing to flirt with . . . whatever they are to her. Neither Michan nor Drayzen has laid any claim to her, but she hasn't been shy about staking her claim on them. Falyn, in her drunken state, whips the blankets off her and sits up before I get to the part about the tree.

"What are you doing?" I barely have to tug on her arm to flop her back into the bed.

"I'm gonna go teach that bitch a lesson once and for all." She struggles to get back up, and a laugh bubbles up in my throat.

"The only lesson you're capable of teaching anyone tonight is gonna wind up involving the toilet if you don't stop thrashing around. You can deal with her later. If you still remember this."

She finally settles and closes her eyes. "I really drank a lot tonight." Less than two seconds later, her eyes pop back open in excitement. "You left before I could give you your present!"

"What present?" I ask in shock. The only person I told about my birthday was Drayzen. "Wait, why did you get me a present?"

"Really? I've been helping you search for your birth family since you got here. You don't think I'd remember your birthday?" she purses her lips. "It's not just from me, though. Everyone helped get it." She gets up, still swaying on her feet but a little more stable than

255

she was when she first got here. Luckily, she doesn't have to go far to retrieve her bag from my floor. As soon as she's back in bed next to me, she holds out a box a little bigger than my hand. I take it from her, still in awe that someone went out of their way to remember my birthday.

Inside the box, nestled between some soft cloth, sits a crystal that looks identical to the one Falyn carries.

"You got me a phone?" It's such a silly response, but my eyes mist up when I pull it out of the box.

"A crystal. But yes," she corrects me. "We all did. If only to keep you from constantly moaning about not having one."

"Funny," I respond dryly. "I don't know what to say. Thank you." I flip it over in my hand, admiring how what looks like nothing but a thin pearlescent piece of glass could be so sturdy and do almost everything a cell phone can without wires and computer chips.

"Happy birthday, Ken." She nestles further into the blankets. "Now finish telling me what happened with Serresa."

I sniffle a little and hope she doesn't notice. "I was gonna go find you guys, but I needed a minute, so I wandered in the trees. Serresa and that asshole that disintegrated my shirt must have followed me because the tree I was leaning against dissolved and I fell flat on my ass."

"That doesn't make any sense."

"What do you mean?" I ask, confused.

"I went looking for you and I found him by the water. When I asked him where you went, he said he saw you walking off into the trees. He couldn't have followed you."

"Then how did that tree dissolve?" She's right, it doesn't make sense.

"Could there have been someone else?"

I think about it for a minute, but I'm positive Serresa was the only other person out there besides me and she doesn't have tower abilities.

"No, it was just us until Michan showed up and scared her off." I think back to what Misara said the day I met her in my bedroom. It feels like so long ago, but she made a comment about not being able to find the right amount. She thought it was because Earth was affecting it, but what if it was me the whole time?

What if there's something wrong with me? Does magic react poorly to me? It would explain why I have abilities no one else seems to possess. Like the fact that I can see and smell magic. Most of the time I'm completely magicless, then when I can manifest, it's a giant display of magic like I can't control it. Then there's that day in class with the wind incident. It was like he couldn't control his own magic. I joke about having broken magic, but what if that's actually the truth? Am I broken?

"What are you thinking?" Falyn interrupts my downward spiral.

"Have you ever noticed magic acts really strange around me?"

"What do you mean?"

"Think about it. You said it yourself that I can do things other people can't. What if there's something wrong with my magic?"

"There's nothing wrong with your magic, Kennedy. You just need more time."

"That's what you keep saying, but I've been at it over a month and nothing has changed. What about that time in class when Lefrin lost control of his magic and manifested an entire wind storm that took him out? That was because of an interaction with me." She opens her mouth to say something, but I keep going. "Then the one time I'm able to manifest, I wind up going so overboard the dean thinks I'm hiding something. Now tonight, Serresa swears up and down she saw me destroy that tree . . ." I trail off.

After that windstorm, Lefrin looked at me like I was the one who did it. When I went to see that healer, she thought mine and Drayzen's wounds were much larger than they were. Now tonight, with that tree. What if it really was me?

"Holy shit, Falyn," I gasp and sit straight up. She startles and looks up at me.

"What happened?"

"The first time I manifested, I grew a flower after meeting another empress. Do you remember that

258

vision I had the first day we met? The girl I grabbed. Do you know what category she has?"

Falyn shakes her head. "No, but I don't understand why that matters."

"I'd bet all my belongings she's a high priestess!"

"So, where are you going with this?"

"Don't you get it?" I'm practically yelling. "The vision, the plant, the wind, the healing, the field, and now the tree. They all have one thing in common!"

"I don't get it because you're not making any sense."

"It was all me, Falyn. I'm the one who manifested all that magic. Somehow, I can manifest other people's magic. I think it only happens after I touch someone. That's the only explanation. And all the times I couldn't do it was because I ran out or hadn't touched anyone."

"That's not possible, Kennedy . . . I don't think." But the look she gives me says she doesn't not believe me either. I may have finally figured out my magic. Too bad it makes me an even bigger freak. Something tells me I need to keep this a secret. Especially from Galen and the elites.

259

CHAPTER SEVENTEEN

I was too keyed up to fall asleep after my revelation and Falyn was too drunk to stay awake, so I spent the night listening to her soft snores until they eventually lulled me into restless sleep.

I wake up to the sound of a pained gasp coming from beside me and open my eyes to find Falyn grasping her head between her hands.

I go get her a glass of water without saying anything because I want her to be fully awake before I reopen our discussion from last night. Taking it from me, she tips her head back and guzzles it until the entire glass is empty. An action that she immediately regrets if her bolting to the bathroom is any indication.

To give her some privacy, I busy myself rinsing out her glass and trying to find something that might help a hangover. I somehow doubt I'm going to find a bottle of ibuprofen hiding anywhere but there's gotta be an Arcanum version of it, right?

I hit pay dirt when I find a jar of tea leaves labeled 'Next Day' mixed in among all the blends in the cabinet. Setting the kettle on the stove to heat water, I grab one of the cloth bags I remember seeing Falyn use the other night to brew the lumi pod. Not knowing how much to use, I fill the bag to the top, then drop it into the now boiling water in the kettle and give it some time to steep.

Falyn is back in my bed by the time I bring the tea tray in for her. She accepts my offering and blows gently on the hot liquid before sipping carefully.

She's immediately wracked by a coughing fit. "What is this?" she chokes out, eyes watering.

"Did I not do it right? I wasn't sure how much to use."

"It's a little strong but also not what I was expecting. I mean what's in it?"

"I don't know. I just got it from one of the jars you keep all your teas in." I shrug my shoulders and lean over her to sniff the tea. It smells bitter and definitely not like something you would want to drink

261

when you're hungover. "I just assumed it was hangover medicine."

"What's hangover?" she asks, scrunching her eyebrows.

"You, Right now. After drinking too much last night . . ." I gesture mostly to the untamed bush of curls she has sitting on top of her head along with the almost black circles under her eyes.

"Oh. You mean consumption sickness. That's not the blend you brought me though, right? I'll have to throw it out."

"No, I didn't see that. I gave you the one that says next day." She chokes on the tea again, then hands it back to me.

"I think you might benefit from this one more than me."

"How's that? I didn't have anywhere near as much to drink as you did." But I take it from her anyway.

"Well, for one, I'm pretty sure that shirt you have on belongs to someone else . . ." She smirks at me.

Shit, I'm still wearing Drayzen's shirt. "I had to get a shirt somewhere, didn't I?"

"Usually when a girl sleeps in a guy's shirt, it's because she also slept with the guy."

My face heats under her scrutiny. "I already told you nothing happened last night. But I still don't see what that has to do with the tea . . ." Before I finish my sentence, I realize what she means. "This isn't for the day after drinking, is it?"

262

She shakes her head no and presses her lips together.

"I gave you anti-pregnancy tea, didn't I?" I can't suppress the snort working its way past my lips.

"Yep. A really strong batch, too. It'll take me years to get pregnant now!" She laughs with me. "So . . . why are you wearing Drayzen's shirt?"

Her question sobers me. "I told you last night. You don't remember?"

"I do, but I also remember when I got here you were wrapped in a towel. So at some point you made the conscious effort to put it back on."

I slump into the chair at my desk. "Ugh. I don't know. Call it momentary weakness. He just smells so good. Can we talk about something else? Like maybe my magic?"

It's Falyn's turn to sober. "We don't even know if you're right. I think we should test it. Maybe get Noric and go bac—"

"No. We can't tell anyone. If I'm right about my magic, everyone will think I'm a freak and scientists will want to do experiments on me and one day I'll wake up missing half my organs. We need to just keep it to ourselves."

Falyn looks at me skeptically. "I have no idea what a scientist is or what you're talking about, but Noric isn't going to tell anyone your secret. We can trust him."

263

"I can't, not right now. Can we just focus on figuring the magic part out first? Then we can think about all the other stuff that comes along with it."

"Fine. But eventually you're gonna have to tell someone beside me, Ken. I somehow doubt this is something we can hide for long."

An hour later we're standing in the kitchen staring at Falyn's plants that line the counter. Well, I'm staring, but she's clipping stems from them and lining the scraps up side by side. When she has about ten, she stops to look up at me.

"Okay, first let's see if you can do anything with them since we slept in the same bed. In case it's just proximity and not touch that triggers it."

I nod my head even though I already know what the result will be. If it was just proximity, then I wouldn't have had any issues manifesting before. I'm literally surrounded by magic everywhere I turn here. Focusing on the first of the stems, I will it to grow into a plant.

When nothing happens, I squeeze my eyes closed and focus harder for good measure. Nothing happens. When Falyn is satisfied that I can't find a drop of magic inside me, she holds her hand out and I take it. The scent of freshly tilled earth washes over me as soon as our skin touches and I know I'm pulling her

264

magic into me. The thought stops me cold and I yank my hand back.

"What's wrong?" she asks, frowning.

"What if I'm actually stealing your magic?"

"Then I would just generate more. I can always recharge."

"That's not my point. What if I take too much and you can't recharge? What if I accidentally strip your magic? I don't know if we should be doing this." The words rush out of me as fast as the panicked thought race through my mind.

"Take a breath, Ken. Let's figure one thing out at a time. Can you make the stems grow?"

I do what I'm told and take a deep breath to center myself. She's right. This is as new to her as it is to me. There's no use panicking over something until it's proven to be a thing. But as hard as I try, I can't push the worry from my mind.

"Ken. Pay attention. We'll worry about that later. We need to figure out the basics first."

"Okay. Give me a second." I shake my hands to release some of my nerves and focus my attention on a stem. The spark of magic is present in my core, so I know without a doubt I'm going to manifest. Tugging gently on the spark, I pull it forward to into my lungs and just like the first time I manifested, I blow a steady breath over a stem, willing it to grow. And it does. So do the other nine. Each one only taking seconds to develop roots and sprout additional stems

265

before leaves unfurl and they all become fully grown plants.

Not just fully grown, but larger and fuller than the plants the stems came from. Falyn watches in awed silence for a moment before speaking. "Gods, Ken. You were right. You know what this means?"

"It means I'm a freak and my magic really is broken," I all but whisper.

"No, Ken. It means you can manifest all magic. All twenty-two categories. There has never been another mage who could do that. There has never been another mage who could do more than three." She fingers the leaves of one of my newly grown plants. "Kennedy. You were right. We can't tell anyone about this."

"Because I'm a freak and they'll strip my powers?" I ask, trying to keep my voice level.

"Yes . . . I mean no! You're not a freak. What you are is probably the most powerful mage to ever exist."

After discussing everything we need to figure out about my powers, we come up with a game plan. We have to figure out how long I can hold magic, if the amount of time I touch someone affects that time, and most importantly, if I'm stealing it or just mirroring it. Then we have to figure out how to hide it from everyone and make me appear as a normal empress and high priestess. None of it sounds easy.

The magic I took from Falyn stayed with me for almost forty minutes. In that time, I grew so many plants we ran out of room. So that's how we find ourselves in the forest behind our house, digging and planting until our fingers blister.

Falyn breaks the silence. "Not to add problems on top of problems, but what are we gonna do about Serresa?"

"What do you mean?"

"Well, I think after last night she's going to be watching you closer than ever. Since you don't have magic always on the ready to defend yourself, we're gonna need to figure it out and fast. During classes you'll be able to consistently manifest now since we sit next to each other, but if she catches you alone, you might not have magic."

What she doesn't say is it'll raise even more suspicion if that were to happen. And if she thinks I can defend myself, she may increase her efforts. Simply put: I'm fucked.

"I'm just gonna have to make sure I'm not alone, I guess."

"Except that pesky issue with you not being in combat and me having sparring sessions after classes more often than not. You can't just hide away in our room every day."

A crazy thought pops into my mind. "There's always Drayzen."

"What do you mean? If we can't tell Noric, then we definitely can't tell Drayzen."

"No. I mean, you guys said it before, but I didn't take you seriously. Drayzen is the best warrior in our school. What if I let him tutor me in exchange for combat lessons?"

"That might work. Partly because you could learn to defend yourself physically, but also because if you're with him, she probably wouldn't try anything."

"It's settled then. Tomorrow, I'll let him convince me I need a tutor."

"Let him convince you?"

"Yeah, it would be suspicious if I brought it up after the number of times I turned him down."

Falyn shakes her head, smiling before rising from the soil and brushing her hand together. "Okay, let's go test if you can drain my magic."

It turns out, no matter how long or how little I touch Falyn, the magic stays the same. She also claimed to not feel any different power wise after we held hands awkwardly for a solid twenty minutes. I went to bed last night feeling way more confident than I started the day and woke up this morning actually excited for classes. Today, I won't look like an idiot. Unless someone brings up the whole topless drunk thing. There's always that.

268

When we get to our first class, there's an excited energy among the students. Everyone is whispering back and forth and something tells me it has nothing to do with the party or my boobs. Thank the triple gods.

"What's going on?" I ask Falyn after we take our normal seats.

"I don't know. Have you checked your crystal this morning?" she asks.

"Oops, I think I left it in my room. I kinda forgot about it in all the excitement. What does yours say?" I ask when she pulls it out of her back pocket.

"The school called an assembly," she replies. Then the blood drains from her face. "The king called an assembly today, actually."

"What? Why would the king have anything to do with the school?" I really wish I had my crystal, because Falyn is taking way too long to share whatever information she's looking at.

"He's here, Kennedy. I don't know why, but the king wouldn't just show up on a whim and call a mandatory assembly."

A thousand scenarios run through my mind at once, but all of them involve him somehow finding out about me. My heart beats an unsteady rhythm in my chest and my palms begin to sweat. "What if he knows?" I lean in and whisper.

"Relax, Ken. We only just found out last night. There's no way this about you." Her logic settles me somewhat when I realize she's right. But even so, I need

269

to do my best to avoid him and his son at all costs. Thinking about Michan brings up a whole new worry though. "You don't think Michan told him what I said, do you?

Falyn rolls her eyes. "I seriously doubt he would come himself to arrest someone, if that's what you're thinking. No, I bet this has something to do with all the missing mages."

"What do you mean, all? Last I heard, it was just a couple students who went missing."

"Yeah. From the school. But more people have been reported missing over the last two weeks from all over."

"What does that have to do with us?"

"I don't know, but I have a feeling we're gonna find out."

Someone comes up behind us and looms over our desks. "The rebels attacked a council member last night," Drayzen announces so only we can hear him.

We both twist around to gape up at him. I'm the first one to recover, but only enough to ask, "How do you know?" He lifts a brow at my question. "Oh, right. Your mom. Are they okay?"

"If by okay you mean currently awaiting their pyre to the afterlife, then yes," he responds.

Holy shit. But I still don't know what that has to do with the king being here. "Do you know why he called an assembly?"

"No idea, but that's not why I came to talk to you." He rounds my desk to the front and leans down,

270

pressing both his palms flat against it to meet my eyes. My heart flutters a little. Probably because I don't like having my personal space invaded.

I lean back in my chair to put some space between us. "What's up?" My mouth is a little dry, so the words come out a little on the husky side.

"My mom is here too. Which means she's going to want to meet you."

I rear back. "What? Why would your mom even know about me, let alone want to meet me?" I glance at Falyn, who looks as shocked as I do.

"Because according to Galen, I started tutoring a promising student who needs a lot of help developing their magic. And believe me when I say my mom is not someone you want to refuse."

"That's ridiculous. Just tell her I'm busy if she brings me up. I am not meeting your mother. Or any of your family, for that matter."

"She's joining us for our tutoring session today . . ."

I grip the edge of my desk and glare up at him. "Our what?" I ask between clenched teeth.

"Come on, Kennedy. You owe me for the t-shirt at the least," he pleads with me, a smirk tilting his lips.

Just yesterday I had decided to cave on the tutoring, but now this really makes me want to forget the whole thing. Unfortunately I don't have a line of warriors waiting to teach me how to defend myself, so I'm forced to admit I kind of need him. I sigh heavily.

271

"Fine. You can tutor me on one condition, and it has nothing to do with your clothes."

"Why do I have a feeling I'm going to regret this?" he asks, finally pulling himself up and out of my space.

"I want you to combat train me, too."

He winces. "That's not a good idea."

"You don't think I can do it?" I cross my arms over my chest, ready to be offended.

"I'm a warrior, Kennedy."

"So? Does that make you above teaching someone the basics? I think you'll survive having to demean yourself just this once." Falyn shoots her foot out and kicks me in the shin.

"What the hell was the for?" I move my glare from him to her.

Drayzen laughs and shakes his head. "I think she's trying to tell you the same thing I am."

"What? I don't get it." I suddenly feel like the butt of a joke I don't understand.

"I'm a warrior. Meaning I have unmatched strength. If I were to train you, there's a real chance I could hurt you."

"Oh."

Drayzen doesn't have time to say anything else because students begin getting up from their seats to head for the arena. It's the only place large enough to house the entire student body. Falyn gets up, so we follow her. We can pick this conversation up later.

The three of us find a spot in the back of the crowd. A podium stands in the center of the room, so everyone gathers around it, but there seems to be an invisible wall that everyone automatically knows not to cross. It gives a solid ten feet of space between anyone at the podium and the audience around it.

I'm not sure why Drayzen is still with us and not currently looking for his besties in the crowd. I'm assuming it has everything to do with our conversation not being finished. He must really need me to put on a show for his mom. I'm hyper aware of how close he's standing. I can feel the warmth radiating from him and I'm surrounded by the same scent I shamelessly fell asleep with the last two nights in a row.

What is wrong with me? I'm standing at what may be a historical event and will soon be in the same room as a king. Yet all I can think about is the man standing next to me.

Someone bumps into Falyn, sending her into my side and causing a domino effect. I go sprawling straight into Drayzen's arms. Thankfully, he has fast reflexes, or I'd be on the floor instead of pressed against his chest.

He stares down at me, a small muscle twitching in his jaw. I'm tempted to reach up and smooth a finger across it, but quickly realize that would be insane. I pull back and nonchalantly straighten my clothes like I'm not the tiniest bit affected.

"Good morning students. I apologize for the circumstances in which I'm forced to visit you, but unfortunately drastic times call for drastic measures."

CHAPTER EIGHTEEN

The voice coming from the center of the arena sends chills down my spine, breaking the moment of whatever that was between Drayzen and me. I whirl around to see who's speaking and find an older version of Michan standing at the podium surrounded by warriors, including Drayzen's mother. I don't think I've ever had such a visceral reaction to just the sound of someone's voice. Especially not someone I've never met, even if something about him is oddly familiar.

His dark hair and eyes match those of Michan's, but I don't think that's what I find so familiar about him. I just can't place it. "Some of you may have heard by now about the attacks on two of my council members," he continues above the murmurs of the crowd.

I look behind me at Drayzen because he only mentioned one, which means either he didn't know or for some strange reason decided not to be totally truthful. He's focused on the podium and doesn't see my look.

"While we weren't able to catch the people who did it, that doesn't mean I don't know who it was." He looks out to the crowd, making eye contact with several people before continuing. "We live in dangerous times. The rebels have grown more brazen in their acts against the crown. They seek to end the prosperity I have built for you all. We cannot allow this to happen." A smattering of applause sounds, but he holds his hand up to silence it. "Mages are going missing all over the realm and I have no choice but to see the rebels most recent actions for what they truly are."

I look at Falyn, who's watching the king speak with rapt attention, worrying her bottom lip between her teeth so hard I'm surprised she hasn't drawn blood.

"Make no mistake, this is an act of war."

Voices rise in the crowd, but not enough that I miss Drayzen swearing behind me. He must have expected this to happen, because there's no surprise etched on his face. The only thing indicating any emotion at all is the hard line of his clenched jaw.

"A war I worry may not be in our favor as our magic continues to fade into the ether. I don't claim to know the will of the Esotera, but I doubt this was what they wanted when they gifted us so long ago." More murmurs of agreement float through the crowd. "Since before I became king, the mundanas have sought to destroy us and take what is rightfully ours."

I lean toward Falyn's ear. "What does that mean? What have they taken?" She doesn't respond because the king quiets the crowd and begins speaking again.

"We have to be ready. Every person needs to know how to best defend themselves and to defend the crown when the time to do so arrives. It's much closer than any of you can imagine."

I don't like the sound of this, and when I skim over the crowd and find the faces of Rostan, Sona, and Ciena, I can see they don't either. Drayzen continues to watch impassively while Falyn has finally drawn blood on her lip.

"That's why I've felt it necessary to implement some changes in your schooling, starting immediately."

My stomach drops. This is definitely not a good thing. I hadn't noticed until now that Michan

277

stands behind his father close to the podium. His back is stiff and his eyes are focused straight forward. Next to him, a small woman wearing a thin gold band around her head reaches up and rubs his arm. He smiles softly at her before wiping the emotion from his face and returning his attention to the king's back. It has to be his mother. If he's not the prince, then does that make her not the queen?

"We will start with mandatory level testing of every student."

"What does that mean?" I hiss at Falyn.

"I don't know. Shh." She glares at me.

"Before now, we've never had anything that could definitively read to any accurate degree the power level of a mage. But thanks to a small group of hierophants working with some of the realm's best temperances, we have developed a way to do so." He waits for the crowd to settle before continuing.

"From here on out, the only magic we want to focus on developing is for students that score above a five."

Falyn's face drains of blood. But I don't have time to think about what this announcement means for her.

"We need you all at your most powerful as soon as possible if we have any hope of preserving our magic and our race. For this reason, class structure will be changing."

None of this makes any sense. Why would everyone need to be at their strongest? The general population doesn't fight wars here as far as I understand. That's for the warriors. People born under the emperor classification.

"The only way we can ensure the continuation of magic for our people is to ensure the continuation of the strongest of our people."

The silence in the arena is deafening when he pauses his speech to look around.

"For this reason, the trials will also be moved up. We can't afford to wait. In four months' time every student will compete against each other in the same the trial regardless of year." I gulp back the dread rising in my throat. Four months? I've only just discovered my magic and now I'm expected to be able to use it successfully against students who have been training for two, three, or even four years?

Falyn reaches over and squeezes my hand. I know we're both thinking the same thing. Neither one of us is prepared in the slightest and four months isn't going to change that.

"I know this may sound an impossible task for some of you, and it very well could be," he continues, his pep talk far from encouraging. "But I have confidence these new processes are exactly what we need to strengthen our magic and our communities."

What he doesn't say is that his new processes involve sending off even more people to live in mundana villages. All around me, people are clapping, and I wonder if they're thinking it through. What do they plan on doing with the students who test below a five? Will they no longer have a place in the school? Since our schooling will only focus on honing powers that test above a five, does that mean they won't have any classes to prepare them for the upcoming trials? I send up a silent prayer to whoever is listening. Please let my friends score above a five. The prayer feels selfish, but I can't imagine not having any of them by my side. Even if it's only to see me off when I inevitably get stripped and shipped away.

The king concludes his speech by announcing that the testing will start tomorrow instead of classes and that classes will be canceled until all students have been tested. I follow Falyn on numb feet as she heads to where everyone else, but Noric is standing. Behind me, Drayzen calls my name, but I don't have the mental capacity to deal with anything else right now. I need to find my footing after that rug was just pulled out from under me.

No one says a word when we're all standing in a circle until Falyn breaks the silence. "Where's Noric?"

"Right here," he says, appearing from closer to the podium. Falyn shoots him a quivering smile. Besides me, she's the only other in our group who is at risk for scoring below a five. My gut twists on itself just thinking about it. Even more so when Noric reaches over and grasps her hand. They don't let go until we've made it outside.

"You'll be fine. I've seen you manifest and there's no way you're coming in under a five," I offer

280

Falyn as we all walk in the direction of mine and Falyn's house. I guess we're sticking together.

With classes canceled and the school on lockdown, there isn't much we can do except sit around and wonder what the trials are going to be like. According to the group, past trials were more of an obstacle course type thing. The goal being to not finish last but also demonstrate your ability to manifest your magic. The way the king phrased it in his speech, it sounds like we're going to be pitted against each other and will have to fight for our spots in the school. Not only does it sound dangerous, but also a bit psychotic on his part. Convincing Drayzen to combat train me has now become more important than ever.

Shit. Drayzen. "I gotta run, guys. I don't want to blow you off, but I'm about to be late for my first tutor session." Falyn waggles her eyebrows and I glare at her before heading back the way we just came.

When I make it back to the courtyard, both Drayzen and his mother are already there, having what appears to be a heated discussion. ". . . wasting your time." I can only make out the last bit of what she's saying before they stop talking to look at me.

"Hey," I say, looking back and forth between them.

281

"Hey, this is my mom, Shanlee." I offer her a nod but don't say anything. "You ready?"

"You're late," she says in greeting.

"Yeah, it's been a weird day." I shrug, then turn to Drayzen. "Where do you want to do go?"

"Isn't that something you both should already have figured out?" she interjects.

I meet Drayzen's eyes and lift both my brows because if this is how our whole session is gonna go, I'm leaning toward skipping it all together. Luckily, he understands my silent message and answers her. "There are several spots we can choose from for her to practice empress magic."

We need to figure that out soon, because the magic I borrowed from Falyn is only going to last for so long. He leads us down one of the off-shooting paths of the courtyard then steps off the trail after passing two buildings set up much like the two worldly houses. There's an eye symbol etched into the front of both the structures facing each other but other than that they're identical to the one I live in. I'm assuming these are the mental order dorms.

Beyond them, a thin dirt trail leads to a small clearing in the surrounding woods. A large boulder marks its center, large enough for several people to sit on. It's all very picturesque.

Drayzen pauses at the boulder and offers me his hand to help me up onto it, but the look his mother shoots us prevents me from grabbing it. I climb up and sit cross-legged, waiting for him to decide what he wants me to do.

"I want to gauge how effective your magic is without being able to touch what you want to grow," he explains when I awkwardly clear my throat.

"So, no starting out with the easy stuff, huh?" I tease.

"Easy doesn't teach you control," his mother interjects once again, and I'm super tempted to use the same vine trick Serresa's lackey got me with the day I had to go to the healer. She's lucky I have no idea how to do it.

"Okay, what do you want me to do?" I ask, shaking out my hands and reaching for the spark of magic churning in my core.

"I came out here a couple weeks ago and noticed a group of trills digging up some wild sweet root. I want you to replenish the area for them."

"It's like you're speaking a foreign language. I have no idea what trills or sweet root are, so you're gonna have to elaborate." Beside us, Shanlee clears her throat, and I roll my eyes.

Drayzen's eyes silently plead with me to ignore her before replying. "Trills are a small furry animal that tunnel and live under the ground in the forest. They only eat plants but their favorite are sweet root, which is the long purple root they serve a lot in the commissary."

I know exactly what he's talking about because they're one of my favorite things to eat. They're very

283

similar to carrots but the sweetness gives way to a horse radish kick with each bite. I nod and focus on the ground. I've only ever manifested through my breath or fingers, so I'm not quite sure how to direct my magic without them.

Tugging on the spark, I pull my magic forward and begin sending it through my arms to my fingers like I normally would, but then stop. I have no idea how to send it outward from here. I open one eye to find both Drayzen and his mother watching me so I do the only thing I can think of and imagine it shooting from my fingers the way Serresa's light magic did that night she attacked me in the woods. I very much dislike the fact that she's the inspiration behind my manifestation right now, but if I ask Drayzen how to do it, I'll have to deal with Shanlee too and I'd rather eat rocks.

The magic flows through my fingers, but as soon as it's beyond my fingertips, I can't feel it anymore. I watch the ground for any sign of new life growing, hoping my magic will just continue to obey my wishes after leaving my body, but not so much as a blade of grass is moving.

"Well, that's rather disappointing, isn't it?" Shanlee destroys my concentration and my magic snaps back to become the tiny spark in my gut.

"You know what's disappointing?" I turn to her, ready to tell her exactly how I feel about her commentary, but Drayzen quickly interrupts.

"Tell me how you were directing your magic."

I waver but decide it's not worth the headache and turn back to him. "Through my fingertips."

"Okay, so next time try turning your magic into a blanket before sending it outward."

I try to envision what that would look like, but come up with nothing. "Blanket. Got it," I say even though I don't because I'll be damned if I let Shanlee make another snide comment about my use of magic.

Closing my eyes, I reach for my magic again and pull it forward. Blanket... how do you turn magic into a blanket? A blanket is made to cover your body, right? I send my magic to course through my entire body until I'm buzzing with the energy of it. Now I just need to send it outward. Somehow.

I picture my magic leaving my body and floating softly to the ground below me. My skin tingles as my magic pulls away. Excited that it's working, I open my eyes to search the ground but don't make it that far because I can see my magic floating off my skin like steam from a hot shower. Unfortunately, as soon as it leaves my body, it dissipates into nothing. The blanket visual isn't working.

A soft snort of derision comes from Shanlee, but it only serves to make me more determined than ever to do this. Sending my magic out through my limbs is obviously the wrong way to approach this, so I pull it back and try another tactic.

Gathering the spark, I pull it into my chest and let the magic build until it becomes an orb of solid magic. I see it as a ball of bright lights spinning in beside my heart, not unlike the orb that floats above the heads of the Esotera statues in the courtyard. Once it feels like a tangible object, I stretch it. Imagining not a blanket but a net. I can feel the weight of the net and know I only need to toss it.

I send it outward and instead of dissipating like before, it coats the ground just beyond the boulder and sinks into the earth. My lips turn up in a triumphant grin when everywhere my magic touches, new life springs from the soil. The grass grows taller, flowers bud, and even a sapling takes shape.

"I did it!" I can't help but celebrate the small victory. Shanlee can shove it.

"No, you, in fact, did not do it. I believe my son asked for sweet root." Okay, what is this woman's problem? From the moment she met me, she hated me, and I've barely said two words to her. "I'm going to speak to Galen about ending these sessions. You should be focusing on your own magic, not someone else's. Especially not someone who has zero control over it."

I watch a muscle in Drayzen's jaw tick. I guess saying no is an option for him now. I wonder if she has enough pull that Galen will reassign me or even just decide to forgo the tutoring at all. With all the changes happening in the school, I doubt I'll rank very high in importance.

"I think I've seen enough for today. I'll see you for dinner tonight," she tells Drayzen and leaves us to watch her back until she disappears from sight.

I turn to Drayzen as soon as I'm sure she's out of earshot. "You know, nobody would blame me for being pissed at you right now." He cringes a little, but I continue. "Instead, I feel kinda sorry for you. Is that what you grew up with?"

"I swear she's not always like this. She just has very specific expectations for me and doesn't like it when anything threatens to change the course she planned out."

"How does you tutoring me affect your future in any way?" I ask. It's not like my shortcomings are going to rub off on him.

"It's not the tutoring . . . actually, never mind. Let's just try again with the sweet root. I think in the excitement you just forgot to focus on what you wanted to grow."

I reach for the spark, but it's gone. Crap, has it been forty minutes already? "Actually, I was hoping to continue our conversation from this morning." How am I going to hide my forty-minute magic limit?

"I already told you I don't think it's a good idea. I could hurt you and I really don't want to have to explain to Maylah every day why you're constantly needing healed."

Thanks to his mom, I don't really have leverage to use anymore since he may not be required to tutor me after today, but I really need him to say yes.

"Are you saying you lack control? Does your mom know?" I slide down from the boulder and he grabs my waist to steady me. I'm not a small person by

287

any means of the word, but his hands make me look tiny in comparison. I shiver. "Look between the trials being moved up and everything with Serresa. I really need help." I opt for the truth. "I trust you to not seriously injure me—" he opens his mouth to interrupt, but I talk over him. "If at any point it becomes dangerous, I promise I won't argue if you decide to stop the training."

He doesn't answer for ten beats of my pounding heart. It feels like forever. "Fine. But I can call it off at any point, not just for hurting you. If you want this to work, you have to take it seriously and do everything you're told."

"Deal!" I reach out to shake his hand, but like high fives and fist bumps, it's apparently not a thing here, so instead he clasps the tips of my fingers and immediately lets go when I pump my hand. I shake my head in amusement. "We can start tomorrow?"

"Testing starts tomorrow. We can start the day after, but we're still magic training too."

I groan at the reminder of testing tomorrow. I'm screwed unless I can figure out a way to ensure I have magic to draw on before it's my turn. There's no guarantee that Falyn will be able to help.

When I get home, everyone has already left, and Falyn is sitting on the couch waiting for me.

288

"How did it go?" she asks.

"I hate his mother. That's how it went."

"That good, huh?" she laughs. "Did your magic last long enough?"

"No, but I managed to avoid having to manifest again once it was gone and got him to agree to combat training, so it wasn't a total waste of time. Unless you ask his mother. I'm sure she'd tell you differently."

"Oh look, I found your crystal," Falyn says when a faint glow emits from between a cushion and the back of the couch. I reach into the crevice between the two and pull it out. I have no idea how it got there.

The only person who contacts me on it is Falyn, so I'm a little surprised it's glowing to notify me of an incoming message. I double tap the flat surface to see who sent it, but it just says "friend".

The message is simple, but even so, it takes a second for comprehension to kick in.

Use the Bracelet.

CHAPTER NINETEEN

I show Falyn the message before tapping out a response.

Who is this?

"What bracelet?" she asks while I wait impatiently for the next message to come through. I must have forgotten to mention that part of my experience the night Rostan and I went to get the lumi pod.

"The high priestess from the market gave me a bracelet the night I went with Rostan. You know, the one who found me on Earth?" It was only a couple days ago that we went to the market, but it feels like months have passed since that night.

"Why?" She frowns up at me.

"I honestly don't know. I shoved it in a drawer and forgot about it. He told me not to touch it until I needed it, whatever that means."

I hurry to my room to grab the box and bring it back out for Falyn to look at. My phone glows again just as she opens the box.

A friend. Put the bracelet on just before testing begins tomorrow. The stones hold empress and high priestess magic for you to draw on.

I show Falyn the message and she pulls the crystal out of my hands to type out a response.

I'm not doing anything with the bracelet until you tell me who this is.

We both hold our breath until a response comes through.

It's your choice whether you use it or not. Just know you have friends among the rebels.

Who are the rebels?

No response.

"It has to be Bren, right?" I ask Falyn, who's still staring at my crystal screen.

"I'm sure it is." She pauses. "Kennedy, he knows about your magic."

I take the phone back from Falyn.

291

I know this is Bren. If you know about my magic, then you must know more. Tell me how to find my family.

Finding my family feels even more important now than it did before. For entirely different reasons. Do they have the same power I do? Is that why they left me behind?

"I'm not using the bracelet until I know what the hell is going on and why people I've never met have any interest in me," I tell her.

What we know is you can't trust anyone. The king has ulterior motives. Motives that will prove to be life threatening to you if you're not careful. Use the bracelet.

Before I can respond, the messages disappear from my crystal, leaving not a single trace of anything we said.

"That was really weird." Falyn pulls the bracelet from the box to inspect it. The light reflects off the green stones causing them to look almost crystalline.

"Do you think he's telling the truth? I mean, he did say not to trust anyone and I'm feeling like he should go to the top of my list of people not to trust."

"I think we should take it with us just in case, but if it is what he says it is, you can't touch it until it's time for your testing." She puts it back in the box and closes the lid.

The mention of tomorrow sobers both of us, and Falyn's face pulls down in worry.

"Have you ever been worried about your power levels until today?" I ask her.

"Not really."

"Exactly. The first day I met you, you told me yourself that you'd fall at about a five or six on the scale. The testing doesn't change that."

"You're right. I'm worrying over nothing." She doesn't sound convinced, though.

"We should go for a run. We haven't done that together since Brextin removed me from combat. It'll be a good way to work off some of the anxiety and I can tell you all the reasons I hate Drayzen's mom."

Falyn and I run until our legs are jello and we're just shy of collapsing. Only then do we go back home to shower and change before dinner in the commissary.

The rest of our group is already digging into their food by the time we load up our own plates and sit down. I don't think anyone is in the mood to talk after the events of the day, so we all eat in silence.

I wish there was a way to find out how tomorrow is gonna go. It would be nice to know what the testing entails and how long before we know the results. More importantly, how invasive is the test? Will it hurt? Is the entire school going to be watching each other?

A hand reaches out and snags the bread off my plate, but I'm too slow to stop him.

"That's mine!" I growl at Noric, but he smirks and shoves it in his mouth whole.

293

Falyn laughs and snatches her own bread, shoving it into her mouth, before he can make a grab for it. I eye everyone else's plate and reach across the table to steal Rostan's while he's still watching Falyn do everything in her power not to choke on the fist-sized chunk in her mouth.

I'm a little more delicate with the bread and rip off half of it between my teeth. But trying to prevent my death via bread was the wrong approach because someone took the remaining piece from my hand before I could swallow it. Rostan glares at me as he stuffs it in his mouth. Meanwhile, Ciena and Sona watch with amusement in their eyes, both clutching their own bread to their chests as if it's the most valuable thing they own. Maybe it is with Noric sitting at the table.

I laugh once I manage to swallow and toss what looks like roasted squash at Noric. He catches it midair and pops it into his mouth. I just shake my head.

"I swear the amount of food you eat is a power in and of itself," I tell him. "If they were testing that tomorrow, you'd score at least a twenty." He smiles and shoves a gigantic bite into his mouth, proving my point.

We go back to eating, but the mood is much lighter than it was when we first sat down.

"What do you think tomorrow will be like?" Rostan asks. "We should take bets on power levels."

I immediately jump at the chance to make light of the whole situation. Otherwise I'll never be able to stop worrying about it. Skimming the students still eating dinner, I stop at a table not too far from our own. I only know one person at the table, but I tip my chin in that direction.

"I'd say that whole table scores in the six to seven range, but I'm hoping the redhead in the center chokes and fails to manifest her magic at all."

Falyn looks over at the table and snorts. "If she chokes, you won't be able to show her the same kindness she showed you once the trials start."

"Good point." I wonder if I'll ever get over being trapped by those damned vines. Maybe it's a good thing I'm still holding on to it. It'll fuel the rage when I get to pay her back.

Sona nods at a table behind me. "What about them?" I don't have to turn around to know who she's asking about. All three of them have been staring at us since Falyn and I sat down.

"Michan and Drayzen will be tens, I'm sure," Falyn immediately chimes in.

I risk a glance behind me and make eye contact with Drayzen. What is it about that man that makes me so hyper aware of him anytime we're in the same room? I push the thought away and turn back to my friends. "I'm betting Serresa scores a ten, too," I say begrudgingly. She might be a bitch, but she's a powerful one.

"I'm hoping for an eight, but I'll be happy with anything above a seven." Noric turns the conversation to our own levels.

I look at Falyn to gauge whether this is something she wants to ruminate about. She shakes her head to tell me not to make a big deal about it.

"Six for me," Ciena says and doesn't sound the least bit worried about it. I wouldn't be either if my gift was turning into a giant cat that can kill with a single flick of her tail.

"My tower will for sure score at least an eight, but my high priestess will be low. When I manifest, my visions are short and confusing, if I get any at all." Sona shrugs her shoulders as if she doesn't care, but she's not fooling any of us. Her parents both carry two powerful categories and her only goal is to match them in strength.

"What about you, Kendee?" Noric asks, concern etched on his face. "Now that I've seen you manifest, I'm betting you're about to become one of the elite," he adds, using the nickname I gave Michan, Drayzen, and Serresa.

I scoff. "Not a chance."

"Are you still having trouble manifesting?" Rostan frowns at me.

I look at Falyn, feeling a little guilty for not telling anyone my secret. I'm not really close to Sona and Ciena, but I've come to think of both Rostan and Noric as close friends.

"Kind of. I guess we'll see tomorrow." I skirt around his question. "What about you?"

"Nine maybe ten." He says it so confidently we all take notice. We knew he was going to score high, but I don't think I really spent any time thinking about how high.

Noric reaches out to fist bump him and Rostan high fives it. I groan because it seems no matter how many times I try to explain the concept to them, they just don't get it.

A small chirp emits from my crystal, waking me up from the strangest dream.

Drayzen and I walk along the sandy beach beside the lake. The sun is only half visible over the water, turning it different shades of orange and pink. When the wind whips my hair across my face, he reaches out and smoothes it back, his hand cupping my jaw gently before pulling away.

He smiles softly at me and leans forward. I close my eyes and wait to feel his lips against my own, but suddenly he sweeps my feet with his own and I land flat on my back, the wind knocked out of me.

"You let your guard down again," he says, towering over me, blocking the last of the sunlight and offering his hand.

"You cheated," I grunt back at him when I can finally draw a breath. I grasp his hand like I intend to let him help me up but at the last second, I twist the lower half of my body so my legs are in front of his and use them to do to him exactly what he just did to me.

Only he falls forward instead of backward, but the end result was the same. Now we're both lying in the soft sand next to each other and I don't feel as embarrassed by falling for his trick.

"You were saying?" I ask through my laughter.

He rolls to his back and tries to poke me in the side, but I grab his hand before he can make contact. He uses that to yank me closer, and I wind up sprawled across his chest, staring into his eyes. He combs his fingers through my hair, and I lean into his touch . . .

The dream felt way too real for comfort. My skin tingles everywhere he touched me. Almost as if I can still feel his hands. But I don't have time to lie in bed and question my sanity for having the dream.

Today is testing day.

I can hear Falyn already banging around in the kitchen, no doubt making her morning cup of tea. I miss coffee. And soda . . . I really miss soda. Her morning teas don't taste bad, but they don't have that jolt of caffeine I took for granted living on Earth. A huge yawn overtakes me. I know I got plenty of sleep because Falyn insisted we go to bed early last night. But for some reason, it doesn't feel like I slept at all.

Groaning, I slip from my bed and make my way to the bathroom. A shower will help chase away the lingering sleepiness. I hope.

Both of us get ready in record time and once Falyn pulls my bracelet from its box and slips it into my pocket, so I don't touch it, we're ready to go. The walk to the arena feels like we're marching to our doom, but I don't voice the thought because I know she's already freaking out about the whole thing.

Even though we've already tested the theory, and Falyn swore up and down I was only copying her power and not stealing it, I'm very careful not to touch her. I refuse to take any risks today.

When we arrive, the arena is already full of students milling around, waiting for someone to take control of the chaos. On one side of the arena stand two makeshift boxes with doors about the size of a small room. I breathe a tiny sigh of relief for the fact that it looks like testing will be done in private.

Since there's only two testing rooms, it's going to take them the whole day to get through every student. I point along the wall where Noric and Rostan are standing and we push our way through the crowd to stand beside them.

"Did they already start?" I ask no one in general.

"Yeah, it looks like they're just grabbing people at random and sending them in to be tested," Noric answers.

Perfect. I'm not in a hurry to go in, so standing on the outskirts and just watching for a while sounds like a good idea to me. "Where are Sona and Ciena?"

Rostan points toward the boxes and I do a quick pass of the crowd until I see them both standing toward the front.

"Someone was in a hurry," I joke. "I, for one, am fine with waiting for a while if you guys are."

Everyone nods and settles in to watch as one student after another enters a booth, then re-emerges after just a couple minutes. Whatever the testing entails, I don't think it offers an immediate answer. Their faces are just as nervous exiting the booths as they are going in.

The hours tick away and none of us make any move to pull away from the wall we planted ourselves against until it's no longer feasible for us to stay here. The crowd has dwindled to less than fifty people, so we have no choice but to queue up for our test. I know the only reason Noric and Rostan haven't tested yet is because of me and Falyn. I appreciate both of them for it, but we've put it off long enough.

"Do you want us to go first?" Rostan asks when it's finally our turn.

Falyn shakes her head. "No, we'll go." She steps into hers first because the one in front of me still has someone in it. Rostan pats my back and I give him a weak smile before reaching into my pocket and pulling out the bracelet Falyn slipped in it earlier. As soon as my fingers make contact with it, I'm hit with

300

the familiar scent of wet earth and I know what Bren, or whoever it is, told me in that message is true. It holds magic.

Rostan watches me put the bracelet on and if he thinks it's weird, he doesn't say anything, but I still feel the need to give an explanation. "It's for good luck." He nods his head to the booth in response. It's now open.

I take a deep breath to calm my fluttering nerves, but it does me no good. My mouth is dry, and my heart is pounding in my ears. I have no idea how this artifact is going to react to me, but I can't put it off any longer.

Stepping inside, I find a small desk and one chair. Across from the desk a sign with instructions is hanging from the wall, so I take a moment to read over them. The sign tells me to pick up the device and enter my name and my classifications. *I can do this.*

It looks exactly like a crystal. When I pick it up, I'm almost positive it was a crystal at some point. They must have modified the magic to detect power levels. I snort at the thought because I have absolutely no idea how magic works.

I do as instructed and enter my information when prompted. The crystal's glass surface provides me with the rest of the instructions. The leaf symbol for empress appears at the top of the screen and the device tells me to press my fingers firmly to the thin rectangle and to send a stream of my magic directly into it until the leaf stops moving. I reach for my spark and pull it to my fingertips before sending it into the reader.

The glass warms against my fingers and begins to glow. The empress leaf spins in a circle for what feels like an eternity, all the while the glow of the device continues to increase until it's so bright my eyes tear up and I can't see the leaf anymore. I yank my magic back and hope it was enough, because I have no way of telling if it was done.

After the glow fades enough that I can see the screen, the eye symbol for high priestesses pops up next and it gives me the same instructions. Except I falter because the only magic I've ever purposefully manifested was empress. I don't think the spark would be the same, so I have to take a minute to feel for magic somewhere else in my body. When I get to the crown of my head, I feel it. It's not as big as my empress spark, but when I first felt my empress spark, it wasn't very big either. It must grow as I use it.

Tugging on the tiny spark, I pull it down to my fingertips and direct it in the same way I did the empress magic. The eye begins to spin and the screen glows. Even when the screen gets so bright I can no longer see anything, I continue to feed my magic into the device. If I'm right about my spark growing with each use, I might as well use this time to build up a little high priestess strength.

I quickly realize it was a bad idea when the device overheats in my hand and I have to drop it onto the desk or risk blistering my hand. I really hope I didn't just break it or I'm gonna have to explain myself to whoever is in charge of the testing. That's really not a conversation I want to have.

The device dings and a thank you scrolls across the screen, so I guess I'm in the clear and I step out of the booth to stand next to Falyn. Little white spots still dance in front of me from being blinded by the light.

"You were in there for a while," she says after Rostan and Noric each enter a booth.

"Yeah, I had to figure out how to manifest my high priestess magic. I didn't know how at first." Her mouth forms a little O. "It's fine. I managed. I just wish they would have told us about the blinding light. I would have done something to protect my eyes."

She frowns at me. "What do you mean?"

"The glow . . ." I say quietly, questioning whether we just took the same test. "Did your device not glow?"

"It did. I mean, what do you mean about blinding? Mine definitely didn't get that bright. It was about the same as my crystal when I get a message on it."

"Mine was so bright it made my eyes water and it almost burned me. Maybe it's broken?"

She stares at me for a couple seconds before responding. "I think this is another one of those things we probably shouldn't mention to everyone else."

Story of my life.

Noric and Rostan emerge from their booths, both smiling.

303

"That was way easier than I thought it would be." Noric smiles down at Falyn.

"Yeah, they should warn you about how hot they run, though. When I first picked mine up, it singed my damn fingers."

Falyn's head whips around to look at me and I smile innocently and mouth the word "oops" before shrugging.

"It's probably from how bright they get during the testing," Noric replies.

Oh, thank the gods. I'm not a freak this time.

"It got really bright for you guys?" I ask not able to squash the hope in my voice.

"Yeah, did it do that for you guys too?" Rostan asks.

Falyn jumps in before I can. "Mine got about as bright as my crystal. How bright did yours get?"

"Mine was about the brightness of a moon globe," Noric answers, referring to the lights we use at night to light up our rooms.

"Yeah, maybe a little brighter than that, I think. Do you guys think the brightness level has something to do with the power level?" Rostan asks.

"Maybe, how bright did yours get, Kendee?" Noric looks over at me.

"Oh, um, I guess about the same?" Never mind. I'm still a freak.

CHAPTER TWENTY

Lying by the lake watching bright stars shoot across the deep purple midnight sky is officially my favorite dream. I'm not sure how I'm aware this is a dream, but the soft sand and cool breeze kissing my skin feels too peaceful for me to be concerned with the logistics of it.

Drayzen lays next to me tracing patterns into the palm of my hand with a single finger. I turn my head and find him watching me instead of the stars.

"You seemed really stressed when you got here," he comments.

"I was. Still am, but you somehow make it feel not as bad," I tell him honestly since it's just a dream. "I'm scared about the results for tomorrow."

"Are you still having trouble manifesting?" he asks, concern wrinkling his brow.

"No, that went okay." I reach over and smooth his brow, before giving in to the temptation and cupping his face. "I'm worried what the results will say about me because of what happened with the device."

"What do you mean?"

"It reacted funny and almost bu—"

"Ken, get up already!" Falyn pounds against my door pulling me from whatever the hell that was.

I groan and fold my pillow around my ears to drown her out but she's persistent and lets herself in. Before I can throw my pillow at her, my crystal makes a sound I've never heard before and Falyn stops to look at it.

"That's the school's official alert. Are they sending our testing results through our crystals?" Her voice edges on panic before she forgets about me and races back to her own room.

Just like that I'm wide awake. I snatch up my crystal and try to open the message through my sleep blurred eyes. It's from the front office to notify me I

306

have a meeting with Dean Galen this morning. It doesn't say why or give any information other than the time.

Falyn comes back through my door tapping at her crystal and frowning. "I didn't get anything. What does yours say?"

"I have to go meet with Galen again, but it doesn't say why," I murmur, still staring at the message as dread slowly seeps through me. "What if it's about the test? Do you think they can tell there's something weird about my magic?" I try to swallow but my mouth is a desert.

"Maybe they're giving us our results individually?" she offers.

"Maybe." We both know it's not that or she would have got a message too. This is something else. "Either way, I guess I really do have to get up because it's in twenty minutes."

"I'll come with you and wait outside," she says and I'm about to refuse, but the determined glint in her eyes leaves no room for argument.

I nod. "We can go get breakfast in the commissary afterward." Normally we eat breakfast from whatever the school stocks are in the fridge, but there's no time.

Fifteen minutes later, Falyn is sitting on a bench outside Galen's office and I'm using the tacky knocker to announce my arrival. He opens the door almost immediately and smiles when he sees me.

307

"Ah, good morning, Kennedy. I'm glad to see you got my message." He looks over my shoulder at Falyn. "Is there something you needed?" he asks her pointedly.

"Nope," she replies popping the p and I almost laugh. "Just waiting for Kennedy so we can go get breakfast."

"I see. I won't be keeping her long. You can head over without her, and she'll catch up," he replies. I wonder why it matters if she waits out here for me.

Falyn plants her feet on the ground and bats her lashes up at him. "I'm okay waiting. Wouldn't want Kennedy to get lost. She can get mean when she's hungry."

I shake my head at her in exasperation, but Galen doesn't seem to know how to respond to that, so I'll just call it a win. Especially since all of a sudden, I'm really glad she insisted on coming. I forgot how creepy he is.

After he shuts the door, he gestures toward the chair I sat in the last time I was here. "Does that happen often?"

"What?" Already forgetting about Falyn's remarks.

"Do you get lost often?" He frowns.

"Oh. That. Um, only when I'm hungry?" I don't know why it comes out as a question, but I'm blaming Falyn for this.

"I see." He pauses to sit in the chair next to mine. "Do you know why I sent for you?"

Probably. "No, the message didn't say." I shift uncomfortably in my chair.

"You were raised on Earth, correct? You've never been to Arcanum before you were brought here to go to school?"

"That's right. I thought you already knew all this." Burnt sage permeates the air. He's doing it again. This time I recognize it for what it is immediately. He's using judgment on me.

"You had no knowledge of magic before coming here?"

"If I did, don't you think it would have been way easier for me to get the hang of my magic?" His line of questioning really has me on alert, but I can't tell where he's going with it.

He ignores my sarcastic question and asks another of his own. "A couple days ago, I had a student approach me with some concern about your use of magic. You wouldn't happen to know anything about that, would you?"

"Can't say that I do." Serresa. Of course she would be the type.

"Are you sure about that?" He cocks an eyebrow at me.

"I'm not really sure about anything, if I'm being honest."

"Let me refresh your memory, then. A few nights ago, there was an unsanctioned party by Celestial Lake." Interesting. This is the first time I've heard anyone call it by a name and not just 'the lake'.

309

"Many of your fellow students attended, including yourself." He pauses for dramatic effect, I'm sure, but I don't acknowledge it. I want to know where this is going first. "Setting aside the fact that you allowed yourself to become so inebriated, you bared yourself to everyone there, you were also seen manifesting magic that you haven't registered."

If I make it through this meeting without being kicked from school, I am going to crush Serresa in the damn trials.

"That's not what happened." I bite my tongue and stop talking. I need to be careful how I phrase everything I say.

"So you don't have three categories of magic, then?" he asks, and the scent of his magic becomes overwhelming. I have to hold my breath to keep from choking on it.

I hesitate to answer for a fraction of a second. I better be right about this. "I do not have three categories of magic." It's not a lie. Technically, I have either zero or twenty-two, not three.

He sits back in his chair, a contemplative look on his face. "Serresa must be mistaken then." I knew it was that bitch!

"Is that all you needed from me?" I don't want to be in here a moment longer than necessary.

"That was only part of the reason I asked you to meet with me. I also want to discuss your test results with you. But first I want to ask you one more time.

Have you ever been trained magically here or on Earth?"

"I already said no. I knew nothing about magic before coming here."

"And you have no idea who your family is?"

"I don't even know if I have one, let alone who they are. Why are you asking about my family?"

"Because I'm trying to figure out how someone who went their whole life not knowing about magic can manifest so powerfully, the reader couldn't categorize it beyond a level ten."

Well, shit.

"Obviously there was a mistake. It's not possible to score higher than a ten." At least that's what everyone has told me, so still not a lie.

"I want you to continue your tutoring with Drayzen for the time being, even though you seem to have a handle on your magic. I may check in from time to time to monitor your progress. With the new class structure, I believe you may be a little out of your element, but I'm sure Drayzen will be beneficial in ensuring you're trained for what's to come."

"What does that mean?" Why does everything he says sound so ominous?

"Let's focus on one thing at a time. You're free to go for now. Levels aren't going to be announced until later today, so don't tell anyone you already know yours. I wouldn't want anyone to accuse me of playing favorites." He smiles and winks at me as if we're sharing an inside joke, but it makes my skin crawl.

311

Falyn is still on the bench when I exit Galen's office. She springs up from her seat and we hurry to get out of ear shot before she peppers me with questions. "What did he want? Was something wrong with your test? Did he say anything about your powers?"

"Well, first he asked me about the incident at the lake because apparently Serresa told him I got drunk and stripped in front of the entire school for fun." Falyn growls audibly but I continue over her. "Second, he asked me point-blank if I had three categories, so she must have also told him about the whole tree thing. He was also manifesting judgment again when he asked."

"Oh no. So he knows then? What is he gonna do?"

"I don't think he does. When he asked, I told him I don't have three powers, which isn't a lie, so hopefully it was enough to confuse his power."

"Well, I guess since you're standing here and not halfway to a mundana village, he must have believed you?"

"I think so. But he does know there's something weird about my magic. He said the reader couldn't register it beyond a ten, which I think means I scored higher than that? Except I don't know how because that's supposedly the highest level, right?"

"I don't even know anymore, Ken. It seems like every time I say something isn't possible you prove me wrong." She offers me a small smile.

"He also said they'll be posting the results later today, but not how or where."

"They have parchment in almost every classroom, house, and the commissary that's spelled to display announcements, so that's more than likely what they'll do," she replies and I think back to the map they gave me when I first got here. Probably the same magic.

"Let's go to the commissary, then. I'm not really hungry anymore, but we can at least see if anything has been announced."

The first thing I notice when we get there is the large crowd of people standing near a bulletin board I never noticed before on a side wall. I guess that means results are in and neither one of us is eating.

"Falyn, Kennedy!" Rostan's deep voice booms across the room at us. I can't see his face, but I think the hand waving above the crowd is meant for us. Falyn grabs my hand and pulls me in that direction.

We push through the sea of bodies to stand next to Noric and Rostan, who are already waiting to see their scores. Rostan smiles. "It's fitting that we took our test together, so we find out our scores together too."

I share a glace with Falyn before returning his smile and nodding my head. "How does it work?" I gesture at the board in front of us.

"You just touch your finger to one of the papers and your name and power level will appear," Noric answers and I'm completely underwhelmed.

"That's it?" I ask, not bothering to mask my disappointment.

"What were you expecting?" Rostan asks, smirking at me.

"I don't know, but would it be too much to ask for a glowing light to cascade over us?" I shrug.

Falyn laughs. "Come on, let's just get it over with."

Before we can step up to the board, someone shoulders their way past me, knocking me into Falyn and almost causing us both to face-plant if it wasn't for Noric and Rostan being here to steady us.

"Thanks," I murmur to the guys before turning around to see who shoved us. "What's your problem—oh, of course." It has to be Serresa.

"You're my problem. Obviously." I didn't realize it was possible to glare and roll your eyes at the same time, but somehow, she manages. "I don't know why you're in such a hurry, anyway. We already know you're a waste of magic and belong in the mundana villages. Thankfully, the testing will move that along for us."

"First off, I'd be fine living among humans if it meant not having to listen to your voice every day and second, we were here first." I slip between her and the board, dragging Falyn with me.

We ignore the gasp of outrage behind us and press our fingers to the paper. It only takes a couple seconds for our names to appear, but I grow worried when a number doesn't follow.

314

"Move your finger, idiot. Unless you're worried about what's under it," Serresa taunts.

I don't know what I'm so worried about. I already know my score, but somehow having it on display for everyone around to see makes it feel so much more nerve-wracking. Falyn lifts her finger first and I breathe a sigh of relief. The leaf symbol for empress forms followed by the number six. Noric and Rostan cheer behind her, but it abruptly cuts off when I lift my own finger for everyone to see. Serresa sucks in a breath, and I allow myself a moment of pettiness when I turn to look directly at her.

"What were you saying?"

She doesn't take her eyes off the two numbers next to the leaf and eye symbols of my categories until it fades back into the paper as if it had never existed. Except it did, and I get the feeling it just put an even larger target on my back.

"How are you a ten?" she screeches, breaking the sudden silence around us. Pushing past me, she presses her own finger to the board until her name appears and when she jerks her finger away, there's a nine next to the sun symbol and a six next to the skull symbol of the death category. Her red face deepens in color to almost purple. I had no idea her secondary is necromancy. It makes me take a second look at her. I don't think death is a common magic to manifest, and I find it a little on the creepy side. Especially knowing Serresa has the power to reanimate people. I shudder.

315

As much as I want to rub my power level in her face, I'm choosing to take the high road. The last thing I need is Galen breathing down my neck even harder before I've had a chance to figure everything out.

"Lets get out of here, quick," I murmur so only Noric, Rostan, and Falyn can hear. "I think her head is about to explode and I already showered today."

"We haven't checked ours yet, hang on." Rostan reaches over Serresa's head and presses his finger to the board. A nine appears next to the elemental symbol of the magician and a seven next to the tree symbol of the hierophants. "Nice." He grins and winks at me.

Noric is next, and he repeats Rostan's actions, all the while avoiding eye contact with the still fuming Serresa who watches us with narrow eyes but continues to say nothing. "Eight," he says when he pulls his hand away, "and seven." The guys high five each other and finally get it right for once. Both immediately look to me for approval.

"Can we go now?" I ask, smiling and shaking my head at their antics. I link my arm through Falyn's and tug her with me as I walk away.

As soon as we're all outside, we finally release the laughs we're holding in.

"Have you ever seen someone's face turn that color?" Rostan asks, gasping for breath.

"She looked like freshly dug up sweet root." Falyn giggles.

I'm about to make a comment about rotten fruit when a girl I've never seen before exits the commissary with tears in her eyes. It immediately sobers me. In all my worry over mine and Falyn's scores, I didn't stop to think about what the new rules might mean for other students.

"What do you think is going to happen to the students who score low?" I ask, watching the girl race off in the direction of the courtyard.

"I think that's what we're going to find out today. We have another mandatory assembly in two hours," Falyn says looking at the crystal she pulled from her pocket when it started chirping out the same sound mine made just this morning. I've only heard it twice, but it's already my least favorite noise in the world. Make that two worlds.

We part ways with Rostan and Noric to head to our rooms, the mood officially killed by thoughts of what happens next.

"I was thinking now that I have a better understanding of my magic, I should probably go back to searching books for information on it. There could be something we missed since we didn't know what we were looking for before," I tell Falyn.

She nods. "I was actually thinking the same thing last night. There has to be something we missed. We can go together after the assembly since classes are still canceled." This time, she loops her arm through mine in a show of support. At some point in the last couple months, I went from being someone who

317

couldn't stand people in general to being okay with having my personal space invaded. When did that happen?

"I have to meet Drayzen, so can we do it after that? It's my first official day of combat training."

"I almost forgot about that! Hopefully, he doesn't make you start with endurance again." She cringes.

That thought never crossed my mind until this moment. "Ugh, would it be ridiculous of me to quit after working so hard to get him to agree?"

Less than two hours later, we find ourselves gathered in the arena once again. It feels like it's been weeks since the last time we were here. Even though the king left immediately after his announcement, the podium is still set up, only this time it's Galen standing there.

"Thank you all for coming," he starts. "By now you've all had time to check the results of yesterday's testing, so I'd like to spend some time going over what this means for you."

A hush falls over the gathering students while Galen pauses for dramatic effect.

"We have some very talented mages in our midst, and I want to start by saying how proud I am of our students here."

318

I roll my eyes at his fake attempt at pride.

"I know some of you are worried what the scores might mean for you, but even if you didn't meet the new standard, there's no need to be. Change is a good thing. This change will be a great thing." Who is he trying to convince? "You're still students here and will continue to be students as we prepare for the upcoming trials." A low buzz of relieved murmurs fills the arena.

"It will, of course, have to be in another capacity." He waits for everyone to calm down before continuing. "In trying times such as these, it has become more apparent to the crown that in order to ensure the future of magic, we need to ensure the success of our strongest mages. While those of you who did not meet, the standards will no longer be training as mages, your talents are still needed."

I look at Falyn. Wherever this is going, it doesn't sound good. Why wouldn't they be training all mages? Magic is still magic regardless of the power level, right?

"We are on the cusp of war, and the king's army can no longer only consist of emperors." My stomach drops. "All mages who scored seven and above who pass their trials will be drafted into the king's service upon completion of school. For those who scored fives and sixes, your duty will lie in the continuance of our economies. It will be your magic that grows our food and builds our cities. It will be your magic, our territories run on." I reach over and

319

grip Falyn's hand. It sounds like I just got drafted into the army and I'm not okay. "For everyone else, it will be your great honor to serve these great mages. Whatever they need to ensure their success will be your priority. Together, we will not only save magic, but make our nation the strongest it has ever been!"

CHAPTER TWENTY-ONE

After the assembly, Falyn and I went our separate ways without a word to each other. There's way too much to unpack in such a short time. I don't think either of us wants to talk about it right now anyway. Galen went on and on about what an honor it was going to be for all of us to serve the realm and our king in our new roles, but none of it feels like an honor.

I admit, the rebels' attack on the king's council was horrible, but how does that equate to war? It feels like a huge escalation. I don't believe for one second all of these changes are just in response to the single attack. Something else is going on. I can't help but think of what Bren, or whoever, was messaging me, said about ulterior motives. Did they know this was coming?

I'm So deep in thought, I almost walk past Drayzen, who's waiting for me at the statue. He clears his throat and I jolt back to myself. "Sorry, I was busy having an internal meltdown," I say in a joking manner, even though it's the truth.

"That seems to be a popular thing to do today," he offers in return. "So what'll it be for you? Servant, labor, or are you joining the warrior ranks?" There's an edge of bitterness to his voice that surprises me.

"I take it you're not fond of the changes?" My opinion of him increases slightly knowing he's not a total sycophant. Although I'm not sure I ever thought that in the first place.

"I just think people should have a choice," he says simply and doesn't elaborate. "Are you ready?"

I half expected him to push his original question so when he doesn't I offer the answer. "It seems I'm being drafted into the king's army, whether I want it or not. Looks like this combat training is going to come in handier than we thought."

He does a double take. "You scored above a seven? I guess you didn't have anything to be worried about, after all."

"The way I see it, I have even more to worry about, but I don't think I'm ready to deal with it, so how about you kick my ass instead?" I mockingly punch him in the chest and am immediately relieved I didn't put any force into it. It feels like pressing my fist against a solid brick wall. "Question," I say, staring at his chest. "During training am I going to be expected to hit you?" I ask, only half joking.

He frowns. "That's kind of the whole point, isn't it? How else would you learn?"

"How exactly do I do that without breaking my hand?"

He tips his head back and laughs. "I can turn it off. Emperor magic manifests a little differently. The strength and shield aspect of it is always on unless we pull it inward. When you reach a point that you're ready to spar, I'll be as soft as you. Probably not as weak, though." He pokes one of my arms and I glare at him in indignation.

"What do you mean when? Don't we have to fight in order for me to learn how to fight?"

"If you tried fighting anything bigger than one of those right now, you'd lose." He says pointing to a small round creature that looks like a hairy basketball walking on four legs as it scurries away from us. "We need to build your strength first, then we can move on to the hitting." I'm just about to open my mouth to argue, but he talks over me. "You swore you'd follow my instructions, remember? This is the only way it'll work."

323

"Fine," I grumble. "For the record, I could take whatever that thing is—"

"An ostalo."

"Whatever. How do you propose I build muscle? Do you have a weight bench or something?"

"A weight bench?" he questions, looking at the benches surrounding the courtyard as if trying to figure out what they have to do with building muscle. He doesn't respond to my request about animal names.

"Never mind." I laugh. "Just tell me what you want me to do."

Twenty minutes later, we're standing in the soft sand next to the lake and he's pointing to the ground while I stare at him in disbelief.

"Really?" I groan.

"Yes, really. I need to see what I have to work with. Do you need me to show you how?"

As soon as we got here, he demanded I start our session with as many chest lifts as I can do before collapsing. At first, I wasn't sure what he was talking about until he pointed at the ground and the realization set in. Pushups. He wants me to do pushups.

"No," I reply, lowering myself to the sand. "I was just making sure I heard you right." I line my

324

hands up under my shoulders and push away from the ground before slowly dropping back down. After five, my arms are burning and after eight, they're trembling. I don't make it all the way back up on the tenth one. I truly am pathetic.

Collapsing, I roll to my back and stare up at his smirking face. If my arms didn't feel like jello, I'd do something about it. Probably.

"When you can do fifty without collapsing, we'll revisit the topic of fight training," he says, not bothering to hide the amusement in his voice. "Get up, let's see what your legs can do."

Even though I'm aware that expression is probably unique to Earth, I can't seem to fight off the heat rising to my face. An image of me jumping up to wrap my legs around his waist flashes through my mind before I have the chance to push it down.

"What's wrong?" he asks and another smirk spreads across his face. He knew exactly what he was saying.

Refusing to rise to the bait, I smile up at him before standing. "Guess you were right about me needing to build up some muscle. I'm already hot and sweaty and we just got started." I dust off the front of my shirt and soft leggings. "Where do you want my legs?" I ask innocently and stare at him through my eyelashes. Two can play this game.

He clears his throat and says, "You're fine . . . um . . . right there." I scratch a fake itch on my nose to

325

cover my smile. "This time, you'll do as many knee bends as you can."

How did I know he was going to make me do squats next? Torture must be universal. I start the squats and feel like I'm doing pretty well, speeding through them until he places one hand on my lower back and the other over my chest to force my upper body into a straight line. The burn comes after just a few rounds in this position. I power through it, though. I'm determined to do fifty on the first try. Or maybe twenty-five. Twenty-five seems reasonable. I count them out in my head and as soon as I hit twenty-five, I push him away. He doesn't let me rest for too long before he has me start all over with the pushups. After three rounds of each, I'm dying, and he hasn't let up once.

"Okay, I get it. This is gonna be harder than I thought." I pant. "But I thought Brextin's running trail was impossible the first time I ran it, and it only took me a month to get conditioned enough to run it without issue, I'm even more determined about this than I was about that so throw whatever you have at me."

He nods. "Good. Let's start for real, then."

How was that not for real? What have I gotten myself into?

Dragging my tired body into the shower after getting home seems an almost impossible task. I can barely feel my legs and arms and if it wasn't for how itchy my skin is because of the sand sticking to my sweat, I would forgo it altogether. I just want to fall into bed to live out my days as a boneless lump.

Unfortunately, I still have things to do today. Like hit the books with Falyn and possibly plan our escape into the mountains, so I never have to fight in a war that makes absolutely no sense to me. I should probably move that to the bottom of my list though.

Scrubbing away the sweat and sand from my workout with Drayzen, I think about my dream. It seems we always find ourselves next to that lake, whether we're awake or sleeping. Although today was much different from the vibe in my dream last night—

I drop the cloth I'm using to scrub my arm with. Earlier, Drayzen said I didn't have anything to be worried about after all. As if we had a conversation about that. Except the only conversation I've ever had in which I admitted my fears to him was in a dream. Damn it. I should have realized those dreams felt too real.

I jump out of the shower and shout for Falyn after I wrap myself in a towel. She bursts into my room in full panic mode. "What's wrong?" she asks, searching for my invisible attacker.

"Drayzen is a moon. That's what's wrong. The last two nights in a row, I've had dreams about him and I thought it was just my libido working overtime, but

327

I just realized it was him all along. He's invading my dreams, and I almost told him everything!"

"Why would you think that? He only tested for one power. Sona and Ciena were there when he got his results. Just a single ten."

I hesitate. Could I be wrong about this? I search my mind for an explanation of his comment and come up with nothing. "No, I'm almost positive he's a moon. During training, he referenced something that happened in my dream . . . the dream he gave me, I mean."

"What did he say? I'm sure there's an explanation."

"You mean besides the fact he's using my dreams to spy on me? I knew he was reporting to Galen. I shouldn't have let my guard down."

"Calm down, Ken. You still haven't told me what he said."

"I told him I scored above a seven and he said there was nothing for me to be worried about after all. Except I never told him I was worried about it. Except in my dream."

Falyn heaves an exasperated sigh. "Ken, everyone was worried. I'm sure he was even worried. Anyone who saw you the last couple days could tell you were on edge. It wouldn't take a hierophant to figure out why, either."

"I guess," I reply, still a little doubtful, but her words take a lot of the steam out of me. If he's not a moon, then that means those dreams are all me. That sounds like something else I need to put away for another day.

"Also, why would you think a dream about Drayzen is your libido's doing? What kind of dreams were they?" She tilts her head, waiting for my reply.

"Never mind that part. Don't we have some books we should be reading right now?"

"Are you planning on wearing that to the library?" she asks pointedly.

I look down at my towel and note the puddle of water under my feet. "Good point. Give me ten minutes."

It only took me five minutes to get dressed, but I used the other five to collect my thoughts. I'm not totally convinced she's right about Drayzen, but I'm also not totally convinced I am either. I may have to wait for another dream to find out the truth.

"I still don't know what we're looking for. I mean, yes, we know what your magic is, but I think if we had come across any explanation of it before, we would remember something like that." Falyn snaps the book she's pouring over shut and leans back against her chair.

"I guess it was kind of dumb of me to think we'll find anything different. I just hate not having any answers. Especially now that all this is happening. If I

329

can't figure out a way to permanently have access to magic, I'm screwed. I might as well just ask to have my powers stripped now."

"You've got to stop thinking like that. We'll figure something out. What about the mysterious friend from those messages?"

"You mean the person who either is a rebel or knows them? What could they possibly do to help?"

"They knew how to help you access magic for the testing. Maybe they can help you with the rest," she doubles down.

"And probably get me thrown in prison while they do. No way. I have way too many eyes on me right now." I rub the spot between my eyes that has already started pounding.

"Ken, how am I supposed to help you if you turn down every suggestion? How is anyone supposed to help you if you refuse to bring anyone but me in on it? I really think we should tell someone else. I'm not saying shout it out for everyone, but if two heads are greater than one, imagine what three or even four could do for you."

"I'll think about it." I give in a little because she has a point. I just need to be sure about anyone I decide to spill my secret to.

While she continues to pour over another book, I pull out my crystal. My mysterious friend hasn't tried to contact me since the day I was told to wear the bracelet and since the messages disappeared along with the contact information, I have no way of reaching out to them.

After an hour, I decide to give up. I don't know what made me think the books would be helpful this time around. I'm grasping at straws.

"Fine. Let's do it your way. But only Noric for now. These books aren't going to help us, but maybe he can. If nothing else, maybe he can figure out how they made that bracelet." Falyn's grin stretches from ear to ear. She's been dying to tell him, but I swore her to secrecy.

"I'll tell him to meet us in our room," she says immediately.

My stomach is an instant mess of nerves. I should have expected her to pounce on it so quickly. Before she can send the message, a shadow falls over our table and I look up to find Michan standing next to us.

"Hey," he says, reading over the book titles scattered across the table. "What are you guys up to?" He grabs a book and flips it around to read the cover out loud. "Manifestation through the years."

I grab the book from him and add it to the pile I'm already gathering to put away. "We were actually just getting ready to head out after a study session," I say quickly, hoping he lets it go at that. "I don't think I've ever seen you in the library." I really hope that didn't come out as accusatory as it sounds to my ears.

331

"I was actually looking for you. I heard about your test results and wanted to say congratulations," he replies.

"Why?" The question springs free before I can stop it. "I mean, thank you, but with how we left things after the party, I'm a little surprised."

Falyn clears her throat. "Ken, I'm gonna head out. Don't forget about our plans," she reminds me before carrying her pile to the cart designated for unshelved books. "We'll just wait for you back at the house." She stresses the word 'we' and I know she's not letting me out of doing this tonight.

"I was a little surprised you scored so high." He ignores my comment and gets right to the point of his being here.

"You and me both," I mutter almost completely under my breath. "I'm assuming you scored high also?" I ask, already knowing the answer.

His proud grin confirms it. "Same as you, actually. Double tens." I hope he isn't expecting the same congratulations he gave me. I honestly can't think of any reason it calls for that.

"So you'll be joining the new and improved army too, then?"

"You say it like it's a bad thing."

"You don't think it is?" I question.

"The only purpose is to create order in the realm again. I don't think we'll be doing much fighting, if any at all. Once the mundanas realize they're no match for us, they'll back down again."

332

"Mundanas? Don't you mean the rebels?" If my suspicions are correct, I don't think it's only mundanas who joined the rebels, but I'm not about to be the one to burst his bubble. Besides that fact, he makes it sound like the true intent of this war is to squash the mundanas in general.

"Same thing." He waves his hand in indifference. "Either way, it's over before it even starts, and we'll be able to focus on the things that actually matter. Like strengthening our magic."

"Doesn't it feel wrong to fight against someone who has no way of defending against magic?" I can't help but ask.

"They're not defenseless. They proved that just a few days ago by murdering members of my father's council." His lips press into a flat line.

I hold up my hands in a gesture of truce. "I wasn't trying to make you mad. I think I'm still just trying to adjust to all the changes."

If it's as easy as he thinks it will be, then why does the king need such a large army? None of this is adding up. I don't know which of us is delusional, but I don't think it's me. The king isn't building a massive army just to scare the rebels into submission. There's more to this and I have a feeling it's going to result in a lot of deaths.

"Can I ask you something?" The sudden change in his voice derails my train of thought.

"Sure?"

333

"Have you ever tried looking for your family here to find out how you wound up on Earth?" I don't know how we went from talking about war to this.

"I did when I first got here, but I don't really have anything to go on, so I had to give up. Why do you ask?"

"Just curious, I guess." Something tells me he's asking out of more than curiosity, but I give up on trying to figure things out anymore.

"I should probably get going. My friends are expecting me . . ."

"Sure," he says and offers a smile. "I guess I'll see you in class tomorrow, then."

"Yep. I'll be there," I reply, trying not to sound as awkward as I feel.

I feel a little unsettled by our conversation. Or at least the last part of it. His question about my family came out of nowhere. Before I exit the library, I turn back to look at him. He's shuffling through the books Falyn and I put on the cart. He reads each title and flips through a few pages before moving on to the next. I duck out of the library before he catches me watching. *I wonder what he's looking for.*

CHAPTER TWENTY-TWO

When I get back to our room, Noric is already sitting on the couch next to Falyn. They're sitting so close, Falyn might as well be on his lap. They're so engrossed in each other they don't hear the door open, and spring away from each other like a couple of teenagers caught in the act as soon as they notice me.

"Don't you have a room?" I ask Falyn just to watch her face turn red and laugh.

"We were just talking," Noric defends her, but his own face is a shade pinker than usual.

"Is that what they're calling it now?" I ask innocently and wink. I almost miss the pillow arcing through the air, aimed directly at my head.

"I'm just kidding!" I call out as I head into my room to grab the bracelet.

"Can you tell what this is?" I ask Noric, handing it to him when I return.

He takes it from me and frowns after a few moments of rolling it round in his hand. "It's an artifact, but it feels different."

"What do you mean different?" I ask. Does he mean the magic is different?

"I mean, it doesn't feel like just temperance magic. I can feel empress magic too . . . and something else."

"High priestess," I say and his snap to mine.

"Yeah, how did you know? What is it?"

"It's used to store magic. Or it was anyway. And I know because it's mine." I take a deep breath. Falyn better be right about this.

"I don't understand." His eyes bounce between me, Falyn, and the bracelet still in his hand.

Here goes nothing. "You know how I had so much trouble manifesting my magic until recently?" I ask, and he nods. "It's because I'm not really an empress. Or at least I'm not only an empress."

336

"I know. You're a high priestess, too. What does that have to do with the bracelet?"

"That's the thing. I'm not. My magic manifests differently than everyone else's. I kind of don't have magic unless I get it from someone else." I'm screwing this up, but I don't know how to explain it.

Falyn sighs and rolls her eyes at me. "Kennedy has all the categories," she announces, simplifying it to a single sentence.

Noric laughs, but when we don't join, he stops abruptly. "You're serious?" He takes a long look at me, as if expecting to see an outward sign. "It's not possible to have all the categories."

"Well, somehow it is because I do . . . kind of," I say.

"How do you kind of have all the categories? That makes absolutely no sense." He leans forward in his seat, waiting for my answer.

Maybe it'll just be easier to show him, so I reach over and grab his arm for a second. He frowns, but doesn't pull away. "What are you doing?"

"Okay, so we've established that I'm for sure an empress and a high priestess, right? The test proved it," I say, releasing his arm and standing up. Closing my eyes, I search inward for the magic sparks I haven't felt before. I don't know how temperance magic works, but I might be able to fumble through his hermit manifestation.

I find one spark in my gut right where I would normally feel empress magic and somehow instinctually know its temperance magic. I ignore it and keep looking until I find another spark at the base of my throat and tug at the thread to send it outward into my limbs. If hermit magic is astral projection, I have to figure out how to separate my mind from my body. I think.

A wave of dizziness cascades through my body. Only it's not exactly dizziness. It's more like my cells feel the way static sounds. I take a deep breath and imagine splitting into two people. The static lessens as half of me peels away from the other half. A soft gasp fills the room, and I know I've succeeded.

When I open my eyes, I see double and a wave of true dizziness sweeps over me. "Whoa," I say, and it sounds like there's an echo in the room. There's two of me and somehow I'm both seeing and talking through both of my bodies. There has to be a way to detach myself or I'm going to make myself sick. "A little help, Noric?" Both me and my other me ask at the same time.

Noric stands and circles my double before reaching out and poking her in the shoulder. I feel it in my own shoulder, causing another wave of dizziness to crash over me. My body double snaps back like a rubber band and I stagger back doing my best not to fall on my ass.

"Okay, that was not as much fun as I imagined it would be," I say, sitting back down. "How does that

338

not make you sick every time you do it?" Noric is too busy staring at the space my double had just occupied a minute ago to answer.

"Noric?" Falyn reaches out and taps his back.

"How does it work?" he asks, whirling to look at us. "Since you had to grab my arm, I'm assuming you take magic from other people?"

"I don't take people's magic," I snap a little defensively. "The best we can come up with to describe it is I mirror it. You still have yours, I just copied it. But unless I touch someone, I don't have magic."

He looks down at the bracelet still clutched in his hand. "That's why you have the bracelet," he murmurs to himself. "How did you get the magic into the bracelet?"

"That's actually why we decided to tell you. We don't know and were hoping you might," Falyn supplies the answer.

"Oh." He sounds a little disappointed, and it takes me a second to figure out why.

"I struggle with trust issues. Falyn wanted to tell you from the beginning, but I wouldn't let her. I'm terrified they'll cart me off somewhere to perform experiments on me," I explain. "I don't want to be labeled the freak the rest of my life."

"You think I'd tell someone?" he asks, hurt lacing his voice.

"No!" I reply a little too loudly. "I just needed time to adjust and figure everything out before I told anyone else."

He nods his head in understanding and I breathe a sigh of relief that he's not going to stay mad at me. "So you can do this with any category?" he asks, bringing us back to the topic at hand.

"So far, I've manifested empress, high priestess, magician, star, tower, judgement, and now hermit."

"So if you have to come into contact with the magic in order to use it, how long does it last?"

"Falyn and I spent a day experimenting, and I was able to hold on to the magic for about forty minutes each time, so not long. Which is why I need a way to store magic or I'm gonna be screwed for trials."

"Forty minutes of manifesting or just forty minutes in general?" he asks, and it gives me pause. I see where he's taking this line of questioning.

"Forty minutes of manifesting. We never checked to see what happens if I don't use it . . ." I look at Falyn. Maybe we should have brought him in sooner.

"You should probably figure that out while I see if I can figure out how to copy the temperance magic in the bracelet." And just like that, Noric is already over the shock of my magic and willing to help. I officially understand what Falyn sees in him.

We spend the next couple of hours until dinner doing exactly what Noric suggested. At the

340

three-hour mark, the spark of empress magic is still shining brightly in my core after not being used, but Noric hasn't figured out how to imbue the stones with magic yet.

Dinner passes in a blur because I'm anxious to get back to our room and continue working on my magic. Falyn and I both give Noric a run for his money on how fast we finish our food. By the time he clears his plate, there isn't anything left on ours for him to steal, and I can't help but snort at his disappointment.

Rostan is the only one who seems to notice something is up with us. "Do you guys have somewhere you need to be or something?" he asks, staring pointedly at mine and Falyn's plates.

"No," Falyn replies a little too quickly. "I was just hungry and want to get to bed early since classes start up again tomorrow." It's a flimsy excuse, but he seems satisfied with it.

Falyn's crystal chirps out the school's official notification and she pulls it from her pocket. "They assigned me a new class," she says, frowning.

I look over her shoulder to read the message. "They took you out of combat? What's magical agriculture?" I ask.

"I don't know, I think it must be something new," she responds, frowning.

Everyone else reaches for their own crystals. "I didn't get any changes," Rostan says, holding up his own for us to see.

Once again, I don't have my crystal on me. I don't think I've even seen it since this morning, and I offer Falyn a sheepish smile when she rolls her eyes at me, knowing exactly why I haven't checked it.

"Where did you leave it this time?" she asks.

"I left it on my bed. I'll check it when we get home." I shrug.

"I didn't get any changes either," Noric says holding his crystal up too.

We linger a little longer, discussing what Falyn's schedule change means. We decide it has something to do with our new roles. Since there's no expectation for Falyn to join the king's new army, they've probably decided she doesn't need to learn combat. Although I'm still confused, since combat was a class for everyone before the king decided to expand his army. There was never an expectation of anyone but emperors to join the ranks until now, and they still offered it. I was under the impression it was to help us pass our trials.

"We should probably head home." Falyn nudges me when we run out of theories.

"I'm gonna head out too," Noric says when we get up to put our trays away.

"I guess we'll see you guys tomorrow at lunch?" I ask. This is probably the least subtle exit any of us has ever taken, but oh well.

"Have you checked?" Falyn asks once we're on the path to our house, Noric walking beside us.

"I still have it. I think we're at the four-hour mark?" I reply checking for the spark of empress magic. "So if we can figure out how to store magic in that bracelet, I could potentially store some in my own body then have a back up to use when that runs out." I'm feeling a little more optimistic about the trials. This new development doubles the amount of time I can manifest magic.

"That's assuming I can figure it out," Noric grumbles.

"I have faith in you." I bump my shoulder into his.

When we get back to our dorm, I head straight for my room to grab my crystal. I don't have a message from the school, but I do have one from my mystery friend.

Tomorrow everything changes.

I read the message twice, but it doesn't make any more sense the second time than it did the first. Taking my crystal back into the living room, I show Noric and Falyn the message.

"Who's that?" Noric asks.

Falyn and I catch him up on everything from how I got my bracelet to meeting Bren in the marketplace and our theory about him being part of the rebels group. After we're done explaining everything, he sits back in amazement and scrubs a hand across his face.

"So the rebels know about you and your magic and they're the reason you're here?" He shakes his head. "This all sounds . . ." he trails off.

"Yep," I reply. "That about sums it up. We just don't know why."

"What do you think they mean about tomorrow?" Falyn asks, bringing my attention back to the message still displayed across the screen of my crystal.

"Your guess is as good as mine. But we already know about one change." I flop against the back of the couch. "Your new class, I mean."

"True, but somehow I don't think that's what they're talking about," Falyn says dryly.

"I'd ask if I thought for one second I'd get a straight answer." I sigh. "I guess we'll just have to wait and see what happens."

"Do you think once the king has his new army, the rebels will really just back down?" I ask Drayzen as we sit in the sand side by side watching the water lap at our bare toes.

"I don't know what to think anymore. But I do think we're only being given half the picture and there's more to it than what we're being told," he replies and laces his fingers through mine as if he's done it hundreds of times before.

344

I know I should call him out about these dreams, but at the same time, I don't really want them to stop. Not that I'd ever admit that out loud.

I let myself scoot closer too and lay my head on his shoulder. "I have a really bad feeling about all of this."

"What do you mean?" he asks and wraps an arm around me.

I take a deep breath before answering because I have absolutely no proof of what I'm about to say. "I think the king wants to eliminate mundanas all together."

His arm tightens around me, but he doesn't reply. We sit and watch the sun disappear until the stars take its place before he finally says anything. "I think we should wait and see what happens before we try to make any guesses about the king's motives."

I pull away to look at him. "You think I'm being overdramatic, don't you?"

"No, I just think we don't know everything, so anything we say is just guessing, right now."

"You're right," I concede, and stand up to brush off my shorts.

"Where are you going?" he asks, frowning.

"I don't want to think about the king or the army anymore. I just want to do something fun for once." I smile and unbutton my shorts.

"Doing what exactly?" He watches my fingers with rapt attention.

345

"Not that, you perv. Let's go swimming." In a matter of seconds, I'm down to just my underwear and bra. "Are you coming?" I call over my shoulder as I wade into the cool water until it's chest level, then dive under.

By the time I resurface, he's already in the water, swimming toward me with determination in his eyes. I tread water and wait for him.

"I'm not giving you my shirt this time," he says when he stops just in front of me. "If you lose your shirt again, you're just gonna have to deal with it."

I splash him in the face. "You know, that wasn't what you think it was, right? I didn't get drunk and take my clothes off in front of everyone just for the fun of it."

"Honestly, I did think that at first, but not anymore. What did happen?"

"Serresa had someone disintegrate my shirt to embarrass me."

"I wondered if she had something to do with it." He pauses. "But at least something good came out of it."

"What? From where I'm standing, nothing good came out of me flashing the whole school." I glare at him.

"Oh, not for you. I meant for me. I got to see your boobs." I gasp in mock outrage at his words and sweep my hand out to send another wave of water at his face.

"Not fun—" He grabs my wrist and yanks me toward him, cutting off anything I was about to say.

"No, not funny. But definitely something I haven't been able to stop thinking about. I didn't expect

346

that as my reward for throwing the party for you." He winks.

My brain is a little addled from his nearness. "That party was for me?" I ask, not sure if I'm understanding him correctly.

"Yeah, you seemed sad about your birthday . . ." he trails off and shrugs.

Warmth spreads through my stomach at his confession. That's probably the sweetest thing anyone has ever done for me. I'm two seconds away from closing the last bit of space between us and giving into the temptation of finding out how his lips would feel against mine when I have another thought.

"Is that why you keep bringing us back here? Have you been hoping for a repeat this whole time?"

"What do you mean me? You're the one visiting me, not the other way around . . ." he says, cocking his head to the side in confusion.

"Kennedy! Get up already!" Falyn shouts through my door and I jerk to a sitting position in my bed. What the fuck?

I don't have time to think about what Drayzen said in my dream because I have to rush to get ready or risk being late. I skip showering and go straight to my closet to get dressed. It feels like my first day all over again. Except this time, I know better than to wear the uniform.

We make it to our first class with only seconds to spare and have to pass Drayzen and gang to get to our seats. He and Michan nod at me as we walk by

347

while Serresa gives me her customary glare. If it really was Drayzen in my dream, his nod gives nothing away. Neither does the bland facial expression he seems to wear ninety-nine percent of the time.

Since I'm so busy searching his face for any hint of recognition, I don't notice how fewer people are here than usual until I'm sitting down. The class is missing half the students I'm used to seeing. I'm guessing Falyn isn't the only student to get new schedules.

It's the same thing in History of Magic and even though it's not normally a class I have trouble focusing in, today is different. Professor Monyae insists everyone sit closer to the front of the room since half the desks are empty and I find myself being pointed to a desk directly next to Drayzen while Falyn has the pleasure of sitting next to Serresa and Michan behind me. I'm not a fan of the new seating arrangement and, judging by the tight expressions on their faces, neither are Falyn and Serresa.

Drayzen barely glances at me before focusing front and center for Professor Monyae's lesson. I almost choke on my own tongue when he tells us the story of the original moon and how she got her magic. Of all the origin stories, he had to pick dream walker magic today.

I look at Drayzen out of the corner of my eye, but he's fully focused on the front of the classroom. In fact, it's like he doesn't know I exist. Maybe Falyn was right. He's not a moon and I'm just looking for any excuse I can grab ahold of to avoid having to admit I find him attractive. I have the emotional development of a twelve-year-old.

Falyn kicks the back of my chair and I realize I've been staring at him for a while now. My face heats when a smile twitches at his lips. This asshole isn't as focused on the front of the class as he'd have me believe.

I spent the rest of class being hyper-aware of him sitting next to me. Every time he shifts in his seat, my eyes are immediately drawn to him. I spend more time than I care to admit, just tracing the lines of corded muscle in his arms and admiring the shape and size of his hands. By the time class is over, I can't tell you a single thing the professor talked about, but I can tell you Drayzen has a tiny freckle in the corner of one eye and a birth mark on the inside of his wrist. I'm a complete disaster.

I'm relieved when class is finally over, until I remember my next class is the replacement combat class. Which means it's another hour and a half of Drayzen, only this time we'll be alone. My stomach flutters and I groan inwardly at myself. *Get a grip, Kennedy.*

I don't wait for Falyn to get out of my seat and rush for the door. I need a few seconds away from him to clear my head. She follows behind at a much slower pace and emerges from the classroom with a giant grin on her face.

"Don't even think about saying it," I warn her.

349

"You mean don't tell you to get a room?" she asks innocently, referring to the exact words I used with her and Noric last night.

"Whatever," I growl. "Get it over with, then."

Before she can say anything else, Serresa's whiney voice floats from inside the classroom. "She's practically stalking you. Don't be surprised if your things go missing when she builds her Drayzen shrine. She already took a shirt. I bet she sleeps in it every night."

I press my lips together when my face goes hot all over again. If only she knew how close to the truth that statement is.

"Give it a rest, Ser," Michan says just as they step through the door together. "Your jealousy is starting to grate on my nerves." Her mouth snaps shut just as mine pops open. Michan is the last person I expected to defend me.

Then I realize he's not defending me at all. He's frowning at Drayzen as he says it. Michan is jealous of Serresa's crush on Drayzen. It's amazing what you can learn by stepping back and watching.

"You ready?" Drayzen asks me, clearly annoyed. So much for keeping our sessions on the down low.

"Um, I guess." I shrug before waving to Falyn and following him toward the courtyard. I can feel the heavy glare of Serresa's eye on my back when we walk away. Perfect.

Drayzen speed walks all the way to the giant boulder he brought me to that day with his mom and doesn't say a word the whole time. I have to half jog just to keep up with him. "What's your problem?" I finally pant when he stops.

"I just needed to get away from her. Sorry, I didn't mean to make you suffer in the process," he apologizes.

"Oh. I thought maybe you were mad at me since you barely acknowledged me in class," I reply. "Not that I expect you to act like we're best friends or anything." I add because I don't like how put out I sound over the fact.

"Serresa hasn't left me alone since she found out her parents are in the middle of negotiating marriage between us," he says, and it takes everything in me not to keel over even though he acts like it's no big deal.

"You're marrying Serresa?" My voice comes out high pitched and way more anxious than I mean for it to.

"Not if I have any say in it. Why would I be mad at you?" he asks, completely jumping over the bomb he dropped at my feet.

"I don't know. It just kind of felt like we were strangers in class today." I shrug.

"We are though, if you think about it. We've only talked to each other a couple times, and it's only ever been school related," he replies, and I realize he's right. "Unless you're talking about your little moon walking trips into my dreams?"

CHAPTER TWENTY-THREE

First off, you're the dream walker. I have two categories already." I put a fist on my hip so he knows I'm not messing around. "And second, if I was a dream walker, why would I be invading your dreams? Like you said, we're practically strangers."

"Oh, so it makes sense that I would invade yours, but not the other way around?" he asks pointedly.

"You're the one who admitted he couldn't stop thinking about my boobs." I lift my eyebrows at him.

"I guess that means I'm the one who was about to kiss you in the water too, right?"

"That was just . . ." I fumble for something to say because I have no reason for that other than being caught up in the moment.

"Just what?"

"Never mind. My point is that I'm not the moon. When you figure it out, I'll be waiting with an "I told you so" on standby."

He just shakes his head at me. "I'm not going to say anything about you having a third, if that's what you're worried about."

"I already said I'm not the moon. The only one with a secret category here is you." I cringe inwardly at my blatant lie.

"Since there's no way to prove it right this second, why don't we get started," he says, ignoring my comment.

"I was just thinking I haven't been tortured enough today. Let's do it."

After another session of intense muscle building, I'm drenched with sweat and running late for lunch. If there's anything to miss about Brextin's class, it's being able to shower after combat. I don't have the same luck with Drayzen.

Falyn wrinkles her nose when I sit down, but I choose to ignore it in favor of shoveling food into my mouth at hyper speed. I'm under strict orders from Drayzen to eat as much protein as possible so I opted for a bowl filled with some kind of noodle and lots of summer beans which I'm pretty sure is this realms version of a chickpea. At least I hope it is, or there's zero protein on my plate.

"Say one word about my smell and I'm going to hug you so hard," I warn her and the rest of our friends snicker when her mouth snaps shut before it fully opens.

Once I'm halfway through my food, I finally slow down and look up from my plate. I'm surprised when I see a lot of empty tables around the room.

"Is no one eating lunch today?" I ask, looking around.

"I don't know, but it's not just the commissary. Did you notice morning classes? Half the students were missing from those too," Falyn replies, frowning.

I set my fork down. "I did notice, but I thought it was just classes being reassigned.

"It's everyone who scored under a five that's missing," Rostan leans in and lowers his voice.

"What do you mean missing?" I've suddenly lost my appetite.

355

"Not really missing. They're all being schooled separately from us. They're being housed separately, too." All our crystals ding except for Falyn's.

I have mine for once and pull it out to see what the school is announcing now.

Starting tomorrow, all students who receive this message will no longer be taking practical applications. Instead, please report to the designated area of campus to begin battle applications of your primary category.

A list of categories and their designated areas follows the message. I look up at the rest of the table. "Did you all get switched to battle applications?" I ask.

"So, I guess Falyn isn't the only one who's taking new classes then," Sona says, and there's an excited glint in her dark eyes. The girl does love violence. It must be a trait of towers.

"Speaking of," I put my crystal away and look at Falyn. "What was your new class like?"

"It was okay, I guess." She looks down at her plate, refusing to look at anyone.

"You guess?" Noric asks, concern lining his forehead.

Falyn looks up at us and attempts a smile, but mostly fails. "I'm sure it was good for anyone who wanted to work with crops after finishing school." She shrugs. "The whole class it set up to teach us how best to use our magic to encourage crop growth for maximum yields," she says bitterly.

"Why would you need to know that?" I question her.

356

"Because according to my new professor, that's exactly what I'll be doing. When Galen said our powers would be what keeps the realm going, I think he meant literally. Through our labor."

"So not only does he tell us who we can marry, but now he tells us what we're allowed to do with our lives? How is this okay? We're an entire nation of people who live solely at the whim of one man."

Flynn claps her hand over my mouth. "Ken, you can't talk like that."

I glare at her but nod my understanding. "So if the more powerful mages are meant to protect the realm while the midrange keep it running, where does that leave the lower power levels, or even the mundanas?" I ask, but nobody seems to have an answer for me.

I take another look around the room, my stomach twisted in knots. I don't know if it's just because of how empty the commissary is, but it feels darker in here somehow. It's definitely a lot quieter.

Everything seems to fast forward. Between my new classes, training with Drayzen, and spending all my free time with Noric and Falyn testing different aspects of my magic, the weeks blur by. It's hard to believe it's been two months since everything changed.

The school still feels really empty, but I've grown used to it. And even though we've been separated from the lower-level students, I see them going from one class to another on occasion, which makes me feel a little better about the whole thing. Not completely because I don't understand the necessity of separating everyone, but at least I know they weren't shipped off to mining camps as cheap labor or anything.

Noric still hasn't figured out how my power bracelet was made. Since I'm the first mage that we know of who requires anything like it, there's probably not a single temperance who does. Besides the one who made it and I'm not engaging with any of the messages they send.

"You're unfocused," Drayzen says right before he sweeps my legs out from under me and I hit the ground hard enough to punch the air out of my lungs.

"That was rude," I gasp out then backward somersault to my feet and further away from him.

He nods in approval and stalks closer. "When you're fighting, your mind has to be fully focused on your opponent. You act like this isn't something I've been drilling into your head for the last two months."

I back away, looking for an opening, but he's not making it easy. You'd think after two months of spending five days a week with him, I would be able to read him better. Impatient to pay him back, I kick out with one leg, but he's ready and grabs my ankle. When he doesn't release it right away, I lift a brow and stand awkwardly with no way to release myself. As he's proven time and time again, my strength is nothing compared to his and I'll never beat an emperor by trying to fight them as an equal.

He's always telling me to find a weakness and exploit it.

I smile when I realize what his biggest weakness is. He's scared of hurting me. All it would take is a split second of him forgetting to pull back his power and I'd be toast. With that in mind, I drop boneless back to the ground. If he continues to hang on to my ankle, he'll break it. He registers it immediately and releases my foot.

"Wha—" he starts to ask, but I'm already moving.

I hook my legs behind him almost exactly the way I did the first night he entered my dream. He doesn't fall for it this time and side steps before I can put any force into it.

"Nice, but part of an emperor's magic is being able to remember and analyze every move someone uses against you. I knew you were going to do it probably before you even did." He smirks and offers his hand, but I'm not done. Gripping his forearm, I let him pull me up, then use the momentum he creates to swing his arm behind his back. It confuses him just long enough to slam my heel into the back of his knee. When he staggers, I kick out again and get the second knee. He drops, but I forgot to release his arm in my excitement over getting the upper hand and he grabs a

359

hold of mine and twists his body around as he goes down, taking me with him.

"Now what?" he asks when we're both on our knees facing each other.

"Now I do this," I reply, thinking as quickly as possible.

I reach for the empress spark I've been carrying with me since this morning and dig my fingers into the ground. Several thick vines shoot up behind him and wrap themselves around his arms and legs, giving me precious seconds to get away.

I have just enough time to land a solid kick to his stomach before he rips through my vines and gets to his feet. "Good," he says before launching himself at me.

I dodge out of the way and let his momentum carry him past me while slamming my elbow between his shoulder blades and sending him stumbling forward again.

"Finally!" I shout, pumping my fist in the air. It took the better part of an entire month to get a blow on him and today I got three. I'm calling it a win.

"If this was a real fight, that little victory dance would have gotten you killed," he says in his stern instructor voice, but it's ruined by the fact that his lips are twitching.

"Yeah, yeah, yeah." I roll my eyes, still grinning. "Say it."

"I'm not saying it."

"You told me if I could land a blow in the first month of actual combat training, you'd say it. Don't make a liar out of yourself."

"Fine." He sighs heavily and purses his lips. "You're a badass warrior goddess and I should be kneeling at your feet."

"Was that so hard?" I ask, struggling to hold back my laughter.

"On that note, we should probably head to lunch." He shakes his head at me. "If I'm being honest, you're learning so fast. Sometimes I wonder if you're an emperor."

If only he knew how close to the truth that is. My smile falters. It's getting increasingly harder to hide my abilities from my friends, including Drayzen. Not because I'm accidentally manifesting anymore, but because the guilt is riding me so hard.

"What's wrong?" Drayzen asks me, bringing me back to the present.

"Nothing. I think today exhausted me more than usual." The lies never end with me, I guess. "Also, do you think I'm an emperor the same way you thought I was a moon? Because we know how that turned out, don't we?"

"Are you ever going to let that go?" He bumps me with his shoulder.

"Probably. Just not today." I laugh, but it sounds empty even to my own ears.

"What's going on?" I ask no one in particular as soon as I get to the clearing where they hold my battle applications class.

There's at least double the amount of students I'm used to seeing and everyone is looking around, confused.

"I have no idea. They must have opened it to lower levels for some reason," a girl says behind me, and I take another look at the students I don't recognize. She's right. They're all lower-level mages.

"I have an exciting announcement!" Professor Ishynt claps her hands together, pulling my attention from the group of newcomers to her. "Now that you all have a grasp on using your magic defensively, it's time to start learning how to use it offensively."

Low murmurs rise behind me, but the sound of blood rushing to my head makes it impossible to hear what's being said.

"These lovely students have volunteered to help you all in your endeavors, so let's make sure we thank them, shall we?"

She can't possibly mean what I think she does. The students she's referring to all look like they'd rather be anywhere but here. "How exactly are they going to be helping us?" I ask, but I'm pretty sure I already know the answer.

"You're going to practice on them, of course." She smiles as if it's a good thing. "Your goal is to subdue them, and their goal is to not be subdued."

A few of the students gasp and she holds up her hands. "Now don't worry, we have healers on standby should it come to that. It's for that reason I don't want anyone holding back. You can't learn to wield effectively if you're too busy trying not to hurt someone." She stares directly at me when she says it.

"I'm not doing that. Why can't we practice against each other?" I speak up again. It would make way more sense to practice against someone near my power level than someone much weaker.

Professor Ishynt frowns at me and presses her lips together in a thin line. "We can't risk one of you becoming seriously injured," she says, as if it's the most obvious thing in the world.

"But you can risk them?" I am beyond bewildered by her logic.

"I already said we have healers on standby, and this isn't a choice, Miss Marston." She looks down her nose at me. "You will participate in class, or you'll find yourself out of school entirely."

I keep my mouth shut, but I have no intention of using my magic against someone who can't defend themselves against it.

"Okay, everyone pair off and finds a spot with plenty of room for movement. Remember, the goal is to subdue your opponent any way you can," Ishynt says.

While everyone else steps forward to find an opponent, I stay right where I am. This is absolutely barbaric and I'm not going to do it. I don't care if that means they ship me off. At this point, I have to wonder if it wouldn't be better to be a mundana.

"You have to." A guy's voice interrupts my thoughts. "You're not the only one who gets punished if we don't fight," he adds bitterly.

"They would punish you?"

"No, having to stay here pretending to still be a student is our punishment. If we don't participate in this, our families receive the punishment for us."

My jaw drops. "You can't be serious."

His hands light up with a soft, familiar glow just before he lifts them and pushes his palms outward toward me. I dodge the blast of light just in time to avoid having my face melted off. I'm not fast enough to avoid the blistering heat searing up my shoulder. Hissing against the pain, I check the wound and find the skin already blistering. I hate suns.

"What the—?" I'm cut off when he sends another blast at me. I dive for the ground to get out of the way.

Around us, everyone else is already in full swing. It's not all magic either. Several pairs are going at it in physical fights and a couple lower-level students are running for cover into the trees. The worst thing they could do when running from an empress.

A booted foot appears by my head, but I refuse to get up and fight back. I won't be responsible for hurting someone for the sake of hurting them.

"Get up," he says.

"I'm not going to fight you. If the object of this lesson is for you to avoid being subdued, then you win. That's gotta earn you something, right?"

"You don't get it. The only object of this lesson is to show us how weak we are compared to you. How we no longer fit into the new society. You think you're helping me, but I'm already screwed. After school, we're being stripped no matter what we do. But if I don't serve a purpose while I'm here, my family gets stripped too. Fight me!" His foot comes down on my wrist and the sound of my bone snapping registers just before the pain does. "If you're so much better than me, then prove it."

My eyes water from the pain and blur my vision, but the glow of his magic flares and I realize I don't have a choice. Cradling my wrist to my chest, I roll, doing my best not to put any weight on it. The flare of light misses me by mere centimeters. He's still advancing on me, so I kick my leg out and land a blow directly into his stomach. He doubles over, trying to catch his breath, and I use the time to pull my empress magic through my limbs.

"I'm not better than you," I say, calling up sleep spores from the soil around me. "You're a little cranky when you miss your nap." I crush a few of the mushrooms between my fingers and blow the spore plume directly into his face. Thank you, Falyn, for teaching me how to grow them during a rough week of sleepless nights.

He crumples to the ground next to me, unable to fight the effects of the sleep spore and I let out the breath I've been holding. He's subdued.

Ishynt watches from across the clearing, obviously not happy with my performance. I stand and dust my pants off with my one good hand as if I don't have a care in the world. I'm well acquainted with her power trips by now and I know she wants me to ask for a healer, but I won't give her the satisfaction.

I use my magic to create a brace by weaving together thick blades of grass and wrapping them around my hand and wrist before stepping over my fallen opponent and finding a spot out of the way of the other students fighting around me.

It's not going well for the lower levels. They're doing their best to hold back the onslaught of magic being thrown their way, but the majority of them are either on the ground injured or trapped in nets of plant growth. A few are even suffering much the same way I did the day I got caught in the thorny vines of one of Serresa's lackeys.

One in particular isn't even struggling, but that isn't stopping her opponent from pulling the vines tighter around her until her face turns purple and she's gasping for breath. The blood dripping down her legs becomes a stream as the thorns grow in size and dig deeper into her skin.

"That's enough!" I yell at the empress wielding the magic, but she's too far gone in her victory and doesn't hear me. Rushing to the girl wrapped in vines but having no idea how to help her, I do the only thing I can think of and wrap a hand around the vine. I pour my borrowed magic into it and accelerate its life cycle until it begins to wither and die, allowing the girl to suck in a much needed breath. I must have been seconds too late because even though she got that breath, her eyes flutter shut before she collapses to the ground unconscious. Thankfully, still breathing.

"Are you trying to kill her? She was subdued." I whirl on the empress and when I'm met with a smirk of satisfaction, I lose all sense of myself. Calling every last bit of power I have left, I send it outward with a thrust of my hands and thick roots rip from the ground under my feet to follow the path my hands create. They wrap around her ankles before retreating into the large hole they created when they tore through the earth at my command. The hole isn't large enough to fit her whole body, but she soon finds herself half buried and unable to free herself from the punishing grasp of my tree roots.

Professor Ishynt appears before me and grabs my broken wrist to yank me toward her. I grit my teeth against the unexpected jolt of pain. "What do you think you're doing?" she hisses at me.

"I'm doing what you should have. She almost killed her, and you stood by and watched," I spit and pull my hand from her grasp.

"That isn't for you to decide. If you ever undermine me in my class again, I'll—"

"You'll what?" I interrupt her because I'm too far gone in my anger to care about consequences right now. "Last I checked, I'm a ten and you're what? A seven at most? I'm pretty sure that makes you much more expendable than I am." Then I leave her to watch me walk away. I really need a healer and as far as I'm concerned, class is over.

CHAPTER TWENTY-FOUR

Why do you keep rubbing your wrist like that?" Drayzen plops down in the sand beside me. I didn't realize I was rubbing it, but I guess it still feels a little sore even after a visit to the healer.

"Let's just say I refused to participate in battle applications today and paid the price." I wince, remembering the whole ordeal.

369

"I thought you said you liked the class," he replies, probably confused by the fact that I refused to participate. He's right. I did like learning how to use my magic defensively. But that was when my focus was protecting myself, not hurting someone else.

"I did until today. You're lucky you still just take straight combat instead of battle applications."

"Why? What happened?" He takes my wrist in his hand and gently rotates, looking for my phantom injury. After he's done inspecting it, I expect him to let me go, but instead he holds my wrist in one hand and uses his other to rub circles over it in a light massaging motion.

"They brought in the students who tested under five and basically used them as target practice to teach us how to manifest offensively."

Drayzen drops my hand, and it bounces off his knee, sending a wave of pain through my arm. "Sorry." He picks it back up when I hiss. "They did what?"

"That was pretty much how I felt about it. It was horrible. But the worst part is it didn't matter if I refused because they were desperate to fight to save their families."

"What do you mean?" He goes back to massaging my wrist and his warm strokes send goosebumps up my arm, almost causing me to forget what we're talking about. "Kennedy?" he prompts.

I jerk my eyes away from his large, callused hands and force my brain to focus. This is important.

"The guy I was paired up with said if they didn't agree to it, their families would be stripped."

Drayzen jerks back. "That can't be right."

"He also said after the trials, all of them are being sent away and stripped."

Drayzen stands up, the reason this whole conversation started forgotten as he paces in front of me. "Why would they do that?" he asks, clearly distressed about it. Then his face loses color and he whirls on me before crouching so we're eye level. "You have to participate. If they're willing to strip hundreds of mages for the sole reason of not being blessed with enough power, they won't hesitate to do the same to you."

I open my mouth to argue, but he rushes on before I can get a word in. "No. Nee. I know you hate it and I know you have your opinions about the kingdom and its laws, but promise me you'll do everything you can not to be stripped."

"I can't do that. I won't kill someone just to prove I'm more powerful. How could you even suggest it?"

"I'm not suggesting you kill anyone. Just play along. We can't afford to lose—" he abruptly cuts himself off.

"Finish your sentence, Drayzen. We can't afford to lose what? And who's we?" I lean forward. "Why is it so important to you that I stay here and play along? For two months now, you've been on my ass about practicing my magic and learning to defend myself. I know these sessions aren't Galen mandated anymore, so why do you continue them?" The questions I've been

371

asking myself for the last couple months start pouring from my mouth. Within days of the new announcements, I got an alert on my phone saying the tutoring will no longer be required of me with the new class structure, but Drayzen never mentioned it once. He continued to show up daily at our sessions. Sometimes twice a day if you count my dreams.

"I didn't mean to say we . . ." he trails off and takes a breath. "Please, Nee. Don't do anything that's going to get you kicked out. I—" he stops again. I'm suddenly hyperaware of how close our faces are when I feel his breath whisper across my cheek. All I would need to do is lean forward the tiniest bit . . . Drayzen must be thinking the same thing because his eyes move to my mouth before sliding back up to my own eyes.

"You what?" I whisper when he reaches up to toy with a strand of my hair that came loose from the messy bun I sleep in.

"I can't afford to lose you." His hand moves away from the lock of hair between his fingers and cups my face. I lean into it, closing my eyes and allowing myself the brief moment of giving in. When I open my eyes, he's staring intently at me. Almost as if he's searching my face for an answer to a question he never asked. He doesn't have to though, because I know exactly what the question is and my body is screaming yes. Seeing the answer on my face, he closes the tiny gap between us to brush his lips, feather light, against my own.

"Damn it, Ken! We go through this every day. You really need to go to sleep earlier or something!" Falyn pulls me from the dream and I've never wanted to throttle someone so much in my entire life.

"I'm up," I growl at her through my bedroom door and roll out of bed to my feet. "Next time just leave me," I grumble when I jerk the door open to glare at her.

"What's your problem?" She glares right back, and it takes the steam out of my annoyance. It's not like she knows what she interrupted. I haven't told her about my nightly dreams with Drayzen since that first day. At first, I told myself it was because they weren't important, but truthfully, it's because I'm afraid if I talk about them, they'll stop, like every other good thing in my life.

"Sorry, I didn't sleep very well."

"Should we culture some more mushrooms?" she asks, frowning in concern.

"No!" I reply way more vehemently than I mean to. "I mean no, it's okay. I'm sure I'll sleep better tonight." The mushrooms are great for getting solid sleep, but I learned they also block a moon's ability to walk in your dreams.

"Okaay," she draws out the word like she doesn't believe me, but luckily drops the subject. "Well, hurry up or we're gonna be late. Again."

The morning ticks by with agonizing slowness as I count down the minutes until my session with Drayzen. When I'm on my way to meet him at our

373

boulder, a message comes through on my crystal from him.

"Coward," I mutter after sliding it back into my pocket. He's canceling today. Or maybe it's not him being a coward. What if he just got caught up in the moment and realized after Falyn broke our dream that he wasn't that interested? And now he's searching for a way to let me down easy. We've had a few moments in the months since he started training me, but he's never acted on them. Have they all been in my head?

I'm so lost in thought as I wander back toward my dorm to wait for lunch, I run right into Rostan. He wraps his hand around my biceps to keep me from falling backward and laughs.

"I called your name like three times, but I guess you didn't hear me," he says, letting go of me once I find my balance. "What are you doing?"

"Drayzen canceled our session, so I was just gonna hang out at home until lunch. What about you? Aren't you supposed to be in class right now?"

He shrugs. "I have History of the Realm and Elwin never notices if you're not there, so I mostly don't go."

"You rebel," I respond, and his smile falters for a split second. "I mean, for not going. I wasn't implying you're a member of the rebels or anything," I rush to explain.

"Relax, Ken. I know what you meant." But his smile doesn't quite reach his eyes. "If you're still in the

374

mood for a combat session, we could always spar," he offers.

I find myself not opposed to the idea. "Magic free?" I ask because I'm still traumatized from yesterday's applications class.

"Sure. Where do you usually go?" he asks, looking around.

"We can just go to the clearing behind the worldly house," I suggest because somehow I've come to think of the boulder as mine and Drayzen's spot and it feels wrong to take someone else there.

"Can I ask you something?" I ask Rostan as we begin the short walk.

"Sure?" He frames it as a question.

"If you had feelings for someone, how long would it take you to do something about it?" I cringe as I ask because it feels ridiculous to even bring it up.

"What do you mean?" He looks at me and frowns.

"I mean, if you had feelings for someone, why would it take you a long time to do anything about those feelings? Like what would be a reason for you to not make a move? Or does the fact that you don't make a move mean you actually don't have feelings for that person?" I rush to get it out. I'm such a loser.

He stops walking and faces me. "Is this about Ciena?"

I stop too. "Huh?"

"Never mind. What were you saying?"

375

"Oh no, you're not getting away with it that easily. What about Ciena?" I demand. "I'll tell you mine if you tell me yours."

He groans. "Fine, let's get to the clearing first."

As soon as we find a spot, I plop down cross-legged on the grass. "Okay, spill."

"Nope, you asked first, so you're spilling first." He follows suit and sits facing me with his legs stretched out in front of him.

"Fine. I was talking about Drayzen."

"I knew it. You're not as subtle as you think you are with all the staring and daydreaming every time he's around."

"Whatever. But seriously. We had an almost moment last night and now today he cancels our session without giving me a reason. That means it was all in my head, right?"

"How did you see him last night? I thought our rooms sealed for curfew now," Rostan asks tilting his head.

"Oh . . ." I probably should have thought it through before telling him that part of it. "We didn't technically see each other last night. Drayzen's secondary is moon." I don't think it's common knowledge that he manifested a secondary, so I hope I'm not outing a secret.

"And he visits your dreams?" Rostan questions.

"Yep, for about two months now."

"Does he do that a lot?" Rostan wags his eyebrows at me.

"It's not like that, but yes. He visits almost every night. All we do is talk, though. He's never tried anything more."

"Ken, if he's expending the energy to visit you every night, it's not for friendship."

"Then why would he cancel our session? It makes no sense. Unless he's having doubts. Maybe he thought he was interested, but realized otherwise." The thought is too depressing. Not just because I'm finally admitting my interest in him, but because I've suddenly become the type of person to pine over a guy.

"Believe me, he's interested. Drayzen doesn't strike me as the type to not know his own mind," he says, nudging me with his booted foot.

"I would have said the same thing about him, but now I'm not so sure." I suddenly don't want to talk about my Drayzen problems anymore. "Anyway, what's this about Ciena?"

Rostan leans back in his hands and stares up at the sky. "I honestly don't know. Before the testing, I thought there was something there. But it's like as soon as she found out I scored a ten, all of a sudden I don't exist for her anymore."

"You kind of don't," I tell him, knowing exactly where Ciena's head is.

"What's that supposed to mean?" He frowns at me.

377

"Think about it, Rostan. You're a ten. She's a six. Allowing anything to happen between you is just setting herself up for future disappointment when you're out of her league. Literally. Even if you guys try to make a go of it, a relationship between you is officially against the law."

Rostan jerks to a sitting position. "That thought never crossed my mind. I'm an idiot."

"Not an idiot. Maybe a little thick, but not an idiot." I smile sadly at him.

"I don't care about the stupid laws," he says vehemently. "Neither does my family. We never have. And now with the prophecy coming—" he snaps his mouth shut.

"What about the prophecy? You mean that stupid note on the statue? What does that have to do with anything?" I ask, intrigued why after months he's suddenly bringing it up again.

"It's nothing. I shouldn't have mentioned it."

"Oh no, you don't get to do that. Something is happening. Between the rebels getting bolder and the new inscription laws and changes in society structures. It feels like we're seconds away from exploding and I want to know what's going on."

He sighs heavily. "I don't really know anything except the high priestess guild has been really focused on it lately."

His answer doesn't feel like the whole truth, but I let it go in favor of asking a more pressing question. "Why now? I thought everyone said the prophecies in that journal have all been disproven."

"Now they're not so sure. They now think the prophecy is specifically about the king and what's been happening."

I never read the full thing, so I have no context for what he's saying other than the one line written on that paper. "How so?" I ask.

"My father thinks the loss of magic is actually punishment and the king's new laws are going to do the exact opposite of what he's claiming and speed up the loss of magic instead of saving it."

"So why don't they just make some lumi pod brew and get some answers," I ask, wondering why it's not a common practice.

"They've tried that, among other things, and hit a wall every single time. Whatever is coming isn't solidified yet, or maybe there isn't a future. Who knows? But the high priestesses aren't seeing much of anything right now. Nothing useful anyway." Both of us go quiet for a bit. Someday I would like for my future to not feel so bleak.

When I've had enough of feeling sorry for myself, I interrupt our depressing silence. "I thought we came out here to spar. Unless you decided getting your ass kicked by a girl is too humiliating." I smirk at him.

"There's zero chance of that happening. Let's go."

After lunch I don't feel like attending Ishtyn's class. After yesterday, I'm not sure I ever want to attend again. Regardless of what Drayzen wanted me to promise. Instead, I find myself walking to the healer's building. Maybe I can check on the girl from yesterday. She was pretty bad off when I walked away from class, so there's a good chance she's still healing. There's no way she's back to full health already.

There's no one in the healer building when I walk through the door. That seems entirely impossible, considering half the student body is being used for target practice now. Injured students should be filling the beds. They're all empty.

"Kennedy! How's your wrist today?" Maylah asks, walking out of the back room with a basket of supplies in hand.

"You made it good as new," I reply, smiling at her and rotating my wrist for her to see. Only the smallest twinge of pain ghosts through my arm. "I can't believe it was broken just yesterday."

"Even though I mended the bones, they'll still be weak for a while, so you better not be doing anything to reverse all my hard work," she replies in the same stern voice she used on Drayzen all those months ago when he came in with that burn on his chest.

I cross my heart but quickly realize she has no idea what that means so I nod my head. "Wouldn't dream of it." I look around again, but no injured bodies have suddenly appeared in the beds lining the walls.

"Where is everyone?" I ask.

"In class, I imagine. Where you should be unless you're injured . . ." she says, clearly wondering why I'm here.

"No, I'm fine. I was just coming to visit someone I thought would be here. You don't have anyone here at all?"

She cocks her head to the side. "No, actually, it's been calmer than it's ever been the last few months. I'm starting to wonder if my job is in danger."

"That makes no sense. Your beds should be full of students right now. They said you're on standby."

"Standby for what exactly? You're the only student I've seen in the last few days."

"Is there another healer building?" I'm pretty sure I already know the answer, but I hope I'm wrong.

"No, just this one. What's going on? Why are you so worried about empty beds? This is a good thing. Working as a healer is probably the only time someone could say not having work is a good thing." She laughs, but I'm too confused to find the joke in it all.

"Yesterday in battle applications, they brought in the lower-level students to give us practice in using our magic defensively. That's how I broke my wrist."

381

Maylah frowns at me. "That doesn't seem like the smartest way to approach defensive magic."

"That was my thought. But we were all told there were healers on standby so not to worry about injuring anyone."

"Well, this is the first I'm hearing of it." Her eyes narrow. "When did this start?"

I tell her everything. My refusal to participate, what my opponent told me, then ended with telling her about the girl I was trying to check in on. With every word, her face darkens until I can practically see the steam rolling off her.

"No one was brought in to me. I didn't even know this was going on. Do you know her name?" she asks her need to offer healing to the injured evident on her face.

"No, I just assumed they would all be here." What the hell is going on?

"Is it possible the injuries weren't as bad as they seemed?" she asks the same question I've been asking myself since seeing the empty beds.

"I don't think so. She was twenty times worse than that night I came in with the thorn injuries."

Maylah's face shuts down. "I'll look into this, Kennedy. You should probably get to class before it becomes a problem for you."

"What about—"

"I'll find out who it is, I promise. I just don't think it's a good idea for you to be asking questions. I'll

382

let you know what I find, but you just focus on school. You have trials in less than two months, after all."

Her voice leaves no room for argument, and she shoos me out the door before I can list all my reasons for needing to help find out what happened. Why does it feel like I'm being shut down the moment I start to question things? Like everyone around me knows more than they're letting on and I'm in a constant state of being on the outside looking in. I'm tired of it. If she thinks I'm just going to drop the subject, she's wrong. She's not the only one who can ask questions around here.

CHAPTER TWENTY-FIVE

Figuring out what's happening to the lower-level students is proving way more difficult than I anticipated. After two weeks of only half participating in battle applications and watching new students replace the injured ones on a daily basis, I know something is wrong. When I ask Professor Ishytn about it, she's puzzled why I would even care.

Maylah doesn't seem to have any answers for me either and is suspiciously quick to change the subject or let me know she's much too busy to talk. Although, I have yet to see an injured person cross her threshold.

Drayzen is another story. He's acting like nothing happened between us, but there's a distinct distance in the way he speaks to me. He hasn't visited me in a dream once since the almost kiss. Our sessions are all about business with little to no time to talk about anything else, so I haven't found an opportunity to broach the subject with him.

Falyn, Rostan, and Noric seem just as concerned about the whole thing as I do, but they're hitting the same brick wall I am. The four of us spend all our free time looking for the missing students. We've even gone as far as to try visiting the buildings where they're being housed, but we haven't been able to make it past the warriors who patrol that area of campus. Whatever they're doing with those students, it's obviously something they don't want anyone to know about.

"There's three students in my magical agriculture class I haven't seen all week," Falyn says on our way to history of the realm. "Do you think it has anything to do with the missing lower-level students?"

"I don't know how it could, since they're not the ones being used for target practice." But I honestly wouldn't put anything past the school at this point. The student body gets smaller and smaller every day. "If you have their names, we can check what rooms

385

they're in and make sure everything is okay," I add when it doesn't seem like she agrees with me.

"That's what I was thinking of doing after classes are over. I just didn't want you to think I was ditching our study session."

"I'll go with you. I'm not in the mood for a study session anyway. I've decided to give them up. If we were gonna find something, we probably would have by now."

Falyn gives me a sad smile. "We'll figure this out, Ken." She hesitates a little before continuing, so I know what she's going to say before she says it. The same discussion we've had multiple times over the last couple of months. "Have you given anymore thought to contacting them?"

"Not since the last time I refused." I roll my eyes at her. I want to get mixed up with the rebels about as much as I want to live in a realm ruled by the King Gefred. Which is to say zero. "Why do you think this group is contacting me of all people? I should be the last person on their radar, considering I lived my whole life on Earth. The whole thing is fishy if you ask me."

"Fishy?" Falyn asks, wrinkling her nose at me.

"It smells bad, I mean," I explain.

"You can smell them?" Her frown deepens, and I sigh. Why is it so hard to remember that Earth sayings almost never translate here? I spend more time explaining the expression than actually getting my point across.

"No, I just think it's suspicious that they keep reaching out to me like I'm someone important. With my luck it's some kind of trap Galen is setting to get me stripped and shipped."

Falyn's mouth forms an O. "I hadn't thought about that." Then she shakes her head. "If Galen wanted you out, I doubt he would need to do all that to accomplish his goal."

"Either way, I just don't really see a point."

"You're forgetting something kind of important, though," she says. "You are someone important. You're the only mage who holds whatever magic you have, and they seem to have more answers than anyone. I think as much as you say you want the truth, you're more afraid to find out than not." With that, she enters the classroom we just arrived at, preventing me from being able to respond.

Drayzen is already in his seat when we sit next to him and nods blandly at me when I collapse into my chair, still annoyed at Falyn for being right. "What's wrong?" He leans over, asking quietly.

"Nothing." I say without looking at him. He annoys me too. Both of them are on my shit list and I'm stuck between them for the entire class. Perfect.

I've never paid so much attention to History of the Realm until today and when the class is over, I hightail it out without so much as a glance at either one of them, then proceed to ignore them all through our next class. Unfortunately, my third class of the day is my session with Drayzen, so ignoring him isn't an option anymore. But if he wants to keep things completely professional, I can do that no problem.

As soon as we're at the boulder, I begin my stretches in silence waiting for him to begin the sparring session. I've been looking forward to this all day if I'm being honest. I have some built up energy that could use an outlet.

When he stands and faces me, I don't wait for his signal. I jump directly into a defensive pose and stalk toward him, looking for an opening. He smirks, and I let out a small exhale, refusing to acknowledge the small flip my stomach just did.

"Whatever you're mad about is making you sloppy," he says, pointing at my feet that are too close together to maintain proper balance if he rushes me.

I widen my stance before responding, "Who said I'm mad?" I lunge forward but retreat before making contact. He was expecting it, and I would have eaten dirt if I went through with it.

"No one said you're mad. I can just see it in your face. You're unfocused and it's going to get you hurt."

"I'm perfectly focused," I retort and make my move by kicking out sideways, then pulling back when he reaches out to block me, leaving his chest unprotected. As fast as I can manage it, I lunge forward on the same leg I kicked with, aiming my fist for his solar plexus. He sidesteps easily and grasps my forearm in his hands before using my own momentum to swing

388

me around and plant his foot on my ass, pushing me away from him. I stumble, but catch my balance.

"See? Sloppy." He's right. Between the missing students, him treating me like a stranger, the upcoming trials in less than two months, and Falyn's insistence over me contacting the stranger who keeps messaging me, it's a wonder I can think straight at all.

"Fine. Maybe my head isn't in it today." I back away from him and drop my hands to my sides. "Can I ask you something?"

He eyes me wearily, but nods his head.

"What do you know about the missing students?"

His eyes widen slightly at my question. "Nothing." He says it so fast I'm almost positive he knows more than nothing.

"Now the truth," I respond dryly.

"I don't know what you mean. Are we sparring or not?"

"Not. I want to know what you're hiding." I hop up onto the boulder and cross my arms over my chest.

He kicks a rock before coming to a decision about what to say. "Look, I only know what I've heard other people talking about and I'm not even sure any of it is factual . . ." he trails off and runs a hand through his dark hair.

"What have you heard?" I instantly perk up.

"All I know is Galen has been pulling students into his office for interviews. I have no idea if it's even related to students going missing or not, because this is the first I've heard of anyone missing."

"It would be a really big coincidence if it wasn't. Do you know what students he's been pulling in?"

"No, but a couple days ago someone in combat was pulled out for an interview, but she came back. That's the only reason I even know about the interviews. That's what she called it anyway."

"What does that mean? Is he interviewing people for jobs? I thought everything was already decided for us."

"I don't know, she didn't say what it was about, but whatever it was had her pretty shaken up. The rest of class she was unfocused and ate the floor so many times it was as if she had no previous training."

"Weird. But since she came back, maybe it isn't related. Was she in combat yesterday?"

"Yes, and she was fine."

I glare at him because none of this explains his reaction to my first question. "But what aren't you telling me? There's a reason me asking you that question made you think about Galen's interviews."

"Because afterward I overheard a couple of guys talking about their friend who was called in but they hadn't seen all day." He pauses, like he's choosing his next words carefully. "I didn't think anything of it at the time and I don't actually know if this person is missing because I don't even know who they were talking about, but it seems like it might be related."

390

I'm really starting to wonder what we're going to find when we visit the rooms of the girls Falyn told me about earlier. Another thought occurs to me. "What about the lower-levels? The ones who get injured? None of them have returned to battle applications. They just keep sending new ones."

He frowns. "That I don't know anything about. I would assume they just require extra healing since they're going up against mages almost twice their strength."

"That's the thing, I thought that too, but when I went to check on one of them, Maylah had absolutely no idea what I was talking about. She hasn't been healing any injuries."

"That can't be right. They must have another healer on hand."

"Where though? There's not another star building and I seriously doubt they have someone making house calls. Not to mention the fact that Maylah said she was going to look into it and now she's doing everything in her power to avoid having to talk to me. We're not even allowed to go to their dorms. Every time we try, warriors stop us."

"How about I see if they'll let me through so we can put this to rest and focus on what you should be focusing on?"

His offer makes me smile. His one-track mind is so different from the one-track mind of literally any other guy I've met. "Do you think they'll let you through?"

"It's worth a try. Sometimes having the mother I do opens doors that would otherwise be closed." He shrugs, but I know it bothers him to use his mother's name for anything. He spends a lot of his time trying to prove he's nothing like her, even though the path he's taking is almost identical to hers.

"Thank you," I say simply.

He smiles at me, and I expect him to demand we spar again, but instead he just sits next to me on the boulder. "How has it been going with batt app?" he asks, surprising me.

"First, nobody calls it that, and second, is this now a catch-up session since you've been all but ignoring me the last two weeks?"

"I haven't been ignoring you. We see each other every day."

I arch my brows at him. "Seeing and speaking are two completely different things and there has been very little of the talking going on." Especially when you take into account that he stopped visiting me in my dreams. I don't want to say that part out loud and wind up sounding like I expect it from him.

The silence drags out between us for a moment before he responds. "Things have been a little weird, right?"

"Not things. You." I laugh to play it off.

"I guess I've been preoccupied lately." He sighs.

"With what?" I ask, feeling a little guilty for not checking in on him because I'm too busy worrying about my own issues.

"Nothing important, really. But back to my original question about batt app."

I roll my eyes at him both for the obvious change of subject and his insistence of using the stupid nickname. "I'm participating. Kind of."

"What does kind of mean?" he questions.

"I'm doing what is being asked of me . . . just not the same way everyone else is doing it. Ishtyn wants us to subdue our opponents, so that's what I'm doing. I'm just getting really good at doing it without actually hurting them." I shrug.

"And how are you doing that?"

"Sleep shrooms, wildflower nets, shrub cages . . ." I tick off a few of my more creative offensives.

"Wildflower nets?" he questions, cocking his head.

"Yeah, I just grow them weaved together to wrap around my opponent. It's effective and pretty." I laugh.

Drayzen sighs. "Are you trying to get kicked out?"

"I'm doing what's asked of me. If she wants to kick me out for that, then so be it. Besides, it makes me the most wanted partner in my class. I'm pretty popular."

"Why do you always make light of being kicked out? It's not an empty threat, you know?

You're risking losing your powers and who knows what else."

His reply sobers me a little. "I'm not making light of anything. I don't want to get kicked out or be stripped, but I will never be the kind of person who is okay with hurting someone for my own advancement. Ever."

"I know, that's what I'm scared of." He nudges me with his shoulder.

"Why are you scared? It's not like I'd take you down with me. I doubt they're so serious about the new order that my punishment would extend to my friends."

"That's not what I meant."

"What did you mean then?" I question, hopeful he might say I'm more than a friend and give me even the tiniest sign he might have feelings for me.

"Just that someone needs to be worried about you because you obviously aren't." *I guess not.* He's officially giving me emotional whiplash.

"Well, don't worry about me. I'll be fine." I slide off the boulder and shield my eyes from the sun to look up at him. "We should head back. It's almost lunch and I'm starving."

It's probably just wishful thinking, but I swear I see disappointment on his face.

Lunch is uneventful, other than the longing looks between Noric and Falyn, and Ciena and Rostan. I swear the moon cycle must be affecting everyone's hormones because I did my own fair share of longing glances. I'm almost grateful when it's time to go to battle applications and I might get to beat up on someone. Kind of anyway.

I know something is up as soon as I get to class and Ishtyn's eyes find me. There's no mistaking the satisfied glint I see there. Especially not when she smirks and claps her hands together to get everyone's attention before speaking. "Some of you have been doing amazing, but others still seem to be struggling a little"—her eyes find mine to let me know she's specifically talking about me—"so we're going to try something new today. I'm assigning your opponents to you today instead of letting you choose your own. This will ensure you're being paired with someone who will challenge you in areas you may be struggling with."

I look at the fresh batch of lower-levels and wonder what she has in store for me. One of them, a guy I've never seen before, is staring right at me and I know without a doubt I've already been paired with him. Especially after he covers his nose and mouth with a bandana before stepping forward to stand in front of me.

His body swells to two times its width before reducing back to its normal size. My magic is telling me he's an emperor. I guess Ishtyn doesn't know my primary instructor is an emperor or she wouldn't be so sure this would teach me whatever lesson she's hoping it does.

He doesn't wait for introductions or even for the professor to tell us to start before he swings a meaty fist directly at my face. Thanks to my experience with Drayzen, I know there's no point in trying to block the blow, so I scramble to duck his fist and get behind him. He's unprepared for the foot I plant in his lower back, pushing him off balance before I dance back out of his reach.

He whirls on me but doesn't advance. He's just realized I'm going to be a harder opponent than he thought and has to take a second to size me up. I let my hands drop loosely to my sides in a relaxed pose so as not to give anything about my fighting style away. One of the inherent abilities an emperor has is to immediately find weakness and they have some sort of sixth sense for knowing exactly what their opponent will do next along with how to best counter it. My only advantage in this fight is that he knows nothing about me other than what Ishtyn told him.

He doesn't take long to study me before he moves forward and puts me on the defensive. I can't win this fight with combat. He can overpower me in seconds, so I'm forced to spend most of my time dodging his kicks and blows instead of actively trying to figure out how to subdue him.

"We don't have to do this, you know," I say, already out of breath and just a little bit afraid.

"That's where you're wrong. I'm here specifically for you. You'll find I'm not as easy of a take down as the lower-levels."

The way he phrases it gives me pause. He's talking about them as if he's not in their group and if that's the case then I may be in trouble. "What level are you?" I ask afraid of the answer but needing to know.

"You'll just have to find out for yourself. If you can survive long enough," he replies just before lunging at me and catching me off guard. His fist connects with my stomach, and I double over fighting both through the pain and for my breath. His arm comes down over my back and I crumple to my knees but have just enough wit to tuck and roll before his booted foot can make contact.

In seconds, I'm back on my feet and putting as much distance between the two of us as I can. Where I'm standing now gives me the perfect view of Ishtyn watching us with rapt attention. There's no concern on her face like you would think a teacher would have for her student. No, it's satisfaction and even a little joy. I'm screwed.

The emperor keeps advancing on me and I keep backing away, but I know I need to come up with something soon. When he allows a little extra space between us, I risk a quick pause to pull my magic through my body—something I should have done in the very beginning. It flows outward from my gut soothing some of the ache from his punch in its path.

397

I send some outward to the soil beneath his feet and roots spring from the ground to wrap around his ankles, allowing me a few more feet of distance before he rips through them with a single shake of each leg. How the hell am I supposed to fight against this?

He closes the gap between us, and I find myself backed against a tree at the edge of the forest surrounding the clearing we use for class. His shoulder tenses slightly and I know he's about to swing at, so I think fast.

I create a hole in the tree behind me and when his fist swings out, I duck so he punches through the tree instead of my face. I send a burst of magic to close the hole around his wrist and bring my knee up as hard as I can to catch him in his groin. He's expecting it though, and twists out of the way so my knee slams into his thigh and it feels like I hit solid steel, sending arcs of pain through my leg.

While he's working on pulling himself free, I grow the thickest vine I can and wrap it around his body and the tree no less than thirty times, until all you can see are his feet and the top of his head. Satisfied it should hold him, I turn my back to seek out Ishtyn. I want to see her face when she realizes her plan didn't work.

The cracking sound behind me doesn't immediately register and by the time I realize what it is, it's already too late. The emperor grabs the back of my neck and lifts me straight into the air, so my feet are dangling above the ground. "You probably should have run," he says before flinging me sideways against a second tree with all the strength of what I now assume to be level eight, if not higher.

My body slams against it and this time, the cracking sound doesn't come from the tree. I slide down the trunk, scraping the side of my face against the rough bark, and hit the ground in what feels like agonizing slowness as pain tears through my body. My lungs refuse to fill, and my breath sounds wet to my ears. What I can hear through the ringing anyway. The emperor stalks toward me and I try to get to my feet, but nothing seems to be working.

He crouches down so we're eye to eye. "I was asked to give you a message." I flinch away from the warm breath washing over my face, but he grabs my jaw in one giant hand and squeezes until I'm sure he's about to break it. "Participating is not an option. If you continue to ignore your duty to the king, being stripped is no longer the worst thing that can happen to you."

He doesn't look away, and I know he's waiting for me to acknowledge his message. I nod through the pain and his hand tightens on my jaw, causing tears to form. Breathing is getting harder with each passing second and the edge of my vision is going dark.

He finally shoves my head back, slamming it into the tree, and releases my jaw before standing and letting out a disgusted sigh when he notices the blood on his fingers. He walks away, but I can't rise to follow. Every breath feels like knives, as I steel myself to pull

399

away from the tree at my back. My body is unresponsive to my need to get up and be okay. This can't be the thing that puts me down. Not after all my hard work and especially not after I let myself choose to stay and make a life here. I urge myself to get to my feet, but nothing seems to be working. Turning my head, I try to take stock of the injuries I can see. My arm hangs, twisted at an odd angle. And my head feels like it weighs a hundred pounds so it flops to my chest, sending shooting pain through my skull. Soon the pain winks out, leaving only relief as the world stops spinning, and darkness sweeps in to claim me.

CHAPTER TWENTY-SIX

The first thing I notice when I wake up is the unfamiliar ceiling above me. Natural wood panels stretch as far as my eyes can see. A white curtain is pulled closed around my bed, telling me I'm lying in one of the beds in the star building. The panel directly above me has a large dark knot in it and I focus on it, trying to piece together how I got here. I remember my conversation with Drayzen about the missing students, and my walk to battle applications, but after that, everything is blank.

Muffled breathing comes from my right and when I turn my head, it feels like someone stuffed it full of cotton. I'm surprised when I find Drayzen sleeping in a chair next to my bed. Half his face is pressed against the hand propped up on the bedside table to support his head. It doesn't look the slightest bit comfortable, but he's fast asleep.

The room is mostly dark, the only illumination coming from the moon globe on the wall above my head that's set to quarter strength. The rest of the room beyond the curtain sounds empty and still. It must be late. I take the opportunity to study him while he's completely unaware. I trace the thin scar from his ear, down his stubbled jaw, to his mouth that even in sleep is set in a grimace.

I've never seen him with stubble. It actually looks like it's been a couple days since he last shaved, but that can't be right because I just saw him this morning and I'm almost positive he didn't have stubble. I don't have long to think about what that could mean before my eyes grow heavy and I can't fight the pull of sleep.

When I wake up again, my head feels normal, and the aches are almost completely gone from my body. Falyn is sitting in the chair beside my bed, flipping through a book and humming under her breath. I must have made a noise because her head jerks up and she beams at me.

"Kennedy! How do you feel? I was starting to think you were never going to wake up." She sets the book down on the table and scoots her chair closer to my bed.

When I try to respond, my tongue feels thick and dry, making speaking almost impossible. Falyn seems to know exactly what I need and rushes to fill an empty cup sitting next to a pitcher of water before handing it to me.

After I chug the whole thing in just a few seconds, I feel slightly more capable of forming words. "Shouldn't you be in class right now?" My voice sounds rusty, and I clear my voice before trying again. "What happened?"

She gives me a sad smile. "There's no school today. You don't know why you're here?"

"Why did they cancel school this time?" I ask, slightly panicked because the last time they canceled classes everything changed and not in a good way.

"They didn't, Ken. You've been out for four and a half days. You missed the whole week of classes."

"How is that possible?" I ask, trying to wrap my brain around her answer. I sit up but have to lie back down when a wave of dizziness hits me.

"Maylah said no sudden movements right after waking up." She looks at me sheepishly when I glare at her too late information. "Sorry, I forgot to warn you."

I stare up at the knot and strain for the memory that would tell me why I was here. I got to battle applications. I remember Ishtyn watching me and having a bad feeling . . . The emperor. I jerk upright again, this time ignoring the dizziness.

"Please tell me that bitch is fired."

"Who?" Falyn frowns at me in confusion.

"Ishtyn, of course. Who else would I be talking about?"

"How is you felling a tree on yourself her fault?" Falyn questions and I can literally feel my blood pressure climb.

"Is that what she said happened?" The scorn making my voice sound husky.

"Is that not what happened? You were really bad, Ken. I thought you were going to die." Her lower lip trembles and her eyes shine from the moisture building in them.

"Hey, I'm fine now. See?" I tell her.

"You are now." Maylah pulls back the curtain around my bed. "Thanks to several hours long healing sessions to repair your destroyed lungs, the bleed in your brain, and the multiple bone breaks."

I cringe hearing the truth of my injuries. "Thank you," I say and mean it.

"I just came to say you're good to go when you feel like getting up. But it took two healers to fix you, so I better not see you in here again." She gives me a stern look before patting my hand. "I'm glad you're okay, Kennedy."

"Me too," I respond.

She smiles then leaves me to change into the clothes she set on my bed when she opened the curtain.

404

"So what happened?" Falyn asks as soon as she's out of ear shot.

I tell her everything. And the further I get into the story, the redder her face becomes until she's pacing back and forth in anger. "I knew you weren't that clumsy. When she called me and I got here, there were a couple of lower-levels here. I'm pretty sure they brought you in, but were acting really strange when I asked them about your class. It was almost like they didn't want Ishtyn to know they had brought you."

"That doesn't surprise me at all. I bet she left me there to die," I say bitterly, but the thought actually makes me sick.

"Should we go to Galen?" Falyn asks.

"Not a chance. There isn't much that happens in this school without him knowing about it."

"Well, you can't go back to that class, Ken. What if it happens again?"

"I don't have a choice. Before I passed out, the emperor told me it would get much worse if I refused to participate again. I think not going would be considered not participating." The thought of having to see her again makes me nauseous and sweat beads on my forehead.

Once we're back in our dorm, Falyn forces me to lie down in my bed even though I feel totally normal. But when I hear Noric and Rostan's voices coming from the living area, I decide maybe it's worth the argument. I don't want to spend the whole day in bed.

As soon as I emerge from my room, all three of them go quiet and I narrow my eyes at them. "What were you just talking about?"

"Nothing really," Noric replies. "Glad to see you up, though."

"Bull. What don't you want me to know?" I turn my gaze on Falyn because she's the easiest to break and I'm rewarded when it only takes about three seconds of eye contact for her to sigh and fold.

"We're not hiding anything from you. Mostly," she says and sits down on the couch. "Just hiding it for now because you're in no condition to be up and about, and I know you won't stay home if you knew."

"My condition is fine. You heard Maylah. She said I was clear."

Falyn presses her lips together before replying. "If you come, you're only allowed to sit and watch."

"Watch what?" I ask and look at the guys who have yet to offer anything.

Rostan starts to answer when he feels my gaze, but Falyn holds her hand up to stop him. "Nope. Promise first or we're not going, and we won't tell you."

I look at Noric, but he refuses to meet my eyes. Of course, he would side with Falyn. When Rostan shrugs and gives me a half smile, I know I'm not getting anything from him either. "Fine. I'll sit and watch and not participate in whatever it is you guys are up to. Now what is it?"

"Actually, it's probably easier to show you than to explain it," Rostan answers. "We were going to skip today, but since you know, now we can all just go."

"You guys are being really weird about this, but fine. Let's go."

We have to walk all the way to the lake since we don't have active portals on campus anymore and it's a lot farther than I thought. By the time we arrive, I'm out of breath and exhausted. Maybe I'm not as fine as I would have everyone believe. But when I see what they brought me to, all thoughts of my exhaustion fly from my head.

I've never been to this area of the lake; it looks like it might be on the opposite side of where we had that party and the class where I first manifested my magic. The shoreline is less sand and more rocks, and the forest is overgrown. This is definitely not an area people frequent often, but somehow that makes me like it more.

The thing that catches my eye, though, is the fact that there are at least twenty other students already

407

here, if not more. And all of them are practicing battle magic. "What is this?" I turn to Falyn.

She smiles. "Ask Rostan. This was all his doing."

Rostan shrugs off her praise. "I wouldn't say that exactly, but it was needed."

"But what is it?" I ask again because they still haven't answered my question.

Rostan looks at the students with what can only be described as pride before he points to a small patch of grass. "Sit. Don't try to deny how much that walk took out of you. I can see it on your face."

I open my mouth to argue, but he lifts an eyebrow, and I know I won't get anything out of him until I do. "Happy?" I ask once I lower myself to the ground and angle my body to watch the students.

He sits so he's not towering over me while Falyn and Noric join the others. "When they changed Falyn's class to that magical agriculture, it got me thinking. These new trials aren't set up for success. The only students who have half a chance of passing are the higher levels like us and maybe some of the sevens from the mid-level group. The rest are being thrown to the wolves. They need someone to step forward and offer them a chance to pass."

His response blows me away. "So that's what this is? You're teaching everyone to use battle magic?"

"Kind of. There's a little more to it. I accidentally discovered something when I was browsing some books in the library."

408

"What do you mean?"

"I picked up a random book sitting on a cart in the library and my hierophant manifestation activated. I'm not sure why because I wasn't actively trying to use it, but I guess that doesn't matter. The book was about the different manifestations and how they can complement each other."

I'm almost positive I read that one during one of mine and Falyn's research attempts, but I'm pretty sure it was a dead end. It was all about how mages can combine their magic to amplify each other, but we already know that. We did it with the lumi pod not too long ago and whoever sent me that bracelet obviously did it.

"Like when we made the lumi pod brew," I respond, nodding my head.

"No, at first that's what I thought too, but then I realized it wasn't talking about multiple mages. It meant a single mage combining their manifestations to complement each other."

I frown because I'm not sure exactly where he's going with this. "What do you mean? How can my high priestess and empress magic work together? They're nothing alike."

"How do you feel about a demonstration?" he asks, a giddy smile on his face. His excitement is contagious, and I smile back but shake my head.

"I don't think I'm up to doing more than sitting here and looking pretty," I joke.

"Not you. Hang on." He gets up and walks toward a girl and says something to her. She nods, then the two of them approach another guy and the three of them come back to stand in front of me.

"Nee, this is Cas," he says, gesturing to the girl, "and Flit." Now pointing at the guy. "Cas is a high priestess and a wheel." He continues. I shuffle through my knowledge of the different manifestations and find the answer buried in my brain. Wheels can manipulate time. "Flit is an emperor and a temperance. The important thing for you to know is Cas is a level five in both her manifestations, while Flit is one of our few level sevens. Before we start, I want to know who you think would win in a fight between these two," Rostan asks.

"The emperor." I don't hesitate. Having been on the wrong side of one of these fights, I already know the outcome. "I don't think this is a good idea," I tell them, my heart already racing at the thought of her going against an emperor. I wipe my sweaty palms against my pant legs and try to gulp back my panic.

Rostan frowns. "Can you guys give me a minute?" They nod and wander a few feet away. "Nee, what's wrong?"

"You can't make her fight an emperor, Ros. Pick anyone else." My voice comes out shaky and high pitched and I hate myself for not being able to hide it better.

410

"I didn't think. I'm so sorry. We don't have to do a demonstration, I can just tell you," he says, sitting next to me again and rubbing my back.

I look up to find Cas and Flit watching me. Cas steps forward. "I heard about what happened to you. Would it make you feel better if I told you Flit won't be able to lay a hand on me? Even if he puts everything he has into it, which he won't because he would never intentionally hurt someone."

I eye her skeptically but find nothing but belief in what she's saying on her face. "How can you beat an emperor?"

"If you'll let us show you, I can promise this will be nothing like your experience."

I must be crazy, but I believe her. "Okay, show me," I breathe out, praying I don't regret this.

She smiles and beckons Flit over. Rostan stays beside me, continuing to offer comfort.

Between one blink and the next, Flit lunges at Cas, swinging his fist directly at her. She easily sidesteps him, so he stumbles past. The stumble was fake on his part because he kicks his leg out behind him, aiming at her stomach and I grip Rostan's hand tightly in my own, forcing myself to keep watching. His kick misses because she takes a small step backward out of his reach and smiles.

Every move he throws at her, she doesn't even break a sweat avoiding. By the end of their ten-minute battle, he's panting and sweaty and she looks bored. He takes one last swipe at her and this time she puts a little speed into her sidestep to get behind him. She reaches under the back of her shirt and pulls out a wooden dagger, sticking it against the back of his neck in one fluid motion. "I win," she says, then pulls the dagger away and bows.

I jump to my feet and run toward her. "How?" It's the only thing I can manage to get out.

She laughs and slides the dagger back under her shirt. "I combined my magic."

"I don't understand," I say, looking between her and Flit.

"I'm a high priestess and a wheel. Because of this, I figured out how to create a time portal in my own mind that I can look through any time I please. I can only see a few minutes into the future using it, but it's enough to tell me every move he's planning to use against me. I know his plan of attack before he does." She smiles sweetly at Flit, who blows her a kiss. "It's only a matter of creating an opening for myself that could render him dead or unconscious. The only problem with emperors is it's almost impossible to knock them out, hence the dagger to the back of his neck."

"That was probably the most impressive thing I have ever seen in my entire life," I tell her honestly. "This is the kind of stuff you guys are practicing out here?" I turn to Rostan, who nods his confirmation. "So you took the mid-levels from having zero to very little chance of surviving the trials to being powerful enough to actually win the damn thing?"

412

"I wouldn't go that far. I just gave them a fighting chance."

I collapse to the ground next to him and wrap him in the tightest hug I've ever given anyone. Actually, I can't remember a single hug I've initiated in my life. But it's well deserved. Rostan has just become my hero.

The students continued practicing for another hour before Rostan announced it was time to pack up if we didn't want to be noticed getting back to campus. Once we got closer to the school, we had to split up. Falyn and I could still walk together since we live together, but if all four of us are seen together, it would be questioned.

Once Noric and Rostan part way with us, she turns to look at me with a serious expression. I haven't stopped grinning for the last hour, but the look she gives me is enough to wipe it from my face. "What's wrong?" I ask.

"That's not the only thing we needed to tell you, but I wanted you to see the good stuff first."

"What do you mean? Did something happen?"

"Kind of. You know how we were going to go check on my classmates the day you were injured?" I nod, so she continues, "I went by myself when you

413

didn't show up. I didn't know you were hurt at the time and thought you just forgot. Their rooms were empty."

"I'm sorry, Falyn. Were they stripped?"

"That's the thing. I don't think they were."

"Why do you say that? Do you think they just got kicked out?" I frown, confused.

"No, their families haven't heard from them either, so they assumed they were stripped. But Ken, there hasn't been a transport to the mundana villages in over a month."

"How do you know that?"

"My parents are the transport, remember?" she replies. "But that's not all of it. You know the emperor who demonstrated with Cas today?"

"Flit?"

"Yeah, he was one of the students pulled into Galen's office for an interview. Only it's not interviews. Galen is asking questions about connections to rebels. They think there are rebels on campus, and I think the mid-levels who aren't coming back after the interviews are students he suspects of being involved."

"So then what's happening to them?" I ask.

"Flit's father is a warrior stationed at the palace. Flit thinks the students are being taken there, but no one can seem to come up with any explanation as to why."

If Flit knows, then surely Drayzen would know the same thing. After all his mom is the king's right hand. Has he been lying to me?

CHAPTER TWENTY-SEVEN

There's no way Drayzen didn't know about the students being shipped off to the palace. His mom is way too close to the king and I know they talk regularly. He once told me she talks about her duties pretty often as a way to prepare him for when he takes over. My only question is, why would he keep it from me? Unless this whole time he really has been keeping an eye on me for Galen. But even then I can't figure out what purpose it serves. As far as everyone is concerned, I'm a nobody. Or at least I should be.

I took sleep shrooms to prevent Drayzen from entering my dreams. Not that he's been doing that lately, but I didn't want to take any chances. I'm not sure I want to speak to him until I know for sure what game he's playing. So when I wake up, I feel well rested and even a little excited about the day. I can't wait to go back to the lake and watch again. I only wish I could participate, but I'm not a hundred percent when it comes to energy and I don't want to risk accidentally manifesting the wrong magic in front of so many people.

"What time is everyone meeting today?" I ask Falyn as soon as she emerges from her own room, looking not even remotely rested.

"Honestly, we haven't really set times or days. People just show up all throughout the day when they have time, so there's been a constant stream of students."

"Wait, so there's more people than what I saw yesterday?"

"Oh yeah, there's at least double that, if not more. Rostan tried to keep it small so we wouldn't get caught, but more people show up every day. It's been less than a full week and we went from a group of ten students to this."

"That's amazing," I say, but she's not paying attention to me anymore. She's only got eyes for her crystal and whatever message she's typing out with a worried frown on her face. "What's wrong?"

"I haven't heard from Noric." She sets her crystal down and begins heating the water for her morning tea.

"It's still really early. He's probably sleeping."

"No, I mean he never called me last night when he got back to his dorm and I haven't heard from him since the lake yesterday."

"Is that unusual?" I ask.

"He calls me every night before we go to bed, so yes, it's unusual."

"I'm sure he just forgot, and we'll see him at the lake," I offer, and she nods.

By the time we make it to the lake, Falyn's worry has her practically buzzing with energy. There's about ten students already there, including Rostan, but none of them are Noric. Falyn doesn't waste any time running up to him.

"Hey, have you seen Noric since last night?" she questions without so much as a hello to him.

"No, why?" Rostan frowns.

"He's not answering his phone, and he never called me last night." Falyn pulls her crystal out to tap out another message, presumably to Noric.

418

Rostan checks his and shakes his head. "He hasn't messaged me either."

I can see the panic rising in Falyn's eyes and I grab her crystal from her to call Noric instead of messaging. The line doesn't even ring, which means it's not on.

"Ken, we need to go check on him."

"Okay, just take a breath. We'll go right now. I'm sure he's just sleeping, Falyn." I hand the crystal back and cast only the briefest longing look at the battling students.

"I'll come too," Rostan offers, but I shake my head.

"No, you stay here in case he shows up. Besides, this is your show. You should be here to support everyone."

He nods but looks almost as worried as Falyn, who has already started walking back the way we came. I jog to catch up with her.

"I'm sure everything is fine, Falyn."

"I have a really bad feeling about this," she says in almost a whisper. I don't dare agree with her out loud. Even if my own gut is churning as we speak.

Falyn knocks loudly on his door. He's in the guy's worldly dorm so it's just across the path from ours. Shuffling sounds from inside and she lets out a breath. "Thank the three," she says and waits impatiently for him to answer.

It's not Noric who answers, though. It's his roommate.

"Hey, Falyn, Noric isn't here. I think he must have left early because I haven't seen him since yesterday."

"He came home last night, though?" she asks hopefully.

"I'm assuming he did, but I didn't hear him come in, why?" His brows tug down in a frown when he realizes where this is going.

"Do you mind if we come in? He borrowed a book from me and I really need it back," I jump in and ask. If Noric really is missing, the last thing we need is for everyone to find out.

"I guess. I don't think he would mind." The guy shrugs and opens the door wider for us to enter.

The layout of their dorm is identical to ours. When you enter, you're immediately in a living area and behind it is the kitchen and dining area. On either side of the living area, there are doors that lead into the bedrooms. Noric's room, like mine, is on the left.

His bed is neatly made and there's no evidence that he slept in it last night. Falyn's face falls as soon as she gets it. I look around hoping to find some indication of where he could be, but his room is very sparse. The only thing that looks out of place is a half made bracelet and several polished stones sitting on his desk.

Falyn and I see it at the same time.

"Do you think that's—" She pauses to make sure Noric's roommate isn't listening in.

"That's exactly what I think it is," I say, not letting her finish her thought.

She reaches over to pick up one of the larger stones and hands it to me. After holding it for a few seconds, I search inward for any spark it might have created but find nothing. I shake my head. He hasn't figured out how to do it yet.

Falyn takes another look around, but since neither one of us have training as detectives, we have no idea what kind of clues we should be looking for. She sighs and tries to give me a shaky smile, but the quivering in her lips makes it almost impossible.

We're just about to leave his room when I remember my excuse for being here and I swipe a book from the shelf above his desk.

"Did you get it?" his roommate asks and I wave my book and nod my head to show I did. "Do you guys want me to tell him anything when he gets back?"

"That's okay, Kase," Flynn says as we walk to the door. "We'll just send him a message on his crystal. Thanks."

Falyn is a mess by the time we make it back to our room. She's listed about ten different scenarios and all of them ending with her never seeing Noric again. I have a feeling I know what happened to him, but I don't want to say anything out loud until I know for sure. No doubt Falyn is already thinking it and I'm not going to validate her worry.

"I'm gonna go talk to Drayzen and see if he knows anything," I tell her after watching her send yet another message to Noric. She stands, but I wave at her. "No, you need to stay here in case he comes looking for you. For all we know, he just has a broken crystal and a really busy morning. It shouldn't take long." She sits back down on the couch and stares at her crystal.

I don't know what else to say, so I pat her shoulder before I leave.

It doesn't take me long to get a hold of Drayzen. He responds to my crystal message immediately and I ask him to meet me at the boulder. He's already there by the time I arrive.

"Hey." He reaches out to grab my shoulders and check me out. "How are you feeling? Are you supposed to be up?" As he bombards me with questions, he gently grabs my jaw to turn my head and look at the side of my face.

"I'm fine." I shrug his hands off and take a step back. I need to be able to think, and when he's that close, things get all jumbled in my brain.

He frowns when I pull away. "What's wrong?"

"If I ask you something, can I trust you to answer me honestly?" I ask.

"Of course. What's going on?"

"How long have you known what's been happening with the missing students?" He flinches, and my stomach turns in disappointment. I really wanted to be wrong about thinking he knows. "I was hoping when I asked you that question, you would have no idea what I was talking about."

He sighs. "Kennedy—"

"No, don't Kennedy me. I feel like it's a simple enough question. I'm not looking for your reasons or anything else. I just want to know how long."

"I was gonna tell you, but then you got hurt and I didn't see you at all yesterday."

"The day I got hurt when you offered to check the lower-level dorms, did you already know?" He flinches again. "Never mind. Don't answer that."

He lifts his hand toward me, but I take another step back. I'm not sure how to process all the emotions going through me right now, but I came here for a reason. I can dissect later. "One of my friends is missing. Can you find out if he's been shipped out?" He hesitates, and I hold my breath for his answer.

"I'll ask around, but I really don't know how far I'll get, so I'm not making any promises."

423

The little voice in my head urges me to tell him I wouldn't trust his promise anyway, but I should probably hold my tongue on that for now. "Thank you." I don't give him the opportunity to say anything else. I need to get back to Falyn before she tears the school apart looking for Noric and gets herself shipped out.

We spend the rest of the day in our dorm pacing. Rostan checks in multiple times but nobody has heard from Noric and the longer he's gone, the more on edge Falyn is. It's getting increasingly harder to convince her and myself that he'll be back.

"Listen, I know what we've heard about the interviews and everything, but Noric isn't a rebel, so even if he was pulled in, there would be no reason for him to be shipped out." I say for what feels like the twentieth time today.

My crystal dings, saving me from having to see the disbelief on her face. I snatch it up and swipe to my messages and smile when I see what Drayzen sent me. I hold it up for Falyn to read.

Noric wasn't shipped off, but he was pulled in for questioning.

No sooner had she read it when a knock sounds at our door and Falyn half runs to fling it open.

Noric is standing there looking exhausted and maybe a little pale, but normal. Falyn jumps into his arms and wraps her legs around his waist before crushing her mouth to his in one of the most R rated kisses I've ever seen. He supports her tiny frame with ease and returns the kiss until I have to clear my throat loudly to get them to pull away from each other.

"If all I had to do to finally get to kiss you was get pulled in for questioning by the dean, I would have done that a lot sooner," he tells her as he places her back on her feet. It earns him a fist to his stomach.

"That's not even a little bit funny," she tells him before dragging him into our dorm so she can close the door. "You were gone a really long time, and we thought you had been shipped off." Falyn's lip trembles.

"I know, I'm sorry," he tells her and wraps his arm around her shoulder. "I actually went off campus after I left you guys last night. I found someone willing to open a portal for me so I could find that Bren guy you said made your bracelet."

I sit down on the couch and slide over to make room for them.

"And?" I ask. If he figured out how to make it, then half of my problems are solved. He smiles.

"And yes. I know how to use stones for magic storage now."

"That doesn't explain the other twelve hours you were missing." Falyn glares at him.

"Bren made me stay overnight. He said it was too dangerous to transport back on campus until today, and since he's a high priestess, I chose to take his word." Then he leans forward a little and clasps his hands together. "But Kendee, we really need to talk."

"About what?" I don't like the lines on his forehead and nothing good ever started with those words.

"I was halfway back to my room when they found me and said I had to report to the dean's office. I thought it was because I got caught sneaking off campus and was being questioned about rebels like everyone else. But Galen didn't ask me a single question about me leaving or my possible connection to the rebels."

"Then what did he ask?" I know without a doubt I'm not going to like his answer.

"It was all about you. Everything he asked was about you." My heart falls into my stomach.

"Like what?" I can actually feel the blood draining from my face.

"He wanted to know about your magic and if I had seen anything weird. He asked if you've ever talked about your time on Earth and whether you knew anything about your family."

My mouth goes dry. Does Galen know about my magic?

"Kendee, I really think you should reach out. No more excuses. Bren told me to tell you he'd be waiting for you to contact him."

426

That asshole. I bet he knew everything that happened today before it happened and, of course, he wouldn't give me a heads up. The least he could have done was warn me. If he thinks this is going to make me want to contact him, he's wrong. I can't trust him. I don't think I can trust anyone at this point.

"Ken, I don't think you have a choice anymore. We need to know how all this ties together and what it has to do with you. Bren seems to be the only one with answers, and that's what we need. You can't keep going through this blind," Falyn chimes in.

I sigh heavily because they're right. I pick up my crystal and type out a message, thankful that he stopped wiping my phone after every message.

I need answers and you seem to be the only one who can give them to me. But I have stipulations.

I stare at the screen and wait for his response to come through. Falyn scoots closer to me so she has a view of my screen as well.

What are your stipulations?

I look at Falyn because I actually hadn't thought of what I was going to say other than demanding the truth. She takes my crystal and types out a message.

I want the full truth about everything. Not half answered questions. Only after I know everything will I consider hearing you out on anything else. If you leave anything out, I will walk away and never look back.

I nod and she sends the message.

427

"I have a feeling they're willing to do just about anything to get you on their side," Falyn explains. "They'll agree to this if they want you as bad as I think they do."

The minutes tick by slowly, but finally a response comes through.

Meet in two hours at the lake where students have been practicing.

Both Falyn and I jerk our heads up to look at Noric when the message comes in.

"What is it?" he asks.

I show him and he frowns. "Add that to your list of questions. How do they know what we've been doing?"

I nod and make a mental note to question how much Bren can actually see or if he has spies inside the school.

"We should go get something to eat before we head to the lake," Falyn says and Noric jumps up so fast he almost tips the couch back.

"I'm starving," he groans and both Falyn and I roll our eyes because when is he not?

We're almost out the door when my crystal chirps again.

Don't bring your friends. Maintaining our privacy is imperative.

"Absolutely not," Falyn growls when I show her the message.

"He said our not my," I point out. "I bet it's because someone I'm meeting is from the school. I don't think I'm in any danger and you're right, I need to know. I'll be careful."

She doesn't look convinced, but I'm determined now.

I don't think I've ever eaten so fast in my life. I arrive before whoever I'm meeting does, which was my intention when I inhaled my food. As much as I love Noric and Falyn, watching them make googly eyes at each other isn't conducive to the frame of mind I need to be in for this meeting. I want to make sure I have all my questions ready to go when they show up.

Even though I'm early, it isn't long after I arrive that I hear the sound of footsteps approaching. I turn around expecting to see Bren, but it's Rostan who greets me.

"What are you doing here?" I ask, looking around to make sure there's no one else coming. I need to get rid of him quickly or they're going to think I brought him against their wishes. "You're not holding a session now, are you?" That would be the worst possible thing to happen.

"No. No session tonight," he responds and bends down to pick up a rock. He skips it across the calm waters before picking up another.

"Rostan, I don't want you to take this the wrong way and I would love to hang out, but I'm kind of meeting someone here and I need to be alone when that happens." I opt for as close to the truth as I can get without spilling my guts. Chances are he'll think I'm meeting Drayzen and leave right away to give us privacy.

"I can't leave yet, Nee." He gives me a sad smile,

"Why not?" I ask, confused.

"Because he's with us." Another voice sounds out from behind me, and I turn to find Bren and Aarond approaching.

CHAPTER TWENTY-EIGHT

This is a joke, right?" I stare at Rostan in absolute disbelief.

"I'm really sorry, Kennedy. I couldn't tell you until we knew you wouldn't turn anyone in. I never actually thought you would, but I take my orders from Bren." He nods at the older man standing beside Aarond. I nod my at Bren but glare at Aarond. Of course he would be a rebel. I still haven't gotten over the fact that he's the one who brought me into this mess.

"Aarond, I wish I could say it's good to see you, but we both know that would be a lie so in the interest of being truthful tonight I'll just say go away."

Aarond smirks at me. "Unfortunately, if you want your answers, I'm gonna have to stay."

"And why's that?" I cross my arms over my chest.

"Because I'm the hanged man who dropped you off on Earth twenty-two years ago."

I'm completely speechless after he drops that bomb on me. For a few seconds anyway. Mostly because I'm contemplating whether I should act on the urge to punch him. He's known this entire time what my goal was when I got her and not once did he think to mention that little tidbit to me.

The short bark of laughter that flies from my mouth has nothing to do with finding humor in the situation. "So all this time, you've known exactly who I am and who my parents are?"

I take a step forward and it's not until Rostan puts a hand on my shoulder that I realize my hands are clenched and I'm dangerously close to acting on my urge. I whirl on Rostan and shrug his hand off my shoulder. "No, you don't get to calm me down. I thought we were friends and this whole time you had information that could have helped me."

His face pales. "No, I swear I had no idea who you were until a few weeks ago when Bren told me.

432

And I've been asking him almost daily when I could say something. I hated keeping you in the dark."

"He speaks the truth, Kennedy. He has been asking incessantly to talk to you, but I swore him to secrecy until the time was right," Bren says, bringing my attention back to him.

"What does that even mean? Who gets to decide the right time? You? Because the right time would have been months ago when I got here. So why now? What's changed?"

"Everything has changed, Kennedy. It's no longer safe for you here. It's no longer safe for most mages but you especially."

"Why isn't it safe?"

"Because the king is closer than ever in his search for ultimate power and by now your dean and his son have reported everything they've learned about you to him."

"There's no way they've learned much of anything. Neither one of them have any idea about my magic." I look at Rostan feeling a little guilty over my own hypocrisy. "The only thing either of them know is that I'm from Earth and I'm a level ten in two categories."

"That's the problem," Aarond butts in. "We didn't think you would go around telling the entire school that you're from Earth. We also didn't have a choice about enrolling you because as soon as you manifested magic your name went on a master list of mages."

433

"How is this my fault?" I question him with every ounce of scorn I'm feeling. "If you had just told me the truth from the beginning or at least told me I couldn't tell anyone then this wouldn't even be a problem right now. What I don't understand is why the king would be so interested in a mage who was raised on Earth and why that puts me in danger."

Aarond is about to reply when Bren holds his hand up and stops him. "I can see this is going to get out of hand very quickly so let me start from the beginning." He waits for my nod of acknowledgment before he continues, "When Aarond was just a couple years older than you are now, he met a star woman who tasked him with a dangerous but necessary job. You see, King Gefred has spent every moment of his life since taking the crown searching for a way to keep it. Forever. He believes that if he can imbue himself with the power of the gods, it will not only grant him immortality but make him the strongest mage to walk Arcanum. In his search for ultimate power, he has done many despicable things, but the worst is perhaps the two-year string of kidnappings about twenty-four years ago."

I don't think I'm going to like anything they have to tell me but I'm hanging on with rapt attention. "And what do the kidnappings have to do with his search for power?" I ask, not seeing the connection.

"Just listen to what he's saying and you'll find out soon enough," Aarond cuts in and I shoot him a glare but stop talking.

434

Bren picks up where he left off. "The rebels weren't really an active group when the king began blaming them for the kidnappings. Not in the organized sense of the word anyway. But he needed someone to blame that would turn suspicion away from him and so he, in effect, created us. He gave us a reason to band together and fight against him." He pauses to make sure I'm still paying attention.

"He would send his most trusted warriors into villages in the middle of the night to find and take women of child bearing age away from their lives and their homes. My wife was one of these women. I didn't know it was him of course, but I suspected. It wasn't until many years later that I met Aarond and my suspicions were confirmed. The king was performing experiments on these women."

My stomach rolls with nausea when I realize where this is going.

"He was trying to create a child who could hold more than three categories. If he could figure out how to do it at conception then it could possibly lead to figuring out how to do it to himself. And if he holds every category of magic, then he would be more god than mage. What they don't teach you here is that the strength of your power is directly related to how strong the essence of the gods is inside you."

This is too much. I can't organize the jumble of thoughts in my mind right now because what he's implying can't be right.

435

"That's where Aarond came in. The star woman he met was the palace healer. She couldn't tell anyone what was happening because the king held her daughter and threatened to kill her should she speak. The king was breeding the women he kidnapped. Forcing them to carry children, sometimes his, sometimes other mages, sometimes a combination of both."

I gulp and interrupt him. "Breeding? The king was forcing himself on these women to impregnate them?"

"Not physically no, but it makes no difference how it was done. By magic or by hand, it's the same thing and each time a child was born from his acts, the result was a mundana. All but two. And each time a mundana child was born, he commanded the healer Anzlee to dispose of them. But being who she is, Anzlee could not bear to cause death, especially not in someone so young and innocent. So she handed them off to Aarond, who transported each child to Earth where they might have a chance at a good life."

He gives me a minute to wrap my brain around what he's telling me before he continues.

"You were different. They couldn't sense your magic when you were born, so it was assumed you were also mundana. Your brother on the other hand, while not a success in the way the king wanted, was at least born a strong mage with two categories. The king kept him instead of ordering his death."

"My brother," I echo his words. Then the comprehension sets and I feel like I can't breathe.

"Breathe, Nee." Rostan grips my shoulder and turns me toward him so I have to look into his eyes. "You're okay. Take a breath."

I do what I'm told and suck in a heaving breath. "The king is my father and Michan is my brother?" I'm hyperventilating now. "And the woman he forced to bear me? What happened to her?"

Bren looks at me with years of sadness shining in his eyes. "My wife. She never came home. Nor did any of the other women."

"I'm sorry." I don't know what else to say. I am sorry. Both for his loss and my own.

He shakes his head and gives me a small smile. "I am too. But we don't have a lot of time before you two have to be back in your dorms so we need to keep going if you want the whole truth."

I don't know if I want any more truth tonight if I'm being honest. But I nod my head anyway.

"Besides the fact that I was born the way I was, what does any of this have to do with me?" I ask and Aarond scoffs at me like I should already know the answer.

"Because you have what the king wants," Bren replies, sending goosebumps down my arms. "And by now he knows who you are and will want to know why you showed zero magic at birth but now hold two ten categories."

"Simply put, he'll either see you as a danger to himself or a way of achieving what he wants, and neither of those scenarios end with you living happily ever after," Aarond adds. I'm sure just to see me squirm. It worked.

"So what do I do?" I ask but it all seems pretty hopeless at this point.

"You come with us. We'll figure out a way to hide you until we can figure out the role you play in the prophec—"

I interrupt Bren before he can finish. "The role I play? I have nothing to do with this prophecy and I definitely don't want anything to do with the rebels. Especially not after your stunt with the council members that got this ball rolling."

"That wasn't us," Rostan tells me. "Another lie created by the king to sow fear and distrust. He killed his own council members. Specifically the two who opposed him."

"Fine, say I believe you. I am not prophecy material. You're betting on the wrong person. What does the full prophecy say anyway?"

"The high priestess who wrote it down said she saw a magicless future. Too many feel it's their right to the essence of the gods and do nothing to remain worthy of such gifts. Magic fades not because of who we make our lives with or the actions we take. Rather, it's our lack of action to better ourselves and our neighbors' lives. Each of the twenty-two were gifted because of great deeds. And over time, that magic has faded to almost nothing because we're not keeping it alive. It goes on to state that although it started with twenty-two, it ends with one. We believe you're the one. The one who ends the fading of magic with a great deed."

I snort. If only my fifth grade teacher could hear this now. She would have thought twice before telling me I'd amount to nothing.

"Yeah, no. I'm not your one. The king is your one. You're trying to read way too far into the prophecy when it's being literal. Magic ends with one. Whatever he's trying to accomplish is going to be the end of magic."

We all stand here looking at each other for a few seconds then Aarond laughs. "Either way, you're still the one, Kennedy," he says through his mirth.

"How do you figure that?" I ask, still glaring at him. I'm not sure I have any other facial expressions when it comes to Aarond.

"Because if he succeeds, you're the only one strong enough to stop him. Even if he doesn't succeed, you may still be the only one strong enough to stop him."

Rostan and I had to run the whole way back to avoid getting caught out after curfew. Falyn is pacing back and forth in the living area when I get back and we stay up until the early hours of the morning discussing everything I found out.

I refused to go with them. I don't want to leave my friends behind to bear the weight of what looks like a pretty bleak future. Bren told me I would be fine at least up to the trials as long as I'm careful but after that I'm going to have to make a choice, and if I want to stay alive then my choice will have to be leaving. By the time we finally go to bed I don't feel any better about anything and the one person I want to talk it through with I can no longer trust.

I'm not sure who I can trust anymore.

"Did Noric make it back okay?" Drayzen lowers himself to the ground next to me.

I forgot to take the sleep shrooms before passing out and it left my mind wide open for him.

"Yeah," I reply stiffly but refuse to look at him.

"Good."

Neither one of us says anything for a while. The moon makes the lake look almost silver in color and I focus on that trying to ignore the pounding of my heart at his nearness.

"Listen, Kennedy. I know I messed up by not telling you the truth. I don't have an excuse other than the fact that I was afraid of what you would do with the information."

440

I let myself look at him. "What does that mean? I'm not a child who needs to be minded. I'm perfectly capable of making rational choices."

"I'm not saying you're a child. But you're wrong. You don't make rational choices when it comes to helping other people."

"What is it you think I was going to do? Run off to the palace and try to rescue everyone? Come on, Drayzen. I'm not that stupid."

"I don't think you're stupid," he growls in frustration. "But I was right. You almost got yourself killed by refusing to use your magic on people."

"You can't use that as an excuse. You withheld the information before that even happened. Unless you're a high priestess now too?" I ask sarcastically.

"No, but I do know you. I know exactly the kind of person you are even if you try to hide it under all the sarcasm."

"And what kind of person am I?" I scoff.

"The kind who risks her own life for her morals and sense of right and wrong."

"That's where you're wrong. I didn't know I was risking my life. Because this whole time I thought I was playing one game and it turns out everyone around me is playing a completely different one. But now I know."

He frowns at me. "Know what?"

"Never mind. My point is that I thought we were friends but if it was so easy for you to keep something that big from me I'm not so sure anymore."

441

He flinches. "It wasn't easy. I wanted to tell you—"

"I am so tired of hearing people tell me that. Is just a little bit of honesty too much to ask?"

"I could say the same thing to you," he returns and my heart jumps in my throat at the implication that he might know what I'm hiding.

"What do you mean?" I choke out around the knot that has seemed to form in my throat.

He opens his mouth then closes it and I wait in dread to hear him say it. "Nothing, it's not important." But the disappointment in his eyes tells me otherwise. "For the record, you are so much more than a friend to me," he adds softly.

I swallow the lump in my throat and it turns into a million butterflies taking flight in my stomach. Now he says it, when nothing can happen between us. When the last thing I can allow myself to do is care for yet another person. Whoever said it's better to have love and lost is a liar. So I take a deep breath and do what I have to do, no matter how much my heart—my whole body—is screaming for me not to.

"I'm sorry, Drayzen. This isn't going to work." Then with everything I have, I wrench myself awake and out of the dream he created for us.

Time seems to speed up. Between the practice sessions with Rostan's group of students and doing everything in my power to avoid Drayzen, weeks go by. It only took him a month to get the message I was sending. I have to keep reminding myself I may not survive the year and it's better this way. So, every night I use the sleep shrooms to keep him out of my head and I don't go to our sparring sessions anymore, opting to spar against the group who practice at the lake.

I'm improving every day. I've learned that I have to be touching something in order to manifest my high priestess magic but it extends to anything I grow. So when I'm fighting someone, as long as any part of them is touching something I've created, I can do something pretty similar to what Cas did with hers and see a few seconds into the future. No one has been able to touch me since. It's looking more and more like the mid-level students are going to dominate the trials. The high-levels aren't going to know what hit them.

"You're not paying attention!" Falyn yells at me and stomps her foot.

"I am too," I reply automatically.

"If you were paying attention I wouldn't have been able to dress you in a grass skirt and flower bra." She gestures to my body and I look down. Sure enough, I'm wearing plants over my clothes like I'm about to attend a luau.

When I look back at her she's struggling to hold in her laughter. "Fine," I grumble. "I wasn't paying attention. But in my defense, we do this so

443

much lately I can kick your ass with my eyes closed so I was just giving you a fighting chance."

"Ha ha," she replies sarcastically. "Let's go again. We don't have much time before we have to head back."

I spread my legs and get into my fighting stance, but when I see Drayzen over her shoulder I almost keel over.

"So this is where you've been hiding?" he asks, looking around.

"What are you doing here? Are you following me?" I demand.

"It was the only way I could figure out what you've been doing," he replies, crossing his arms over his chest.

"And why exactly would you need to know that? This is none of your business." I put my hands on my hips. We're going to have to find a new spot now. I look over at Rostan who's watching me with a question in his eyes. I shake my head to let him know I don't need help and he sends everyone home.

"You shouldn't be participating in this. You have battle applications and our sessions for combat tutoring. This isn't safe."

"You don't even know what this is, so how would you know if it's not safe?" I cross my own arms over my chest.

"I know that if everyone leaves as soon as I get here and you have to do it in a remote area then it's probably not something you should be doing."

"Again I ask you why you're here?"

"I've been trying to talk to you for weeks now but you won't even look at me"

"Maybe it's because I don't want to talk to you," I tell him.

"I know hiding that from you was wrong but don't you think you've punished me enough?" he asks and I almost cave.

"I'm not punishing you, Drayzen. This isn't even about you, really. I just have a lot going on right now and I can't handle it all."

"If it's not about me then why do I seem to be getting the brunt of it?" he challenges and steps closer. I force myself to focus on his face and not the way he smells.

"The brunt of what exactly? Because I quit our sessions? I'm trying to do something good here and I'm learning while I'm at it."

"What good are you doing here besides risking getting caught and shipped out? Or is that what you want? Because from where I'm standing everything you do seems to lead down that road."

"I'm just one person. Did you see how many people were here when you came? Every single one of them is at risk of getting shipped out. More so than I am because they don't have the magic to back themselves up. What makes me more important than them?" He doesn't seem to have an answer for me so I continue, "This isn't about me and it's not about you. You're so focused on me passing the trials that you've

445

forgotten there are hundreds of other students in our school who are going through the same thing. Why are you so bent on helping me and not them?"

"Because you're important," he says, and I'm so tired of hearing that. I walk past him intent on heading back to my dorm but his next words stop me in my tracks. "You more than anyone need to make it through trials."

I whirl on him. "What does that mean, Drayzen? Why me more than them?" I march forward so our faces are only inches apart and I'm staring directly into his gray eyes. I half expect him to tell me he's either a member of the rebels, or working for Galen, maybe even the king but at least it'll finally be out in the open.

"Because I need you to get through it," he all but whispers. His eyes drift down until they land on my lips. He reaches up to grip my shoulders with both hands. I don't know if it's to keep me from walking away again or if he's as desperate for contact as I am.

"You need me to? Why? What benefit could my passing possibly have for you?" I breathe out, not daring to hope he means exactly what I think he does.

One of his hands slides upward along my shoulder until it reaches the back of my neck and he uses it to pull me in closer. "Because I need you," he says just before he closes the remaining distance between our mouths and swallows any response I might have.

446

His lips are firm and soft at the same time. Demanding and giving all at once. I part my lips without thinking about it and wrap my arms around his neck to pull myself closer until there isn't a centimeter of space between our bodies.

Nothing could have prepared me for the feeling of his mouth against mine. It's exciting and new but makes me feel like I'm right where I belonged this whole time. His warm tongue brushes against my own and I wonder how I went this long without kissing him. He groans and slides his hand down my back to grip my hips and pull me impossibly closer. It takes entirely too long for me to remember that my chances of surviving past this year are next to none if what Bren told me is true. Starting anything with him would be a mistake.

Even if I do make it, I'll have to leave. Letting this happen with Drayzen will only make leaving that much harder and I can't do it. As much as I want this, I'm only setting myself up to be hurt and I'm tired of hurting. I'm tired of not having control of the things that happen in my life.

The realization over falling and losing Drayzen sends my mind into a frenzied panic. I press my hands against his chest to put some space between us. One second, we're wrapped in each other's arms and the next he's flying backward and landing on the pebbled shore ten feet away. I lift my hand to my swollen mouth in terror over the realization of what I just did.

Somehow I activated the emperor spark. "Drayzen . . ." I trail off because I don't know how to explain to him what just happened.

Swallowing back my shock and the sharp ache of longing, I turn and run.

CHAPTER TWENTY-NINE

We need to test this out before we rely on it," Noric says, handing me a stone bracelet similar to the one Bren gave me.

I close my fist around it and am immediately assaulted by the smell of wet earth and lemongrass. "I can already tell you it works," I tell him, feeling my two most used sparks come to life inside me. To demonstrate, I touch my finger to the soil of one of

Falyn's many plants and grow another one right beside it.

"She's not going to be happy about that. You know she doesn't like overcrowding her babies." Noric grins.

I shrug and put my finger to my lips, but not before Falyn walks out of her room to witness it.

"Don't encourage him to keep secrets from me!" she scolds me. "Also, looks like you're gonna spend your afternoon repotting."

"Sorry, no can do. We need to save all our energy for the trials tomorrow," I say, suppressing my twitching lips.

"Whatever. Are you guys ready?" She blows out a breath.

"I really hate assemblies," I grumble. "This school's track record really sucks with them."

Noric laughs and grabs Falyn's hand to pull her after him to the door.

"This one hopefully won't hold any surprises. All it's for is to let us know what to expect when the trials start tomorrow. If anything, it'll just be boring," he says.

"I want to know what your definition of boring is." I glare at Noric after we leave the arena.

450

The assembly was anything but boring. In fact, I don't think anyone expected it to go the way it did. Dean Galen was practically giddy when he announced the new rules. With every word he spoke, my stomach dropped further and further until it felt like it was sitting directly on my feet.

The trials will happen in two phases. The first starting tomorrow will allow for groups of four to compete with each other. I knew immediately that it would be me, Falyn, and Noric, but I wasn't sure whether Rostan would want to be a part of our group or if he would opt to be with Ciena's. Knowing him, he'll go to her first, but knowing her, she'll find some way to get out of it.

From Galen's explanation, it sounds like a deadly version of capture the flag. Only it's not flags, it's medallions with the king's crest stamped on them. They're hidden in the arena somewhere and it'll be up to us to find them. There will be fewer medallions than groups, so we'll have to battle against each to get them. You can hold as many medallions as you can find and although any team that makes it to the end holding a medallion, passes to the next phase, the students on the team with the most medallions will be given something extra to help them through the second phase of the trial which will occur four days later.

We are allowed to use and do anything to secure a medallion for our team, as healers will be on standby to help should anyone get injured enough to need it. That's the most concerning part of the whole announcement. I've been given that same line before and it was a lie. Knowing I'll be going against the very students I've spent so much time practicing with leaves a bitter taste in my mouth.

The second phase is everyone for themselves. The goal will be to get from one end of the course to another before the timer counts down two hours. He didn't say how long the course is or what obstacles besides each other will stand in our way, so it doesn't sound promising.

The walk back to our room is a quiet one filled with tension as we all contemplate what tomorrow will hold for us, but when I see Rostan standing outside the door to our building some of the tension eases away.

"You joining the team?" I ask.

"Looks like it," he responds with a half-hearted smile.

"She'll be fine," I whisper as I walk past him to enter the building.

We spend the rest of the afternoon discussing strategy. Thanks to Rostan's practice sessions, we already know how to work as a team, and I feel confident we'll get through tomorrow. But my confidence doesn't curb the twisted gut feeling I have.

"Whatever happens, we stick together," I say vehemently. I don't know why I feel the need to say it, but it feels too important to ignore.

The three of them eye me for a few seconds before nodding their consent.

I don't think any of us slept more than a couple of hours. Rostan and Noric never left to go to their own room, and we all camped out on the couch and floor of mine and Falyn's living space. The time to get up and get ready came way too fast for my liking.

All of us decided against eating anything before the trials because, as Falyn so eloquently stated, "vomiting on our opponents won't do anything but make them mad." The way my stomach is feeling, vomiting isn't completely outside the realm of possibility.

When it's time, we join the hundreds of other students making their way to the arena, which is no longer completely enclosed. The back wall holds two pocket doors. Something I've never noticed before today, but it stands open to reveal the forest behind the arena.

There isn't an opening ceremony or fanfare of any kind to begin the trial. One second, we're all gathering inside the arena, and the next Galen's voice booms out that the trials have begun.

Everyone rushes forward, creating a bottleneck at the back of the arena. Since we were some of the last to arrive, we have to wait longer to begin our search for a medallion. I lean in so my three partners

453

can hear me. "Come on, let's go around." I gesture to the door we came in and the four of us run for it.

As soon as we're outside, we head for the forest behind the arena, but instead of going the same direction as everyone else, we skirt the edge and cut in further down. Hopefully far enough down that we can avoid having to fight anyone right away.

Our plan works for the most part. Even though we can hear students moving through the trees around us, we can't see anyone.

"Does anyone know what the medallions look like or how big they are?" I ask, looking around us but not seeing anything. Everyone shakes their heads and I sigh. "I guess that would be too easy, right?"

We venture further into the trees, scanning high and low for anything that doesn't look like it belongs. It's twenty minutes before we hear the first scream. I flinch and send a panicked look over to Falyn. She reaches over and squeezes my hand. "They have healers, remember?" That somehow doesn't make me feel any better about it.

Another twenty minutes goes by and I'm kicking up large stones and searching crevices in every tree trunk I pass when Noric yells out. "Move!"

I don't know who he's talking to or what's going on, but I don't hesitate. Just as I push away from the tree, a small fireball hits it, right where my head was. I whirl around to find another group of four creating a barrier between me and my friends.

The girl who threw the fireball already has another sitting in her palm, ready to throw. I react without thinking and dive for the ground just as she sends it my way. I know from experience my magic isn't super effective against someone wielding fire, but I send it out anyway. I create a wall of dense shrubs between me and them to give myself a little time to get away. On the other side, I hear a few grunts before the sound of bodies hitting the ground. I panic and rush around to make sure everyone is okay, only to find Rostan with both his palms pressed against the soil and his eyes glowing white while Noric and Falyn watch.

"People always forget lightning strikes from below," he says grinning, and claps his hands together to get rid of the clinging dirt. I eye the four students wearily, but Rostan pats my shoulder. "Don't worry, it wasn't nearly strong enough to seriously injure them. They'll probably wake up pretty quick, so we should get out of here.

Before we get too far, I suddenly remember the whole point of today. "Wait!" I stop moving. "We didn't check them for a medallion." I turn back and run as fast as I can. I almost feel guilty when I find a small gold coin attached to twine around the magician girl's neck. But then I remember she tried to kill me with that fireball and I yank it from around her neck hard enough to snap the twine.

When I make it back to them, I hold it up with a triumphant grin, but Falyn isn't happy.

455

"You're the one who made us promise to stick together and then you just run off like that?" she yells at me.

My smile fades. "You're right, I'm sorry. Next time I'll wait for you guys," I reply, feeling thoroughly chastised.

I'm wrapping the twine around my own neck to tie it there when the ground underneath us rumbles and splits open right under my feet. I topple over and, in the process of trying to catch myself, wind up flinging the medallion in the air. It lands just a few feet away from me, but it's far enough away that I can't reach it with my outstretched arm.

A pair of unfamiliar shoes race past me, and someone stoops to scoop the medallion up before running back the way they came. Luckily, both Falyn and I are quick draws and vines and roots that pop around the person's feet send them sprawling to the ground much in the same manner I went.

Noric's astral projected self pops into existence right in front of the guy and lunges to steal the medallion back from him. I'm just about to cheer when the tree next to me cracks and falls sideways with me and Falyn right in its path. I shove her aside and do my best to dive out of the way, but a branch hits my shoulder, sending searing pain through me. I'm no stranger to broken bones thanks to battle applications class, so I'm positive that's exactly what I'm dealing with.

I clench my teeth against the pain and get up, clutching my arm to my side. All three of my partners rush to my side to check on me, but only Falyn makes it, because Noric and Rostan are waylaid by the partners of the guy who initially stole our medallion.

One is obviously the tower who knocked the tree on me and Falyn and when the other two grow larger then shrink back down to their normal size, I yell as loud as I can at Noric and Rostan, "Emperors!"

They both dance out of arm's reach to avoid being crushed by the two emperors, just as Falyn and I pull thick roots from the ground to wrap around their ankles. I know it won't hold them forever, but it might give us enough time to get away.

We run. I clutch my arm to my chest in hopes of limiting the jostling but the pain is almost unbearable and I fight back the urge to scream. There's enough screaming happening all around us to last me a lifetime.

Once it feels like we're far enough away, I stop and lean against a tree to catch my breath. "How much farther do you guys think it is to turn the medallion in?" I pant.

Falyn is busy creating a sling for my arm and doesn't answer, while the guys just look at each other blankly. Right. We have no idea. Only that it's in a clearing somewhere on the other side of the forest from where the arena is.

"Here, put this on." Falyn slides the makeshift sling over my head and shoulder and carefully puts my

457

arm in it. I do my best not to flinch, but I don't think I'm being very convincing.

"Alright, we need to move again if we have any hope of making it to the end," I say and pull away from my tree reluctantly.

Noric shoves the medallion in his pocket so it's not visible and we set out at a fast pace. The smell of multiple kinds of magic is overwhelming to my magical senses and I wrinkle my nose against it. "There's a lot of people near here," I warn everyone.

"I don't see anyone," Falyn says, looking around.

"I can smell their magic. It's really strong. We need to keep moving, but stay alert," I tell them, thankful to have friends who trust me enough to take me seriously.

The forest around us has gone quiet and I know that's not a good sign. The only sound is our heavy breathing and the leaves being crushed under our feet.

"Maybe I should astral project and run ahead?" Noric asks.

"Can you be hurt in your astral form?" I ask.

He hesitates to answer. "Yes, but if I see anything, I can fall back in the blink of an eye so I don't think anyone would have time to hurt me." I don't like the idea, but I have to admit being able to see what's ahead of us is really tempting.

"Okay, but since you're still not a hundred percent at controlling both bodies at the same time, let

458

me and Falyn try to erect some protection before you go." I reach for my spark but find nothing, so I hold my hand out for Falyn. She understands exactly what I'm asking and laces her fingers through mine long enough to top me off, then we grow several bushes around us. Not enough to completely enclose ourselves because we want it to provide a hiding place, but still look naturally grown. We tuck into them and I nod at Noric. "Okay, if you feel a pinch, come back in a hurry," I tell him. It's not technically separating, so it should be fine, right?

I'm grateful for the momentary reprieve of not having to move my throbbing arm and release a sigh of relief. But it doesn't last long before we hear approaching footsteps. Rostan holds a finger to his mouth and we nod in acknowledgement. A whimper follows the footsteps, but they move past us. I can't see who it is, but Falyn's eyes widen when she's able to see them from her spot in the bushes.

"It's Cas," she whispers and starts to move, but I reach over and shake my head at her. "Ken, she's hurt pretty badly."

A thump and a grunt follow Falyn's panicked words, and she doesn't hesitate to leave our hiding spot. Rostan and I give up and stand as well. Cas is laying in the dirt about twenty feet away and Falyn is crouched at her side, crying. I don't need her to turn around and tell me why. I can already see it in Cas's lifeless eyes.

"I told you we'd find more this way." That voice is the last one I would ever want to hear right now. Serresa. Rostan and I both whirl on her, our magic already queued up to fight back. Beside her stand two people I don't know, and Michan. While her hands are glowing, his are covered in the inky blackness of his shadows. I gulp back my fear and the soothing sound of Rostan's lightning crackles next to me.

"You don't want to do this, Serresa," Rostan warns her, but she only smiles at him.

"That's where you're wrong," she says, looking only at me. "I've been wanting to do this for far too long." Her hands flare brighter for a moment before a stream of light arcs just over my shoulder and I realize too late she's not aiming at me, but at Falyn behind me.

"Falyn, move!" I scream, desperate for her to be able to react in time. As much as I want to look back, taking my eyes off the group in front of me is the wrong thing to do. Already tears are streaming down my face, because Falyn has yet to tell me she's okay.

Neither Rostan nor I wait for them to make another move. He shoots a bolt of lightning directly from his palm into the center of the group and all four of them are forced to separate to avoid being fried to a crisp. I've never seen him do that before, but I don't have time to stop and admire. I use the distraction to cage two unknown mages by tying them together with the thickest vines I've ever created. Then I grow the vine up and around the highest branch I can find and use it to hoist them a hundred feet into the air. Even if they can get out of the vines, it'll result in broken bones at the least.

Meanwhile, Rostan is keeping Serresa at bay by trading streams of light with streams of lightning. Neither one of their magic hits the target. Michan has yet to do anything, seemingly content to watch the fight and not participate. Actually, he's not watching the fight, he's watching me.

"You knew this whole time, didn't you?" I ask him because I can't resist.

"I did." He doesn't bother to lie or make excuses, which I might admire him for if it wasn't for the fact that if he knows about me, then he knows everything his father has done.

"You're okay with it? Everything he's done and continues to do? None of it bothers you?"

The tiniest squinting of his eyes tells me he might not be as unaffected as I think. The shadows around his forearms swirl in agitation and I wonder if he plans on using them.

"I am what I have to be," is his only answer.

"No," I reply bitterly. "You are what he made you."

"There's no difference—"

"Enough talking already and help me!" Serresa shrieks at Michan. "I don't know what the bitch is going on about, but I'm not going to fail because you're letting her distract you."

461

Multiple things happen at the same time, and it feels like it all plays out in slow motion.

Instead of lobbying another streak of light at Rostan, Serresa turns to me with hatred in her eyes. Her hands become blindingly white as she lifts them in my direction.

"Kennedy!" Rostan screams and starts running toward me, but he's too far away.

Michan's shadows pull away from his hands just as a blast of light streams from Serresa's.

It's not true what they say about your life flashing before your eyes when death is near. Because the only two things I can think about is that my own brother is taking part in my death, and I wish I could see Drayzen one last time.

Then everything speeds back up and the shadows I thought Michan was going to send my way, wrap themselves around Serresa and yank her off balance, causing her light to miss. He saved me.

My breath flies out of me in a loud whoosh and I turn to assure Rostan that I'm fine. When I see him, every ounce of magic I hold pours out of me in a bolt of lightning that would make Rostan envious. The lightning hits Serresa in her shoulder to the left of where I was actually aiming. She spins through the air and lands unconscious or maybe dead on the ground.

That beam of light she threw might have missed me, but the new path it took was directly at Rostan. I meet his eyes as he lies gasping on the ground.

Falling to my knees next to him, I grab his charred hand as he releases the last breath he'll ever take.

CHAPTER THIRTY

Smoke drifts upward to meet the clouds. Unshed tears make it hard to differentiate between the wisps of moisture that hang in the sky and what will soon be all that remain of my friends. Ash and smoke. Thirty-two students—people I called friends—lost their lives yesterday. And for what? To prove we can survive a war that doesn't exist?

I want to scream at the crowd surrounding the mass funeral pyre. They should know what they're risking their lives for. Everything that's happened—is happening—to us is for the sole purpose of finding more people for the king to use in his search for immortality and power.

None of it matters. We don't matter. And by the time they see the truth, it will be too late.

My throat burns, but I swallow it all back. Crying isn't going to solve anything. My rage might, though. I have that in spades. So much so that I don't think I'll ever feel anything else again.

I still intend to follow through with the next phase of the trial. But my reasons have changed. Serresa survived my lightning bolt and, with any luck, Michan didn't see that I was the one who threw it. But it doesn't matter, because after I pay her back, I'm leaving with Bren and Aarond. I'm officially joining the rebels because Serresa isn't the only one I intend on paying back. First, I take downher, then we take down the king.

A hand slips into mine, lacing our fingers together. On my other side, an arm is thrown over my shoulder. For a moment, I allow myself the tiny comfort being offered before I pull away from both Falyn and Noric. Comfort and mourning can come later. Not yet. First, I have things I need to do.

We need to pull you out before the next phase.

A message comes through on my crystal and I ignore it, just like I ignored the previous ones he sent with similar warnings. I'm not leaving.

Kennedy, the king knows everything. My sources say he's on his way to witness the trial. In all my years, he hasn't ever done this.

I toss the crystal on my bed. There's no point in reading the rest of the messages. I'm not going anywhere yet and there isn't a damn thing he can say to change my mind. It's still early evening, but the only thing I want to do is sleep. It's the only time I don't have to think about it. The only time the look in Rostan's eyes doesn't play on repeat inside my head.

I curl up on top of my blankets and reach for the stash of sleep spores I keep on my bedside table. Crushing the heads of two of them, I inhale the spores deeply, then wait for oblivion to take me.

"We should just let her sleep," Noric whispers from my doorway.

"She's been sleeping for over sixteen hours. Look at all the sleep spores laying on her floor," Falyn whispers back. I woke up once and re-dosed myself.

"You know I can hear you guys, right? And Noric's right, you should just let me sleep. Wake me up when it's time for phase two." I roll away from them.

"Phase two starts tomorrow, Ken. Don't you think you should prepare yourself a little bit?" Falyn says gently and comes to sit beside me on my bed.

"The only thing I need to be doing right now is sleeping." I crush the head of another sleep pore before she can stop me.

When I wake up again, my room is pitch black. It's so quiet I can hear my own heart beating, and I count the beats out in my mind. I probably shouldn't take another sleep spore, or I'll risk not being able to wake up in time for phase two. When Rostan's eyes flash through my mind, I do everything I can to push the image away, but they refuse to go.

He died trying to save me. The least worthy person in this realm. Rostan had already done more good for other people in the last few months than I will in my whole life. He died because I was too weak to protect myself. He died because I was too slow. He died.

The single tear that rolls down my cheek breaks the dam I've been trying so desperately to hold together. I suck in a heaving breath, but it's too late,

467

and the sobs tear their way up my throat and demand release.

I don't hear my bedroom door open, but my bed dips under Falyn's weight just before her hand begins stroking my hair. No matter how hard I cry, it doesn't soothe the ache in my soul over the knowledge that it's my fault he's dead. I don't think anything can.

Falyn and I get up like it's just another day. We don't talk about last night or even the last few days. We don't need to. It's a constant cloud looming over me, trying to crush my chest and steal my breath.

When a knock at our door interrupts our morning, I look at her and ask, "Was Noric coming over before the trial?" She shakes her head and shrugs.

It's not Noric standing at the door when I swing it open. It's Drayzen. The sight of him makes my heart jump, but I push it down and drink in the view, committing it to memory because I don't know when I'll ever get to see it again.

He doesn't bother with niceties and pushes his way inside before I can offer the invite. He whirls on me as soon as he's inside. "I don't think you should compete."

I shut the door behind him before responding. "If I don't compete, then I get stripped and shipped,"

468

I say, raising one brow at him. "What happened to me out of everyone needing to survive?"

He flounders. "We can just leave. Together. We'll find somewhere to hide and figure things out, but you can't compete today, Kennedy."

I have to admit the idea is really tempting, but I know in the long run it'll just make things worse. We'll spend our whole lives running and trying to stay one step ahead of whoever is chasing us. "You know we can't do that. Are you really going to give up everything you've worked for? What is this really about? What's going on, Drayzen?" I know well enough by now that he wouldn't be suggesting something so crazy if he wasn't truly worried.

He paces back and forth in agitation. "Because you're not safe, Kennedy. Something is happening and even though I don't know the specifics, I do know you're at the center of it."

"How?" I question as the ever present lump in my chest grows in size.

"I just do. Please, Kennedy, don't compete," he begs me before reaching out and clutching my shoulders.

"The truth, Drayzen. What aren't you telling me?" After I get over the initial shock of what he's saying I realize there has to be more. We've shared one kiss, I don't think that equates to running away together in any realm. He's really starting to scare me.

He sighs and scrubs a hand across his face. Whatever it is, he's terrified. "I received orders from my mom today. And I know I'm not the only one."

"Orders for what, exactly?" I pull away and crush my arms over my chest to stave off the chill that starts forming.

"The focus of the last phase has changed. Lasting to the end isn't the only goal now." He stops talking and I clench my teeth.

"What's the new goal?" I ask, knowing if I check my crystal I won't have a notification.

"You, okay? You're the new goal, Kennedy. You're not allowed to survive."

"I really don't think you should be doing this," Falyn says when we enter the arena a couple hours later.

"I'll be fine, Falyn," I assure her for the hundredth time. "There's something I need to do before I leave." I haven't told anyone about my plans. I don't want to see the disappointment in their eyes when they find out.

"You can just message Bren and have him pull you out now," she urges me. "Nothing is more important than your life."

470

"That's where you're wrong," I tell her matter-of-factly. "You guys are, and I can't leave until I know you'll be safe."

"What does that mean?" I just shake my head, so she continues. "What about everyone else? Are we more important than them? Because you have a chance to save everyone and you're too focused on revenge to see straight."

I should have known she would figure out what I need to do. "I have to, Falyn." It's the only thing I can offer. I can't explain how it feels like I'm fighting to draw in every breath I take. I can't explain how it feels like those labored breaths are clutched in Serresa's hands. She is all I can see right now. Her and Rostan's eyes.

Falyn sighs in disappointment, but I don't turn to look at her because my entire world has just narrowed to a single person standing across the arena. He's staring directly at me, so I lift my chin and meet his eyes. I want him to see my face. I want him to know exactly who I am and how I feel about him, and I want him to be afraid when he finds out his plan didn't work. I want the king to know exactly who's coming for him when this is all over.

This phase started in exactly the same way as the first one. Only it was the king who announced the start instead of Galen. His voice still echoes in my ears as I race through the forest, looking for the one person I'm focused on. We're not allowed to work together, so Falyn and I had to split up immediately or risk being pulled. My stomach is in knots, but I have to believe she'll be fine, or I won't be able to focus.

I have the spark of magic she gave me before we parted, plus the bracelet Noric gave me as backup. It won't last me the full two hours but with any luck I won't need it to.

A twig snaps behind me, and I whirl on the person trying to sneak up on me. It's a student from one of Rostan's sessions and as soon as our eyes meet, he lifts his hands in truce and nods his head. I blow out a breath and nod back. We won't be fighting each other.

I run into my first fight only a few minutes later when I'm pushed to my knees by a gust of wind and suddenly all the air in my lungs is pulled out, leaving me gasping for a breath I can't take. I stare at my attacker and remember the first time I met him months ago when Serresa sent him to mess with me at my desk. He didn't come across as someone who could take another life, but I guess neither did I.

I snake a root around his ankle and tug, so he falls backward with a jarring thud and loses his focus. When I'm able to suck in my first breath, I do it in great heaving motions, like I'm swallowing the air. But I don't have time to linger over the relief of it or even to run over and add his power to my own for fear of him waking up.

I know I should tie him down, but it'll just be leaving him to die if anyone comes across him and I can't bring myself to do it. Luckily, he doesn't chase after me and soon I find myself alone again, so I allow myself to pause and catch my breath.

I should have known better. Standing in the open like this was bound to get me caught. And worse, it's not just one set of footsteps I hear approaching, it's at least four. Maybe five. I spin around, but it's too late to run because they've surrounded me. Michan, Serresa, two I don't recognize . . . and Drayzen.

I stare accusingly at him. All his talk this morning about leaving and getting me to safety, yet here he is with the very people he knows are tasked with getting rid of me. He doesn't meet my eyes, instead he fixates on a point over my shoulder, his jaw clenched and ticking.

Gathering up the vestiges of my courage, I arrange my features in what I hope is a smirk. "Fancy meeting you, of all people here, Drayzen. Them, I expected, but you?" I can't keep the hurt out of my voice, but it doesn't matter.

He doesn't respond, but Serresa does. "Did you think he would choose a nobody like you? It would be cute if it wasn't so sad."

Four of the five move forward to surround me while Drayzen lingers behind, watching me with hard eyes as if to say he warned me and I didn't listen. I take

473

a step back from Serresa and wind up back to chest with one of the two I don't recognize. He grabs my arms and yanks them behind my back so hard I have to bite my tongue to keep from yelping. An emperor. Serresa laughs and something about it is so familiar I almost forget what's happening. This was my vision. The one I had the first day I arrived at the school.

It feels like years have gone by since that day, but it's only been months. The thought is cut off when Serresa lays her palm against the skin of my exposed stomach where my shirt has ridden up. At first it just feels warm, but the heat increases until it's unbearable and I have to scream from the pain of it. Only then does she pull back, leaving behind a red, blistered imprint of her hand.

Drayzen steps forward, but I shake my head. I don't want, nor do I need help from him in any way.

"Is that all you have?" I spit at her. If I have to go, it won't be cowering and afraid. She's going to have to look me in the eye. She just smiles and drags a hot finger down the side of my face. I can smell the burning flesh but refuse to give her the satisfaction of screaming again.

I struggle against the hands still holding me, but it's no different from an ant struggling under the weight of a foot. Useless.

Michan watches her and makes no move to help me again. "What was the point of saving me the other day if you're just going to stand by and watch today?" I shout at him.

474

"I'm sorry," he says. "This is the way it has to be."

Serresa watches our exchange with confusion in her eyes, but stays quiet.

"Says who? Our father?" I don't know why I felt the need to let everyone know the truth, but he wasn't expecting me to just lay it out there like that. Neither was anyone else. Drayzen's eyes widen in shock, Serresa gasps audibly, and the hands holding me loosen the tiniest bit, giving me my chance.

Drawing on the emperor spark courtesy of the very hands holding me, I yank myself away from him and spin to plant my foot directly in his abdomen. He goes flying backward while everyone else looks on in amazement.

Turning to Serresa, it's my turn to smile. "Did Michan forget to tell you? Not only do we share a father, but he's the reason you've all been tasked with ensuring I don't make it. Isn't that right, Michan? You told your father about my magic, but you failed to mention it to anyone else."

I stalk forward, but Serresa is too stunned to realize the danger she's in. I don't make it far. Someone grabs a handful of my hair and yanks me backward. I can feel a clump rip away from my scalp so I lean into the hand.

The next thing I know, I'm on the ground watching a booted foot come down full force toward my stomach. I barely manage to roll away in time.

475

The sound of a fist hitting flesh rings out and I look over to see Drayzen attacking Michan, and Michan doing everything he can to fend him off. I've never seen Drayzen like this before. Deadly and powerful. It might actually be the hottest thing I've ever seen. Michan's shadows are barely managing to pull him away.

My momentary distraction costs me. The emperor hauls me to my feet and pulls my arms back in exactly the same way he held me before. The second guy lifts a hand that morphs into sharp claws, and I know exactly what he's planning on doing with them. I look at Drayzen, who's fully focused on his fight with Michan and can't help me.

Just before the clawed hand swings down, Serresa shouts, "Wait!" He stops immediately. "This is all mine," she says, pulling massive amounts of power into her hands until they're so bright tears spring to my eyes.

I squeeze my eyes shut because no matter what I thought earlier about forcing her to meet my eyes, I don't actually want to see it coming. Everything fades away. The only sound I hear is my rapidly beating heart and panicked breaths. The back of my eyelids are red from the brightness of her light, so I know she's close even though I can't feel the heat yet.

Then my body starts to warm and I know it's almost over. It takes me a few seconds to understand the warmth is coming from inside me and not outside. It's growing hotter with every passing second until I feel like I'm being burned from the inside out. The pressure of my magic builds until it's so painful to hold on to that I have no choice but to shove it outward. It leaves my body with an ear shattering boom, and everything goes black.

When I come to, I'm lying on the hard ground in the fetal position. I can't hear anything over the ringing in my ears, and everything around me is nothing but a hazy blur.

I fumble to my feet but trip over someone's leg and fall forward onto the ground again. A wave of nausea rolls through me and I dry heave a few times before I feel like I can get up again. Thankfully, when I do, I can see a little better. Four bodies lay still in awkward angles on the ground. They're covered in angry blisters with black edges, and some of them are missing patches of hair. I can't tell if any of them are breathing.

Drayzen. I walk up to each body, trying to hold back the nausea from seeing their burned faces. None of them are him. And I'm pretty sure they're not breathing. Losing my battle with nausea, I bend over and retch air into the soil again. It's not until I hear a groan behind one of the trees that I'm able to control it and stand back up.

"Kennedy?" I rush to his side and tears spring to my eyes when he looks a little beat up but not burned or dead.

"I'm here." He sits up in a panic and looks around. "They're dead, I think." I tell him and he relaxes against the tree.

Then he bolts up again. "You need to go, now!" He rises unsteadily to his feet and grabs my hand before pulling me after him.

He sways on his feet, but it doesn't stop him from moving forward.

"Drayzen, stop. We need to get you help. You're injured." He doesn't pay any attention to me. So I shout his name louder. "Drayzen! Stop!" He finally hears me and spins around.

"Don't you get it, Kennedy? We can't stop. We have maybe five minutes before someone finds us after that blast you caused." I flinch back. "Kennedy, you're an echo. That makes you the number one priority on the king's list of people to get rid of."

I gape at him as he pulls me forward again. An echo. Falyn and I never thought to name my magic, but I guess there might already be a name for it.

"So you know, then. But how do you know what an echo is?" I ask, practically running to keep up with him. We're almost to the clearing where our boulder sits, and I have to wonder why we're going there.

"There's not enough time to explain," he says and just as we break through the trees, he pulls me into his arms and crushes his mouth to mine in a kiss so deep, I forgot the question I asked in the first place. It's not until someone clears their throat behind us that

I'm able to pull away and stare at him, breathless and wanting more. Drayzen cups my jaw in a gentle hand and presses his forehead to mine before turning me around.

Bren and Aarond stand near the boulder, waiting for me. I look between them and Drayzen, trying to wrap my brain around the fact that Drayzen not only knows them, but brought me to meet them.

"How?" I ask him. He just shakes his head.

"There really isn't enough time. You have to go." He nudges me forward then speaks so quietly I'm afraid I imagined it. "I love you, Kennedy." Then he melts back into the trees, leaving me with the two men who started it all.